"A KISS FOR LUCK," WHIT SAID TO HER.

He stared at her lips, the color of a rose just before sundown. He needed to know her taste, her warmth, when his own world felt so flavorless and cold. God, he wanted that, wanted her mouth against his, and the sudden strength of that want hit him like a cannon.

At that word, *kiss*, her gaze went directly to his mouth. And heat and heaviness shot directly to his groin. Desire gleamed in her eyes.

Which she quickly shut away. Her expression cooled as her gaze moved up to his eyes.

"It would be a shameful thing to kiss you in front of my family. But I will wish you *kosko bokht*." There was something almost sorrowful in her words, in her eyes, as she stared up at him.

He felt it then. An icy sense of premonition sliding down his back, like a cold hand tracing the line of his spine. Though he was not a superstitious man, just then some strange other sense of foreboding tightened his muscles and bones. He had the oddest desire to stay in the encampment and avoid the ruin.

Books by Zoë Archer

The Blades of the Rose
Warrior
Scoundrel
Rebel
Stranger

The Hellraisers
Devil's Kiss

Published by Kensington Publishing Corporation

DEVIL'S KISS

The Hellraisers

Zoë Archer

ZEBRA BOOKS
KENSINGTON PUBLISHING CORP.

http://www.kensingtonbooks.com

ZEBRA BOOKS are published by

Kensington Publishing Corp.
119 West 40th Street
New York, NY 10018

All Kensington titles, imprints, and distributed lines are available at special quantity discounts for bulk purchases for sales promotion, premiums, fund-raising, educational, or institutional use.

Special book excerpts or customized printings can also be created to fit specific needs. For details, write or phone the office of the Kensington Special Sales Manager: Attn.: Special Sales Department. Kensington Publishing Corp., 119 West 40th Street, New York, NY 10018. Phone: 1-800-221-2647.

Zebra and the Z logo Reg. U.S. Pat. & TM Off.

ISBN-13: 978-1-4201-2227-5
ISBN-10: 1-4201-2227-4

First Printing: December 2011

10 9 8 7 6 5 4 3 2 1

Printed in the United States of America

For Zack, always

Chapter 1

The Gypsy girl cheated.

James Sherbourne, Earl of Whitney, could not prove it, but he knew with certainty that she cheated him at piquet. She had taken the last three hands, and his coin, brazenly. Whit did not mind the loss of the money. He had money in abundance, more, he admitted candidly, than he knew what to do with it. No, that wasn't true—he always knew what to do with money. Gamble it.

"How?" he asked her.

"How what, my lord?" He liked her voice, rich and smoky like a brazier, with an undercurrent of heat. She did not look up at him from studying her cards, arranging them in groups and assessing which needed to be discarded. Whit liked her hands, too, slim with tapered, clever fingers. Gamblers' hands. His own hands were rather large, more fitting for a laborer than an earl, but, despite their size, he had crafted them through years of diligence into a gamester's hands. He could roll dice or deal cards with the skill and precision of a clockmaker. Some might consider this a dubious honor, but not Whit. His abilities at the gaming table remained his sole source of pleasure.

And he was enjoying himself now, despite—or *because of*—the cheating Gypsy girl. They sat upon the grass, slightly removed from the others in the encampment. Whit hadn't sat upon the ground in years, but he did so now, reclining with one leg stretched out, the other bent so he propped his forearm on his knee. Back when he'd been a lad, he used to sit this very way when lounging on the banks of the creek that ran through his family's main country estate in Derbyshire. Years, and lifetimes, ago.

"How are you cheating me?"

She did look up at him then. She sat with her legs tucked demurely beneath her, a contrast from her worldly gaze. Light from the nearby campfire turned her large dark eyes to glittering jet, sparkling with intelligence. Extravagantly long black lashes framed those eyes, and he had the strangest sensation that they saw past his expensive hunting coat with its silver buttons, past the soft material of his doeskin waistcoat, the fine linen of his shirt, all the way to the man beneath. And what her eyes saw amused her.

Whit wasn't certain he liked that. After all, she was a Gypsy and slept in a tent in the open fields, whilst he was the fifth in his line to bear the title, lands, and estates of the earldom that dated back to the time of Queen Elizabeth. That merited some respect. Didn't it?

"I don't know what you are talking about, my lord," she answered. A faint smile curved her full mouth, vaguely mocking. The sudden desire to kiss that smile away seized Whit, baffling him. He enjoyed women—not to the same extent as his friend Bram, who put satyrs to shame and even now made the other Gypsy girls at the camp giggle and squeal—but when gambling was involved, Whit usually cared for nothing else and could not be distracted. Not even by lush, sardonic lips.

It seemed he had found the one mouth that distracted him.

"I know you aren't dealing from the bottom of the deck," he said. "I have had the elder hand twice, the hand with the advantage. We know what twelve cards we both have. Your sleeves are too short to hide cards for you to palm. Yet you consistently wind up with one hundred points before I do. You must be cheating. I want to know how." There was no anger in his words, only a genuine curiosity to know her secrets. Any advantage at the card table was one he gladly seized.

"Perhaps I'm using Gypsy magic."

At this, Whit raised one brow. "No such thing as magic. This is the modern eighteenth century."

"There are more things in heaven and earth," the girl answered, "than are dreamt of in your philosophy."

Whit started at hearing Shakespeare from the mouth of a Gypsy. "You've read *Hamlet*?"

Her laugh held more smoky mystery. "I saw it performed once at a horse-trading fair."

"But you *do* believe in magic?" he pressed. "Gypsy curses, and all that."

Her slim shoulders rose and fell in a graceful shrug. "The world is a labyrinth I am still navigating. It is impossible for me to say I *don't* believe in it."

"You are hedging."

"And you're *gorgio,* and I always hedge my bets around *gorgios*." She gazed at him across the little patch of grass that served as their card table, then shook her head and made a *tsk* of caution. "They can be so unpredictable."

He found himself chuckling with her. Odd, that. Whit thought himself far too jaded, too attuned only to the thrill of the gamble, to enjoy something as simple and yet thrilling as sharing a low, private laugh with a beautiful woman.

She *was* beautiful. Perhaps under the direct, less flattering light of the sun, rather than firelight, she might not be as pleasing to the eye, though he rather doubted it. Her cheekbones were high, the line of her jaw clean, a proud, but proportioned nose. Black eyebrows formed neat arches above her equally black eyes. Her mouth, he already knew, was luscious, ripe. Raven dark and silken, her hair tumbled down her back in a thick beribboned braid. She wore a bright blouse the color of summertime poppies, and a long,

full golden skirt. No panniers, no stiff bodice or corset. A
fringed shawl in a vivid green draped over her shoulders.
One might assume such brilliant colors to jar the eye, but on
the Gypsy girl, they seemed precisely right and harmonized
with her honey-colored skin.

Rings glimmered on almost all her slim fingers, golden
hoops hung from her ears, and many coin-laden necklaces
draped her slim neck. Whit followed the necklaces with his
eyes as they swooped down from her neck to lie in sparkling
heaps atop her lush bosom. He envied those necklaces, settled smugly between her breasts.

Whit had a purse full of good English money. He wondered if this girl, this cheating, sardonic siren, might consider a generous handful of coins in exchange for a few
hours of him learning the texture and taste of her skin. Judging by the way she eyed him, the flare of interest he saw
shining in her gaze, she wouldn't be averse to the idea.

"For God's sake, Whit." Abraham Stirling, Lord Rothwell's
voice boomed across the Gypsy encampment, tugging Whit
from his carnal musings. Bram added, "Leave off those dull
card games for once and join us."

"Yes, join us," seconded Leopold Bailey.

"We've wine and music in abundance," said Sir Edmund
Fawley-Smith, his words slurring a bit.

"And dancing," added the Honorable John Godfrey. Someone struck a tambourine.

The men's voices blended into a cacophony of gruff entreaty and temptation. Whit grinned at his friends carousing
on the other side of the camp. True to form, Bram had his
arms around not one but three girls. Leo and Edmund busily
drained their cups, whilst John received instruction from a
Gypsy man on how to properly throw a knife.

Hellraisers, the lot of them. Whit included. So the five
friends called themselves and so they were known amongst
the upper echelons of society, and with good cause. Their
names littered the scandal sheets and provided fodder for the

coffee house, tea salon and gentlemen's clubs, their exploits verging on legendary.

Bored with London's familiar pleasures, the Hellraisers had all been staying at Bram's nearby estate, spending their days hunting, their nights carousing. Yet they had soon tired of the local taverns, and the nearest good-sized town with a gaming hell was too far for a comfortable ride. It seemed more and more lately that the Hellraisers grew restive all too quickly, Whit amongst them, seeking novelty and greater heights of dissolution when their interest paled. He was only thirty-one, yet he could gain excitement only when gambling. Lounging in the gaming room of Bram's sprawling estate, Whit and the others had considered returning to the brothels, theaters, and gaming hells of London, but then Bram had learned from his steward that a group of Gypsies had taken up temporary residence in the neighborhood, and so an expedition had been undertaken.

The Gypsies had been glad to see the group of gentlemen ride into their camp, even more so when liberal amounts of money were offered in exchange for a night's amusement. Trick horse riding. Music. Dancing. Fortune-telling. Plenty of wine. And cards.

"How much wine have you drunk?" Whit called to Leo.

It took a moment for Leo to calculate, swaying on his feet. "'Bout four or five mugs."

"Ten guineas says you don't make it to six before falling arse over teakettle."

"Done," Leo said immediately. The nearby Gypsies exclaimed over the absurdly high amount of the wager, but to Leo, and especially to Whit, the amount was trivial.

Whit smiled to himself. Leo was the only son of a family who made their fortune on the 'Change, and he was the only one of the Hellraisers who wasn't a gentleman by birth. He felt this distinction keenly and, as such, met any challenge with a particular aggression. Which meant that Leo took any bet Whit threw his way.

"Your friends seem eager for your company," the Gypsy girl said wryly.

Whit brought his gaze back around to her. "We do everything together."

"Everything?" She raised a brow.

"Nearly everything," he amended. Bram might have no shame, but Whit preferred his amorous exploits to be conducted in private. He wondered how much privacy he could secure for himself and the girl.

A striking older Gypsy woman walked up to where he and the girl sat and began scolding her. Whit could not understand the language, but it was clear that the older woman wasn't very pleased by the girl's behavior. The girl replied sharply and seemed disinclined to obey. The older woman grew exasperated. Interesting. It seemed as though Whit's saucy temptress proved as much as a termagant to her own people as to him. Though Whit wasn't exasperated by the girl. Far from it. He felt the stirrings of interest he had believed far too exhausted to rouse.

"My granddaughter, Zora," huffed the older woman. Her accent was far stronger than her granddaughter's. "Impossible. 'Ere the fine gentlemen come for *dukkering*, and she does not *dukker*."

"What's *dukkering*?" asked Whit.

"Fortune-telling," the girl, Zora, answered. A fitting name for her, perfumed with secrets and distant lands. "Is that what you want, *gorgio*?" She set down her cards, then held out her hand. "Cross my palm with silver, and I shall read the lines upon your hand. Or I can use the tarot to tell your future." She nodded toward a different deck of cards sitting nearby, upon a scarf draped over the grass.

"I don't want to know the future," he said.

"Afraid?" That mocking, tempting little smile played about her lips.

"If I know the future," he replied, "it takes away all of the risk."

This made her pause. "You like risk." She sounded a bit

breathless, more than the heat of the nearby fire reddening her cheeks.

He gave her a smile of his own, not mocking, but full of carnal promise. "Very much."

Zora turned to her grandmother and spoke more in their native tongue. With a loud sigh and grumble, the older woman trundled away.

Whit seized his opportunity. "I can give you five times what you'd win from me if you tell me how you keep winning at cards."

"I thought you enjoyed risk," came her quick reply.

"There's a risk in cheating, as well. Someone might catch you. And if they do catch you, who knows what they might do. Anything at all."

She gazed intently at him, then shook her head, firelight lost in the darkness of her hair. "No. It would be too dangerous to give those skills to a man such as you."

"A man such as me?" he repeated, amused. He set his cards down upon the ground. "Pray, madam, what sort of man am I?"

Her fathomless eyes seemed to reach deep inside him. He felt her gaze upon—*within*—him, a foreign presence in the contained kingdom of his self. After a moment, she said, "Handsome of face and form. Wealthy. Privileged. Bored. Throwing years of your life upon a rubbish heap because you seek something, anything to engage your restless, weary heart and prove you are still alive."

Whit laughed, but the sound was hollow in his chest. He didn't know this girl. Didn't know her at all, having met her for the first time earlier that very evening. She certainly did not know him. He was an *earl*, for God's sake, with a crest emblazoned upon his carriages. No fewer than three substantial estates belonged to him, all of them staffed with small armies of liveried servants.

She lived out of a tent. Whit wasn't sure she even wore shoes.

Yet a few words from her cut him deeply, far sharper than any surgeon's blade, and much more accurate. Why, he wasn't even aware he bled, but he was certain he'd find droplets of blood staining his shirt and stock later as he undressed for bed.

His solitary bed.

"If you won't divulge your secrets with the cards," he said with an insouciance he did not quite feel, "perhaps I can tempt you to reveal other, more personal secrets." There could be no mistaking his intent, the suggestive heat of his words.

She drew in a sharp breath, but whether she was offended or interested, Whit couldn't tell. Despite her insight into him, he possessed none of the same insight into *her*, making her as opaque as a silk-covered mirror. When his physical needs required satiation, Whit knew women of pleasure in London, Bath, Tunbridge-Wells. Actresses, courtesans. He knew their wants, their demands, the systems—both crude and elegant—through which they negotiated their price. A mutually beneficial relationship, and one he could navigate easily.

When it came to offering a night of pleasure to a fiery Gypsy girl, here, Whit found himself happily at a loss. Happily, because he had no idea how she might respond, and the inherent risk made his pulse beat a little faster.

"Would you see me financially compensated for revealing those personal secrets?" she asked, her own voice sultry.

"Absolutely," he said at once. "If that is what you wish." He moved his hand toward the purse he kept tucked into his belt, but then he stopped in surprise when she reached over and clasped his wrist. Her grip was surprisingly strong, surprisingly arousing. He felt her touch spread like a lit fuse through his body, beginning the reaction eventually leading toward explosion. Whit stared down at her hand, her dusky skin tantalizing against his own lighter-colored flesh, then up at her face as she leaned close.

"*Romani chis* are not your *gorgie* whores, my lord. Especially me." Her voice was steady, yet her eyes were hot. "I may lie *to* you, but not *with* you. Not for coin." She released her grip and sat back, and Whit felt the echo of her touch.

"If I were to take any man to my bedroll, it would not be for money."

Which seemed to imply that she *might* share her bed with a man, only without any sort of monetary inducement. That sounded promising.

Before Whit could speculate on this further, Bram staggered over with his arm hooked around the neck of a Gypsy man. The Gypsy looked a little alarmed to be so close to the tall, somewhat inebriated stranger, but could not easily break free.

"Taiso here just told me something very interesting," Bram said. "He said that a few miles from here is a Roman ruin. Isn't that right, Taiso?"

The Gypsy man nodded, though from eagerness to rid himself of Bram or ready agreement, Whit couldn't tell. "Aye," Taiso answered. "To the west. On a hill. Many old columns, and such."

"Bram, if your estate is nearby, wouldn't you already know about a Roman ruin?" Whit asked.

Apparently, this had not occurred to Bram. He frowned. "Must be a new ruin."

The Gypsy girl, Zora, snorted. Whit found himself smiling.

"We should go investigate," Leo said, ambling forward with John and Edmund trailing.

"No!" yelped Taiso. "Ye oughtn't go there. 'Tis a place of darkest magic. The haunt of *Wafodu guero*—the Devil!"

"So much the better," said Leo. "We're Hellraisers, after all."

Edmund and John chortled their agreement. "This place is getting deuced dull," Edmund added.

Whit didn't think so. Though he was uncertain whether the tantalizing Zora might share a bed with him, he wanted to stay with her longer, even if it meant simply talking. He couldn't remember being so engaged in a conversation for a long, long time.

"It's settled, then," declared Bram. "We go to the ruin."

Cheers of approval rose up from Leo, John, and Edmund.

Bram fixed Whit with a stare that held far more strength than one might expect from his inebriated state.

"You're coming, aren't you?" Bram asked. The question verged on a command. In some ways, Bram styled himself the de facto leader of the Hellraisers, even though, as a baron, he ranked beneath Whit. Yet Whit had no desire to lead this band of reprobate men—he wanted only the thrill of the gamble—and so left the decisions to his oldest friend.

Yet it was all a ruse. Bram mightn't say so, but he *needed* to have Whit with him during their many escapades, and if Whit refused to go, Bram would stay.

Whit looked at Zora, who watched the whole exchange with an incisive, speculative gaze. "What say you, Madame Zora?" he asked. "I could go to the ruin, where the Devil is rumored to reside, or remain here, with you. Shall we wager it on the flip of a coin or turn of a card?"

Her expression turned opaque. "The disease of your boredom has nearly claimed you if you can't make decisions for yourself."

He didn't care for the edge of censure in her tone. Whit spent much of his time avoiding anyone who might reproach him, which was why he hadn't seen his sister in nearly a year. It was not this Gypsy girl's business if he liked to gamble. It was no one's business but his own.

Resolved, Whit smoothly got to his feet. He hadn't been imbibing at the same rate as his friends, so the world remained steady as he stood. "Let's see where the Devil lives."

Bram exhaled, as if holding a breath in anticipation of Whit's answer. Seeing Whit make his decision, Bram grinned his demon's grin, the same he made whenever he was on the verge of doing something truly fiendish—like that time he entertained an entire troupe of ballet dancers in his London town house.

Zora arose to standing in a sinuous, graceful line.

"A kiss for luck," Whit said to her. He stared at her lips, the color of a rose just before sundown. He needed to know her taste, her warmth, when his own world felt so flavorless and cold. God, he wanted that, wanted her mouth against his, and the sudden strength of that want hit him like a cannon.

At that word *kiss*, her gaze went directly to his mouth. And heat and heaviness shot directly to his groin. Desire gleamed in her eyes.

Which she quickly shut away. Her expression cooled as her gaze moved up to his eyes.

"It would be a shameful thing to kiss you in front of my family. But I will wish you *kosko bokht*." There was something almost sorrowful in her words, in her eyes, as she stared up at him.

He felt it then. An icy sense of premonition sliding down his back, like a cold hand tracing the line of his spine. Though he was not a superstitious man, just then some strange other sense of foreboding tightened his muscles and bones. He had the oddest desire to stay in the encampment and avoid the ruin.

"Time to ride, lads," Bram commanded. He and the other men strode off to where a Gypsy boy had brought their snorting, impatient horses.

Whit laughed at himself, shaking off the sense of dread as he might hand a rain-soaked greatcoat to a servant. Nonsense, all of it. As he'd said earlier, this was the modern age, and the Devil and magic did not truly exist.

He reached out, requesting Zora's hand, and after she slowly gave it to him, he bowed over it and pressed a kiss to her knuckles. Her eyes widened. Beneath his lips, her skin was silk and warmth; he barely resisted the impulse to lick her to learn whether she tasted as spicy as her spirit.

Their eyes met over their clasped hands. "Farewell, Madame Zora."

"Be careful, my lord."

"There's no amusement in careful."

"There is more to life than amusement."

"If there is," he answered, "I have yet to encounter it."

She slid her hand from his, and her gaze also slid away.

"Whit!" came a chorus of voices from across the encampment.

He gave her one last, searching look, as if trying to etch her image on the metal of his mind. A silent entreaty for her to meet his gaze one final time. Yet she would not, staring fixedly at the ground, and the flickering firelight turned her into a distant gold and ebony goddess. He wondered if he might ever see her again. The thought that he might not filled him with an inexplicable anger.

He made one final bow, as sharply elegant as a rapier, then turned and strode off. Whit swung himself up into the saddle. Bram and the others kicked their horses into a gallop. Whit's horse wheeled and danced in a circle as he took one last glimpse of the Gypsy encampment, of *her*, before he set his heels into the beast's flanks. They darted off into the night.

The *gorgios* were gone, having left some hours ago. Yet Zora could not be easy, could not still the beating of her heart or whirling of her mind. She paced as everyone else in the camp amused themselves with music and stories. It had been a good night. The wealthy *gorgios* had thrown coin around like handfuls of dust, and the mood amongst the families was high and celebratory. Even the best day of horse trading and *dukkering* at a fair could not bring in as much money.

Zora alone could not enjoy the remains of the evening. She walked up and down the camp—careful to keep her path behind the men who sat around the fire, as custom and belief demanded. Amongst the Rom, it was considered dangerous for a woman to pass in front of a seated man, though no one explained the reasons why in a way to ever satisfy Zora. That had been her way, since her earliest years—Zora demanding why, and the answer: *because*.

"Sit, girl," commanded Faden Boswell. "Ye make my head spin with yer to-ing and fro-ing."

Zora ignored him. Faden claimed he was the king of their

group, but he talked more bluster than he did enforce order. Everyone knew that Faden's wife, Femi, held the reins of control and made the major decisions.

"She's thinkin' of her handsome *gorgio*," teased Grandmother Shuri. "With the pretty blue eyes and deep pockets."

"He is not *my gorgio*," Zora said immediately, yet she knew the truth. She *was* thinking of him. Whit, his scoundrel friends called him. A suitable name for a man possessing much intellect, yet also ironic, for he squandered his wits on ephemeral pursuits. What drove a man to live from one game of chance to the next? He had wealth, privilege, friends—though those friends were as wicked as demons. Yet he staked his happiness on the brief excitement of the wager.

It troubled her. *He* troubled her, far more than she would like.

There was passion in him—and no true channel for that passion. Nothing that engaged him fully.

No, that was not true. He seemed very much engaged and passionate when he looked at her.

Zora suppressed the shiver of awareness that danced through her as she remembered him. Grandmother Shuri was right. The *gorgio* Whit was indeed a most handsome man, and extremely well formed. He might be a scoundrel of the worst order, but it left no toll upon his face and body. Tall, his broad shoulders admirably filling out his costly coat, his long legs encased in close-fitting doeskin hunting breeches and high boots polished to brilliance.

And his face. She recalled it vividly as the firelight painted him a dark angel. Unlike other wealthy *gorgios*, he wore no wig but pulled his deep brown hair back into a queue. She imagined what his hair might look like loose about his shoulders, and knew he would appear a very incubus, sensually tempting a woman to wickedness. He had a square, strong jaw. A bold, aristocratic nose. Full lips. Dark, slashing brows above eyes the color of the sky at midday. Sharp, those eyes, and hungry.

Hungry for her. He made himself very plain. He wanted her for a night's pleasure. And, God preserve her, she wanted him, too. That lean body. Those clever hands. But she'd spoken true. She was no whore, and would not take his coin in exchange for her body. Even if he had not offered to pay her for the privilege, Zora knew that such affairs with *gorgios* were dangerous for young *Romani chis*.

She might not have taken him to bed, but she had not wanted him to go, either. She enjoyed talking with him, the way in which he truly seemed to listen. He was not afraid or dismissive of her opinions, not like other men—especially Jem, her former husband. Whit's mind was sharp, and he played the bored rogue, but she saw in him a yearning for meaning, for connection to something real, beyond the gloss and polish of his wealthy, wastrel life. She had that own yearning for herself, for a life away from telling fortunes and speaking in deliberate riddles. There had to be more than that.

There had been a palpable connection between her and Whit, which was indeed strange. Two people could not be more different. He lived trapped within walls, and she had the freedom of the road and the sky. He was a wealthy *gorgio* man of privilege, whilst she was a *Romani chi* who wore her wealth around her neck and upon her fingers. The sun and the moon. Yet the connection had been there, just the same.

She could not quite dismiss the disquiet she felt when he and his attractive, scapegrace friends decided to visit the Roman ruin. She might not adhere to the old folk beliefs of her family and the other Rom—it all seemed rather superstitious and silly to her, frankly—but something seemed deeply unsettling and wrong about the fact that the one *gorgio* who lived nearby had never heard of the ruin before tonight. Almost as if . . . it had been hiding, waiting for him and the other men.

"Ach," she growled to herself. "Enough of this." She had grown weary of pacing like a cat and would divert her restless thoughts.

Zora threw herself down onto the grass and shuffled her tarot deck. She did not believe the *dukkering* cards could actually tell the future, just as she did not believe the lines on a person's hand foretold anything. When she *dukkered* for the *gorgios*, she let them focus on the cards or their hands, while she actually read their faces, their postures and silent, subtle, unaware ways that revealed who they were and what they desired. Easy for them to think she had the gift of magic. But all Zora truly had was a knack for seeing people and telling them what they wanted to hear.

Still, dealing the tarot for herself usually soothed her. The proscribed patterns in which the cards were laid. The pictures printed upon their faces, older than history. Calming.

After shuffling the cards several times, Zora began to lay them out in the ten-card cross with which she was most familiar. She did not pay much attention, simply allowing her mind to drift as her hands moved, setting down the cards. When she did finally bring her attention down to the cards, what she saw made her gasp aloud.

Evil. A great evil is coming, unleashed by the five.

Zora shivered. The warning was plain, spelled out in the cards.

She shook herself. Yes, the tarot had its meaning, and she knew what each card was supposed to represent, but they were merely suggestions, not actual truth. Not genuine prophecy of what was to come.

She quickly gathered up the cards she had laid, shuffled them again, then laid them out once more in the cross formation.

Her breath lodged in her throat.

The cards came out the same. Exactly the same. The five of swords. The inverted knight of wands. Culminating in the fifteenth card of the Major Arcana: the Devil. Zora stared at his horned, goatish face contorted in a sinister grin, batlike wings outstretched, as he presided over two figures chained at his feet. A pentacle marked the ground where the chained figures knelt.

Coincidence. That was all it could be. She would prove it.

She scooped up the cards and shuffled them a third time. And for the third time, she set them out. By the time she turned over and placed the final card, her hands shook.

The same. Each and every card. Their meaning clear: *A great evil is coming, unleashed by the five.*

Her heart pounded, her palms went damp, and her mouth dried. She never believed it possible, and yet . . . it was. The tarot predicted the future, a terrible future. Which meant—

Zora jumped to her feet. She ran to her family and the other families who made up their band. At her approach, the men stopped playing their fiddles and took their pipes from their mouths, and the women left off their gossiping. They all stared at her, and she knew that her face must be ashen, her eyes wide. She likely looked like a phantom.

"We have to stop them," she announced without preamble.

"Who?" asked Litti, her mother.

"The *gorgios* who went to the ruin." Her hands curled into fists by her sides as she fought to keep her voice level. "I have seen it. The cards have shown me. If we do not stop them, those five men are going to let loose a terrible evil."

No one laughed. Everyone knew that Zora put no faith in *dukkering* or magic. Yet it was for that very reason that they all took her seriously now. In fact, looks of pure terror filled their faces and the firelight shining in their rounded eyes turned them glassy and blank. Zora stared at them, at the men, and they stared back.

Not a single man moved.

Impatience gnawed at her. She took a step closer. "Why are you all sitting there like frightened goats? Get up! You must ride after the *gorgios* and stop them!"

The men exchanged glances until, *finally,* Zora's cousin Oseri stood up. Zora exhaled in relief, but her relief was short-lived. From the terrified expression on his face, it was clear Oseri had plans only to hide in his tent.

"The *wafodu* is too great," he stammered. "The evil will hurt us."

"So you are going to do nothing?" Zora demanded.

The men all shrugged, palms open. "What can we do against such powerful, bad magic?" someone bleated.

"Anything!" she shot back. But every last one of the men refused to move, while the women crossed themselves and muttered prayers.

There was no hope for it. With a growled curse, Zora turned on her heel and walked into the horse enclosure, but not before grabbing a crust of bread from the cooking area and slipping it into her pocket. It was said that bread held the Devil at bay, and she needed every bit of assistance she could scrounge. She also had her knife, tucked into the sash at her waist.

"Where are you going?" Zora's mother cried.

Zora did not stop until she slipped a bridle onto one of the horses and then swung up onto its bare back. Once mounted, she trotted forward until she stared down at the trembling men and women of her Romani band.

"I'm doing what needs to be done," Zora said. "I'm going to stop those lunatic men before they do something we shall *all* regret."

Despite her fear, she kicked her horse into a gallop. She had never faced anything like this in her life, and had no knowledge of what awaited her. How might she prevent the evil from being set free? All she knew was that she must.

Atop a rounded hill, the ruin formed a dark, jagged silhouette against the night sky, like a creature rising from the earth. As the riders neared the hill, Whit felt himself drawn forward, pulled by a force outside himself. He did not know *why* he had to reach the ruin, only that he must, and soon. His companions must have shared the feeling, for they also urged their horses faster, their hooves pounding beneath them as thunder presaged a storm.

At the base of the hill, all of the men fought to control their shying, rearing horses, trying to urge them up toward the ruin. None of the beasts would take the hill, though it was surely traversable by horse. The men alternately cursed and cajoled. Yet the horses refused to go farther.

"On foot, then," grumbled Bram.

After dismounting, as directed by Bram, the men gathered up fallen tree branches. Bram used skills honed during his time fighting the French and their native allies in the Colonies and quickly made torches from the branches. He set them ablaze with a flint from his pocket.

"Don't we look a fine collection of fiends," drawled Whit. For that is what they resembled as light from the torches bathed the men's faces in gaudy, demonic radiance.

At this notion, they all grinned.

"Shall we investigate, Hellraisers?" asked Edmund.

"Aye," the men said in unison, and Whit felt almost certain he heard a sixth voice hiss, *Yes.*

They climbed the hill, using torchlight to guide them. The shapes of toppled columns and crumbling walls emerged from the darkness, gleaming white and dull as bones. Everyone reached the top and surveyed the scene. Whatever the building had once been, its glory had long ago faded, becoming only a shade of its former self. A strange, thick miasma cloaked the ruin, its dank smell clogging Whit's nose, and it swirled as the five men prowled through the ancient remains. Examining a partially standing wall, he touched the surface of the stone. A cold that seemed nearly alive climbed up through his hand, up his arm, and would have gone farther had he not pulled back.

Their murmured voices were muffled by the heavy vapor, but Leo said, loud enough for all of them to hear, "What the hell is this place?"

"Appears to have been a temple," answered John, their resident scholar. He crouched and brushed away some dirt until he revealed what appeared to be a section of stone floor. "See here." He pointed to the ground as everyone gathered around. Holding his torch closer to the stonework, he indicated the faded, chipped remains of mosaic lettering. "*Huic sanctus locus.* 'This sacred place of worship.'"

"Worship of what?" asked Leo.

"Bacchus, I hope," said Bram. He gazed critically around the ruin, the torchlight turning the sharp planes of his face even sharper, his black hair blending with the night. The light gleamed on the scar that ran along his jaw and down his neck, a souvenir from his military service. "It's dull as church up here."

"What were you expecting?" said Whit. "It's a *ruin*, not a bordello." He thought of Zora, her refusal to take his money in exchange for a night in his bed, and wondered if he would ever see her again. He decided he would, and planned to return to the Gypsy encampment on the morrow, though he did not know how pleased she might be to see him.

Bram made a noise of displeasure and paced away, kicking aside a few loose rocks in his impatience. Whit, John, Edmund, and Leo all exchanged rueful smiles. Of all of them, Bram pushed the hardest for yet greater depths of debauchery, as if continually trying to outpace something that chased him.

The friends broke apart to drift separately through the ruin. Whit ambled toward a collection of five columns that had all toppled against each other, barely standing but for the tenuous support they gave each other. Fitting, he thought. He found himself possessed by the oddest humor, a moody melancholy that sought some means of release. Too late he realized he should have placed a wager with Leo as to what the ruin might have once been. The opportunity was gone now. Perhaps there was something else here upon which he might gamble. Leo had not gotten to a sixth cup of wine back at the Gypsy camp, so that bet could not be won or lost.

A gleam at the base of the leaning columns caught his attention. He slowly neared and peered closer. Yes, something dully metallic appeared on the ground. As he edged closer, he saw that the metal was, in fact, a large, thick rusted ring, the size of a dinner plate. Whit thought at first the ring simply lay in the weeds. A second ring, exactly the same, lay some three feet away. Closer inspection showed the rings were attached to something in the ground. Whit crouched to get a better view.

"Come and have a look," he called to his friends.

The men assembled around him, and the light from their collective torches revealed that the iron ring was affixed at one end to a large, square stone block. Whit handed his torch to Edmund and cleared away the rocks, weeds, and debris that nearly obscured the block, with Bram and Leo assisting. Soon, the block was completely uncovered. It was roughly three feet across and three feet long, with a metal ring set at each end.

"Looks like a door," said John.

"If it's a door," Bram answered, "then we should open it." His voice sounded slightly different from normal, a deeper, harsher rasp.

At once it seemed to Whit to be not only the most sensible thing to do, but the most essential. A burning need to see what was behind the door seized him, as strong as any need to gamble. He gripped one iron ring, and Leo gripped the other after giving his torch to Bram.

"On my count," said Whit. "One, two, *now!*"

Both he and Leo pulled with all their strength. Whit's muscles strained and pulled against the fabric of his shirt and coat, against the doeskin of his breeches as he dug his heels into the ground and fought to wrench open the heavy stone door. He grunted with exertion through his gritted teeth. *Pull, pull!* He had to get the door open.

Bram, Edmund, and John shouted their encouragement, their eyes aglow with the same fevered need to breach the door.

A deep, heavy wrenching sound rumbled up from the ground, as if the very foundations of the world were being rent asunder. Whit and Leo pulled harder, encouraged by the sound. Inches of stone emerged up as the stone slab rose in clouds of dust. Suddenly, with a final growl, the stone broke free from its earthen prison.

Whit and Leo heaved the block to one side, and it thudded on the ground, barely missing John's toes. But John didn't complain. He, like the other Hellraisers, was all too captivated by the sight of the opened door.

A black square, the doorway, and through it the scent of long-buried secrets came wafting up. It wasn't a damp smell, rather hot and dry, the scent of singed fabric and burnt paper. Whit grabbed his torch from Bram and thrust it through the doorway in the ground. The firelight illuminated precipitous stone stairs that disappeared into the gloom.

"A hollow hill," murmured Whit.

"I've read about them." John gazed avidly down. "From ancient legends about fairy kingdoms."

They paused for a moment, each taking in the wonderment of an actual hollow hill. In silent agreement, they descended the stairs. Their boots scraped over the stone, and the sound echoed as they delved farther. They found themselves in an underground chamber. Whit could not imagine what kind of ancient tools had the strength to carve a large chamber out of solid rock, yet somehow, some ancient laborer had done just that. The room itself was almost entirely bare, just a floor and sloping walls that arched overhead. Whit was surprised at the height of the ceiling. He was a tall man, yet he did not have to stoop or bend in the chamber. Instead, he stood at his full height as he and his friends slowly turned in circles as they gazed at the incredible room hewn from a stone hill.

Yet the chamber was not empty.

"We have a companion, lads," said Whit.

At one end of the chamber, on a crude seat carved from solid rock, sat a man—or at least his skeletal remains, remarkably preserved given that they had been buried in this chamber for what had to be over a thousand years if the age of the ruins above was any indication. Whit and the others pressed closer to stare at this new discovery.

"He's wearing the uniform of a Roman centurion," John

whispered. "His helmet has the horsehair crest, he has medals upon his chest, and—this is astounding—his wooden *Bacillum Viteum* stick has not decayed." Sure enough, a knotty stick rested in the crook of the centurion's arm.

"I'm more interested in *that*," said Whit. He pointed to what the long-dead soldier held in his bony hands. A bronze box, the size of a writing chest, with images of twining snakes worked all over its surface. The centurion gripped the box tightly, holding it snug against his breastplate. Whatever was inside the box must have been extremely valuable, valuable enough to consign a Roman officer to death.

Bram stared at the box, then at the faces of his friends clustered around. He grinned fiendishly as he placed his hand upon the box. "Let's have ourselves a look."

Whit stared as Bram forcibly pried the box from the skeleton's grip. The bones cracked as the box was wrenched free, yet Whit did not wince at the sound. All he wanted was the box, to learn what it contained, and he gazed avidly as Bram began to open it.

Be careful, Zora had warned him. Yet he shoved her warning aside. The answers to everything were inside the box.

As the lid opened, the flames from the torches were suddenly sucked inside the box. The chamber plunged into darkness.

Chapter 2

Without warning, Zora's horse surged up, recoiling. She fought to keep the gelding under control, but panic gripped it. The horse reared and whinnied in fear. The animal tossed its head, tearing the reins from Zora's hands, then reared again. She lost her hold and flew from the horse.

She landed hard upon her back, breath forced from her lungs. The night sky stared down, black and empty, as she heard her horse gallop away. For a moment, she lay on the ground, struggling to breathe, cursing the animal. She could not waste any time, so she staggered to her feet.

To go back to the encampment to get another horse would take too long. No help for it but to proceed on foot. After ensuring that her spinning head had settled down to a reasonable degree, Zora began to run. She hoped she would not be too late to save the handsome *gorgio* from himself.

"What the devil?" growled Whit.

"Well, yes," said a voice in the darkness, a voice Whit did not recognize. It sounded cultured, elegant, but held notes of the deepest shadows, impossibly deep, and with a sharp edge like a duelist's rapier. "In a manner of speaking."

Light flared. Not from the torches. From lamps that suddenly appeared along the walls. Whit was certain no lamps had been there when first he and his friends had surveyed the chamber. They gave off a sulfurous light, and shadows shuddered over the walls. It took a moment for Whit's vision to adjust from light to darkness to light again. When, at last, his eyesight adjusted, he thought at first that his senses played havoc with his reason.

He stumbled back, as did his friends. Bram dropped the box with a clatter. A paper scroll tumbled out, and from the scroll emerged a tiny flicker of light, smaller than a firefly, that darted about the chamber. But Whit didn't pay any heed to the flitting light.

A man stood before them. Dressed in debonair black satin, from his waistcoat to his frock coat to his breeches. Rich silver and green embroidery covered his cuffs, the edges of his coat, and the surface of his waistcoat, and the lace frothing at his wrists and neck was gleaming white. His stockings, too, were pristine, and dazzling jeweled buckles adorned his shoes. He wore a nobleman's sword, equally jeweled. Though the man's clothing and sword invited admiration, it was his face that truly arrested the eye. He seemed the same age as Whit, yet the stranger's hair was purely white—and not from powder, nor was it a wig. He wore it tied back and bagged in black silk.

And his eyes were the color of diamonds, the irises colorless, yet burning.

"Holy God," breathed Leo.

The stranger smiled. It was a cold smile, the same one Whit had observed at the gaming table many times, one he had given just as frequently. Full of calculation, a gesture designed to unsettle rather than put at ease.

"Oh, not Him," the stranger said. He looked at each of the men in the chamber, Whit included. "I must thank you, gentlemen. Over a millennium in that wretched box can grow exceedingly tedious."

"Who . . . who are you?" Bram demanded.

The stranger looked droll as he flicked at the lace at his cuffs. "Must I explain?"

Whit's heart beat thickly in the confines of his chest. He thought certainly that what appeared before him must be some variety of illusion, brought forth from either an intemperate night or perhaps some Gypsy's engineered trick, for well-dressed men did not simply emerge from ancient Roman boxes.

"No trick," murmured the stranger, as if reading Whit's thoughts. "No result of too many cups of wine. I am as real as you, Whit."

Whit started upon hearing the stranger speak his name. He'd never met the man before. Not in any ballroom or brothel.

"Of course I know your name, Whit." The stranger never lost his smile. "I know you *very* well, just as I know Bram, Leo, Edmund, and John." He stared at them each in turn, the five of them rooted to where they stood. "Though that"—he gestured disdainfully at the scroll lying on the ground— "kept me prisoner these long years, I still watched, still learned. I might not have had the use of my power, but I could yet gather intelligence as the world changed around me. And you dear Hellraisers have been *most* entertaining and educational."

A snort of disbelief came from Bram.

John gulped, "Are you really . . ."

"The Devil?" finished Whit, hardly believing he spoke such words.

The stranger made a dismissive wave with his pale hand. A black stone ring glinted on his littlest finger. "Such an unappealing name. Without a shred of poetry. If you like, you may call me . . ." He thought for a moment. "Mr. Holliday."

Bram laughed, though the sound was more of a harsh grate than a laugh. "I've heard more truth from a mountebank."

A flicker of annoyance crossed Mr. Holliday's face, but it was gone almost as quickly as it appeared. "You desire proof? As you wish."

The stone chamber vanished. A glittering salon took its place. The walls were covered with gilded woodwork and rich tapestries. Closer inspection revealed that the tapestries depicted vices of the most depraved order, things that shocked even Whit. Crystal chandeliers gleamed with the light of thousands of candles. Music filled the air, though Whit could see no musicians. Elaborately carved furniture filled the room, and upon marble-topped tables rested silver pitchers, goblets, and platters heaped with delicacies. Whit smelled the sweet grapes and savory capons, reminding him that he had not dined. Another table had dice and decks of cards—a temptation.

Women lounged upon settees, their soft limbs and bodies barely hidden by loose, transparent gowns. They stared at Whit and the other men with blatant enticement, offering their own temptation. Bram growled as he stared at them, and the women laughed, their laughter like chiming glass.

"Whatever you want, gentlemen," Mr. Holliday said, "I can provide."

"This could be an illusion," John noted, ever the skeptic. "Something performed with mirrors."

"Of course, a learned scholar would demand further evidence." Mr. Holliday snapped his fingers, and one of the women drifted up from the settee and glided toward John. She wrapped her arms around his neck, pressing the length of her supple, hardly clothed body against his. "Does that feel like an illusion? Or that?" He snapped his fingers again, and another woman swayed toward Whit.

She held out a fig, ripe and purple, and his hand came up to take it. She smiled invitingly at him. He returned the smile, though he wished her hair was black, not blond, her eyes dark rather than blue. The fig felt very real in his hand, and he took a bite. Its sweet flavor flooded his mouth, the most delicious thing he had ever tasted.

Women came to drape themselves against Leo, Bram, and Edmund, pressing offerings of cakes and fruit into the men's hands. As each of them took and ate the offerings, it hit them all.

This was real.

The Devil—Mr. Holliday, as he preferred to be called—*truly* stood before them, released from a prison that had held him for likely over a thousand years. And Whit and his friends had freed him from that prison.

"That is correct," said Mr. Holliday. "Through the munificence of that act, you men have at last liberated me from that most hateful place." He snapped his fingers, and one of the women darted forward to grab the parchment scroll from the ground. She handed it to Mr. Holliday before scurrying away. He held the scroll tightly.

"For that deed alone," he continued, "I must show my thanks. I must bestow a gift upon each of you."

That sounded promising.

"What did you have in mind?" asked Whit.

Mr. Holliday gazed at him, and his gaze held knowledge far beyond anything a mortal man could ever attain. "Your deepest desire." Barely a whisper, these words, yet Whit heard them as clear as if spoken directly to his brain.

For a moment, an image of the fiery Zora flashed into Whit's mind, but he would not allow himself to think of her now.

"It is but a small matter," continued Mr. Holliday, "and I shall make it yours." He strode toward him and shooed away the simpering woman. His diamond-white eyes stared hard into Whit's own eyes, piercing and intent. As he fixed Whit with his gaze, the little will-o'-the-wisp flitted around Mr. Holliday's head. Annoyed, the white-haired stranger swatted at it. The light retreated to a corner of the chamber and Whit thought it flickered angrily.

After a moment, Mr. Holliday's mouth curled into a smile. "For you, my dear Lord Whitney, I shall grant you the ability to control the odds. You can make them good or bad, as you require."

"If that were such a gift," answered Whit, "I should have control of chance all the time."

"Ah, but no," was Mr. Holliday's amused correction. "For a true gamester understands that sometimes it is better to lose than win."

Whit could not deny this. If he won every round, took every hand of cards or cast of the dice, no one would permit him to gamble with them anymore. Yet with a judicious losing streak, he could build false confidence in his opponents, lure them into complacency as they wagered higher and higher amounts, and then Whit could win it all. A greater risk. A greater reward. A greater thrill.

Mr. Holliday knew this, knew Whit, and all from a glance.

As Whit absorbed the implications of having control over probability, Mr. Holliday strolled toward Bram.

"Women," Bram said immediately. He caressed the lush form of the female nestled against him.

Chuckling, Mr. Holliday shook his head. "You already *have* women, Bram. There is no gift in that. No, for you . . ." He stared again with that incisive gaze, this time holding Bram captive with that look. Mr. Holliday boldly stared at the scar that marred Bram's face. "I shall bestow upon you the ability to persuade anyone to do anything. Including the demons who shout in your head. As well as any woman you wish to persuade into your bed."

Bram grinned, clearly liking that potential gift very much.

Then Mr. Holliday ambled toward Leo, who stared back with as much arrogance as he could muster. Another chuckle from Mr. Holliday. "I cannot change the circumstances of your birth to make you a gentleman," he said, and Leo scowled. "However," Mr. Holliday continued, "what I can offer you is the gift of the future. You deal in futures, do you not?"

"How would this gift work?" Leo was ever a shrewd businessman, demanding to know the details.

"It takes but a single touch." A coin appeared in Mr. Holliday's hand, and light gleamed on its surface as he slowly flipped it back and forth across the backs of his fingers. "You've only to touch a piece of money—a bill, a coin—and you will have a vision of the owner's financial future." The coin vanished in a tiny cascade of sparks. "Specifically, their disasters."

"And I invest, or counterinvest, accordingly."

Mr. Holliday smiled. "As you desire. With my gift, you will be able to see into the future, and thus increase your fortune. Then no doors will be closed to you, regardless of your less than genteel origins."

Though Leo did not grin as Bram had, Whit could tell that the idea of finally shouldering his way into the inner circles of privilege strongly appealed to Leo.

"As for you," Mr. Holliday went on, coming to stand in front of Edmund, "your deepest desire has but one face. The face of a woman lost to you."

Edmund inhaled sharply, and no wonder. Many years ago, Edmund fell deeply in love with Rosalind Gautier, daughter of the Marquis of Prestbury, but Edmund was only a baronet, and Lord Prestbury had greater ambition for his daughter. He married her to a duke's eldest son, yet Edmund still stared longingly after Rosalind whenever she sat in her box in the theater or entered a ballroom—much to her husband's chagrin.

"Yes," he breathed, yearning plain in his face.

"She shall be yours." Mr. Holliday said this easily, as if offering a tavern's special meat pie to a hungry customer. Then he turned and strode to John.

"But you," he continued, "you have a different desire, one that encompasses more than just one woman's heart, or the throw of the dice."

John, lips pressed tight, said nothing, though his face was flushed and his breathing rapid. Though Whit kept company with John, the other man was always the most reserved of the five friends, his impulses and needs more opaque in the midst of their carousing.

"For you," continued Mr. Holliday, munificent, "I shall

bestow upon you knowledge of other men's minds. The power and influence you seek so ardently shall be within your grasp once you can read the secret tomes of men's thoughts."

Power? Influence? The first Whit had ever heard of such desire in John. Yet if his friend wanted these things, Whit had no objection and would rather leave these weighty matters to someone who desired them. Unlike himself.

John's eyes narrowed, and then he gave a slight nod, but he could not contain the hunger in his expression. Yes, Mr. Holliday had read him properly, if the look on John's face was any indicator.

"So, what say you, gentlemen?" Mr. Holliday stepped back and opened his arms wide, a host welcoming guests into luxurious accommodations. "Will you permit me to show you my gratitude by granting each of you your heart's desire?"

The tiny wisp of light grew agitated and swooped around Mr. Holliday. He glared at it before backhanding the little gleam. It careened into a wall, then slid to the ground, dimming. What was that thing?

"Everything you ever wanted, my dearest Hellraisers." Mr. Holliday was all polished courtesy again, his voice both calming and smoothly persuasive. "It shall be yours. All I need is your permission."

Whit searched in himself, trying to reason his way toward understanding what was being offered. Yet he could not make his mind sharpen. He would reach toward a question, a thought, and the thoughts kept slipping away. He brought to mind Zora, how she read him so quickly and with such clarity. He tried to mentally call her up, her precision of thought, her judgment. He could not—she glimmered beyond his reach. All he knew was that the gift being proffered was too great, the persuasive qualities of Mr. Holliday's voice too seductive to gainsay. Whit could command the odds as he chose—no gambler could ask for more.

What might he win? *Whom* might he win?

He felt the movement of his neck as he nodded, and saw his friends nod, as well. "Yes," they said in unison.

Mr. Holliday beamed, and the women clapped. "Marvelous. And to seal the bond, I require the smallest token from each of you." He snapped his fingers.

Five men suddenly appeared, all of them dressed as fine as courtiers, all of them seemingly young and hale, just as Whit and his friends were young and hale. Yet though the men had appeared out of thin air, Whit could not find anything particularly remarkable about their appearance. He tried to look at these newcomers in the face, but every time he did, his gaze simply . . . slid away, as if guided.

One of the men came to stand in front of Whit. He held out a hand.

Whit understood. He was to give the token to this courtier.

A voice within him shouted, *No! This is not right.* But that voice grew muddied and dim, driven away by a shadowed tide.

For a moment, Whit deliberated what to give the courtier. He thought of his pocket watch. Nothing he possessed had such worth. Monetarily, it would bring almost nothing, for it was old, dented, hardly the latest in the horologist's art. Yet the watch's value was beyond measuring, for it had belonged to his father, and his father's father. The only true connection he had with his past. He rebelled at the idea of giving it away, even to gain power over chance.

"It needn't be something so important to you as your timepiece," said Mr. Holliday. "Something inconsequential will suffice."

A relief. With a swift tug, Whit pulled a silver button from his coat, then handed it to the man before him. Though Whit could not truly see the courtier's face, Whit felt the man's satisfaction as his fingers closed over the button. Throughout the chamber, the scene was enacted four more times. Bram, Leo, Edmund, and John. They all handed over unimportant objects—the ribbon binding Bram's hair, Leo's

snuffbox, a stickpin from John, Edmund's handkerchief—
and the courtiers who received the tokens pocketed them.

"Wonderful," said Mr. Holliday. A glow emanated from
his black stone ring. It rose up from the ring, then broke apart
into five separate lights. Whit did not have time to duck or
move aside as one of the lights shot straight toward him, just
as the other lights shot toward each of his friends. The light
hit him straight in the center of his chest, making him stagger. A cold radiance spread through Whit's body, seeping
outward, until he felt burning ice in every vein, every bone,
followed immediately by a surge of energy and strength.

The feeling was intoxicating, galvanizing. Whit became
aware of the beat of his heart, the breath in his lungs, his muscles bunching and stretching, his every nerve acutely sensitive. Powerfully alive. The voice inside him, crying out that
all this was wrong, went very, very quiet. As though strangled.

"Splendid." Mr. Holliday's smile widened until it stretched
nearly from ear to ear. "My congratulations, fine sirs. You
have made an excellent bargain." He laughed.

Whit laughed, as well. He could not stop himself. It burst
from him without warning and without end. He felt unlike
himself. Wild, reckless. Capable of anything.

Bram, Leo, John, and Edmund also laughed. Triumphant.
The five friends united in conquest, for they knew that now no
obstacles stood in their path. Their voices sounded odd—as
though they were instruments played by strange hands.

"Stop!"

Whit jerked as a familiar feminine voice rang out. He turned
to see Zora running into the chamber, her skirt swirling, her
braid undone so that her hair flew wildly as she ran. As she
entered the chamber, she started in surprise, gazing at the
elaborately decorated room. She skidded to a halt, gasping for
breath, and Whit realized she held a piece of bread in one
hand, a knife in the other.

The will-o'-the-wisp flared back to life again, then shot

out the same door through which Zora had entered. At the same time, the five courtiers vanished.

Dark eyes wide, Zora stared at Mr. Holliday. Fear tightened her lovely face. And when she looked at Whit, the fear drained away, replaced by profound sorrow.

"Oh, *Duvvel*," she breathed. "I'm too late."

Zora did not consider herself one of the faithful, yet she had prayed without cessation as she had run to the site of the ruin. Her legs had ached, her side had burned—she was far more familiar with riding a horse than running—yet she had forced herself on, determined to prevent disaster from happening. Hope had withered when she found the *gorgios'* five horses impatiently stamping at the base of the hill. She had charged up the slope, even though all of her senses told her it was a place to be shunned. A miasma clung to the ruin, cold, malevolent. She had found no sign of the men wandering amongst the shattered marble and toppled stone. Zora had clung to the slightest shred of fortune that perhaps they had grown bored and wandered off on foot in search of other amusements.

Then she had found the doorway leading into the hill, and hope had died.

Men's voices had drifted up to her as she debated for half a moment. She felt it, the strong, dark power over that place, and it hummed through her body like dread. All the fairy tales she had heard and dismissed as *hokibens*, nonsense, they came back to her in a rush. She recalled one, a favorite of hers as a girl, where a princess journeyed through the underworld to rescue the enchanted prince. The princess had faced awful peril, many trials against a powerful foe. In that story, though, as in all the other tales, goodness triumphed over evil. Zora had to believe she would do the same.

With her heart pounding painfully, she had drawn her knife, pulled the bread from her pocket, and descended the ancient stairs. She did not know what to expect. A crude stone chamber. The relics of an ancient shrine.

Instead, she now found herself in the most ornate room she had ever seen. It was the kind of room *gorgios* liked and the Rom avoided, full of heavy, golden furniture and walls covered with elaborate carvings that resembled rotting vegetation. A choking prison of a room, gaudy and too bright. She couldn't believe what the tapestries hanging on the walls showed, either. Things she knew were physically, if not morally, impossible. In addition to the images of women engaged in licentious pursuits, there were actual strumpets everywhere, hanging like vines off of sofas—and off of men.

Her man. He wasn't *hers*, but she couldn't help but think of him as such.

Whit and his friends were here, in this awful chamber. Waves of sinister energy flowed out from them like contagion. Even Whit radiated this malignant force, and she shriveled inside to see it in him. Whit looked exactly the same, but he was changed, deeply changed.

A man dressed in black wore a ghastly smile. No, he was not a man, but *Wafodu guero* himself. Zora never believed there could be an embodiment of evil. She thought it a story told to children or the gullible, looking for something or someone on whom they could blame their misdeeds. Yet here it was. Here *he* was. And she stood in the same chamber with him as breath burned in her lungs and throat. She felt the truth of her body recovering from its sprint, and this convinced her that she was painfully, miserably awake. The look on his face was triumphant.

She had been too slow.

"Why, *pireno*?" She turned to Whit, and her blood froze to see the fever burning in his blue eyes. Even beneath the glare of the chandeliers, he remained as arrestingly handsome as he had beside the campfire, maybe even more so, all the clean lines of his face, the strength of his form completely revealed. Now that masculine beauty held a great wickedness, a wickedness greater than before, for this was not one man's wasteful pursuits, but the loss of his soul. A loss he did not yet comprehend.

"Because *I want*," he answered her in his rich, deep voice. His eyes raked over her, bold, intent—utterly altered from the way he had looked at her back at the encampment. He was the same, but a different man gazed at her from behind Whit's eyes. The trollop hanging on him giggled.

Zora stormed over and pushed the woman off of him. The tart hissed at Zora as she slunk away, but Zora only looked at Whit. "You don't know what you've done."

His friends chuckled, and the one with black hair rumbled, "We know *exactly* what we've done."

Whit only stared down at her like a shadowed blade. She felt the gulf between them widen. He had done it. Given himself over to a terrible power. He could not possibly understand what this meant, for if he did, surely a man as intelligent as he would never have done it. Trickery of some kind. The Devil was an expert in trickery. Because of his deception, he now possessed five new souls. Including Whit's.

No, she refused to admit defeat. She whirled to face the creature clad in black satin, the thing with eyes of ice and a ravenous smile. Though her hand trembled, she held her knife aloft in one hand, the bread in the other. She would have no allies here. She was alone. Anger and fear surged through her as she stalked to him.

"Undo it," she demanded, hoping her voice did not shake too much.

"Undo what?" the wicked creature asked mildly.

"Whatever it is you've done to him." Now her voice was shrill. "To them. Undo it; take it back."

"My sweet *mushi*," he said, and it startled her to hear him speak the Romani tongue. He spread his white hands. "They merely accepted gifts of gratitude, and of their own free will."

"There is always a price," she fired back. Hoping that the weapon gave her some advantage, Zora brandished her knife. "I demand that you release these men and go back to wherever you came from. Or I shall cut you."

Wafodu guero sighed, then gazed disdainfully at the knife. Zora's hand spasmed. The knife was pulled from her grip by an unseen force. Her weapon flew across the chamber, looking like a child's flimsy toy, before clattering onto the ground. Zora's heart dropped.

"Truly, did you anticipate your fragile mortal metalwork might pose some threat to me?" The beast sounded quite amused.

If a weapon could not harm the creature, perhaps ancient belief could. Zora waved the piece of bread as one might wave a torch, feinting toward *Wafodu guero*'s smirking face.

Yet he did not move, did not shrink back. Only sneered. "And *that* is an insult to my power." He rolled his eyes. "Really, this strains my patience." Another pointed glance from him, and two half-dressed trollops suddenly leapt upon Zora, grabbing her arms. The useless piece of bread fell to the floor. He kicked it away, and light from the chandelier made the jeweled buckle on his shoe glimmer.

Zora's muscles screamed in agony as she tried to break free from the women's hold. The harlots' plump, soft bodies were deceiving, for the women gripped Zora with a vicious strength, their nails digging through the fabric of Zora's sleeves to cut into the flesh beneath. They hissed into her ears, their breath heavy and sweet like rotten flowers. Zora drove her heels against the women's knees and thighs, but they would not release her. No way to get free. She fought on, twisting and pulling as hard as she was able.

"Such a wild little thing," murmured *Wafodu guero*. He turned to the assembled men, who had been watching the proceedings with bemused interest. "What shall we do with her, eh, lads? So fierce. So lovely." Casually, he strolled to Zora. She tried to shrink away, to no avail, and he ran one fingertip down her arm.

Zora shuddered at the burning cold of his touch. She wrenched herself to one side, trying to break the contact. The women held her fast, though, one of them gripping the back of her head, so she was forced to endure the loathsome touch. Zora felt defiled.

"What, then?" asked *Wafodu guero*, turning back to the men and moving away from her. His henchwoman released Zora's head. "I am feeling magnanimous tonight. Thus, I leave the choice up to you fine gentlemen. Set her ablaze? Turn her into a sow? Or perhaps you have . . . other ideas. You are all young, healthy men. I am sure you can think of something."

Zora thought it certain that her heart would burst from her chest. She felt ill. Powerless. These *gorgios*, lost to wicked magic, could do anything to her. Kill her. Or make her plead for death. But she refused to let them see her monstrous fear. It might inflame them further, for malice fed upon weakness. So she tipped up her chin and glared at them with all the heat and defiance she could marshal.

Each of the men stared at her, openly appraising. Whit amongst their number. Silence stretched out.

"Give her to me."

Her gaze shot to Whit. "What?" she gasped.

He did not look at her. Instead, he stared hard at the creature in black. "I want her. Give the Gypsy girl to me."

Wafodu guero laughed, and Zora struggled even harder against the hands that gripped her. Rage blazed through her, scouring her from the inside out.

Zora cursed in English and Romani. Angry, she was so blindingly angry. The cutting edge of betrayal sliced through her. Even having given himself to the Devil, she still clung to a shred of hope that Whit was not fully lost, that his heart—the heart that yearned for meaning and purpose—might yet persevere. They had shared something at the encampment, something beyond attraction.

"You want the girl?" asked the dark-haired *gorgio*, the one with the splendid face and ominous scar. "A pretty enough piece, but you've never been the wenching sort."

Whit crossed to her on his long legs until he stood very close. The heat of his body soaked into her own, and she hated the fact that she needed his heat after the chill touch of *Wafodu guero*. She continued to fight against the demonic women holding her, yet, even in this struggle, she was aware of Whit's height, his strength.

He looked down at her with eyes that searched as well as demanded. The blue of cornflowers, she realized dimly. This man, who had just unleashed the Devil upon an unsuspecting world, had cornflower blue eyes. And, under different circumstances, she might have gladly spent hours admiring them, wondering what thoughts dwelt behind such brilliant color.

Now, she wished she'd never seen those stunning eyes again. Yet she could not turn away from him, held in place more by the intensity of his gaze than the hands of the Devil's strumpets.

"Her secrets," he rumbled, and though his words were for his friends, he continued to stare at her. "I want to learn them."

"What secrets?" she hissed back. "*Card* secrets?"

"*All* your secrets." His words were a dark promise.

Zora swallowed hard. "You will get nothing from me."

Wafodu guero chuckled again. "I do like this. I like this very much. Do you fellows agree? Shall we give the girl to Whit?"

"Aye," the four men answered, grinning.

"No!" Zora shouted. This couldn't be happening. If she hadn't pursued Whit to this cursed hill, she would be preparing to go to Horsham on the morrow, to tell fortunes for the marketgoers, and her mother wanted her back in time to help with the washing, even though Zora hated doing the washing and was never very good at it. Her ordinary life. She wanted it desperately. "Do not do this," she whispered, tears gathering.

Something flashed in Whit's eyes, something she hoped was remorse. She caught a glimmer of the man she had known back at the encampment. Free of the Devil's dark influence. Whit's jaw tightened. Maybe it was not too late. Maybe he could stop this—

"It will be so," boomed the Devil. "I give the girl to you."

The creature clapped his hands, the sound unnaturally loud in the chamber, like the crack of a musket.

Her head spun, everything dimmed and fell away, and Zora knew no more.

Gone. The girl simply disappeared as if dousing a candle. Whit had seen many incredible things this night, yet Zora's vanishing jolted him from his intoxicated haze of power. Even Bram, Leo, John, and Edmund exclaimed in surprise when the girl blinked away.

"What have you done with her?" Whit demanded of Mr. Holliday.

The elegant man held up his hands in a placating gesture. "Be at ease, Whit. Search your pockets."

Whit frowned, but complied. One pocket held his usual equipage—a pearl-handled folding knife, half a cheroot, some coins. But the other . . . He pulled out a playing card, though none had been there before. Intertwined serpents were printed on the back of the card. When he turned it around he cursed.

The card was the queen of diamonds. And the queen looked exactly like Zora. Same wide-set, dark eyes, same tumble of black hair, same lovely features set defiantly, as if daring someone—*him*—to meet her challenge. Whit stared at the card in his broad hand, amazed. It seemed so fragile, nothing but paper.

He glared at Mr. Holliday. "She had better not be hurt." A strange urge had made him ask for Zora, an urge he'd had to obey. Yet he had not anticipated anything like this. Perhaps she would be simply given over to his care. But this . . . He pushed back at the shadowed thoughts and demands swirling through him. He wanted her, but would not harm her. Even a reprobate Hellraiser such as himself clung to a few tattered shreds of honor.

"The Gypsy is perfectly safe," soothed Mr. Holliday. "Merely held in a temporary suspension. She cannot free herself. That power is yours. To release her, all you must do is go to London and place that card upon your own card table. She is bound to the card and will not be able to move more than twenty feet away from it. And if you possess the card, she shall be yours for as long as you desire."

"Knowing Whit," Bram muttered to the other men, "he'll weary of her right after he tups her, then be back at the gaming tables fifteen minutes after."

Whit did not share Bram's opinion. Zora was a complex woman and would hold him longer than any other woman had before. He knew this instinctually as if uncovering a hidden part of himself, a new sense receptive only to her.

"For as long as you want to keep her," Mr. Holliday continued, "the girl will be unable to lie to you. Ask her anything you wish, and she must answer truthfully."

Whit found himself smiling. Ah, but that was a good gift, for he wanted her secrets. Anything she could give him, he wanted.

Carefully, he slid the card into his pocket, for it was a precious burden. He burned to get to London as quickly as possible so he might have Zora to himself. Away from the eyes of others. Only him and her, alone in his home. She was a wild thing, unbroken, and his dark blood blazed to think of the potential. Hell and damn, she would be delicious, exactly what he needed, what he craved. Now he had the power to make her entirely his.

"My thanks, sir," he murmured to Mr. Holliday, and bowed.

"We *all* thank you," added Leo. The other men added their voices to Leo's, all of them bowing.

Mr. Holliday beamed, the most munificent host, as he returned the bow. "It is *I* who offer you my gratitude. I am most eager to learn and discover this modern world, now that you excellent gentlemen have given me my long-denied liberty. As I am sure you are also most eager to explore the world with your new gifts."

The friends shared grins, each of them thinking of yet untapped pleasures and unmet ambitions, all of which they would soon come to realize. Whit felt the presence of Zora close, and the towering heights of anticipation. Her secrets would be his, and probability was also his to command. Part of him rebelled at the notion, but the shadowed voice within him smothered that rebellion. He told himself he could not imagine anything more wondrous or welcome. Just as his friends envisioned what their gifts would bring them.

They had been growing weary of things so easily lately. That would not be the case again.

"If any of you have need of something," Mr. Holliday went on, "simply say, *Veni, geminus*, and one of my attendants shall wait upon you." He gave another sinuous bow, a movement of supreme, unearthly elegance, then patted the scroll he held. "Now I bid you all good evening, Hellraisers." A smile spread across his face. "I shall see you all again."

In an icy mist, Mr. Holliday disappeared. The gilded room and the women within vanished, as well. Leaving the five men standing once again in the carved rock chamber, with only the skeleton and empty box for company. Their torches, lying upon the ground, burst back into flame and illuminated the chamber.

For a moment, none of the friends moved. No one spoke.

"Was that . . . real?" whispered Edmund.

Whit's hand strayed to his pocket and found the playing card. He glanced at it and saw the image of Zora printed upon its face. A hum of awareness traveled the length of his arm, through his body.

"Indeed, it was real," he said. "It *is* real." He returned the card to his pocket, then looked up at the dazed faces of his friends.

"Felicitations all around," Leo boomed.

Everyone joined in, offering each other their congratulations on a job most splendidly done.

"What shall we do now?" asked John.

"What *won't* we do?" Bram returned with a laugh like the bite of a whip. "For me, I shall find the most beautiful, virtuous woman in England and, with my gift from Mr. Holliday, persuade her to share my bed. Then thoroughly debauch her until she is the *least* virtuous woman in England."

"I must find Rosalind immediately," said Edmund fiercely. "And make her mine at last."

"She *is* married," Whit felt compelled to note. The state of marriage meant nothing to Bram, but Edmund had always tread a more respectful path. Or he had, before this night.

Edmund's eyes gleamed with fever. "Mr. Holliday said she was to belong to me, and I will have her, no matter what."

Whit wondered what Edmund's vow might entail, for Edmund had never been a particularly violent man, never joined in when the Hellraisers brawled. But seeing the hectic color staining Edmund's cheeks and gleaming in his eyes, Whit thought those days of passive calm were over.

"I am for Whitehall," said John. He curled and uncurled his fingers in his habitual gesture of contemplation, though there was something manic about his movements now, less controlled. "There are many men whose minds I would know, their plans and alliances. Soon, they will find me a most astute and"—he smiled tightly—"powerful ally."

"There are fortunes to be built," Leo said. "*My* fortunes." He added darkly, "And there are fortunes to be razed."

There were several men of genteel birth who had made it quite clear that neither Leo nor his commoner family were welcome in the rarified air of genteel society, Leo had railed bitterly to Whit and the others over predawn whiskey and cheroots. No mistaking the bloodthirstiness in his voice now, the need to punish. Those aristocratic men had no idea what awaited them, the beast they had thought chained now broken free from its restraints, intent on carnage.

"And you, Whit?" asked Edmund. "What wondrous schemes do you intend?"

"I must go to London posthaste," Whit answered. Bram might ruin reputations, and Leo might trample upon the pecuniary fortunes of his enemies, but the dark voice within Whit demanded that he cut a wide and devastating swath through the gaming hells of London. He could win anything. Not just money, but prized possessions, property and heirlooms. He had Mr. Holliday's gift of mastery over odds. And he also possessed the gift of Zora. Soon, he would learn every one of her secrets. Her card tricks. Her fierce heart. He would have all of her, laid bare for his pleasure.

Whit started toward the stairs that led out of the chamber.

"Enjoy your Gypsy girl," Bram called after him.

Whit paused on the stairs and grinned at his fellow Hell-raisers. "I shall. As we all should enjoy our newfound gifts."

"Now we are Hellraisers in truth," said John, laughing.

Whit smiled, though he did not laugh. "So we are."

"There are no obstacles in our paths," said Edmund.

"Godspeed," Leo called.

"God has *nothing* to do with this." On that, Whit strode up the remainder of the stairs and emerged into the chilled night, utterly transformed from the man he had been only hours earlier.

Chapter 3

Zora's head cleared, vision and sense returned. Yet what she saw next made her dizzy all over again. She knew only that one moment, it had been the middle of the night and she had been standing in that horrible *gorgio* chamber full of heavy gilded wood, a chamber full of reckless men and awful women. The Devil presiding over all of it.

She'd had a dim sense of motion around her, as if she had observed movement on the bottom of the ocean. Voices had come to her, muddied, muted. The words had made little sense. Fleeting impressions of a horse's hooves, land rushing past her, the open country being gradually choked by buildings, until she was in the thick of a monstrous, sprawling city. There had come a distant impression of entering very grand squares surrounded by massive homes. The horse's hoofbeats had slowed, then stopped. She felt herself carried up a flight of stairs.

Then, the next moment, she was in a room.

Spinning around, she found herself not three feet away from Whit. He looked windblown, his mahogany hair coming loose from its queue, his fine hunting clothes travel-worn and rumpled. In fact, he breathed heavily, as if he'd been riding and then running at top speed. He stared at her with ravenous blue eyes—so different from the cautious attraction with which he had regarded her back at the encampment. Though he wore the same face and had the same long, strapping body, he was not the same man who had sat upon the ground, who had played piquet with her and playfully demanded her secrets at cards.

This man standing before her was far more dangerous.

She found herself instinctually backing up, until she collided against some furniture and could go no farther.

"What is this place?" she demanded.

"My home." His voice was rough silk. He gave her a small bow. "Welcome."

Zora cast a quick glance around, assessing. This chamber she did not find half as revolting as the other beneath the ruin. The room in Whit's home was smaller, yet the walls were paneled with rich, dark wood that reminded her of the forest. A fire burned lowly in the hearth, but there wasn't a single cooking pot or tub of washing hanging over the flames. One small table held a chess set, yet the only real furniture in the chamber was a circular table surrounded by half a dozen chairs. Decks of cards were stacked upon the table. Everything in the room was of the finest quality, far more grand and sturdy than anything any Rom might have. The room smelled of strong drink and tobacco.

Through the tall, velvet-curtained windows, the dawn cast pink light. It was still too dark outside for Zora to see exactly where she might be. Somewhere in a large city. Far from home.

Because of Whit. The Whit who had been changed by the Devil's dark sway.

She whirled back to face him. "Let me go," she growled.

The wicked *gorgio* only shook his head, his eyes never leaving hers. "You are my guest."

"Your *prisoner*," she snapped.

He stood between her and the door, and she knew that he could easily catch and overpower her if she tried to bolt past him. So she turned and sprinted across the room, heading for the windows. The wood groaned under her hands as she pushed a window open—the room must never have been aired out, the atmosphere was so close and clinging—and as it opened, a cool dawn breeze flowed in to bite at her flushed cheeks. From what Zora could tell, the room was on the first story, which meant she could easily jump to the ground below. It wouldn't be the first occasion she'd fled a *gorgio*'s home through a window. This time, she did not have a sack full of purloined silver over her shoulder.

She did not care about stealth now. Gritting her teeth, she shoved the window open just enough for her to wriggle through. As soon as she had sufficient room, she put her hands upon the windowsill and vaulted over it.

Or she tried. She slammed into a barrier, then stumbled back to land on her backside. From the floor, Zora glared at the window.

She launched herself at it again. And found herself back on the floor once more, dazed.

With more caution, she stood and approached the window. Brisk morning air wafted into the room, and a leaf torn from an elm tree drifted in, borne upon the breeze. Slowly, Zora reached out, trying to stick her arm through the open window. She could not. An invisible barrier marked the boundary between the inside of the room and the outside. She pressed her fingertips against it and found the barrier to be cold and unyielding like a wall of ice.

Heart pounding, she snatched up one of the chess pieces and tossed it toward the window. The little carved bishop sailed out as if nothing stopped it. Zora stared, hardly believing.

She heard Whit walking steadily toward her. With quick hands and no warning, she grabbed the chessboard and flung it at him. He whipped up his arm to block the game board, playing pieces flying in every direction. Taking advantage of his momentary distraction, Zora shot past him, heading for the door.

He made a feint for her, but she evaded his outstretched

hands, swift as a vixen. They called her that sometimes, her family: a fleet, cunning she-fox. She drew on that part of herself as she ran toward the door. Then she was at the door, flinging it open to reveal an elegant hallway. A brief surprise to find the door unlocked. In a moment, she understood why.

Shoulder first she ran toward the doorway. And smashed against that same cold, immobile barrier. Her shoulder actually ached from the contact. There were no objects close at hand, so she tore off one of her rings and pitched it through the doorway. Just like the chess piece, the ring had no trouble leaving the room. In fact, it bounced off the hallway's wall and then rolled down the length of the passage with a mocking, metallic sound. It had freedom. She did not.

Whit's footsteps sounded behind her, the heels of his boots hitting the wood with the finality of a drumroll before execution.

"The Devil's wickedness," she snarled. She turned to face Whit, her body humming with fear and anger and the aftershocks of trying to throw herself against a magical barricade.

She could hardly believe she lived now in a world where existed such things as invisible barriers and *Wafodu guero*'s magic. Yet it was true, they were real, and she had no means of combating them.

"You are my guest," Whit repeated, as if she had not just attempted to flee and everything that had just happened was merely a lull in conversation.

"Until when?"

"Until I am ready to let you go." He advanced, and she would not allow him the satisfaction of intimidating her, no matter how much more height he had, no matter the coiled strength of his body or the burning intensity of his gaze. She stood her ground, tipping her chin to glare up at him.

She braced herself for his touch. Yet he did not touch her. Only stood very close, close enough for her to catch his scent of leather and warm male flesh, to see the flecks of gold in his eyes, like coins at the bottom of a bright blue sea. This close, she saw the masculine splendor of his face, its bold lines. The tempting contours of his mouth. A series of tiny scars just at his temple, the lingering trace of a childhood battle with illness—which made him all the more human and real.

He stared at her, and she saw a faint glimmering beneath the surface of his handsome face, a kind of distant puzzlement as if he were observing a beautiful yet brutal ritual. There, in those quick moments of wonderment, she saw him. The Whit she had known back in the encampment. Clever, quick of mind. Yearning. Desirable.

He blinked, and that man disappeared.

Now he was a villain. A beautiful villain.

He reached toward her then. She recoiled. All he did was shut the door behind her.

She retreated until the door pressed into her back. He advanced, closing the distance between them. His hands came up to brace against the door. The muscles of his shoulders and arms shifted and tensed, forming solid shapes beneath his coat. Sometime during the night, he had lost his stock, and he stood near enough for her to see the beat of his pulse beneath the corded length of his neck.

Despite the enforced calm of his expression, his pulse throbbed in quick rhythm. He was not as impassive as he seemed.

Her own heart was a galloping horse that ran all the harder at his nearness. Perhaps he wasn't as lost as she had thought, for he might have done a dozen things to her, none of them good. Yet she saw in his eyes, in the press of his lips, a struggle within. Battling the Devil's wickedness.

Maybe there was a chance at freedom, for both of them. If so, she had to tame the creature living in her chest, must control herself. But, even amongst her own people, she was known as too fiery, too impulsive, and so her cheeks flamed and her breath came in gulps as she stared up at Whit.

"'Tis your secrets I want, Zora." He said her name in a husky whisper—the voice of the man she'd known back in the encampment—that shivered up and down her spine.

"I don't want to give them to you," she answered.

A corner of his mouth turned up, sly and sensuous. "You've no choice in the matter. Mr. Holliday—"

"Who?"

"I believe you called him *Wafodu guero*."

"Mr. Holliday," she repeated. Her own smile tasted bitter. "Fitting for him to use a pleasant guise to cloak his evil."

At the word *evil*, Whit did frown. Clearly, he disliked the sound of it. There again, a trace of who he had been emerged. Zora wanted to reach out to that Whit from before. Yet he shook his head as though to dislodge his earlier self.

"Mr. Holliday granted me an additional boon," he continued. "While you are my guest, you must tell me the truth. No false words shall pass your lips." His gaze strayed down to her mouth. She found herself looking at his, the seductive shapes of his lips promising things she would not allow herself to ask for, not from this wicked stranger. She had known him, somehow, before, but now she did not.

The implications of his words unnerved her. Life amongst the Romani was made of spinning yarns and telling *hokibens*, both to the *gorgios* who wanted their fortunes told and amongst the Rom themselves. The Romani were expert fabulists and liars—a justifiable source of pride, it meant they were clever and could be trapped by no one. Yet perhaps this sinfully handsome *gorgio* was himself lying.

He saw that she doubted him. "What is your surname, Zora?"

She wanted to give him the alias she always used, Lee, but instead other words leapt from her mouth as if pulled by an unseen hand. "Grey. I am called Zora Grey." She bit her lip to keep from saying more.

Duvvel preserve her. It was true. She could not lie to him, thanks to the Devil's magic.

Whit smiled, pleased with himself, pleased with her.

There was no way out. Not until she gave this dark stranger what he desired. "It's card secrets you want? As you wish." She ducked underneath the cage of his powerful

arms and strode toward the gaming table. Deftly, she picked
up a deck of cards and began separating out the aces through
the sixes for piquet. As she did this, she noticed a card nearby
lying faceup on its own atop the table. She frowned as she
studied it.

"This queen of diamonds has no picture on it," she noted.

Whit came to stand beside her. He tapped the card with
one long finger, and his golden signet ring gleamed. "This is
what binds you to me. You cannot be more than twenty feet
from this card."

The cards in her hands fell to the table, scattering like dead
leaves, as she reached for the empty queen of diamonds. She
tried to pick up the card. Yet she could not lift it. Nor push it
across the surface of the table. It was as though it weighed
ten stone.

With maddening leisure, Whit strolled over and picked up
the card, then ambled toward the fireplace. He propped up
the card on the mantel, as one might display a hunting trophy.

"Until I say I am ready to release you," he said, giving the
card a nudge to straighten it. "And no earlier."

Zora grabbed the poker and swung it at him. His hand shot
out and grabbed it with surprising speed and agility. She
fought to pull it from his grasp, yet he was too strong, moving
not at all as she struggled to wrest free the long piece of iron.
Her teeth clenched with the effort. All for nothing. He might
be a wealthy *gorgio*, but Whit was not soft, not pampered.
He possessed strength in abundance.

Using every foul Romani word she knew, Zora cursed
him. He merely smiled his devil's maddening, arrogant smile,
delighted with his spirited plaything.

"I'm not a toy," she said through gritted teeth. "Not a doll.
Thoughts and feelings and needs—I have them. And they've
got nothing to do with you."

"Then tell me what I want to know," he answered calmly,
though menace threaded through his words.

Zora released her grip on the poker and stalked back to
the card table. She gathered the fallen cards, snatching them

up with hands that felt like talons. If only her fingers were tipped with cutting claws, capable of drawing blood. She would hurt the madness that held Whit, maybe drive it from his body, his soul. But she had only hands, no weapons against madness. Hot anger surged through her as she shuffled the cards, a bitter current through her body that pooled acridly in her mouth, as Whit came to stand beside her.

"To cheat at piquet is mere sleight of hand," she spat. "The secret of it lies in the shuffling and dealing of the deck." Her hands flew in neat circular motions, the cards in continuous motion.

His brows rose. "Not in marking the deck?"

Though she wanted to mislead him, the honest answer burst from her. "No, that will only get you caught, and is prone to failure if you are given a strange deck of cards. You must practice your shuffling to ensure you get precisely the cards you want at the deal." She demonstrated, allowing herself the momentary diversion of the cheat rather than focus on the intolerable situation in which she was now trapped.

Whit whistled in appreciation as she shuffled and dealt three times, each time dealing hands that made her the winner.

"It takes long hours to get the technique right," she said.

"Yet you've a gift for it." He watched her, his gaze sharp and also admiring. "I have seen many cardsharps, some of the best in England, and you make them look as clumsy as bears."

In his words, his face, he emerged, the same Whit he had been back at the encampment. Untouched by the Devil's influence. It was like catching sight of the sun after a cold, mist-shrouded night. And it was to *this* Whit she responded, gratified by his appreciation. Strange, so profoundly strange, to have found the one man, a *gorgio* at that, who could truly value her skill. She could only wish he hadn't bartered himself to *Wafodu guero*.

"Nonetheless, there must be more to your art than simply controlling the shuffle," Whit pressed.

"As I said, it's also in the dealing," she confirmed. Maybe

she could still reach him, beneath the guise of revealing her card secrets. "You can either deal the second card or deal from the bottom of the deck."

"I know about those techniques—and when we played I watched your hands." These last words were a silken murmur. "I never saw you do either."

She flushed to think of him looking at her hands, curiously intimate. "Simply because you could not see it does not mean it didn't happen. Watch." She immersed herself in the deal, her fingers barely whispering over the cards as she worked.

His hands, large and warm, covered hers. Stilling her. Yet she was far from still. His touch ignited cascades of awareness through her, darkly brilliant. The falsely named Mr. Holliday must have gifted Whit with some other enchantment, some power of seduction, for how else might she explain the hot need flooding her at Whit's touch, the rough desire that spared no thought for her heart or her mind? *He is your captor. Yet there's another man within him, an imperfect, searching man who longs for meaning.*

"Slower." His voice was deep, a shadowed rumble.

She pulled her hands out from beneath his, feeling the drag of his hot skin against hers. Air became scarce, thick.

"Like this." She demonstrated again her dealing technique, slowing down her movements so he might see them. It felt awkward and graceless to slow her actions. Yet she must. She might not reach Whit, free him from the Devil's influence. If so, if he was lost, and the sooner he learned her skills, the sooner she could leave and return to her family, her people.

She went through the process one more time before Whit's hand came to rest atop hers again. And again she felt the heat of his touch travel in incendiary waves through her body.

"Now me," he said.

She pushed the deck of cards into his hand, wanting distance. He gave her none. His tall, masculine presence kept too close as he stood beside her. Now it was her turn to watch *his* hands, large yet dexterous, the tendons of his wrists whilst he shuffled the cards.

Her life was spent studying hands and the lines upon them. They revealed much—not the future, not what was to be, but the person who possessed them, the paths the person had taken and the truths of that individual's life. Grime beneath fingernails, calluses, knuckles swollen from overuse, strength. Soft hands, barely lined, fresh and lavender scented, adorned with rings or very lightly stained at the tips from pinches of snuff. Professional habit had her observing a person's hands within moments of meeting that person.

Hands were not sensual, not alive with sexual promise. They were business to Zora. Nothing more.

Watching Whit work the cards changed her mind. She saw his fingers glide lightly over their printed surfaces and could not stop vivid images blazing through her thoughts. Those long fingers toying with her body, cleverly stroking and touching her to fevered arousal. The breadth of his palm, cradling her head as he kissed her deeply.

She ruthlessly shoved those thoughts aside. Desire was a drug trying to lull her into compliance. He was no longer the man he'd been. Difficult to remember that, when they shared these moments together not as captor and captive, but man and woman, as they had been before.

The erotic potential of Whit's hands captivated her. More than that. In their quick movements and the speed at which he learned this new art, she saw further evidence that his mind was incisive, adept. He might be born into privilege, but he was no thoughtless *gorgio* blue blood, whose brains had been systematically bred out of him. She furtively glanced up at his face. His brows were drawn down, the line of his mouth firm, his blue eyes clear and sharp. He concentrated, giving his full attention to the task of mastering the cards. Nothing so arousing as a handsome man immersed in complex thought.

Within a few minutes, Whit shuffled and dealt with an expert's touch. His movements were as swift as her own.

Had she not known what trick he used with the cards, she would never have realized he cheated.

"An adept student," she said.

She did not realize she had spoken aloud until his eyes gleamed with pleasure at her compliment.

"A skillful teacher," he murmured.

Their gazes connected, held. She felt herself drawn closer, pulled toward him by a force greater than her sizeable will.

She almost forgot. Forgot that she was here *against* her will. She could not rely on him.

Zora glanced away, breaking the connection.

"You have what you wanted," she said.

"Do I?" His question was casual, yet want pulsed beneath.

Her jaw tightened. "My secrets at cards. I've given them to you."

"Is that all of them?"

"Yes. And I can't lie to you, so you know I speak the truth." She tipped her chin up. "When it comes to card games, I have shown you everything I know."

"Not everything." He was an unyielding presence without even touching her. "There are still your secrets to telling fortunes with cards."

She turned back to him. "A nobleman and gambler hasn't a need to *dukker*. You didn't even want your fortune told at the camp."

He gave a shrug that only seemed indolent. Strength and potential simmered beneath the careless movement. "Now I want to know how."

"Let me go," she whispered. "Back to my people. Back to my life." Her eyes grew hot and damp as she stared up at him. To keep herself from placing a pleading hand upon his arm, she twisted her fingers in her skirts. "My family will be worried about me."

Another flare of shadowed regret in his gaze. He looked at her then, *truly* looked at her, and she willed herself still to return his look. Lifetimes passed, or mere seconds. A war was being fought behind the crystal blue of his eyes, where his desires and his principles battled against one another. She prayed that he was not so far gone, that the muscles of his conscience had not withered after probable years of disuse, that he had the strength to fight the Devil within.

His hand drifted up to his coat, finding the spot where a button had once been. The coat was fine, well-maintained. It seemed strange that a button would come loose and fall from it. But its absence seemed to strike a note in him, reminding him of something.

"No." It was he, this time, who turned away. "There are secrets you possess I still want."

Zora shivered, cold. Daylight had nearly broken, and violet shapes emerged outside, revealing themselves to be trimmed hedges of a walled garden, and beyond the wall, the forms of other imposing, heavy *gorgio* homes. The quiet of night slowly retreated. Someone was in the mews between houses, singing as he went about his work. Servants were awakening and making everything ready for their slumbering masters. From the growing sounds of many voices, many carts and carriages in the lane, the multitude of chimneys rising up against the dawn sky, Zora realized she was in London. Not the part of London she knew, not Smithfield for the St. Bartholomew's Fair, not Tyburn to ply the crowds watching the hangings. This was wealthy London—a London she had never known. *His* home. Over which the sun struggled to rise and break from the thick haze of smoke and soot.

"I want to leave," she pressed.

"Perhaps tomorrow. Or the day after that. I have yet to decide." His expression shifted, darkened. A mask sliding into place, obscuring who he once had been. He took her measure again, slowly and thoroughly. A boldly sexual look. As if he imagined the shapes their bodies would make when intertwined. "You intrigue me so."

"God," she said bitterly, "how I wish I didn't."

He took a step toward her. "Come, Zora. It need not be this way between us. We might enjoy one another. I promise you, I can give you quite a lot of pleasure." His confidence was indisputable, and she did not doubt him. He murmured, smiling, his lids lowered, "Let's to bed together."

"Will you force me," she asked, then added acidly, "*my lord*?"

He looked startled. The mask slipped. "Never," he said at once. The notion seemed to appall him.

Good. Maybe there was yet hope for him, and for her. "That is what it will take to get me into your bed." Her voice was cutting. "Force. I won't go otherwise."

His eyes narrowed. "Do you hate me?"

"Yes," she said immediately.

Again, his surprise. As if he found himself suddenly on stage in the middle of a play and discovered he was performing not the role of the hero but the villain. "Do you desire me?"

The magic that controlled her would not allow her to lie. "Yes."

A quick blaze of triumph in his face. "Let me show you how I desire you." He stepped nearer. His head lowered, bringing his mouth close to hers. She felt the warmth of his breath as his lips hovered a scant inch from hers, the heat of his body as strong as a fever. This close, she saw stubble along his jaw, intoxicatingly male, the short dark fringe of his eyelashes, a multitude of tiny details imprinting themselves on her mind and her deepest self.

His kiss would devastate her. She knew that if his lips met hers, she would mistake him for who he had been, not who he was now, and the resistance she needed would burn to ash.

She turned her head to the side. His breath fanned her cheek. "By force alone. That is the only way you'll ever have me."

For a moment, she thought she had pushed him too far. His expression grew shadowed. Animal need gleamed through him, tightening him. He reached for her and she stiffened, readying herself. She would fight him, if she had to.

He did not grab her. Did not haul her to him, or use bruising, punishing hands.

Instead, he ran a fingertip lightly down her neck. She shivered.

"Care to bet on that?" he asked.

She had to answer, yet before she spoke, he turned away.

As if speaking to any guest, he said, "A bedchamber will be readied for you."

The thought of sleeping in a *gorgio* bed, in a *gorgio* house, felt like entombment. She had seen their cumbersome beds and thought them massive and terrifying, especially the ones with hanging draperies like shrouds.

"If I'm held prisoner in this place," she said, "then I will stay in this room."

Of her many responses, this was one he hadn't anticipated. He looked around at the room, frowning. "You can't stay in the gaming room." This was a clear fact to him. Nobody slept in a room not designed for sleeping. Typical *gorgio*.

"Until you let me go, this is where I'll stay." She folded her arms across her chest.

"The other chambers are much more comfortable."

"Not to me."

Whit studied her for half a moment, as though she truly were a fox that had somehow been trapped within his home. A strange, wild creature in a place where it didn't belong.

He bowed, smiling. A gentleman's bow, elegant and effortless, highlighting the sleek muscularity of his body. "As my lady wishes."

"I'm not your lady," she fired back. "Not as long as the Devil has his claws in you."

He frowned, seemingly torn between his two selves. Then he gave another bow, retreating behind his aristocrat's polished veneer. "Good night, Zora. Or rather," he said, eyeing the pale dawn sky, "good morning. If you change your mind about wanting a bed, *any* bed, it's yours for the taking."

She knew exactly which bed he wanted for her. Before she could spit back a retort, he strode from the chamber. He paused in the hallway, and she saw him pick up her ring, then put the bauble into the pocket of his waistcoat before walking off.

The room felt oddly empty without him in it. Of course it would, she reminded herself. The Whit who kept her here was her jailer. The dark magic of the Devil swirled around him like a cloak. She might not reach the uncorrupted man beneath that cloak, which meant she was alone, merely a Romani girl held against her will, far from home, far from her family and friends.

With him gone, exhaustion filled her, weighting her limbs. Zora sank down to the plush carpet. Rest. She had to rest. The night had been long, filled with events she still could not fully comprehend. Had someone told her yesterday that she would come face-to-face with the Devil himself, that she would become the prisoner of a handsome, wealthy *gorgio* who was himself a prisoner of the Devil's magic, she would have laughed and chided the person for telling stories too outrageous to believe.

Now she knew differently.

She rose up onto her knees when she heard the door open. Servants came trooping in, holding blankets, pillows, a chamber pot, a folding screen, a nightstand. Two footmen carried a narrow bed, but the quality of it was fine, the mattress thick. It hadn't been taken from a servant's room. As she watched, amazed, the large round card table was pushed to one side, and the servants began to set up everything as if the game room were, in fact, a bedchamber.

"Why'd the master want this stuff in here?" a footman asked.

A maid shrugged as she tucked sheets into the bed. "Gentry. Who knows why they does anything?"

"It's for me," Zora said.

"Is someone goin' to sleep in here?"

"Me," Zora said again, getting to her feet. She scuttled aside as another footman came in bearing a tray covered with delicious-smelling food. The servant very nearly walked right over her, almost as if he hadn't seen her standing right in front of him.

"Your master is holding me prisoner," she said. She turned to the maid, who shook out a blanket and laid it atop the bed. "Please help me."

The maid continued on in her work, paying Zora no mind.

"Can't any of you help me?" Zora spun to the footman with the tray of food. He set it atop the card table.

"Don't make no sense to me," the footman muttered. "Make up a full breakfast with no one to eat it."

"I told you." The maid adjusted the placement of the pillow. "He's gentry. They get all sorts of odd notions in their heads. He wants the gaming room made up for some pretend honored guest, we just nod an' say, 'Yes, my lord.'" She marched to the window and shut it with a slam.

Zora whirled around, frantically searching the faces of the half dozen servants preparing the room. "Please—"

An immaculately dressed man appeared at the door. "Is everything attended to?"

"Yes, Mr. Kitson," answered the footman who had brought in the food.

"Who's this for, Mr. Kitson?" asked the maid.

The well-dressed man scanned the room, his gaze passing over Zora without as much as a blink. "I've no idea, and it's none of your concern. If you are finished here, then I suggest you leave in anticipation of the guest's arrival."

The servants sighed and filed out of the room, with the finely dressed man shutting the door behind them. Zora was alone again.

She stood by the bed, dazed. Somehow, the magic that held her in this place kept the servants from seeing or hearing her.

In truth, she hadn't been counting on the servants. She counted on herself alone. Always had. For if anyone could figure out a thorny situation, it was her, and she had seen herself through some very sharp thickets.

She would not allow herself to be touched that Whit had seen to her needs, instructing his servants to make the gaming room more comfortable. As if one should appreciate a captor using silken cords rather than coarse rope to bind one's wrists.

Whit belonged to the Devil now. He and his friends were in league with the beast. They had, in fact, set the Devil free. Which meant that something had to be done. Whatever they or the ironically named Mr. Holliday planned, it would not be good. It was very likely disastrous. Of those who knew that the Devil had been raised from Hell, only Zora opposed him. The responsibility fell to her to figure out what Mr. Holliday schemed and how to stop him.

She had to stop Whit. He was a danger. To her, to himself. To the world.

Zora paced to the window, watching the gray dawn. She pressed her hand to the glass and saw a corona of heat mist form around her palm. Trapped.

There was a way to freedom. She knew it. And she would find it.

Even if the Devil himself stood in her way.

Sleep did not come, not as quickly as Whit thought it would. The night had been long, extraordinary, something out of a boyhood fantasy. Yet the fantasy was very real. He had only to go downstairs and look into his gaming room to prove that he did not dream the last twelve hours.

Zora was his. He wanted her, and she was his. That lovely, fierce creature *belonged* to him. The dark part of himself reveled in this. A voice within him, though, growled out that no one could, should, have ownership over another.

He'd surprised himself when he'd bluntly invited her to share his bed. As if unable to stop himself from speaking aloud his desire. But, by God, he'd wanted her from the moment he had seen her in the Gypsy camp, a need that built with each hand of cards they had played, and it could no longer be contained.

Whit kicked off the blankets and stalked to the window. He didn't care that he was nude—his bedchamber was high enough that no one could see in. Hands braced on the window frame, he stared out at the garden below. She had the same view a story below him. He wondered if they were looking out at the same time, if she watched the pathways fill with silver light and heard the sounds of London as it came awake.

He hoped the servants had made the gaming room comfortable for her. He couldn't stand the thought that she would suffer under his care. If she let him, he would give her anything she wanted. A shadowed voice within rumbled, *As long as she remains mine.*

Power suddenly coursed through his body. He was alive with it. Fully alive for the first time in many, many years. He'd never known this sense of possibility, of potential.

He opened and closed his hands, feeling surges of energy coursing through his blood, his muscles and bones. Of what was he now capable? Anything. Everything.

No wonder slumber eluded him. How could he sleep when he knew himself to be on the verge of something monumental? The gift of chance was his, to control as he desired. All over London were gaming hells ripe for harvest. He would claim it all for himself.

With Zora, though, he would take another tack.

Whit rang for his valet. Moments later, Kitson appeared, immaculate as always, even though it could scarce be past six in the morning. He arrived so quickly, Whit was still in the process of slipping on his banyan. Whit had one arm in one sleeve, and the other was bare.

Kitson stared. Normally, the man was as composed as a sonnet, but the valet actually stared openly at Whit. More specifically, he stared at Whit's bare shoulder.

Glancing down, Whit saw what snared his valet's attention. He strode to a mirror atop a dressing table. Stared at his reflection.

Images of flames covered his left shoulder, as if someone had drawn upon his skin. They resembled flames in an alchemical text, entwining over the curved surface of his shoulder. He lightly touched the markings, marveling. They had not been there the day before. But last night, he had been given a gift from the Devil himself. The images must have appeared after that.

He now wore the Devil's mark. What did it mean?

This was not the time to consider it. Whit turned from the mirror and covered his shoulder.

"Has the gaming room been prepared?" he demanded without preamble, securing the banyan.

Kitson recovered immediately, his gaze now suitably disinterested. "Yes, my lord."

"And food was brought, too?"

"Yes, my lord. Are you expecting a guest?"

Whit stared at him. "My guest is already in the gaming room."

"There is no one in there now, my lord. I saw it myself. I heard no one speak." Kitson kept his expression carefully blank.

Whit's mind worked. It was impossible for Zora to have left the gaming room—Mr. Holliday had assured him she could not be more than twenty feet from the card, and Whit himself witnessed her inability to leave or even move the card. She had to still be there.

Yet neither Kitson nor any of his servants had seen her. Or heard her. Which meant . . . she was as a ghost to them. More of Mr. Holliday's power.

Perhaps if Whit were in possession of the card, she would be visible. If that were true, he would need to make preparations for her.

"Send someone to Madame Lyonnet," he said. "She has a

shop on the Strand, I believe. Get everything a pretty young woman could want—gowns, fans, ribbons, underclothes, shoes. The cost doesn't matter."

If Kitson thought this command was peculiar, his impassive expression did not show it. He simply noted, "Such a large order will take some time for Madame Lyonnet to complete."

"Tell her I will double her usual asking price if she can have everything ready within two days."

Kitson bowed. "I shall make that known, my lord. If I may ask, the young woman in question, what are her dimensions? Is she fair or dark? Robust or slight?"

"She is this tall." Whit held his hand up to just beneath his chin, remembering with a frisson of heat how he had to bend to bring his mouth close to hers. "She is slim, her waist about . . ." He had not touched her waist, but he had marked its slenderness well, and knew that she would be lithe and quick beneath his hands. Whit held his palms out to approximate Zora's narrowness, wanting her there and not empty space.

"And her bosom, my lord?" At Whit's brow raised in question, Kitson explained, "Modistes find such details highly important, my lord. To ensure a proper fit."

Whit had not touched Zora's breasts, but he sure as blazes wanted to. "Lush," he said, though the word seemed paltry compared to her delectable flesh, so abundant with vital energy. He had no doubt that she would be soft and sleek and luscious. "And as for complexion, her skin is the color of heather honey, and she has night-black hair and dark eyes." Eyes full of fire and cunning, eyes that taunted and seduced him even as she declared without reservation that she hated him.

She desired him, too. She could not deny that. He relied upon it.

"I shall see to it immediately, my lord. Is there anything else you require?"

"That is all for now, Kitson."

The valet bowed again and left Whit's bedchamber noiselessly. Kitson was the perfect manservant for a nobleman. Discrete, reliable, and utterly disinterested. If he gossiped, Whit never knew, and that was all that mattered.

Alone again, Whit strode back to his bed. He rested his hand atop the rumpled bed linens. He would have Zora here. Whatever vow she made that he could not take her except by force, he made his own countervow. He would not employ the gifts given to him by Mr. Holliday. Instead, Whit would use all his own arts to make her willingly his. Seduction. Beguilement. The interplay between him and Zora was the same as the first few hands of cards, where opponents learned each other, their strengths and flaws, strategies and gambits. She was a worthy challenger.

Whit's attention strayed to the coat he'd thrown carelessly over a nearby chaise. His eye immediately went to the missing button—proof that the gifts bestowed upon him by Mr. Holliday were genuine.

His waistcoat lay beside his coat. From its pocket, he plucked Zora's ring. Such a tiny thing—it wouldn't fit even on his littlest finger. He took from his dressing table a length of leather cord he sometimes used to bind back his hair, then threaded the cord through the ring. He put the cord around his neck and knotted the ends together. Zora's ring lay just beneath the hollow of his throat, the cool metal warming against his skin. Just as she would warm to him.

Whit smiled as his gaze returned to the bed. It was empty for now, but would not be for long. The Devil had given him control over probability, and a beautiful woman, both to do with as he pleased. Whatever Whit wanted could be his. He had only to take it.

"By hell's fire," he whispered, "I will take anything I want."

Chapter 4

Voices sounded on the other side of the door. A man and a woman, Zora judged, with sharp city voices. She recognized them as two of the servants from earlier in the day.

"It's ridiculous, is what it is." The woman spoke lowly, but the complaint in her voice made her nasal. "Nobody's been in or out of here all day."

"Ridiculous or no, it's what the master wants," the man answered, tired and bored.

The door opened, and Zora tensed, pressing herself against the wall. She exhaled after half a moment. There was no need to conceal herself or worry that these two servants posed a threat to her—as far as they knew, the game room in their master's home was empty. Moving to perch on a footstool by the windows, she watched the man and woman enter the room. The footman held a tray with more food, while the maid carried a taper to light candles against the fading daylight. He appeared resigned, while the maid's annoyance was writ plain across her youthful, peach-cheeked face.

"Bring in food, take away food," the maid grumbled. "Make the bed. Empty the chamber pot. Am I supposed to pantomime all of it, like some Italian in the commedia?"

The footman set the tray of food upon the card table, and

his dull eyes barely noticed the tray beside it, until a second later. His gaze snapped back to the first tray.

"Moll," he said.

The maid stood in front of the fireplace, her hands on her hips. "Don't I have enough to do between Mrs. Salter runnin' me near to collapse? Master ain't hardly ever at home, but she wants each chamber cleaned twice daily. If I wanted to be worked so hard, I'd have stayed back in Banbury with my mam and five brothers."

"Moll," the footman said again, sharply.

"What?" snapped the maid.

Wordlessly, the footman pointed at the first tray that once held Zora's breakfast. All that remained of the cakes were scattered crumbs, and smudges of cold grease on a plate marked where the morning's eggs and bacon had been. A film of tea coated the bottom of a dish.

"Ned must've eaten all that." Moll marched over and sniffed disdainfully. "He's always gettin' caught in the larder."

The footman paled. "Ned's been with me in the front hall."

"Somebody else, then. There's fifteen other souls livin' in this house."

"Ain't nobody come in here all day. So Mr. Kitson said." The footman yelped. "Look, Moll."

Both he and the maid peered under the table. Zora had taken the blankets off the bed and made a pallet for herself beneath the card table, and now the two servants stared with growing dread at her makeshift bed.

"You sure nobody's come through?" Moll whispered.

"Mr. Kitson don't lie."

"The windows were closed, too." The maid stared at them now, wide open to let in what fresh air could be found in London. "I closed one of 'em myself."

The unease in their expressions stoked something dark and angry within Zora. She had been trapped in this room the whole of the day, starting at every sound, pacing like a caged beast, alternating among states of fury, determination, resentment, and, worst of all, fear. Seeing vulnerability in the servants' faces made the snapping vixen within Zora lunge.

Jumping to her feet, she grabbed a deck of cards from the table and flung it at the footman and maid. Both servants screamed as cards scattered around them.

"Who threw 'em?" Moll gulped.

"They just flew. On their own."

Zora banished her own fear by preying upon theirs. She gathered a handful of ivory gaming tokens and hurled them at the terrified servants. She yelled, too, though she knew they could not hear her.

Shrieking, terrified, the footman and the maid bolted from the room. A shadowed thrill shot through Zora as she heard them running down the hall. They left the door swinging wide open, which only served as a taunt of Zora's own confinement. She had never been indoors this long, used to living beneath the canopy of open sky, and her caging within this *gorgio* house pushed her near to madness. Her frustration rose up like a baited bear, wanting to tear the throats of the dogs that tormented her. She kicked the footstool, and it smashed to pieces against the marble-fronted fireplace, but still she wasn't satisfied. God, she wanted to tear this whole house down.

"I hope you know of a good placement agent."

She spun at the sound of the deep voice, the same voice that had taunted and inflamed her during her restless attempts at sleep. Whit stood in the doorway, holding a lighted candlestick, and Zora told herself that her heart pounded from anger and being too long confined, not the sight of him, nor the rich resonance of his voice.

He stepped inside the room, shutting the door behind him, but his gaze never left hers. She could not look away from him, either, for she had never seen any man so darkly beautiful in the whole of her life.

Zora had little experience with wealthy *gorgios* in their evening finery. She saw them in their daylight clothing at

fairs and markets, and only sometimes, at night, caught
glimpses of carriages or sedan chairs and their torch-bearing
outriders, a jeweled hand at the window, a froth of snowy
lace draped across a wrist. How the *gorgios* dressed themselves for their nighttime pleasures mattered little, for their
world and her own did not overlap.

A distant edge of her mind wondered if she had denied
herself a great pleasure by never standing outside an assembly hall to see the adorned creatures within. Yet she knew
that, no matter what assembly hall or private ballroom she
might have haunted, from Cheltenham to London, she would
never have seen a sight to rival the man standing before
her now.

His velvet coat and breeches were deepest green, the color
of forest shadows. Light from the candle gleamed and sank
into the fabric's lushness as it stretched across his wide shoulders and clung to his tight, lean thighs. Golden embroidery
traced along the collar and wide cuffs, echoing the glinting,
faultless needlework that ran across the surface of his white
silk waistcoat. Impossible for her not to notice the leashed
strength of his torso, how the silk managed to cover yet powerfully suggest the musculature beneath. The shapes of his
calves made sleek arches beneath his white stockings—a
gorgio he might be, but not one of softness. A minimum of
lace gathered at his wrists and throat, the stock about his neck
almost austere in its simplicity, yet it seemed exactly right, for
the column of his throat and slant of his jaw were displayed
impeccably.

Whit wore no wig, nor did he powder his hair. Instead, he
had pulled his chestnut hair back in a simple queue, tied
back with black silk. He was elegant and beautiful and masculine, surpassing every construct her imagination had built
during their hours apart, and he stared at her as though she
alone could sate his devouring hunger.

God help me, she thought.

She felt almost self-conscious and shabby in her wrinkled, slept-in Romani attire, but reminded herself that it was his doing that had her wearing yesterday's rumpled clothing.

"They are convinced my home is haunted," Whit said. In contrast to his predatory gaze, his words were light, almost casual. He came farther into the room and set the candlestick upon the card table, revealing the scattered cards and gaming tokens.

Zora's dazzled mind belatedly realized he was referring to the servants she had scared off.

"You have the power to exorcise me," she answered.

He did not hear her, or pretended not to. Instead, he began to gather up the strewn cards with the practiced hands of a gamester. As he bent to collect cards from the floor, he caught sight of the bedding she had arranged beneath the table and frowned.

"Is the bed uncomfortable?" he asked.

"Too comfortable."

He understood at once. Had she lain in the bed he provided, she would surrender to its luxury, fall into too deep a sleep. She wanted to be alert, prepared for anything or anyone. Someone could approach her as she lay, vulnerable and unaware, in the bed. Beneath the table offered greater protection. She would not sleep as deeply, and one would either have to remove the large table, or else crawl to reach her.

A look of unease passed across his face. He saw her for what she was: his prisoner, trapped in his home and bound to his will through dark magic. There was nothing existing between them to gain a woman's trust.

She had been missing from her family for nearly a day. Were they looking for her now? Did her parents, her cousins go to the ruin calling her name? She prayed that if they did go to that cursed place *Wafodu guero* had long deserted it.

"I brought you something," he said. He held out his free hand, revealing that he carried a book covered in fine embossed leather. "If you are in need of diversion."

She did not move to take the book, instead crossed her arms over her chest as she stood on the other side of the table.

A wry smile tilted the corner of his mouth, far too charming for Zora's comfort. "Don't you care for Fielding? He's much less of a didactic bore than Richardson. I've even marked some of the good parts. There is a scene at an inn. . . . Just a moment. . . ." He rifled through the pages, searching.

"Bribing your own captive is an odd practice, my lord." When he glanced up, she added, "Besides, it is useless to me, as I can't read."

"You cannot read?" he repeated, almost blank with surprise. She shook her head.

"Can you write?"

"Only this." She traced the form of a *Z* upon the table-top, and even this was an awkward, unfamiliar motion.

"But . . . you tell fortunes using cards."

"I'm not blind, my lord. There are pictures on cards."

He set the book upon the table. For a brief moment, he appeared a little lost, as though he'd awakened to find himself on a boat in the middle of the ocean.

The division between them was not just the span of the polished card table, but of worlds. This house, with its heavy walls and substantial furniture, its servants and staircases, it was everything she was not. He—in his dazzling finery, an aristocrat by blood and bearing—was a breed apart. Chance alone brought them together the other night.

Chance, or fate?

Zora did not believe in fate. Unlike some of her superstitious kin, she believed in choices, the deliberate and precise decisions a person made as he or she journeyed through life. These choices defined a person, not merely the where and when of the person, but the why and who. Whit had made his choice when he made a bargain with the Devil, and now both she and he must live with the consequences.

He saw this, too, as he stared at the useless book upon the table. Doubt flickered across his face. Zora saw it, with a sudden, sharp clarity. Whatever, whoever, he truly was, this role of Devil's agent did not suit him, not really. He could yet be salvaged. She had to believe that.

Or else my heart is a liar.

"Do you hunt, my lord?"

Her question startled him. "Seldom."

"Deer or fox?"

"Grouse." He chuckled at some memory. "Edmund gathered us at his hunting box in Northumberland for the Glorious Twelfth, but due to circumstances from the night before, we slept right through the day."

She could only guess what those "circumstances" might have been. Every word from his mouth proved how unalike they were, yet something within him reached out to her—the questing, hungry self that demanded answers. She needed to find and hold tight to that part of him, for there lay the possibility of escape.

"You've seen a fox hunt, though," she said.

"A few. Not to my taste." He glanced at a painting hung upon the wall. She knew without looking which painting caught his interest, for she had stared at it throughout the day. It showed a nameless man on horseback riding through the countryside. The horse was a beautiful animal, as sleek and glossy as sunlight, and its long legs stretched in the glory of movement. How Zora envied that horse and its rider.

"It was all rather . . . brutal," he murmured. "The hounds, the riders. Chasing a single, small animal with no means of defending itself. No gamble in it. The end result was a foregone conclusion. It could only end in the death of the fox." He turned from the painting to fix her with his cornflower blue eyes. The intensity of his stare verged on frightening. "I swear to you, Zora, I will never hurt you."

His vowed words sent bright thrill through her. But they were only words. Her trade in telling fortunes reminded her that words one person thought meant everything were only pretty, empty trifles to another.

"Yet you do. Every moment you keep me prisoner." She

edged closer, though she kept the table between them. "Worse, you hurt yourself. Can you not see that?"

She watched him waver, standing upon a ledge. Her heart climbed into her throat as he waged a battle within himself. The sun had set, and with the fire unlit, the only source of illumination came from the lone candle, so he was a figure of light and dark, gold and shadow. She had never seen anything as beautiful and frightening.

So much of her life had been spent reading not palms but faces, studying the tiny shifts and changes that altered a person's expression. She saw plainly the struggle in Whit, even though his face was a handsome, stern mask, no doubt the same mask he wore when sitting at the gaming tables. Which way might he turn? Would his better self prevail?

She ventured a risk, edging closer still, and reached out to lay her hand upon his sleeve. Only her fingertips contacted him, the barest presence on his arm, yet it was as if the velvet of his coat were the velvet of his skin, for it was warm. The air surrounding him also held heat and the scent of bay leaves, clove, and male flesh.

He did not move, though she felt the whole of his body tense.

His lips parted, as if he was about to speak, and hope rose up like a bird for she saw in the line of his jaw that he had made a decision. He was not lost. He would let her go.

Before he spoke, a cold wind gusted through the window. It was a sickly wind, full of damp and rot, thick with river stink and human sadness. The candle gutted and went out. Cards flew everywhere, swirling around Whit and Zora like shades. She could not see but felt their edges against her face and her forearms, and she raised her hands to beat them away. Cold crept down her neck. She shivered. Beneath the fluttering sounds of flying cards, beneath the wind itself, she heard whispers. Words without form, yet as sinister as a knife against the spine.

She stumbled through the darkness toward the window.

With several hard tugs, she managed to shut it. The wind cut off, and the cards fell lifelessly to the ground.

The room became very still. Whit was only a large, dark form amidst further darkness.

"My lord?" she asked. Then, tremulous, "Whit?"

A flare and hiss as he struck a flint. The candle lit. It took a moment for her vision to adjust, from light to dark and back again.

Zora's heart sank. The mask was back, and with it, his darker self. He was harder than the flint he now pocketed, his eyes both burning and cold. He looked the same. He looked entirely different.

"I'm not done with you, Zora." He said this with a proprietary malevolence, as if not only she but her name as well belonged to him for his exclusive pleasure. When he made to cross to her, reaching for her, she shrank against the chilled window.

"Only by force," she reminded him.

Despite his profound alteration, he stopped in his tracks. A muscle twitched in his jaw. After a moment, he pulled out a chair.

"Sit," he said.

She sat.

He took a chair for himself, spun it around, and straddled it to face her. His long legs stretched out so that she was forced to tuck her feet back to keep from touching him. Despite the chair having a high back, he was tall enough that he braced his arms easily upon it. The pose was indolent. The shadowed force radiating out from him was not.

"Tell me how to read someone's fortune," he said.

"You have coin in abundance, my lord." He had requested this before, yet still his demand mystified her. "There is no need to *dukker* for money."

His smile, small though it was, softened the severe edges of his face. "Oh, I could just see myself, hoops in my ears, wrapped in scarves. Going from house to house. 'Cross my palm with silver.'" He held out a hand, and the candlelight gleamed on the band of his signet ring. A talented Rom could easily slip the ring from his finger, but finding a buyer for a ring emblazoned with a nobleman's crest would be difficult.

Still, Zora fought her own smile, imagining this vigorously male *gorgio* dressed like a Romani woman and knocking on doors for the promise of a few shillings.

"If not for coin," she asked, "then why learn to *dukker*?"

"Because you know how," he answered, lowering his hand. "And I want every part of you."

The bold simplicity of this statement made her shiver. "I'm more than a teller of fortunes."

"I am well aware of that." His gaze roamed over her, burning her. "Yet this is where I will begin, and then delve deeper."

She did not know if *Wafodu guero* had enchanted Whit's voice, but that seemed likely, since each word from his mouth caused a deep current of heat to rise within her. Protecting herself remained key, however, so she moved on hurriedly.

"There's no magic in *dukkering*," she said.

He raised a brow. "That is not what your fellow Gypsies say."

"The greater the *hokibens*—nonsense—the greater the profit."

"Like gambling. Sometimes it is better to bluff for a higher take."

She nodded. "The true skill lies in the reading of faces, not the lines on someone's hand nor the lay of the cards."

"I know that well from the gaming tables," he said. "To study every aspect of a player's face, the discourse of their body. It's called the 'tell.' I thought after years of experience and training I had no tells, but that is how you were able to cut me so deeply back at the Gypsy camp." His mouth flattened, and she remembered with wounding vividness how she had neatly, callously described his character.

"I was truthful, but not kind." She glanced down at her hands in her lap. "That's the surest way to earn no money."

"No profit in truth." He considered this, and she looked up to see him enmeshed in thought, turning ideas over in his head as one might examine polished gems. "Yet you spoke the truth to me. Why?"

She was tempted to lie, or make some evasion, but the subtle pressure of his magic bore down on her will. It felt like a ghostly hand drawing truth from a locked compartment. Frightening, and unpleasant. An answer leapt from her. "Because I liked you too well to treat you as just another source of coin. You deserved better than that."

His smile was slow and wicked, and more heat kindled inside her. "I liked you, too, Zora. Very much. I still do." The low, carnal promise of his words left no doubt as to his interest.

"The best way to gain what you want is to tell someone what they want to hear." She tipped her chin up. "Shall I do the same with you?"

He rose up quickly, a sleek, agile movement that showed how well his body moved. Zora instinctively recoiled, but he only paced the room, alive with barely contained energy.

"Is deceit all you practice?" he clipped.

Again, she had to respond with truth, which she found ironic, given his question. "Almost always. There are certain routine fortunes I tell, depending on the circumstance. Though people like to believe themselves unique, the truth is that the more I see of the world, the more I understand how very alike everyone is. It would be a little sad, were it not so profitable."

"Are people so easily gulled?"

"You know as well as I that they are." She raised her hands to her temples as though going into a mystical trance. "Three times you have been in great danger of dying."

He stopped his pacing to stand near the fire. "Surely no one falls for such tripe."

Professional pride had her spine stiffening. "I assure you, they do. Everyone likes to think they've encountered danger. Everyone likes to believe they escaped by either wiles or fate."

"Men, especially," he said with a self-deprecating smile. "Plays to the romantic hero in us. Give me another." He gestured for more.

Zora lowered her voice, as she did when customers thought themselves too intelligent for *dukkering*. "At one time, you had great trouble with your family. They treated you poorly."

He nodded, approving. "Clever. Almost everyone has difficulty with their family." Softer, reflective, he added, "Most of mine had the gall to die from fever, leaving me an earldom at the age of sixteen. And my surviving sister has never been particularly shy about her dislike of my fondness for gaming. We have not spoken or exchanged letters in nearly a year."

She wondered if he heard the sadness in his voice, the hints of a boy who too early assumed too great a responsibility. Little surprise that, having suffered loss, he turned to the controlled chaos of gambling, the small deaths and resurrections that came from a roll of the dice or lay of the cards.

"My own family can drive me mad with their nearness," she said. She stared at the heavy walls of the room enclosing her. "I didn't think I would miss them, but I do." It struck her with a surprising ferocity, the keen edge of longing for their familiar faces gathered around the campfire, as they told the same stories and badgered her with the same nagging complaints. *Why can't you be like Doro? She's a good girl, never talks back, never asks too many questions. She's not impulsive. Doro kept her husband.*

Maybe she didn't miss them, after all. Or, at least, she shouldn't.

The shade of regret crossed Whit's face briefly, but it slipped away. "And what of reading palms? Is it the same . . . what's the word . . . *hokibens*?"

His pronunciation of the Romani word was terrible, and she

fought a smile. "There are many things that can be learned from a person's hand."

In two strides, he crossed the room and stood before her, palm outstretched. "Show me."

Sitting made her all the more aware of his size and strength, and her own relative fragility. She was also level with his hips, and of their own will, her eyes moved from the broad, large hand he offered her to his groin. Did the size of his hands reflect the size of his . . . ?

Her face heated when he saw her speculative gaze. *There's only one way to find out*, his eyes said.

Zora cleared her throat and focused on his hand, taking it between her own. It was much bigger than hers, and she cradled it between her two palms. The sensation of his hot skin against hers felt like a cascade of sparks from a stirred fire. It made no sense. She touched the hands of men many times, impersonally, professionally, and not once did any of them affect her as Whit's did. Who would give a man hands such as his, for what purpose, if not to entice a woman or make her think of what his hands might feel like on her body? Perhaps his mother or father had also been in league with the Devil, asking for a child who would one day grow to be a man of darkest temptation.

Through her lashes, she saw color rise on the high bones of his cheeks, a fever-stain of awareness that she shared. In the tendons of his wrist, his pulse beat hard and fast, just as her own raced. It was as if some unseen threads stretched between them, tying them to one another, possessors not only of their own bodies, but each other's.

"Hands are covered with lines," she said, her voice embarrassingly short of breath. With the very tip of her finger, she traced the lines on his palm. His skin was free from calluses save for one upon his index finger where he rested his quill when writing. "Life line, head line, heart line."

"Love?" The word, spoken lowly, held a powerful, seductive resonance. "In the shape of one's hand?"

She looked up at him, but the intensity of his gaze was too much, too demanding. Quickly, she returned to her study of his hand. "Some might tell you that in the course of the line, you would see the person you are destined to love, if that love will be a happy one or full of sorrow. If you cleave to those you love, or whether you play them false."

A question whispered in her mind: Would he be faithful to his woman, or inconstant? Good God, she didn't even know if he *did* have a woman. It was entirely possible. Clearly, he wasn't married, but wealthy *gorgios* had lengthy engagements, and the men kept mistresses.

It did not matter if he was betrothed to a simpering *gorgie* or if he kept dozens of women for his personal pleasure. It did not matter, for he was a wicked man. So she told herself.

"*Some* say," he repeated. "But not you."

"A hand can reveal many things. Age and sex, of course. Whether you're wealthy, or whether you are a laborer. Does ink stain your fingers? Is there dirt beneath your nails? Does your hand smell of perfume or gravy?" She shrugged. "A story is contained in someone's hand, but it doesn't provide prophecy."

"The tell is not only in someone's face," he said, meditative, "but their hands. I see that at the gaming tables, as well. If a man clutches his cards, or holds them loosely. Does he continually shuffle and rearrange them? Is he feeling the cards for marks, or trying to mark them himself?" His chuckle felt like a stroke of velvet along her neck. "Never thought there might be so many parallels between Gypsy fortune-telling and a gentleman's game of chance."

"But I *dukker* to earn my bread," she felt compelled to point out. "If I fail at my work, I might not eat. The stakes aren't so high for you."

"I make sure to keep them high, else there's no enjoyment in it. Come, now." With the fingers of his free hand, he tipped her face up so that their gazes met. "There must be some part of you that enjoys reading people, discerning their secrets. Even, dare I say, manipulating the *gorgios* that come to you for guidance." Small lines fanned at the corners of his eyes as he smiled.

It took Zora a moment to realize that he had not asked her a question, a question she would be impelled to answer. Instead, he had carefully laid out a series of statements, leaving the decision in her hands as to whether or not she would reveal anything of herself to him. She ought not to feel grateful for this—*his* dark magic was what forced her to speak the truth. Yet she did feel a strange gratitude. He wanted her to speak of her own will, and hoped that, if she did speak, she would be honest.

"There is . . . power in it," she admitted.

"To make someone think or do precisely what you want them to," said Whit, "without their ever recognizing how you control them."

She had never confessed that to anyone, not even her mother. The Rom liked getting the better of *gorgios*—cleverness and guile were prized amongst her people—but no one ever admitted that they enjoyed bending *gorgios* to one's will, taking the yielding wood of their minds and carving it into whatever shape one desired.

"Mostly, I tell the same fortunes, harmless things. 'You will have three great chances in your life. Be ready to seize the next opportunity.'"

"Mostly," he echoed, but then noted, "not every time."

"People who come for *dukkering* aren't always shining examples of those manners you *gorgios* prize." She hesitated.

He lowered smoothly into a crouch so that his face was level with hers. A searching need gleamed in his gaze, though his face remained a handsome, hard mask. In the candlelight and darkness his eyes were the deep blue of hidden, shadow-strewn pools, and she wanted to submerge herself in them.

"Confide in me, Zora. Tell me your secrets."

She had no reason to trust him, none at all. Yet the need in his eyes called to her. "An old, rich *gorgio* wanted me to read the cards," she said. "He had been rude to everyone in the camp, calling us a band of filthy, thieving vermin, sneering at our men and leering at our women."

A cold anger hardened his jaw. "You, as well?"

"I am not unused to it." Still, she didn't care to be the object of anyone's vulgar attention, especially not disrespectful *gorgios*. She was surprised, however, to see such rage in Whit, for she truly believed at that moment that if that old, rich man stood in the room, Whit would make him suffer for a long time before ending his life. Romani men took insults to their women very seriously, but never had Zora witnessed anyone other than direct kin be so angry on her behalf.

"Did you get his name?" Whit growled.

She shook her head. "Names aren't often given when someone wants *dukkering*." She added, "However, I did have my vengeance on the old donkey. I dealt the cards and told him that he would fall victim to a terrible property dispute. If he didn't take the proper preventative steps, he would lose his estate and be forced to live off the charity of others."

"The preventative steps were suitably foul, I hope."

"He had to drink tea made from the droppings of long-eared bats, and sew moldy cheese into the lining of his waistcoats."

Whit laughed, and the unexpected sound traveled the length of Zora's body, settling warmly between her legs.

"Appropriate." He chuckled.

"I saw him a week later, walking through the village. People crossed High Street to avoid coming too close. He also looked a little green."

"Drinking tea brewed from bat droppings isn't good for the complexion." Approval and respect had replaced the anger from a moment before. It surprised her how much she enjoyed seeing that in his face, how she enjoyed being the object of his respect. "That was well done. Standing up for yourself."

"You don't think me a mean little Gypsy?"

"I think you are delicious." His gaze went to her mouth.

At the same time, his hand—which she had unknowingly been holding all the while—turned over to grasp her own hands. It wasn't a hard grip, pinching and punishing, but secure, and his hand was so much larger than her own that he easily enfolded her. Only the most blameless innocent could ever mistake the sensual hunger that tightened him now, the desire in his touch. Zora was neither blameless nor innocent.

She felt herself slipping beneath the surface of dark, warm water. It would be so easy to drown in him. She could see he wanted his mouth on hers, and she wanted the same.

Surely, surely, there was good in him. She needed to believe it. If he was a truly bad man, he would not grow so angry on her behalf. He would not take pleasure in her petty revenge, nor be gratified that she had spine enough to defend herself.

He leaned closer until their lips were mere inches apart. All she had to do was tilt her head, just a little, and they would kiss.

"Turn away from him," she whispered.

"From whom?"

"*Wafodu guero*. The Devil."

Whit stilled. "Zora," he murmured, almost a sigh. He turned his head, but he did not move back, did not release his hold on her.

She quickly went on. "There is goodness in you. I see it. I *feel* it." Desperation made her words urgent, but she found that she wasn't pleading so much for her own freedom as she was for his. "Whatever the Devil has given you, it isn't too late to reject his gifts and save yourself."

A shadow passed over Whit's face. "I never said I wanted to be saved."

"But—"

He rose from his crouch and, releasing her, braced his hands on either side of the top of her chair. His looming presence threatened to overwhelm her.

"You do not know me at all," he said, "else you would understand that I want *exactly* what Mr. Holliday has given me."

"What has he given you?"

A dark smile curved his mouth. "Control of the odds."

No greater gift could be offered to a gambler. The need to wager ran through Whit like blood.

He saw that she understood. "Everything I desire shall be mine."

"Not me," she said.

His eyes narrowed with the challenge. "Care to wager on that?"

Enforced honesty made her answer, "No." She added, "However, it will take much more than a roll of the dice or turn of a card to win me, my lord."

"I hope so. For there is nothing so exciting as beating difficult odds."

"In this case, the odds are impossible."

He smiled, purely wolf. "Even better. Makes for a sweeter victory."

"You might use that power against me."

His smile faded. "Never. I swear that. And once I vow something, I do not renege."

Zora cursed the fact that the one time she finally met a man with a spirit equal to her own, they would be set against each other. Cruel, it was. Had circumstance been different . . . But it wasn't different.

He straightened and, stepping back, pulled a timepiece from his waistcoat pocket. It surprised her, that pocket watch, for the case holding it was old and a little dented from use. When he took the watch from its case, she noted that it was well cared for, yet rather plain. Surely a man as wealthy as Whit could afford a new, more ornate timepiece.

"I'm late meeting Bram and Leo for supper," Whit said. He replaced the watch. "We convene at a chophouse before heading off for our night's entertainment. Say the word, and I'll dismiss them." He nodded toward the playing card propped on the mantel. "I can take that, and you can leave with me. You and I can dine in a private room. Make our own night's entertainment." His lids lowered.

She had no doubt that he would make the night very, very entertaining. "Until you wash your hands of *Wafodu guero*, my answer remains unchanged." Which meant that this room would remain her prison, and he her jailer.

"As my lady desires." He bowed effortlessly, one hand pressed to his heart, the other stretched out in a flourish behind him, and his outstretched leg showed itself very finely. A true gentleman's bow, the sort that she had never received. She had to admit it was a pretty thing, yet even this courtliness he invested with potent virility. Strange—the bow did not feel ironic, but rather genuinely courteous.

"Don't wait up," he advised. "I usually come home after dawn."

She stood. "I won't keep your chocolate warm."

He gave a half smile before turning and striding toward the door. His hand on the doorknob, he said, "Speaking of chocolate, I'd advise not frightening my servants with your ghostly hauntings."

"It doesn't matter to me if I scare them."

"It should, as they're the ones who bring you food. Or, I could wait on you."

She frowned. "Teasing your captive is bad form."

"I'm not teasing. It would give me much pleasure to take care of you, Zora." The huskiness of his voice revealed him to be quite sincere.

No answer or biting reply came to her. All she could feel was stunned, uncertain. He was neither hero nor villain, but something in between, and this confused her deeply.

With a final, smaller bow, he left the room. She expected— hoped—to feel relief after he had gone.

Instead, she was beset by a strange and unwelcome emptiness.

Chapter 5

The scent of roasting animal flesh hung heavy in the air of the Snake and Sextant. A burnt carbon smell, strangely both enticing and repellant. Whit wondered if this was the smell of the Inferno, sinners eternally roasting upon spits like so many beefsteaks. It wasn't a pleasant image or thought, so he forced it from his mind as he pushed into the tavern. Though the hour was relatively early, few empty seats remained.

Familiar, this place. Its heavy, scarred floors, its chipped green settles and battered tables, its aggressively cheerful fire that beat back London's gloom but filled the tavern itself with smoke. For years, the Hellraisers had been coming to the Snake and Sextant, fortifying themselves with meat and ale before the night's carousing. To be sure, taverns were more plentiful on Fleet Street, but the Snake's location just off Haymarket won out. Close to Covent Garden, Bram's demand, and a fairly short ride to the clubs on St. James's Street, Whit's demand.

Someone shouted his name. He knew without looking who called him, and from where. Whit began weaving his way through the tavern to find his fellow reprobates. Ensconced at their favorite table sat Bram and Leo. Bram already had a girl upon his lap, her arms around his shoulders as she left red bite marks upon his neck, and Leo wryly watched the spectacle over the rim of his tankard. Like Whit, his friends were dressed for evening.

"Good thing your company is so amusing," Bram said as Whit approached the table. "Else we would have left an hour ago."

"Business kept me at home," Whit answered.

"*Business* has lovely dark eyes, doesn't she?" drawled Leo.

"And a figure to rival Isis," added Bram. He caressed the girl in his lap, his movements habitual, made without thought. Whit could not begin to guess at the number of women Bram had petted in a similar manner, and he was certain Bram had no idea of the tally. "Have you tupped her yet?"

"Given the way Whit looks ready to rip your arms off," Leo said, "I'd wager that he hasn't."

Whit forced his hands to unclench, his snarl to relax. This was new, uncomfortably new, both the sudden surge of emotion and the jealousy. Only the gaming tables ever witnessed or provoked any strong feeling in him. In all other aspects of his life—including women—he drifted in a kind of amicable indifference. Which horse to ride in the park. Whether he preferred that afternoon to practice his swordsmanship or his marksmanship. If Whit picked out an opera dancer for the night's diversion and Bram or Leo lured her away, it mattered not at all. Whit simply found another girl.

It was not the same with Zora.

"Tonight, she enlightened me on the practice of fortune-telling," he said.

Bram shook his head. "Christ, has it been so long that you've forgotten how to bed a woman?"

"Not so long," answered Leo before Whit could speak. "That passel of courtesans at John's place, before we left for the country. As I recall, Whit retired to a chamber with the blond one who had the big—"

"I haven't forgotten," Whit growled, though, in truth, the encounter had left barely a ripple in his memory. That night had been about slaking a body's need, and little else. The moment it was over, he'd dressed and gone to a club, and he remembered more about the sound of dice as he played hazard than the sound of the blond courtesan's voice.

"Then what—" Bram broke off as the girl in his lap attempted to lick the scar that ran down his jaw and neck. He pulled her back. "None of that. Leave us alone, Betty."

"It's Kitty," the girl pouted. True to Bram's taste, she was a very pretty girl, pale skin, fair haired, but Whit could take note of her looks only as if from a great distance. He had but one image, one woman, burned upon his mind's eye, and she was captive in his gaming room.

Bram gently set the sulking girl on her feet. "Go on, now. Bring us steaks, artichoke and oyster pie, and another round of ale."

Whit expected Kitty, or Betty or whatever her name was, to object tumbling from gentleman's paramour to servant in a matter of seconds. But the mulish expression suddenly lifted from her face. After smiling and bobbing a curtsey, she flitted off to carry out Bram's directive.

"Mr. Holliday's doing," said Bram. "That is nothing. Only this afternoon, with our esteemed friend's gift, I persuaded two of London's most obnoxiously virtuous young widows to share my bed."

As Whit sat, he said, "It must have been crowded."

"You've never seen Bram's bed," Leo noted. "There's room enough for a baker's dozen of obnoxiously virtuous young widows."

"A pity there are so few," Bram sighed.

Three full tankards were brought to the table, and as Whit took his first drink, he wondered whether there would ever be enough young widows, pretty barmaids, or opera dancers to satisfy Bram. Even now, after recounting his afternoon with not one but two willing women, Bram all but hummed with a restless, shadowed energy pushing him forward, keeping him from any measure of peace. In an unthinking gesture, Bram ran his thumb back and forth over the raised mark of his scar, as if confirming the presence of a lingering sickness.

If Mr. Holliday's gift of persuasion could not ease Bram's disquiet, could anything?

Unaware of Whit's thoughts, Bram continued. "Spending your nights at hazard and piquet has turned your manners coarse. No wonder you can't get the Gypsy wench under you. Shall I persuade her on your behalf?" His animal grin showed that Bram did not mind this duty at all.

Whit grasped the handle of his tankard so tightly his knuckles whitened. "My thanks, but that is unnecessary. If—*when*—Zora becomes my lover, it will be through my own unaided seduction, not magic."

"Then you'll never have her," Bram said.

Whit's smile felt thin, though he knew his friend meant nothing by his jests. Scant days earlier, Whit could have borne it all—Bram's teasing, the possibility of losing or sharing a woman—without complaint or anger. But in a short span of time, he felt altered, his poles reversed so that his sense of direction found no purchase.

"And what of you?" Whit asked Leo, sitting opposite him. "Have you used your gift in similarly sybaritic ways?"

Leo raised a brow. "I'm no Lothario like Bram. A wonder his cock hasn't fallen off, or he hasn't gone mad from the pox."

"Preventative measures, Master Leo," Bram pronounced. At twenty-eight, Leo was only four years younger than Bram, but that never stopped Bram from addressing him like a youthful novitiate. "There are some women on Half Moon Street who sell the most useful devices—*sheaths*, if you will—of thinnest sheep's gut, which you tie on with a ribbon to your—"

Leo scowled. "I know what they are. Even callow social climbers are schooled in such things."

A reply was prevented by the fortuitous arrival of their food. Betty or Kitty set three steaks before them, as well as the artichoke and oyster pie, ale, and an unasked-for tureen of early spring pea soup. The Snake and Sextant was not the most fashionable tavern in the Haymarket, but the food was good and, with Bram's new persuasive abilities, plentiful.

The girl's ready smile widened farther when Bram dropped more coins than necessary into her apron pocket. When she moved to sidle in beside him, he waved her away. "We want privacy, sweetheart. Don't come back until I call for you."

"Yes, my lord." She sauntered off, happily jingling the coins.

Unlike Bram, Leo, and the rest of the patrons of the tavern, Whit did not stare at her swaying, deliberately provocative progress as she walked away. He would rather watch Zora's unconscious grace than a room full of flirtatious barmaids. Trouble was, Zora's demonstrations of her lithe agility often came when fleeing him.

"The answer is no," Leo said, cutting into his beefsteak. "I haven't been employing my gift to roger the fair ladies of the town." He amended, "Not that I have trouble finding a willing woman, but even if I wanted to use magic to tup a woman, the ability to prophecy future financial disasters by touching coin isn't precisely useful in that regard."

"Than what bloody good is it?" demanded Bram as he sliced the artichoke and oyster pie.

"There's more to life than what's under a woman's skirts," Whit felt obliged to point out.

Bram pointed his knife at him. "I don't trust your value system. Never have. Any man who'd rather spend his nights toying with inconstant Lady Luck rather than the sure thing of bedsport is clearly deranged."

Whit placed his finger on the tip of Bram's knife and gingerly pushed it aside. "None of us Hellraisers are particularly compos mentis. Perhaps that is why we like each other so well, whilst no one else will have us." An image of Zora flared in his mind, her face as she realized that he would not give up Mr. Holliday's gifts. Disappointment, that's what it was. Her disappointment in him.

"I concede the point," said Bram.

"Where are our other Hellraisers?" asked Whit.

"Edmund had to discuss certain matters with his man of

business." Bram added dryly, "And to my utter astonishment, John is attending a political debate."

For a few minutes, the men said nothing as they concentrated on their meal. The food was good, so it absorbed everyone's attention, each of them attending single-mindedly to his meal, as men of a certain relatively young age are wont to do. Though he was a nobleman by birth, Whit preferred plain fare and saved his indulgences for the gaming rather than the dining table. Heavy, rich meals made him feel sluggish and softened his brain, qualities a serious gambler avoided.

What kind of food did Zora prefer? He hadn't asked—perhaps Gypsies liked certain dishes and avoided others—and he wanted to ensure that every courtesy was being extended to her. At the least, judging by the empty tray, he knew that she was eating whilst his guest. And if any of the servants were too frightened to bring her food, Whit had spoken true. He would gladly serve her. In any capacity. Pleasure her for hours, days, if she gave him leave. God, yes.

Pictures and scenes blazed through him. Her sitting on the card table, her skirts around her waist, as he knelt between her legs and savored her. Her bent over the chaise in his bedroom, gripping the cushions, as he took her from behind. The two of them, touching, tasting, learning one another, what gave each other pleasure. His need for her went beyond the physical. Such a fiery creature, this Zora Grey, her intellect as keen as a scimitar and equally exotic. He wanted every part of her, mind and body.

The intensity of this wanting left him burning and taut, hardly aware of the voices around him or the presence of his friends at the table.

He took a cooling drink of ale. Regaining control of himself was imperative if he planned on gambling tonight. A distraction from Zora was not needed.

"What *have* you done with Mr. Holliday's gift?" he asked Leo.

"Spent the day down at Exchange Alley. There were some

business ventures looking for capital, ventures that, thanks to our mutual friend, I foresaw will collapse. My counter-investing will net considerable profits." Leo smiled faintly. "I deal in futures, after all." His smile turned cold. "And a few well-placed suggestions to certain people had them investing in those schemes doomed to fail."

"Certain people," said Bram. "Such as . . . ?"

"Richard Gorely, Bertram Carswell."

Men who had deliberately cut Leo and his lowborn family. Carswell, in particular, had been vocally furious when Leo joined the club of stock traders and jobbers formed a few years earlier. A screed of Carswell's denouncing Leo had been published in a newspaper, and though the name had been barely disguised, the target was clear. Whit remembered the day the newspaper came out, and how he and Edmund had had to physically restrain Leo from challenging Carswell to a duel.

"Carswell would never act on your advice," Whit said.

"Precisely why I gave him the opposite counsel." Leo's hazel eyes held grim satisfaction. "The tea-importing ships he invested in will sink just off the coast of Formosa. The crew shall survive, the cargo shall not."

Whit and Bram shared a look. Though Carswell had a decent income, a loss of that caliber would not be easily endured, and Leo knew it.

"To be sure," Leo continued, "if either of you, or John or Edmund are entertaining ideas for investments, I'd be gratified to advise you. I plan on becoming a wealthy man very soon."

"You already *are* wealthy," Bram noted, gesturing to the heavy gold ring Leo wore upon his smallest finger. His dark gray evening clothes were of the finest silk, and the stones upon his shoe buckles were genuine, not paste.

"Even wealthier." Leo grinned, but there was no happiness in it, only brutal determination. "Speaking of filthy lucre, Whit, have you cut a path of destruction through the gaming hells of London yet?"

This time, it was Whit's chance to grin. "Tonight shall see

me unleash my gift." His heart began to pound at the thought, and he felt a new edge to his old, insatiable hunger.

Bram raised his tankard. "Lads, I propose a toast." When Whit and Leo also picked up their tankards, Bram went on. "To our esteemed mutual friend, Mr. Holliday. We may have liberated him from his prison, but it was he who liberated us from the prison of ordinary life."

"And unleashed us upon an unsuspecting world," added Leo.

"And gave us the means to gain our every desire," Whit said. Leo and Bram had what they wanted most, and now it was Whit's turn.

"I speak on behalf of our fellow Hellraisers who are not here." Bram hefted his tankard higher. "To Mr. Holliday."

"To Mr. Holliday," said Whit and Leo.

They loudly brought their cups together, and to Whit's ears the sound of the metal clashing was the sound of the gates of Hell opening. He smiled.

The hour was late. London's good, industrious, and honest citizens had taken to their beds long ago to rest before the day's hard work. Most of the city was covered in darkness only slightly mitigated by sputtering, weak lamps that threw off more smoke than light. In these shadows dwelled bawds, thieves, and ruffians eager for the unwary or foolish. A world entire lived in this darkness.

Yet the world in which Whit and his friends existed was one of artificial light, artificial everything. The best gambling did not begin until two in the morning, which left Whit, Bram, and Leo several hours that needed filling. First, the Theater Royal in Drury Lane, its stage, performers, and patrons lit by greasy candles. A simulated moon shone down upon pretend lovers shouting out their devotion over the crowd's chatter. No one came to the theater to watch the performances, not truly. Whit spent his time there placing bets from his box as to whether or not a fight would break out amongst the strutting, swaggering young bucks in the pit

over perceived or manufactured insults. He reserved his
power over controlling the odds for later in the evening,
cradling it close like a coveted gem. He wanted to feel its
power for the first time when sitting down to cards, not
thrown around idly on bumptious society pups.

After that, Whit and his friends debated whether to make
the journey to the Ranelagh pleasure garden—Vauxhall
being too far that night—before Edmund and John finally
joined their company, asking them to attend a supper and
ball on St. James's. The five of them went, finding another
brightly lit room populated by actors of a different sort.
Girls barely out of their leading strings were paraded before
gouty old men. There were flirtations and transactions. Be-
trayals and confidences. And all those in attendance pretending that they weren't bored out of their skulls, seeing the
same people at the same places year after year until it took
on a glossy, glassy monotony. Whit did not bother to join the
men gambling in a salon off the ballroom. No one at these
social events played deep enough for him.

Finally—*finally*—Whit broke away, with only Leo for
company. They went to London's most exclusive club, also
on St. James's, a place so new, so sought after that the waiting list of petitioners was rumored to rival *Paradise Lost* for
length and breadth.

He stood now at the hazard table. Lights blazed here, too,
for shadows hid the possibility of cheating. The room was
roasting hot. Men were everywhere, drinking, sweating,
eating. But most of all, they were there to gamble, Whit
amongst their number.

His heart pounded thickly in his chest as he waited his turn
at the dice. Excitement flooded him, stronger than any spirit.
He had played hazard more times than he knew, and the
club's ivory dice were his own bones, yet this night was
vastly different. Just beneath the surface of his skin, he
seethed with new power. A wonder he didn't burn as bright
as the chandeliers suspended over the tables.

"Do you even care?" asked Leo, standing beside him.

When Whit raised a brow, Leo explained quietly, "When I was down at Exchange Alley, knowing what kind of capability I had, it was all I could do to keep from combusting. Had to drink two glasses of wine to calm me down, but even that barely sufficed. But you . . ." He shook his head. "Cool and indifferent as a winter sun."

Whit allowed himself a small smile. "A gamester's old habit. Show nothing on the outside. I assure you that in here"—he tapped the center of his chest—"I'm as chaotic as Bedlam."

"You could apply that same sangfroid and gambling spirit to the Exchange. Investing is merely a variation on this." Leo gazed at the room, the tables where men huddled over games of chance, winning and losing fortunes with dice and cards. Across the chamber, a young lord fresh from his Grand Tour gave a shout of dismay before lowering his head into his hands. A year's allowance gone, and the morrow would find him called before an angry father. The creditors would go unpaid, along with dozens of tailors and wine merchants and horse breeders, arrears in the hundreds if not thousands of pounds.

Tomorrow night, the young lord would be back, begging for credit, hoping for one big win. And the men who ran the club would grant him credit, knowing that he would only dig himself in deeper.

It was not unknown for a man to leave the club completely, utterly ruined. More rare, but not impossible, a fortune made in the very same room.

Which would it be for Whit? The death and rebirth of each night gave movement to his blood, blood that might have stagnated had he not discovered the thrill of gambling.

"The element of risk is there, I grant you," he said to Leo. "But unless the wheel of the ship transporting cinnamon from Ceylon is under my hand, your form of gambling is too removed. I need to be elbows deep in chance. That is how I prefer it. These fellows have the same preference."

Leo rolled his eyes. "You gentry are daft, preferring to

shore up your fortunes through utter luck rather than hard work."

"Work?" Whit pretended to shudder. "With such a stance, you won't make it very far in society."

"Perhaps I won't." Leo's gaze turned far away, his mind preoccupied and brooding. A man at war with himself, desiring acceptance by people he did not esteem.

Were Leo anyone but himself, he would find his life no great hardship. Young and hale, possessing of a sizeable financial estate, and Whit saw how women stared after Leo, sighing into their fans.

But Leo wanted more than the things within his grasp. In that, he was no different from any of the other Hellraisers, Whit included.

At this moment, Whit wanted two things very badly. To gamble. To have Zora. Of the two, one was a certainty. For now. The other would take time, but, though he burned, he did not begrudge the wait. It would make possessing her all the more exquisite.

"My lord," said the man running the table. "It is your turn." He held the dice out for Whit.

With the cool disinterest of a veteran, Whit took the pieces of carved ivory. A satisfying weight in his hand, sending a visceral charge up his arm and through his body. The dice still carried the warmth of the last man to hold them, so they felt alive, almost sentient. Smug little buggers, believing that they alone controlled chance.

Whit resisted the urge to smirk. He would prove them wrong. He placed his bet, setting the gaming tokens upon the table, and a red-faced man nearby cursed softly at the amount. Even Leo, well used to Whit's habits, gave a low whistle. Whit did nothing by half measures, especially this night.

"What is your main, my lord?"

"Six," Whit answered.

Beside him, Leo snorted. "Pity there aren't three dice, that you might cast three sixes."

"I'd hate to be obvious."

The man running the table did not understand the meaning of Whit and Leo's exchange. "Cast, my lord."

Whit held the dice a moment longer. Then cast.

Everything remained the same: the room, the gamesters, the servants moving between the tables to bring glasses of wine. The change came from within Whit, spiraling out. The room now contained probability, an infinite number of probabilities spiraling out from all persons, all things, until the gaming room became an endless sea of chance. The servant could trip upon the raised surface of the carpet, spilling wine and distracting the sallow man playing vingt-et-un, who would lose this hand and, in a foul temper, return home early to catch his wife with her lover. Or the servant could move on without trouble, the sallow man would win and continue playing for three more hours, giving his wife ample time with her paramour.

But these probabilities were nothing compared to the potential that radiated from the gaming tables themselves. The dozens, hundreds of ways a game of piquet could turn, depending on which cards were dealt. Same with the tables dedicated to hazard. A kaleidoscope of odds, dazzling and dizzying.

Power filled him, intoxicating him. He had only to wish it, give one of the spirals of chance the slightest mental nudge, and the outcome would change to suit him. So much possibility. So much potential. Where to begin?

His own odds, of course. As the dice rolled across the baize-covered table, Whit took the helixes of chance and altered them, aligning them. He did not move. To anyone observing him, he stood at the table, hands lightly braced at the edge, and calmly watched the dice tumble. He controlled an invisible force using his will alone. The helix spun and shifted at his command, until—

"Six. The caster has thrown a six. It is a nicks, my lord."

One die had two spots turned up, the other four. He had won the cast.

A few gentlemen close by murmured, "Nicely done," or "Good cast."

Leo said nothing, though he proffered a slightly ironic bow. "And?" he then asked lowly.

Whit felt expansive, larger than time and infinitely more powerful. Capable of anything. He almost wished he could tell the men in the club what he had done, what he *could* do. Level the whole of London through his mastery of chance. Depose kings. Reshape the surface of the world. He would give Zora the shining globe for her plaything.

His appetite for more had always been sizeable. Now, a ravenous hunger consumed him. He wanted everything. He could have everything.

"Ah," said Leo, in the silence. "Now you know how I felt this morning at the Exchange."

"A wonder you didn't tear the city down," breathed Whit.

"Nearly did, but only the ruthless application of restraint kept me in check. Between the five of us Hellraisers, I doubt anything can stop us."

A wild laugh nearly escaped Whit. However, like Leo, he wrestled himself under control so that, instead of laughing, he merely smiled. "Nothing shall," he said.

A night of immeasurable, dark joy. Whit had never experienced its like, not during his school years, nor the time he'd spent on the Continent, nor even during the wild and riotous nights here in London with his fellow Hellraisers. No, this night had been different.

The exercise of his will, his power, given strength and form by that iniquitous benefactor, Mr. Holliday. How had Whit existed without this gift? Only a few days earlier, he had moved through his life in what now appeared a shadowed half existence, content with mere trifles. On this night, and for all the nights to come, he controlled the outcome of a hundred, a thousand futures.

He played at hazard again. This time, he wanted to test the capability of his magic. He called six as his main again but changed the outcome so that he cast a seven. Neither a win nor a loss, it permitted him to cast again but with seven as his new main. He rolled the dice and plucked the strands of probability so that seven came up on this cast. Another win. Bright, hard pleasure knifed him. Beside him, Leo chuckled. Whit knew Leo well enough to understand that anything subverting the dominant order pleased the younger man.

As a game of chance, hazard offered many possibilities of success and even more of failure. He once had enjoyed the game's complex structure, its almost arbitrary rules about what numbers one should and should not cast, depending on the chosen main. Before, it had been about navigating the treacherous waters of probability and luck. Now it became a dance, with figures and patterns over which he held sway—turning, shaping outcomes to suit his needs.

Losing, as well. Whit sensed the man running the hazard table growing restive as Whit continued on his roll. He had been winning for too long. The manager of the club circled the room's perimeter, feigning indifference but his attention was actually fixed on Whit. Whit thought of Zora—how she read the subtle shifts within people as attentively as a scholar read a book.

"Have a care," Leo said in an undertone.

"Already attended to," Whit answered.

On his next cast, he called nine as his main. As the dice tumbled across the table, Whit delved into the swirl of chance, altering its course.

The dice came up with eleven.

"A throw-out," said the table runner with obvious relief. "I am sorry, my lord," he added unconvincingly.

Whit made a small show of frowning and muttering a curse. Within, however, he wildly celebrated. He could win or lose as he desired. Truly, anything was possible.

It was the same at the card tables. For hours, Whit played piquet, loo, and vingt-et-un. Instead of shifting the movement of the dice, he delved into the turn of the cards, and this he enjoyed for its infinite possibilities and combinations. Which number or suit or face card he needed. When to have a strategic loss. A learning process, yet here was the thrill he had never experienced at university, educating himself on the most judicious and profitable uses for his magical gift. He created an alchemical process, combining his own knowledge of gambling with the new gift. Zora's knowledge was an additional ingredient. The end result was not lead into gold, but a stake of a few hundred pounds into tens of thousands of pounds.

The value of the money itself was nothing to him. Only the thrill and heady power of manipulating chance to his advantage. A framed painting upon the wall depicted the goddess Fortuna, blindfolded, scattering coins as she balanced precariously upon a globe. She bestowed her gifts without favor, immune to mortal influence or desire.

Studying the painting, Whit permitted himself a small, vicious smile. He had toppled the goddess from her perch. She had no power over him anymore.

I have killed an ancient god. Where once there were deities, the Hellraisers reign.

He almost pitied the world. Almost.

Hours later, Whit stood outside the club, amazed how little anything had altered. From the noxious puddles in the street reflecting the gray dawn, to the nodding coachman awaiting him, to the deliberately imposing façades of buildings fronting St. James's Square, the world was almost exactly the same as it had been the previous day.

He felt a bizarre urge to stop a passing costermonger, shake the man by his shoulders, and crow about the wondrous new world he had created. Instead, Whit and Leo donned their tricorn hats and stood quietly, their breath steaming in the frigid air.

"I feel as though I should ring the bells at St. Paul's," Whit murmured.

Leo offered a rueful grin. "Been fighting that urge ever since yesterday. But now"—he yawned hugely—"Mr. Holliday's gift or no, I haven't seen my bed in far too long. Are you for home?"

Home. And Zora. It was a measure of how entranced Whit had been with his power that she had only infrequently entered his thoughts as he had sat at the card tables, existing as a warm, luminous presence hovering at the edges of his consciousness. Now, fresh need surged, only temporarily dammed. He saw her dark eyes, heard her low, husky voice, and it was all he could do to keep from knocking the coachman from his perch and driving himself home at a breakneck pace.

"Home, my lord?" said the coachman, snapping Whit to wakefulness.

"I think I've done all that I care to," said Whit. He felt not dissimilar to the sleek matched carriage horses that steamed and stamped in impatience.

"At the club, anyway," added Leo.

"Can I give you a ride home?" Leo's residence was in Bloomsbury, a distance most would traverse either on horseback or by carriage.

"These peasant legs of mine find pleasure in walking. Enjoy your Gypsy girl."

Already stepping into his carriage, Whit paused, one hand upon the top of the door. Enjoy her? She was more than a momentary pleasure, some exotic delicacy to be sampled before moving on to the next flavor. He had only to think of her and a primal hunger gripped him, something that would not be slaked by taking her once or twice. More than fancy, more than lust. This he already knew, though he had not even tasted her mouth.

"Good night, Leo," he said.

"Good morning, Whit." Leo strolled off, whistling.

The ride to his town house in Berkeley Square was brief, yet Whit churned in a fever of restiveness. When he did at last arrive, he did not wait for the carriage to stop, nor the footman to open the carriage door. Instead, he flung the door open and bounded up the steps. He took no notice of any of the footmen or maids he passed once he was inside. He strode quickly to the game room, not pausing as he handed off his hat to a waiting servant. As he neared the room, his heart throbbed with each step.

He paused outside the game room just long enough to give a tap on the closed door. No sound from within. Panic gripped him. Was she gone? It could not be possible.

Fear dissolved when he opened the door, stepped inside, and saw Zora sitting by an open window. The fire in the grate burned low, and no candles were lit. It hurt to look at her, the dawn light tracing silver and smoke along the bold, feminine lines of her face. She had her legs drawn up, her arms wrapped around them, as she perched upon the chair. Her head turned toward him when he entered, eyes flaring bright. Other than this, and the small tightening of her hold around herself, she did not move.

Whit shut the door behind him, but when he turned back to her, he did not close the distance between them. He wanted to look his fill, behold his treasure, his prize. Zora.

She stared back. Her gaze traveled over him, seeing, no doubt, his evening finery a little less pristine after a night's adventure. She lingered longest on his face. A keen, exacting stare—one he was coming to know well. It cut him open as surely as an anatomist studying a specimen. His heart exposed to her. An exquisite pain.

"A successful evening," she said. Her voice stroked him with its velvet timbre.

He strode to her. "A miraculous evening." He tried not to see her minute flinch when he reached for her, but she relaxed when he only took a lock of her black hair and wound it around two fingers. His thumb caressed the heavy, silky strands.

She raised a dark brow. "*Miraculous* implies the work of the Divine."

"Another kind of divinity. Ah, Zora," he breathed, crouching down so that their faces were level, "I wish you could have been there to see it. To see me."

"Even if I left this room, I don't think the places you frequent would admit me."

That made him pause. Slowly, he unrolled her hair from around his fingers, and it pleased him that the locks continued to hold the shape. He needed something of him to affect something of her, no matter how small.

"Women are not admitted to gentlemen's clubs," he said, "but, on my arm, you could go anywhere your heart desired." This was not entirely truthful. As Whit's mistress, she might be able to attend the theater or visit the pleasure gardens of Vauxhall and Ranelagh, but no aristocrat or person of gentle birth would admit her to his private residence.

"I want to go home." No pleading in her tone, only a statement of truth. Nevertheless, her words were a cold knife cutting through his euphoria.

"See what I have for you." From his pocket, he withdrew a sheet of paper and held it out to her. "Take it."

She eyed the paper warily, then, slowly, her slim hand reached out and took hold of it. Briefly, her gaze flicked down to the paper, then back up. "I can't read this."

Ah. He had forgotten. It was widespread for people of the lower orders to be illiterate. Whit ventured to guess that at least half his servants could barely write their own names. Country folk were often unschooled in their letters, as well. Yet he placed Zora far above the ranks of ordinary people, even above the gentry he knew. Here was evidence that she was no paragon, but a genuine woman of circumstance and flesh. A fact both discomforting and alluring.

"It is a draft from the gaming club," he said. "Tonight, I won ten thousand pounds."

Her lush mouth parted in surprise. "Ten thousand—" She blinked.

"That's more than a bishop makes in a year." He folded her hands around the paper, and she was delicate but strong beneath his palms. "Yours," he said.

Her night-dark eyes went round. It took her a moment to speak. "You are giving it to me?"

"Everything," he answered, rough and urgent. "I will give you everything. This night's work was all for you." His words came faster as excitement built in him as he relived the events of the past few hours. "If only I had the means to show you, to let you experience what I experienced. It's incredible, Zora. And beautiful."

"There's no beauty in such wickedness," she said. "Using magic to cheat."

His patience frayed slightly at the edges. "This, from the woman who happily tells lies to any willing fool."

She tried to tug her hand back, but he maintained his hold. "No, your pardon," he said, forcing down his temper. "That was ill spoken of me. But, Zora, this gift of mine is not wicked, it's wonderful. And I want to share it with you."

No answer from her, only her continuing stare as if she could uncover a deeper truth—or other self—within him.

"This ten thousand is yours." He tightened his grip. "No more *dukkering*, or living out of a tent. No more horse fairs or roaming from town to town."

"No more being Roma," she answered bluntly.

He smiled. "Sweet, wild creature. I would never take that from you. If you wish to *dukker*, you may certainly do so. I can give you a tent made of silk, gilded fortune-telling cards, and more gold around your neck." With the tip of one finger, he lightly touched the coin-laden necklaces that hung so deliciously between her breasts. The chains held her body's heat, as if forged from her golden skin.

"You must think very little of yourself," she said. "Offering me money to couple with you."

He reared back as if she had slapped him, releasing her.

"You mistake me." He rose up and paced away. "I won't lie and say I don't want you in my bed. But I'm not paying you to fuck me."

Her mouth compressed at his coarse language. She unfolded herself and stood, holding out the draft. "What is this, if not a whore's payment?"

"Keep your legs together and keep the damned blunt," he bit out. "I want you to have the money whether you become my mistress or no." He gave her a hard smile as he planted his hands on his hips. "Trust me, love, I've enough confidence in my skills as a lover. Bribes are unnecessary."

She stared down at the draft. A struggle waged within her, her shoulders tensing, her brows drawing low. As she debated, Whit's own tension raised yet higher. He did not lie. The money would be hers, even if she rebuffed his advances. But, by the Devil, he did not want her to.

The moment stretched, tightening. *Say yes*, he urged in his mind.

Zora raised her gaze to him. Her eyes were dark and rich. "Temptation comes in beautiful guises. You. This." She held up the draft. "You tempt me so."

"A mutual condition."

She moved away from the chair. But she did not come to him, as he urgently wanted. Instead, she laid the draft upon the card table. "I won't accept this."

Disappointment gutted him. From the heights of his earlier exhilaration, the plunge down was far, the crash painful. Anger and dismay. He was not accustomed to being denied, especially something he desired this badly.

"What the hell do you want?" he demanded.

"To go home." His question forced her to answer honestly, but it wasn't what he hoped for. She took a step toward him. "More than that, I want you to renounce *Wafodu guero*. Return the dark magic he gave you."

"Impossible," he said.

"What do *you* want?" she asked, echoing his question.

He strode to her so that only a few inches separated them.

This close, he caught her scent of smoke and forest. Her heather-honey skin was dusky, luminous. To resist touching her was beyond him. He feathered caresses down her cheek, along her neck. Barely, he suppressed a groan. If just the feel of her skin against his fingers felt this good, how much better, how sweet and delicious would she be wrapped around him as he sank himself into her?

"I want to touch you everywhere," he rumbled. "I want my tongue in your mouth. I want my cock inside you. I want to make you come so many times, you forget your own name and know only mine."

Her breath hitched, her eyes darkened. Lush color stained the high crest of her cheeks. The tip of her tongue darted out to wet her bottom lip. She did not touch him, yet she did not push him away either.

"Zora." Her name was like incense and secrets. "Do you want to kiss me?"

Magic compelled her to answer truthfully. "Yes." She held his gaze. "I wanted to kiss you soon after I met you. Because I saw not just a handsome man, but a man with a hunger like mine. A man with a need for answers. A questing soul."

He found it difficult to draw air—his heart beat too fiercely. Nothing compelled her to say these things, for she had answered his question. Her words were freely given, and that made them all the more precious.

"I wanted to taste that hunger," she murmured. "I wanted to know if my lips could answer those questions. If this man whom I saw could be my counterpart, the companion on my own quest." Her eyes were dark and inescapable. He felt himself falling deeper, deeper, and did not want to stop his fall.

"I saw that it could be so," she continued. "I see it now, for I've never met a man like you, and I never will again. There is no one such as you. Just as there is no one such as me."

Whit had no protection from her. He did not want protection. He threaded his fingers into her hair as he cradled the back of her head. He wanted—*needed*—her mouth. Brought his own close to hers, close enough to feel her breath upon his lips.

Her hands came up to wrap around his wrists, her thumbs brushing against the thunder of his pulse. "Yes," she whispered, her eyes drifting closed.

Their mouths met. Words, details glinted through him like dropped gemstones. *Soft. Lush. Spice.* Her lips were wonders beneath his own. Full and silken, pliant yet bold. The initial kiss saw them both with lips closed, but it took only a moment's contact before they needed more, and opened to each other. With a groan, he felt her tongue touch his, a velvet stroke that reverberated through his body in sumptuous, heavy waves. She moaned in ready response.

Her taste intoxicated. A woman's taste, bold and demanding. He met her demand with his own. They sought out answers and found them in each other. The kiss deepened, and her hands moved from his wrists to his shoulders, pulling him closer. Their bodies fit together, as perfect as music. She was curved yet strong, possessing enough softness so that his tight, hewn body found precisely the place it most belonged.

Yes. Here, was his answer. And it made him greedy for more.

His cock was thick, insistent, rising up between them to cradle against the curve of her belly. She rocked into him and he growled. He needed inside her in every way.

She pulled back, only slightly, yet to lose her mouth felt like the cruelest wound. "Whit," she breathed. "I can't lie to you, but your kiss does not lie to me. I knew it wouldn't. The man I wanted at the camp is still here."

"He never left," Whit rasped.

Her hand drifted from his shoulder to stroke his face. He leaned into her touch, craving it. "You've no need for magic. Not when there is a whole world between us to explore. You can surrender *Wafodu guero*'s magic yet gain so much."

A new tension tightened his body. "Don't ask that of me."

"There is strength enough in you," she persisted. "In each of us."

"And if I want everything?" His words were a harsh grate in his throat. "Power *and* you?"

Her hand dropped from his face, and her other hand slid from his shoulder to flatten against his chest. Though she trembled slightly, he still felt a subtle exertion of pressure as she held him back. "One or the other. But not both."

Whit released her. He had never faced an obstacle as impassable as Zora's will. This frustration, this consuming, thwarted need—he'd never known it until now, and it stoked a conflagration of rage. He grabbed the bank draft from the table, strode to the fire, then threw the draft upon the flames. Zora gasped. He did not trust himself to speak, so he watched the edges of the paper blacken before the whole document writhed in the fire, reducing quickly to ashes.

He sent her one last, searing gaze before slamming from the room.

Chapter 6

Zora was being punished.

Or rather, it felt like punishment when Whit did not visit her once during the day. She stared out the window and watched an orange tabby cat hunting in the garden. When the cat lost interest, it lightly leapt over the wall, free to come and go as it pleased. She envied that cat.

Servants came and went, most in states of terror as they brought her food, emptied her chamber pot, and even brought in and filled a hipbath. Zora had eyed the bath warily. If she wanted to use it, she needed to strip, which left her vulnerable. The servants might not be able to see her, but Whit could.

The worst of it was that Zora had been unable to decide if she liked that idea or not.

God, that kiss . . . Not once throughout the day did she forget it. Her mouth still felt his, she still tasted him—brandy and tobacco and man—and her body demanded more. Worse than the needs of her body were the needs of her heart. She had kissed Whit to make a point, to prove that he was still the worthy, searching man she had desired at the camp.

Unfortunately, she had been right. And she wanted that man, her hunger even greater. It could be so good between them. Could be, but never would, not when he refused to turn from the Devil. Hairline cracks spread through her heart as she thought of the loss, made all the more difficult by her continued imprisonment.

She had to focus on the mundane to keep from surrendering her sanity. So, she had taken a chair and wedged it beneath the doorknob. Whit possessed enough strength to knock through that small defensive barrier, but he hadn't used violence against her. Not yet. So she had peeled off her rather limp, stale garments and taken a bath. Lavender had perfumed the water. It had smelled of heaven and felt even better, especially after days trapped in a room she was beginning to despise.

After her bath, Zora had donned her musty clothing reluctantly, then removed the chair from beneath the doorknob. A few minutes later, more frightened servants had come in, muttering in fear to see the obviously used bath. They had taken the tub away and left several paper-wrapped packages in its place.

"Whoever's here," a shivering footman had said, "I was to tell you that these things is for you." Then he had scuttled away like a rat fleeing fire.

She had cautiously unwrapped the parcels, chary of what they might contain. While she doubted someone had wrapped up a bundle of adders, it would have been reckless to simply tear into them. Slowly, so slowly, she had untied the blue silk ribbons on one package. The magpie in her loved the ribbons—so sleek and beautiful, yet used for such a practical purpose! Zora would have gladly woven the ribbons into her hair, or trimmed a bodice with them. These wealthy *gorgios* baffled her.

The ribbons had come away and she had peeled back the heavy paper. Then gasped aloud. Unable to contain herself any longer, she had lifted up the contents.

A gown. Perhaps the most lovely gown Zora had ever seen. Certainly the most luscious she had ever touched. Golden silk, trimmed with deep coral-colored ribbons and rosettes. Heavy pleats fell from the shoulders; the fabric would trail and pool sumptuously behind the wearer. The vivid color would flatter her dusky skin, much more so than the pale, insipid hues many *gorgies* favored.

Unable to resist the lure, Zora had torn into the other parcels.

"God save me from such beauty," she had whispered in the Romani tongue.

More gowns, each of them glorious. Colors had dazzled eyes too familiar with the dark shades of the masculine game room. Sapphire, emerald, ruby. Dresses the colors of gems, of precious things one wanted to both flaunt and hoard. Adorned in ribbons, embroidered with minute, perfect stitches. Heavy and ethereal in her hands. More than gowns, there had been stomachers covered in embroidery and silk bows, whisper-thin chemises trimmed in lace, stockings, garters, nightgowns, back-laced corsets, petticoats. Two fans of ivory. Three pairs of slippers ornamented with glittering buckles that were not paste. The parcels had held everything a woman could ever desire.

Everything a *gorgie* could desire. Zora was not a *gorgie*, but she had not been able to stop herself from holding the emerald-colored gown to her body. Her heart had sunk when she realized that the gown would fit her perfectly, even without the confining corset. Somehow, without Zora ever being measured, the seamstress had created a faultless wardrobe and of the precise range of colors that would complement Zora best.

Zora had been glad there was no mirror in the gaming room. It would have been physically painful to see how well the gowns would flatter her, luring her into trying them on, knowing that she could not accept them.

"Damn you, Whit," she had muttered, then laughed mirthlessly. He had already damned himself. He didn't need her to do it for him.

She had reluctantly folded everything, though it had been beyond her strength to repack the clothing in its paper and retie the ribbons. Touching the gowns, the chemises, had been torment enough. The Rom lived fairly simple lives, the needs of staying mobile preventing any of them from acquiring all the possessions that *gorgios* seemed to think were required. Zora preferred her freedom to being weighed down by objects, clothing, property. But she was still human, still a woman, and sometimes craved beautiful things.

She would be beautiful, too, in the gowns. What woman did not want to be beautiful? To have a man stare at her as if she contained the entire world, and he would do anything, anything to have her?

Unfair of Whit to tempt her like this, when his kiss had been temptation enough. She would not fall, as he had done. And when he came to her that day, she would tell him exactly that.

But he never did come. She remained alone in the gaming room.

She ought to be grateful. This was peace, free from Whit and his handsome face and strong, lean body, his kiss promising her things she should not want, yet, *Duvvel* help her, she did.

I want to touch you everywhere. I want my tongue in your mouth. I want my cock inside you. I want to make you come so many times, you forget your own name and know only mine.

Just thinking of his words made her heart pound and heat gather between her legs. To remember his kiss made her long for his hard, hot body over her, beneath her. For the man he could be, for the potential of them—together. A potential that would go unmet. And this fueled her anger.

She paced the gaming room, feeling like a wild horse in a narrow corral. What did he mean by staying away? Was he trying to show her how much she needed him? Was it an exercise of his power over her? Of a certain he must be angry with her for making him choose between her and the dark magic, for deliberately showing him everything that he missed because of his choice. But it was impossible to accept him as her lover—not under these circumstances. Surely he saw that.

Logic meant nothing, not as long as he remained loyal to *Wafodu guero*. And that would never change. His face last night had convinced her. All but glowing with power, with feral joy after using his dark magic to win at gambling. They had kissed with blistering intensity, yet he would rather control the odds than allow the passion between them to flower.

"Ten thousand pounds," she said aloud. She could support not only her family, but her whole band, for the whole of their lives. A fortune. But the money was tainted by darkness. If she had accepted it, she would have damned herself and her family. Was that what he wanted? To drag her down with him?

Zora picked up a ceramic vase perched on a side table, then flung it against a wall. The sound of shattering filled the room, and pieces of pottery fell to the floor in jagged shards.

She didn't feel any better. In fact, the bits of destroyed vase bothered her, and she knelt to collect the pieces. As she gathered them in her skirt, her finger caught on one of the sharp edges.

Cursing, she held up her finger for inspection. A thin cut ran along the tip of her index finger. Blood welled, and a single crimson bead dropped on the floor.

She ignored the cut and finished cleaning up the pieces of the vase. Unsure what to do with them, she put them in a little pile in a corner. One shard she kept, however, tucking it into the pocket of her apron. Anything that could serve as protection she would keep. She would just have to be careful not to cut *herself* while using her improvised weapon.

Night fell in darkening waves. Sounds of the city changed. The working folk began to head for home, whilst the wealthy *gorgios* began to stir for their evening's amusement.

Whit would be going out, as well. He was a creature of night. Perhaps he had gone already. The thought was distressing, and the very fact that it *was* distressing bothered her even more.

She had sought to tempt him with her kisses, yet *she* paid the price now, wanting him, wanting what could never be.

Zora lit candles to counter the rising darkness, wondering how she would pass another night. How she would try not to dwell on his mouth or the feel of him against her, his very obvious arousal that stoked a fire within her. How she would resist the temptation of trying on the beautiful gowns. How else she could plot her escape. Magic held her here, and she possessed none. Days ago, she did not believe in magic. Now she fervently wished she had some of her own.

She paced. Then stopped when she sensed something—*someone*—standing outside the door. The tread had been quiet, but she felt him near. A masculine presence, bold, powerful. Whit.

Her body tensed as her heart began to pound in expectation. Yet the door to the gaming room remained closed.

Slipping off her shoes, Zora noiselessly walked to the door. She could open it. Reveal him. She did not. Instead, she pressed her palm to the wood.

He was just on the other side of the door. She could not leave, but he could come inside. She wondered what he wore this night, what splendid finery emphasized his strength, the male beauty of his form.

They stood like that, her on one side of the door, he on the other.

Come in. I don't want to see you. I don't want to kiss you. I need to.

Her heart pitched when, finally, she heard him move away. His steps retreated down the hallway. A door somewhere opened and closed. She thought she heard him speak to someone. And then . . . he was gone.

Disappointment speared her, made even worse by the fact that she shouldn't be disappointed. He was her captor. Her tormentor. The cohort of the Devil.

Zora pushed away from the door and paced to the window. She stared with burning eyes at the growing gloom outside. If ever she had doubted her resolve to escape, now she knew it for certain. There was no hope for him, for them. She needed to get away from this place and from Whit. The question was, *how*?

So absorbed was she in her thoughts, she did not look at the blood she had dripped upon the floor, nor the flickering glow that now grew around it.

It would be a bad night for gambling. Though Whit lived for the thrill of gaming, like any seasoned gambler, he knew that one needed to be calm and composed to win. Emotions clouded judgment, and one's odds decreased as a result.

Except he controlled the odds, no matter what tumult he might feel. He could stride into the club in the foulest of humors and still emerge a winner.

He was due to meet Edmund, Bram, and John for supper. Leo had another engagement. Yet, when Whit marched down the steps of his town house, he growled up at his waiting coachman, "White's." Then he flung himself into the carriage and sat, brooding, as the footman closed the carriage door after him. The coachman clicked his tongue, flicked the reins, and they were off. Whit could just as easily have walked the distance from Berkeley Square to Chesterfield Street, but such were the privileges of wealth and birth that he could make use of his healthy, strong limbs only when he damn well felt like it.

Whit didn't care that he was abandoning his friends. He didn't care that it was far too early for decent play at the gaming tables. All he needed was the comfort and pleasure that could be found in gambling. Using Mr. Holliday's gift would ensure that Whit would win, and that would bring him relief. Relief from his anger, his confusion. His need for Zora, and the pain her deliberate manipulation caused. It was a blazing brand that hurt him far more than he ever could have anticipated.

The elegant lanes of Mayfair rolled past him: gentry in their sedan chairs; wide, brightly lit streets. He saw none of this. Zora's dark eyes haunted him, her lush mouth, the opiate of her kisses. Her cruel words kept scoring the raw flesh of his heart. *One or the other. But not both.*

He slammed his fist against the side of the carriage. The vehicle immediately slowed.

"Drive on," he barked.

The coachman quickly obeyed, and soon they were en route once more to the club.

What bloody right did she have to make him choose? To show him what could be, and then ruthlessly steal it away? She could not judge him. He was a peer of the realm. She admitted to lying, to cheating. When he'd accepted Mr. Holliday's gift, Zora had not been uppermost in Whit's thoughts, but now that she was his, he would make use of his power to make her life a goddamn sodding paradise. If she'd let him.

Clearly, she wasn't going to take anything from him. He cursed her pride and strength, even as he marveled at and admired it. Pride he had in abundance, being an earl, but strength . . . That quality eluded him. At least, when it came to denying himself the pleasures of gambling. Or denying himself anything.

He'd been strong today, though. He had forced himself to sleep, to eat, to conduct matters of business, and to meet in the afternoon with Leo for coffee and intelligence. All this he had done and not gone to see Zora once, whilst his muscles and bones and heart demanded he do just that. To see her. Listen to her voice. Talk with her. And, God, to kiss her. Even as her kisses maddened him, she yet gave him a sense of peace and rightness he had not known . . . perhaps ever.

The carriage slowed, then stopped. A liveried footman opened the carriage door and murmured, "Welcome, my lord." If the servant was surprised to see Whit so early, he gave no indication, just as a well-trained servant kept counsel.

Saying nothing, Whit strode up the stairs and inside the club. He handed his cloak and hat to a waiting footman as the club's manager walked up briskly, all smiles.

"Greetings, my lord. Are you here for supper? We've a

lovely cold collation, or I am certain I can prevail upon our cook to prepare a special—"

"Hazard," Whit said.

The manager did not blink. He smiled wider and unclasped his hands. "Right this way, my lord."

Time lost its significance, as it always did when Whit immersed himself in the tide of gambling. He submerged in a deluge of odds and numbers, cards, dice, bet and losses. The dizzying, intoxicating kaleidoscope of probability that he now controlled. In his mind, the club itself vanished, the men in the club becoming fragments: hands, eyes, voices. Someone gave him a glass of wine. He supposed he drank it, because a moment later, the empty glass was taken. Perhaps he ate. He wasn't certain. The mania had him. Nothing else mattered.

Two thoughts consumed him: to gamble, and to put Zora from his thoughts. One was easily accomplished. The other proved as tenacious as a rose's thorn digging into the twitching, angry muscle of his heart.

I will level this club. I will raze London. It will be entirely mine. Then I shall make you choose, Lady Gypsy. Passion and prosperity with me. Or nothing at all.

"Jesus, Whit, you look like hell." Bram's sardonic voice barely cut through the haze of risk and odds.

Whit only grunted in response as he studied the cards in his hand. The game was Pope Joan, and permutations of probability swirled about the round staking board.

"How long has he been here?" That was Edmund, sounding concerned.

"Five hours, my lord," said the club manager. "He goes from one game to another. We cannot prevail upon him to stop, not for a minute."

"Come, Whit," said John, even-tempered and sensible. "Lord Abeldale is hosting a rout. His gatherings are always amusing. There may be cards."

"And willing women," added Bram. "Not a Gypsy amongst them."

Whit played his ace card, winning the contents of the Intrigue compartment in the staking board. He did not have many cards remaining, and he rearranged the odds to ensure that he would play his last card before any of the other players, thus winning the game.

"I don't think he heard any of us," Edmund said.

"Whit." Bram took hold of Whit's arm, but Whit shook him off without ever letting his eyes leave the card table.

"I heard you," he growled. "Just don't give a damn."

The voices of his friends continued to rise and fall around him. He paid no attention. The game was everything. At some point, his friends left, knowing that only outright bodily force could pry him from the table. His eyes were hot and sticky. Smoke from pipes and cheroots filled the club, yet he barely blinked as he sank deeper into his mania.

This he could control. *Here* was where Whit commanded everything. Even the uncertainty of fortune bent to his will. No man could resist such a lure, and neither did he.

A baron's son bet and lost a prized racehorse to Whit. From a squire worth five thousand pounds a year he won a seaside cottage. Someone's ruby stickpin now resided in Whit's pocket, beside his pocket watch.

He knew an inanimate object could not feel or think, yet somehow he sensed disapproval emanating from the pocket watch—the manifestation of his father and grandfather. They would not have condoned his actions this night. He told himself he did not care.

After he had exhausted his interest in Pope Joan, the hazard table claimed him next. He had enough sense to deliberately lose his first and second casts, and, to make the display more convincing, bet decent-sized amounts. He was vaguely aware of the club manager sighing in relief before fading back to attend to other duties.

Once the manager had gone, Whit decided it was time to

dig back into the business of winning. He wagered a smaller amount on his next cast.

"Eight," he announced as he shook the dice in his hand.

The dice tumbled from his palm. Wanting to prolong the play, Whit adjusted the patterns of probability so that the dice came up reading seven, enabling him to cast again. So he did. He would need to cast a seven this time in order to win.

Clattering against each other like teeth, the ivory dice rolled. Whit delved into the protean eddies of probability. He manipulated chance, arranging it precisely as he needed.

The dice stopped their tumble. He reached for his winnings, but the man running the table coughed politely.

"Pardon, my lord," he said, somewhat embarrassed. "But you cast a twelve. It is a throw-out."

Whit's gaze moved from the dice to the man's reddening face, then back again. He blinked to clear his eyes. Yet the markings on the dice did not change. Two sixes. Not the three and four he needed. The numbers he had guaranteed would turn up in his cast.

Whit stood dumbstruck, frozen in place, reaching out foolishly for a prize that was not his.

He had lost.

Something flickered in the window's glass. A gleam. Zora thought at first it was only the reflection of a candle. No. The light actually *grew*. Was something on fire?

She spun around, then stepped back, knocking into the wall behind her. Her lips parted, but no sound came out. Instead, she could only gape.

Silver light appeared as an orb as big as a billiard ball, hovering inches above the floor. Above the droplet of blood Zora had spilled earlier. As Zora stared, the orb of light grew larger, lengthened. No heat came from it, but its radiance filled the room, chasing shadows that lurked in corners.

Zora gulped. Was this more of *Wafodu guero*'s dark magic? She had to defend herself, but how? Reaching into her pocket, she pulled out the cutting shard of pottery. It was no match for the Devil's power, yet she needed some sense of protection, no matter how illusory.

The light steadily increased in size until it was almost as tall as Zora. She squinted, shielding her eyes, as a person's figure coalesced within it. The light gathered, took shape, until it formed . . .

A woman.

Zora actually found herself taking a step closer to get a better look, even as her mind shouted that she must be cautious. Yet she could not contain her curiosity.

The woman wore one of those long, draped tunics Zora had seen on ancient statues and figures adorning fountains in public squares. Some of her dark brown hair was piled up in an elaborate style, a kind of fillet holding it back and up, while the rest hung in waves over her shoulders and down her back. She was beautiful, as elegant and lovely as those statues, and her gray eyes seemed to peer deep into time as she scanned the room.

The woman was also completely translucent. Zora could see right through her to the wall.

A bavol-engro. A ghost.

Zora recited old Romani incantations against evil, incantations she never believed in nor tried to memorize. Now she wished she had paid more attention when her grandmother had attempted to instruct her in Romani lore—back when Zora did not give credence to things such as magic and evil. She knew differently now, yet too late. All she could recall were jumbled phrases, shreds of belief she tried to use as shelter. To no avail. The ghost did not disappear, did not even flicker. She continued to hover just above the ground as she stared at Zora.

"Go from here, spirit." Zora attempted a command, but her voice shook as much as her knees.

To her shock, the ghost answered.

"She can see me?" Her voice held a strange accent, a little like the Italian commedia actors the Rom sometimes met in their travels. The ghost at first sounded as though she were a great distance away, but, as she spoke, her words grew stronger.

Zora could only nod.

"And . . . she hears my voice?"

"Y-yes."

The ghost held up her own arm and stared at its gleaming translucency. "She sees. And I have form." Lowering her arm, she drifted toward Zora. Her eyes beseeched as much as her outstretched hand. "Touch. So long. It has been so long since I felt another's warmth."

Zora skittered away as the ghost floated toward her. When the spirit passed through the solid form of a chair, she stopped in her progress and stared down in shock.

"Form, but no substance." She whirled away from the chair, pressing her knuckles into her eyes. "The punishment, it does not cease. Punished for my transgressions."

Zora did not know what to believe or what to trust. *Wafodu guero* was a liar, a trickster. This mad spectral woman could be one more of his ruses to lead her down dark paths. Whit had been taken in, but Zora needed to remain wary, for his sake as well as her own.

"Transgressions?" she asked guardedly.

"Pride. And greed," answered the spirit, distracted. She suddenly grew agitated once more, spinning back toward Zora. "Am I too late?"

"I don't know." Zora could hardly believe she conversed with a ghost, if that's truly what this creature was. "Too late for what?"

"Too late for what, she asks. Does she not know? I do not believe she knows. She must." The spirit's lovely face grew stern. "To defeat the beast that has been set loose upon an unsuspecting world."

Wafodu guero, Zora thought. "He is your master."

The ghost gave a riotous laugh before choking it back. "Not my master. No. *I* sought to be mistress over *him*."

"Who are you?" Zora demanded.

"Names? What are names? Alone, who has a name? Once, others called me Valeria Livia Corva." Her voice grew wry. "Other names, too. When they thought I did not hear, but I heard. Yes, and marked them well. Wicked woman. Priestess of Hecate. Worshipper of the dark forces and chaos."

Zora's head spun as she tried to puzzle out what she saw, what she heard. Truly this spirit—if that's what she was— had lost her mind. "This makes no sense to me."

"We are of a kind, her and I. Am I here? Do we converse? Is *she* real? My memory, my . . . sanity, it is a liquid thing." The ghost pressed transparent hands to her temples. "I remember . . . the prison being opened, and I was free. But so was he. And there were men. The ones who had freed us. The girl was there. And then . . . she summoned me. Yet"— she glanced around, her eyes attempting to focus—"I know not this place."

"This is the home of one of those men. We're far from where this all began. How did you come to be trapped with the Devil?" Zora would ferret out the truth, if it existed.

"The Devil," the spirit repeated, her mouth twisting. "So that is what he is called now. I have my name. Valeria Livia Corva. He has his names, his faces, all different. They were different then, when I knew him."

"A long time ago," Zora guessed.

The spirit gazed about her, uncertain. "I do not know *when* we are. Once, I lived. A woman of flesh and appetite. Many appetites. Food. Men." She smiled at some wicked memory. "All of them mine. Anything for a daughter of Rome here in Anglia, this cold, cold outpost of the Empire. Worshipping my own gods. The dark gods of the natives."

Images appeared in the air between Zora and the ghost: a statue of a triple-faced goddess holding torches, a goat-horned, bearded man, and twisting, seething shapes of implike creatures. All of them radiating sinister energy. Instinctively, Zora clutched the shard of pottery, seeking its protection.

"They told me. Mother. Father. Said I wanted too much. What did I care what they thought? More. Always more. That's what I wanted." Disgust laced the ghost's voice. "Greedy girl, vain woman—lured by darkness. Now, what have I? Half life. Nothing. Half of nothing. Is half of nothing still nothing?"

Zora thought of Whit and his friends, how they had been tempted by *Wafodu guero*. If there were answers in this mad spirit, she must find them. "You summoned him," she deduced. "To gain power."

"Oh, power is a delicious thing." The ghost gave a low, voluptuous chuckle. "Sweet and edged, like a knife of sugar."

"How did you do it?" Zora pressed, trying to guide Valeria Livia Corva toward a measure of clarity.

"The door between the worlds was sealed tight. Locked. He would not come. I had to open the door." She admitted with a measure of bitterness, "It took more power than I had. What wasn't mine, I stole."

The images shifted and transformed into two women. One was fair, dressed in a different style of tunic, with elaborate metal bands around her arms. The other had dusky skin and dark eyes, wearing bright silk and golden jewelry. Something about the dark-skinned woman felt familiar to Zora, though she was certain she'd never seen her before.

"A captured Druid priestess and a slave from India," said the ghost. "Possessors of powerful magic. Proud women. Strong women. They fought against me. Their courage and pride, they meant nothing to me then. I took their magic." She mimed reaching out and grabbing something, and her voice was cold with anger—toward herself.

Zora knew deception. It was her trade. The ghost's fury with herself did not seem feigned, nor fully a delusion created by her madness. But *Wafodu guero* was a master at manipulation and deceit.

"Their power was mine," the specter said, "and I used it. Pushed the portal open. The portal between the worlds." The vision of the captured women dissolved into ghostly flame. "The Dark One crossed through. From his world of darkness into our world of light. Evil in his eyes, no promised power.

The future writ large in letters of fire." She waved her hand, and a cascade of sparks fell to the floor.

Zora started forward, seeking to extinguish the sparks before something caught fire, but they were only phantasms that vanished the moment they touched the ground.

The ghost, lost in her memories, paid no heed. Her eyes were wide with horror as she relived releasing the Devil.

"He comes!" she cried. "He will enslave us all. Make this earthly plane into another Hell. Fool, fool!" She knocked her fists into her forehead with such force, Zora believed the ghost might injure herself—if she weren't already dead. "My fatal mistake. I did not realize. Not until this moment as he steps from the underworld."

"Too late," Zora could not help but say.

The ghost seemed to recall herself, and smiled bitterly. "The Druid and the Indian slave, they were better women than I. They found reserves of courage, and magic. And allies."

As she said this, the images of three armored men flickered in the air, their swords upraised as they fought against an unseen enemy. Zora had never seen soldiers in action, not with this kind of intent and purpose, and it awed her to see them in true combat. The two women joined the fight, with bolts of magical energy streaming from their hands. Even though the five people battled with every ounce of their strength, they all sustained terrible wounds, and blood poured like autumn rain.

"Did they win?" Zora asked, unable to keep herself from being drawn into the story.

"Win, lose, win, lose," said the ghost airily. "They are the same. The words mean nothing. Small words."

"What happened to the Devil?" pressed Zora, gritting her teeth.

"Forced back through the portal." The spirit shook her head. "It cannot close to keep him in. Someone must shut and lock the door from the inside."

"Sacrifice themselves." When the ghost did not answer,

Zora stared at her, and the tight, drawn expression on the specter's face provided the answer. "You."

"Never have I done anything for anyone but myself. My last act as a living woman—my first selfless deed."

The shapes in the air changed once more. Zora watched as the figure of the priestess hurled herself into a gaping, fiery gateway, pulling burning gates behind her.

"Terrifying," said Zora.

"No words can describe the feeling, the fear." The ghost's voice shook with it even now. "Precious life. I did not want to end it."

"Yet you did." Zora considered the ghost. Perhaps this was more trickery, but if it was, the deception was artful and tugged hard on her heart. Was the crazed ghost's story of self-sacrifice true? Zora wondered if she, herself, would have the courage to face death—and possible eternal torment—to do what must be done. She could not stop herself from asking, "What's it like? Death?"

The ghost turned to look out the windows, but light from the candles turned the glass reflective, opaque. There was only darkness and flame.

"This is not the peace of death," she said, her voice hollow. "Not dead. Not alive."

It sounded awful to Zora. "You were trapped, just as the Devil was. Just as I am." She added quietly, "If you speak truly."

"The girl of warm flesh and cold heart calls me a liar," the ghost muttered to herself.

"I think that where *Wafodu guero* is concerned I must remain on my guard."

The priestess's mouth curved into a cynical smile. "She has wisdom, this girl. More than I ever did."

"It was hard won."

"As was mine," said the ghost. She gazed at the reflection of the burning candles. "I thought to imprison the Dark One. So I did. One final spell, just as I crossed the threshold. Binding the Dark One to a hidden prison. Our prison. Mine wasn't the only life surrendered that night. A centurion guarded the prison, allowing himself to be buried alive in order to keep it safe."

An image of a box appeared. Zora recognized it from the underground chamber where she had found Whit, his friends, and *Wafodu guero*.

"The soldier simply died after a time. Not me. Not the Dark One. Him and me. Me and him. Forever and ever and ever." The spirit's voice went far off, her eyes empty. "No one to speak to. No one to touch. The world changing around me. Figures on a distant shore. Such transformations I could never have believed. This is my eternity, watching the passage and shift of time." Pain laced her words. "Endurance. All I knew. Trapped in a dream from which I could not wake."

No wonder the spirit had gone mad. Zora both condemned and pitied her, if it was possible to feel both emotions at once.

"One consolation. One small gem I clutched to myself. Believing the Dark One was as trapped as I. There was little comfort in it. Trapped in between," she said hollowly. "Forever."

"But not forever," Zora noted. "You've been freed."

The ghost blinked, as if coming back into the room, into herself. "Am I free? And who freed me?" She seemed at a loss. "These men?"

Once more, the images in the air changed, transforming now into the strong, bold figure of a man Zora knew very well. His square jaw, the sensuous curve of his lips, his clever blue eyes that gleamed with a ravenous need for *more*.

"Whit," Zora whispered.

This image of Whit was flanked by his four friends, each of them shadowed by hunger.

"*Why* did you open that cursed box?" the specter demanded of the images.

Again, the ghost's pain and confusion seemed real, even as she mistook her own illusions for reality. Zora could only venture a guess to answer her demand. "Because they have everything, yet it isn't enough."

"We share that complaint." The specter reached toward

the images of the men, but they dissolved into nothingness. She stared down at her empty hands. "And we share recklessness. They do not know. Could they? No—how would it be possible for them to understand? What they let loose upon the world. Their lives and many more imperiled."

Zora's chilled blood cooled even further. If this was deception, if the ghost was a minion of *Wafodu guero*, it was a cunning deceit, disguised by lunacy. "What will happen?"

The ghost looked bleak. "These gaps in my mind—the storm comes through. Rain upon the floor, only cold water and wind. No knowledge. Yet the Dark One is clever. Subtle. He chooses his pawns well. Hands tied, others will do his work for him. Men of strength and power."

"Whit's friends are indeed men of strength and power— just as he is strong and powerful." She had felt his power even without the dark influence of *Wafodu guero*.

"Precisely what the Dark One needs."

"Needs to do what?" She feared what lay in store for Whit. What sins he might commit.

The specter turned and held Zora's gaze. It felt like the icy hand of eternity clutching at her.

"To unleash Hell on earth," said the ghost. Eyes burning with sudden clarity, she floated closer to Zora. "But the girl and I are going to stop him."

Whit staggered from the table. Direction and comprehension both failed him as he wove through the club. Noise, noise on all sides. Voices, glasses, rolling dice. Someone spoke to him but he heard nothing, only formless sound. The many candles threw everything into glaring relief. His limbs felt heavy and numb, barely under his control. Somehow he managed to gain enough balance to find a spare room off the club's main hallway.

As Whit opened the room's door and then closed it behind him, the flame of a lamp within guttered. Misshapen shadows writhed upon the walls.

Unwanted detritus from the club formed a small chaos. Tables and chairs jumbled together, other pieces of random furniture, paintings, candlesticks. The window, bare of curtains, looked out onto a narrow alley. He stood there for a moment, his breath coming harsh as his head spun.

He needed Zora's steadiness, but she was not here.

"*Veni, geminus*," Whit rasped.

The scent of burnt paper filled the room. And then a man stood in the room with Whit. The man's face was a blank; or, rather, Whit could not truly see his face, for his gaze kept sliding away every time he tried to focus on the man's facial features. By his fine clothing, Whit recognized him as one of the courtiers who had attended Mr. Holliday in the underground chamber, the same courtier who had procured a token from Whit. A button. Whit had given the courtier a button from his coat, and in exchange, he had received the gift to control chance, with the markings upon his skin as signifier.

At the time, Whit had believed his gift was infallible. And it had been, up to a few minutes ago.

"A pleasure, my lord," said the courtier. He bowed elaborately.

The gallant gesture meant nothing. "I would not have wagered your master's gifts to be so faulty."

"Oh, never faulty, my lord." The courtier's voice was polished glass. "Always perfect."

"There was nothing perfect about what happened just now at the hazard table. Except I felt like a perfect fool." He took a step toward the courtier. "If probability is mine to control, then how is it that I lost when I had no intention of losing?"

The courtier sighed, as if about to explain once more a lesson that had already been taught. "Power over the odds is yours, indeed, but only . . ."

"Only . . . ?"

"If you are going to win something that truly matters."

Whit foundered. "The stake at the hazard table was five hundred pounds. That is no small amount."

The courtier made a sound of dismissal. "A trifling amount for you, my lord."

"And everything that had come before? This?" He fumbled in his pocket and pulled out the ruby stickpin. "This does not matter, yet I won it."

"You *needed* that win, just as you needed the racehorse and the seaside cottage."

"Again, both valueless to me. I can buy as many damned horses or cottages as I please."

The *geminus* looked at him with almost pitying eyes. "The things themselves did not matter. You needed the *win* to soothe the turmoil in your heart. The win of five hundred pounds would do nothing for you, not here." The courtier tapped the center of Whit's chest, and he reared back, away from its touch.

True—he had placed the bet for the five hundred pounds when he cared little for the outcome. Yet the fact that he lost at all was still profoundly wrong. He was not supposed to lose. Ever.

"'Tis only money," continued the courtier, then added with a smile in his voice, "And it is not gambling if you win *every* time. Where's the thrill in that?"

Whit felt the air leave his body, as if he was clutched in a giant fist and squeezed until his bones turned to pulp. "Mr. Holliday said none of this," he managed to choke out.

"A very busy man, is Mr. Holliday. Certain small details escape him from time to time."

"This is more than a *small detail.*" Whit wondered what other *small details* he and his friends had not been informed about, what hidden traps into which he had blundered. Zora's warnings sifted through his mind, her continual pleas for him to repudiate Mr. Holliday and his gifts.

The courtier effected a shrug. "You are a gambler, my lord, as is my master. As I am. The pleasure comes from never quite knowing what may happen. Shall we lose everything? Shall we gain a valuable prize?"

None of the courtier's hypothetical questions carried an ounce of significance. Whit paced in the cramped, cluttered room, his mind feverishly working as he struggled to make sense of everything. The hidden defect in Mr. Holliday's gift revealed a greater flaw, something cancerous eating Whit from the inside out.

Seeing that Whit was not paying him any mind, the courtier tsked. "See here. This very night I have truly gambled and won." From an inside coat pocket, he plucked out a shining disk the size of an old five-guinea coin. The object was not made of gold, however, but a material Whit had never before seen. It literally glowed in the courtier's hand— a soft, warm radiance that seemed out of place held between the courtier's fingers, as if his touch sullied it somehow.

Whit knew what it was. Felt it deep within himself, an understanding that was the worst kind of knowledge.

A soul. A human soul. He could not believe that he looked upon such a thing, that it was at all possible, and yet here it was.

"Ah." The courtier gloated. "Explanations are unnecessary. Mr. Holliday was right. You are indeed clever, my lord."

Mouth dry, Whit asked, "What will become of that?" *And what will become of the person who gambled and lost their soul?*

The courtier held up the gleaming soul, then tucked it back into his pocket. A chill crept through the room, seeping deep into Whit's flesh, and deeper still until he felt entombed in ice.

"Like any man of means," answered the courtier, "Mr. Holliday safeguards his property. I, like my fellow *gemini*, maintain a vault where the tokens are kept. This ensures that when the original possessor of the token breathes their last, they become Mr. Holliday's property, as well."

He made it all sound like a neat, efficient transaction. It was anything but that.

Zora's warnings sounded louder than ever. Whit had been

blind—by vanity, by greed—but she had seen. *Reject his gifts. Save yourself.* But he had not. He'd reveled in those gifts, until not but a few minutes ago.

She knew. Somehow she knew.

Whit and the other Hellraisers had made a terrible mistake. A mistake that cost them everything, and for which— he saw now—they would pay. Eternally.

How could he have been so blind? So arrogant? But he had been drunk on possibility and power, too intoxicated with potential to remember the experienced gambler's axiom: You can never beat the house at its own game.

"Good God," Whit muttered thickly.

"He has nothing to do with this," said the courtier, very pleasant, "and nothing to do with you. As of a few days prior, Lord Whitney, you and your friends belong to us."

Ravaged, Whit looked up at the courtier. A curse broke from his lips and his heart stopped in the midst of a beat as he finally saw the face of the Devil's minion.

It looked exactly like Whit.

Chapter 7

Zora stared at the priestess's ghost, hardly believing what she had just heard.

"You truly *are* mad," she said. "*Wafodu guero* is the greatest evil. Defeating him isn't possible."

The specter laughed, as if the fragile tether of her sanity broke. "The bird hunts the tiger. Water burns and fire quenches. The impossible is possible." She laughed harder.

Zora cast a nervous glance toward the door, cursing the magic that kept her imprisoned in this room with a mad ghost. She had no idea what a deranged phantom might do.

The ghost's laughter abruptly stopped, and she narrowed her eyes. "Tell me your name."

Zora hesitated. Giving one's name surrendered power, so all the old tales said.

The priestess muttered irritably. "I have told her mine. Valeria Livia Corva. Livia. She gives me nothing."

"Zora," she said after a moment.

"A good name," the ghost whispered to herself. "Strength in it. I will need strength if this is to be done. Give her power. Can I?" She cupped her hands and began muttering under her breath, her words strange, the language she spoke even stranger. As she did this, light gathered in a ball between her hands, colors swirling over its surface like oil upon water.

Zora's heart pounded as she edged as far as she could from Livia. Though the priestess seemed to have no physical body, she possessed magic—magic that could hurt Zora. Was there nothing she could do to protect herself? Damn Whit for trapping her here, with no means of escape.

"Keep that away from me," she warned, but there was nothing with which she could threaten the ghost.

"Allies. The warm girl and I. Zora and I against the Dark One." Livia hovered closer, her expression determined. The ball of light collapsed, winking out, and the ghost glowered down at the space where it had been. "Come back to me." She stared up at Zora. "For your own good. For everyone's good."

Zora tried to dart away, but no matter where in the room she went, nothing held the priestess back. The spirit glided through furniture as if it weren't there.

"Wasting time," Livia growled. "There had been so much time, spilling everywhere, but now it is precious. Every moment lost. The Dark One's power grows."

"I can't fight him!" cried Zora. The last time she had faced *Wafodu guero*, her meager attempts to combat him did nothing. The Devil had bound her with his magic, and she had no means of stopping him.

"Stop evil from blighting the world," said Livia.

"I'm powerless. I cannot *do* anything."

"She is frightened," Livia snarled to herself. "Timid girl."

No one had ever accused Zora of being timid. But she had gone against the Devil once before and lost. All she had were useless crusts of bread and harmless knives. Another round against *Wafodu guero* would likely see her dead, or worse.

Livia stopped her pursuit and narrowed her gaze. Her expression sharpened, becoming clearer. Calculating. This frightened Zora even more.

"She will not be courageous for the world, then. But what of her handsome friend?"

This stopped Zora's flight like a hand pinning down a fluttering ribbon. "Whit?"

Livia smiled shrewdly. "The heart gives pause."

"What about Whit?" demanded Zora.

"He casts the dice. He is lost. Perhaps he is not lost. Perhaps the girl may make her wagers and win him back."

Zora's already racing pulse sped faster. Her mind worked, sorting through possibilities. Saving herself *and* Whit. He didn't believe he required saving, but Zora knew differently. The man he truly was still existed within him; their kiss had proven that. He needed to be rescued from himself—if it was not too late.

"You may be mad," she muttered at the ghost, "but you're cunning."

This pleased Livia, and she preened. Under other circumstances, Zora might admire the priestess's guile, but she did not appreciate her role as the one being manipulated.

The problem with manipulation was that it worked.

"Even if I wanted to help," Zora said, "I've nothing that can stand against *Wafodu guero*. The 'magic' I use for *dukkering* isn't real."

The priestess suppressed a flare of triumph in her gaze. "Draw it forth. Bring it into being." She closed her eyes, drawing into herself, then reached out one hand toward a burning candle on the other side of the room. The flame bent to her, flickering.

Zora watched, stunned, as the flame lengthened, stretching from the candle across the length of the room all the way to the tips of Livia's fingers. The flame actually went into the ghost's body, as though Livia *drew the fire into herself.* She murmured words in an ancient tongue, her transparent body glowing brighter as the flame suffused her. The ghost was some kind of conduit, channeling not water but fire.

Chanting louder, Livia opened her eyes. They literally burned. She turned her fiery gaze to Zora, who edged back against the wall.

What have I done?

The ghost held up her other hand and pointed it at Zora. A streak of fire leapt from Livia's hand—right toward Zora.

Zora did not scream, but she turned and pressed herself

to the wall, seeking shelter. The fire covered her in heat. She braced herself for pain. Yet it did not come. There was intense warmth, but her skin did not burn, did not blister. Her clothing did not catch to drift in scorched flakes. Pulling back slightly, she gazed down at herself and gasped. The fire was going *into* her. Just as it had with Livia. Her body drew in the flame, suffusing her with heat, and she felt it illuminate her veins, her breath and being.

It felt . . . incredible.

Livia's chanting reached a peak as the fire permeated Zora. The priestess shouted one final word, *"Incendium!"* and the fire vanished into Zora.

For a moment, Zora could only stand there, panting, staring down at herself. Bright power coursed invisibly through her. Slowly, eyes wide, she turned around to face Livia.

The ghost seemed paler, drained by channeling magic. She flickered much as the candle flame had flickered.

Zora held up her shaking hands, but they shook not with fear, but with energy. Flames suddenly danced on her fingertips. Reacting instinctually, Zora flung one hand away, trying to shake the fire out. But the flames did not die. They leapt from her fingers onto a nearby curtain. The fabric quickly began to burn.

Not wishing to set the whole house ablaze, Zora grabbed a pitcher of water and dashed its contents over the burning curtain. The flames went out, leaving behind singed, wet fabric.

Zora dropped the pitcher. She could not believe that she had just set fire to something *using magic from within herself.*

She whirled to face Livia. "What manner of evil is this?"

"Not evil," the spirit answered, her voice somewhat faint. "Fire quenches the darkness." Then the ghost disappeared, as if she could not sustain herself after using so much energy.

Zora was alone again. With a new power. If this was, in fact, sinister magic, it hid its darkness well. She felt strong, capable of anything, alight with her own power like a torch in the depths of night. Was this how Whit felt? Potent and alive? If so, she had not given enough credence to how difficult rejecting such power would be.

She stared down at her hands, and flames again appeared on her fingertips. She *could* master this. She had the strength. Her whole tribe lived on the strength of the fire that burned in the middle of their encampment. Fire fed them, kept them warm, beat back the darkness. It ran within her, veins of fire, giving life.

Glancing around the room, she spotted a discarded newspaper tucked beneath a chair. She reached one hand toward the newspaper, concentrating. Fire stretched between her fingers and the periodical. She cried out with surprised triumph when the newspaper's edges blackened, and then the whole of the paper caught. It burned so quickly, it turned to harmless ash before it could set anything else aflame.

She turned in place, taking in the details of the gaming room. Her prison for the past few days, and a place she had come to hate. A roof over her head, blocking out the life-giving sky. Heavy walls that penned her. The trappings of *gorgio* life that were alien and unwanted, forced upon her. Surges of energy filled her, demanding an outlet. She wanted to set fire to the whole room. Burn the house down. Wipe clean the slate of wickedness.

Yes, destroy everything.

She shook away that insidious voice. As much as she disliked Whit's servants, she had no wish to kill them and was no murderer. There was no proof that if she set fire to the gaming room she would not burn with it. She went and opened the window, then tried to stick her hand outside. She met with the same resistance she always did from the invisible barrier.

This place was still her prison. Whit had not released her.

She strode to the fireplace and stared at the mantel. One object commanded her attention. The playing card. The object that kept her anchored, unable to break free.

Zora picked up the card, stared at it. Nothing, up to that point, had been able to destroy it.

Flames curled up her fingers. The fire felt clean, pure. With bone-deep understanding, she knew this magic was not evil, but gave her the power to combat wickedness. And she would fight, now that she had the means.

The playing card burned.

Whit reared back, slamming into a table. Something atop the table fell and shattered. The noise of breaking glass filled the tiny room, but to Whit, the sound was far away. He heard only the roar of blood in his ears as he stared at his exact duplicate. From the color of his hair to the breadth of his shoulders to the minute scars left behind after a youthful bout of smallpox, the courtier was identical to Whit.

His twin.

Geminus.

It stared back at him with a mild, vaguely patronizing smile. God, to be smiled at by a creature that wore his face—the experience went beyond uncanny into the realm of the ghastly. He vaguely remembered some old tale told to him by the groundskeeper at his family estate. Beware the *fetch*, the groundskeeper had said. To see one's double was a sign of approaching death.

He'd laughed then, believing himself too old to be frightened by superstition.

"Come, my lord, there is still much gambling to be done this night." The *geminus* gestured toward the door. "Now that you know the parameters of Mr. Holliday's gift, it shall be easily managed." It took a step in Whit's direction.

With a sound like a cornered tiger, Whit surged. He slammed his shoulder into the advancing *geminus*. The double staggered, falling back into a collection of chairs with a grunt. Whit tore open the door and ran down the hallway.

Shocked exclamations burst from men he passed as he

ran. He paid no heed, not to them, not to the alarmed servants. His throat was dry, his pulse racing. Footmen barely had time to open the front doors of the club before Whit rushed through them. After the heat of the club, the night air bit against his flushed cheeks. His cloak and hat were still inside.

He didn't care. He did not wait for his coach. For the first time in years he *ran*, full out, tearing through the streets of Mayfair. Only one thought coursed through his mind: *Get to Zora.*

He needed her. Her guidance, her strength. Somehow, she had seen the danger he had not. She would know what to do, how to fight his way free.

A cold, sticky sweat filmed his body by the time he reached his home. He vaulted up the stairs, taking three at a time. Shouldering past a surprised footman, Whit sped toward the back of his house. Toward the gaming room.

His steps faltered as he noticed the gaming room door wide open. Zora always kept it closed. More icy fear scraped down his neck. He surged into the room, then stood there, stunned.

The room was empty.

"Zora," he said. Then again, louder. "Zora!"

No answer. Though the room was small, he tore through it like a tempest: knocking over the card table, pawing through the pallet she had devised beneath the table, kicking aside the folding screen. Yet everything proved his greatest fear; she was gone. Nothing of her remained. The parcels of new clothes had been opened but left behind.

Holy God, has something happened to her? Has Mr. Holliday taken her? Hurt her?

Rage filled him, the likes of which Whit had never experienced, all but paralyzing in its intensity. If any harm befell her, nothing would stop him from exacting vengeance. He didn't care if he faced the flames of Hell itself. Nothing and no one hurt Zora. And God help anything and anyone who did.

Whit grabbed a chair and, with a roar, threw it against a wall. It broke apart into splinters.

He spun, seeking some other outlet for his fury, and that's when he noticed it. The empty mantel. The playing card—Zora's card—was gone.

In two strides, he stood at the mantel. His fingers rubbed against the stone and came away smudged with ash.

"My lord?"

Scowling, ferocious, Whit pivoted at the sound of his valet's terrified voice. Kitson stood in the doorway, pale and shaken. If the unflappable valet showed this much fear, Whit must have been a truly terrifying spectacle.

"Did you see her?" Whit demanded.

"N-no, my lord," stuttered Kitson. "But some of the footmen did. A Gypsy girl . . . She bolted from the room. Ran out the front door without saying a word. No one saw her come *in*, my lord. I searched the room. Nothing was stolen, so she did not break in. Not for that purpose."

Whit's hand strayed to the hollow of his throat, where Zora's ring nestled against his skin. Having this small token of her brought him a fragment of peace, but it was not enough.

"Wake the grooms. Have them saddle the fastest horse in the stable." When Kitson hesitated, Whit roared, "Now, damn it!"

The valet bolted.

The moment Kitson left, Whit slammed from the gaming room and up the stairs to his private chambers, casting off his expensive garments heedlessly. Refined silk and gentlemen's buckled shoes would not serve his purpose. He needed doeskin breeches, stout boots. His hunting clothes.

"By Hell's fire," he snarled to himself, "I will find her."

The strange city loomed all around Zora, huge, dark, ravenous. She did not know where she was, only that she must run fast. No time even for joy at being, at last, free.

This was London. Coal smoke and river stench choked the air and blocked the stars. The sky gave her no guidance.

Where was she? Massive homes towered on all sides, as large as palaces. Not the London she knew, the horse fairs and markets at the edges of the city. As she ran, she passed a few linkboys with their smoldering torches guiding sedan chairs, and one watchman made a halfhearted attempt to grab her. Otherwise, the streets were empty and silent, save for the sounds of her feet on the pavement. Nothing looked familiar. She found herself caught in a nightmare of wrong turns, dead ends, giant squares, and fenced parks. After days inside, her eyes still would not be able to make sense of the darkness. She ran like a fox searching for a place to make a stand.

Lord save her, this city was a maze from which she could not escape. Instinct guided her. London was *Wafodu guero*'s pleasure garden. It reeked of vice, of wickedness, the faces of the buildings streaked and grimy, as if sin itself ran down the brick and plaster. She could not face the Devil here, where he had so many possible allies. She needed open spaces, clean air, not a sky choked with smoke.

The best thing was to run, and run fast. But where?

Think, Zora. Her family had often approached London from the south, their caravan moving through tracts of open land before buildings began to crowd in. *South, then.*

A giant river confounded her progress. Fortunately, she could swim, but she did not trust the stinking, black water. Up to the northeast, she saw a bridge.

By the time she reached the bridge, she was too tired to marvel at its size, its stately arches or high walls. She ran across it, dodging people still going in and out of the shops lining the bridge. With every step closer to the opposite bank, Zora felt her heart throb. It was too far to open space. She hadn't even left London, yet.

Not impossible. She must push herself to the limits of her endurance, even as her body ached from weariness. Too long had she been trapped, immobile. Powerless. Not any longer.

A fresh surge of energy washed through her as she reached

the southern bank of the river. She sped on through suburban developments, houses and other buildings coming less frequently. Before her, a large field opened up. It stretched wide and dark around her. Up ahead lay a crossroads.

"Zora!"

She spun around at the sound of Whit's voice. Her eyes had adjusted to the darkness, so she saw him plainly. On horseback, thundering toward her, he seemed a figure of ancient myth and fevered intent. Even across the field, even in this darkness, she felt his gaze on her, pulling on her, as though he had loosed an arrow and it plunged straight into her chest.

Zora could not move as he rode closer. His presence stunned her into immobility, but her traitorous heart leapt with a complicated joy.

He pulled up hard on the reins, his horse dancing and snorting around her. Before the animal came to a total stop, Whit leapt down from the saddle and strode to her. His gaze was hard, tense. Yet not angry. He seemed both relieved to find her and, strangely, afraid. She resisted the urge to throw her arms around him, though it took far more strength to hold herself back than she liked.

He was armed. Not with a gentleman's dress sword, but with a dangerous curved sword the likes of which she had never seen. A pistol also bulged in his coat pocket. He must believe she would put up a tremendous fight, to arm himself thus.

They spoke, their voices overlapping.

"How did you find me?"

"How did you break the spell?"

"Something has happened." He reached for her. "I need—"

A chorus of male voices shouted from the other side of the field, calling Whit's name.

Both Zora and Whit turned to face the newcomers. A new current of fear flooded her as she saw Whit's four friends, all on horseback, all riding straight toward them. Bringers of the end of the world.

And bringers of the end of her brief freedom, as well as the possibility of her stand against the Devil. She whirled to Whit as she felt the cut of betrayal. She had thought him better than this—but perhaps his kiss had been false. "Needed reinforcements to steal back your prize?"

He scowled at his approaching friends. "You do not understand."

Before she could demand an explanation, the men were upon them. Like Whit, they, too, jumped down from their horses. They formed a ring around Whit and Zora, a shadowed, confining circle whose presence stole the very breath from Zora's lungs. Four men, each exuding sinister power. Whit moved closer to her, shoulders squaring, almost as if trying to protect her.

Why would he protect her when he had enlisted his friends to drag her back to captivity?

"The hell, Whit?" the dark, scarred one asked hotly.

"I ask you the same damned question," Whit shot back.

"We were told we had to find you," said a younger blond man. "That you were in peril."

"Told by whom?"

The dark one jerked his head toward a mounted figure that Zora had not seen. When the figure drew nearer, sedately walking his horse forward, Zora gasped. She could not believe it.

The mounted figure was *Whit*. Yet it wasn't. Whit stood beside her, his hand on the pommel of his sword. Her gaze flew back and forth between the two Whits. The one next to her wore serviceable hunting clothes, while the other Whit had on evening finery. Save for the manner of dress, the men were identical.

"God protect me." She gulped.

"You see it, too?" the Whit standing beside her demanded.

"Your brother?" she tried to guess.

He shook his head. "None of my brothers survived childhood."

Yet when the mounted man spoke, it had Whit's voice. "If you continue on this path, Mr. Holliday will be extremely displeased."

"We have his gifts," said Whit's scholarly friend, placating. "There is no need to earn Mr. Holliday's disfavor."

"*Look* at him," Whit growled, pointing at his elegantly dressed double.

The four friends glanced at the Whit on horseback, then back at the Whit standing next to Zora.

"What of him?" The dark man frowned. "He found us, told us you were in danger."

"*He* is the danger," answered Whit.

The double merely sighed as Whit's friends looked plainly baffled.

Realization hit Zora. "They cannot see," she murmured. For some reason, Whit's friends did not perceive that the man on horseback looked, and sounded, exactly like Whit.

When she spoke, the double turned its gaze on her, then narrowed its eyes. Cold, calculated hatred. Instinctively, Zora edged closer to the Whit beside her.

She remembered, belatedly, that she had power of her own. Yet when she reached for the magic that Livia had given her, she found . . . nothing. Just cold ashes where brightness had once been. Perhaps the priestess's own magic had been too weak to grant Zora anything lasting.

Damn. Zora would find more comfort in knowing she could set someone on fire.

"*She* is the threat," the double said, as if reading her thoughts. "She leads Lord Whitney astray, jeopardizing not only him, but all of you."

"The Gypsy girl?" asked the young blond man. A puzzled frown appeared between his brows. "She has influenced him with her feminine ways."

"Now she has a power far greater than a woman's wiles," corrected the double.

Zora almost corrected him, since she had no magic anymore. But it was better for an enemy to think her more powerful than she truly was.

So the double must have believed, for it continued, "And she means you all great harm." It added with icy menace, "Unless you destroy her."

"Wait—" cried Zora.

A hiss resounded loudly in the field. Whit unsheathed his sword. He took up a ready, fighting stance.

The sight astounded Zora. He was defending her. Skillfully. For a gentleman and man of leisure, he made a remarkably convincing warrior.

"No one bloody touches her," he warned, his voice low and edged.

Shocked silence followed. Whit's friends stared at him as though he had suddenly grown claws and fangs. Zora, too, could not believe that Whit had actually drawn his sword against his friends. It was clear that they cared about one another with the fierce friendship that men cultivated over many years. It was also clear that no one ever expected Whit to position himself against them.

But he had. To protect her.

"Whit . . ." The dark man was stunned, uncomprehending.

"He's been beguiled," the double snapped. "He knows not what he does. Disarm him before he hurts someone. Before he hurts himself. *Now.*"

Whit's friends reluctantly obeyed the double's command. They slowly advanced on Whit, hands upraised, as if approaching a cornered animal. One of them said soothingly, "Be at ease, Whit. We only seek to help you."

"Step no closer," Whit warned. Yet he hesitated, plainly reluctant to lash out against his friends.

God above, Zora thought, *if only I had the fire magic given to me by that damned ghost!*

Fire . . . A fire always burned in the middle of her band's encampment. Images of the campfire flickered in her mind, warming her. She had thought of her band's fire at the moment when Livia had first given her this magic, *felt* that fire burning within her. The strength of her people.

Yes . . . she understood now. She needed a font for her magic, something from which she could draw power. If she could reach her band's campfire, her power would be restored, fortified. She would have a way to fight *Wafodu guero* and his minions. Fight for herself. And Whit. He defended her against his friends and his double.

She had been right about him all along. Even though she could not trust him, he was worth saving from the Devil.

Now! her mind shouted. While everyone, including the double, was distracted. She hated leaving Whit, but if she reached the campfire, she could return to help him. She could not voice her plans, lest the double or his friends hear.

Fast as a thrown knife, she bolted between two of the men, evading their outreached hands. She ran toward the waiting horses. Shouts sounded behind her, but she would not allow herself to turn, to see. Instead, she leapt onto one of the horses in a flurry of skirts. Someone, she could not tell who, made a grab for the reins, but she pulled them away and blindly kicked out. Her heel connected with a solid torso, and there was a gasped oath. It wasn't Whit's voice. There were sounds of struggle, of men grappling.

The horse impatiently danced beneath her. For a moment, Zora wavered. She did not want to leave Whit, not like this, but then she heard the *other* Whit, the double. It shouted orders to Whit's friends, commanding them to stop her.

One of the men—the dark one with the scar—ran up beside her horse. He reached out and grabbed one of the reins. Trapping her in place. She pulled hard, trying to break his hold, but his grip was like iron.

Whit appeared, his face a mask of fury. His sword made a bright arc as he swung it. Zora braced herself, waiting for his friend's scream of pain as the sword hacked into flesh.

It never came. Instead her horse danced backward. Looking

down, Zora saw she held only one taut rein. Whit had cut the other, freeing her.

For a moment, no one moved, no one spoke. Whit had come within a hairsbreadth of severing his friend's hand. Though he hadn't, the action spoke clearly. *I will cut you down if I must.*

It had to be now. Zora dug her heels into the horse's side and galloped off into the darkness.

Whit watched Zora clear the edge of St. George's Fields. The night swallowed her retreating figure.

He swore, then started toward his horse.

"Good God, Whit." Bram clamped a hand around Whit's arm. Only a moment ago, Whit had raised a sword against his friend, had nearly cut off the same hand that held him now. His closest friend. But Bram had threatened Zora. That would not stand.

"No time for this," Whit said through clenched teeth. Though his friend had strength in abundance, Whit shook him off.

"If she's a poisonous influence," said Leo, "you are well to be rid of her. You raised steel against us. *For her.*"

"She stole my horse," John said, staring angrily at the place where Zora had vanished.

"Zora isn't poison," Whit growled. "She's the antidote."

"That's not what he said," noted Edmund, and pointed at the *geminus*.

Whit could not control the hard pound of his heart, nor the comingled rage and fear that turned everything hazy. The world was chaos, and he swept up in its madness.

His friends could not see it. They had not the means to recognize the *geminus* for what it was.

"There is not one word from that *thing's* mouth you should believe," he spat.

The *geminus* tutted, as though mildly disappointed, but Whit could see the enmity and determination in its gaze.

God, he stared into a warped mirror to look upon himself, but not himself, and the sinister gleam in its—his own—eyes.

"You are overwrought, and misled," the *geminus* reproved.

"More falsehood," said Whit. He kept his saber drawn. The blade he had won in a game of piquet ages ago from a Prussian hussar. Before setting off in pursuit of Zora tonight, Whit had grabbed it rather than his rapier, knowing he would need a far more brutal and effective weapon for whatever he might confront in the night. He had never once believed he would ever use it against his friends. He never thought he would do *anything* in opposition to them. It was difficult to believe that he did at this very moment.

A week ago, he would have laughed and said it impossible. Now he understood that *impossible* meant nothing. A world lay within *impossible*.

"The gifts Mr. Holliday gave us are flawed," he said. "Everything is flawed, and we are damned."

His friends—Bram, Leo, Edmund, and John—stared at him in bafflement, still mired in shock that not only did Whit have his steel drawn against them, but that they had scuffled in earnest. Tension hummed through all of them, like a sword beaten too long upon the anvil and ready to break.

"Explain," demanded Leo.

Whit feinted with his saber. His friends leapt out of the way. He took advantage of the path opened up to him and moved cautiously but quickly to his horse, keeping his friends at a distance with his brandished sword. Even as he did this, he was conscious the entire time of Zora getting farther and farther away. Knowledge of London and his control of probability had allowed him to find her once, but he feared if she disappeared into the countryside, he would never see her again. He could not allow that to happen.

"I'd say that you should ask *that*," Whit said, swinging up into the saddle, "but he cannot be trusted. None of us can be trusted." Not even himself.

"Goddamn you," snarled Bram. "Tell us what you mean."

"I am losing time. We are all losing time." He directed the point of his saber in the direction of the *geminus*. "Don't listen to that creature. All of our souls are imperiled, and we've only ourselves to fault."

"Lord Whitney is clearly misguided," drawled the *geminus*. "But—"

Whit cut off Edmund. "We must each find a way, any way, toward salvation. I only pray that we are not too late." He glanced down at his friends, the four men he trusted more than any other, men he loved like brothers—better than brothers, for they did not have the weight of blood or familial expectation and disappointment—and with whom he had done everything. Including damnation. Could any of them be saved?

"Farewell, lads," he said. Ironic, the words of polite leave-taking, with his sword still drawn. He did not trust any of them. Not anymore.

Before any of the Hellraisers could move, Whit kicked his horse into a full gallop. He might never see his friends again. Or, if he did, they might meet as true adversaries. The pain of tearing himself from them hurt worse than any bullet or slash of a blade, yet he had to. He needed to find Zora, for he understood intuitively that she held not merely answers, but salvation.

Zora strained to hear the sounds of pursuit over her horse's hoofbeats. Nothing. Yet she remained vigilant. Hours she had been riding, through sleeping villages and farms, skirting around larger towns. The more she rode, the more she recognized, and that gave her some cheer to know she neared her family and would see them soon. True, she would not be able to linger with them, but after days apart from her kin, even a few moments might serve as a balm. And then she must turn around and take up the fight for Whit's soul.

He had followed her, defended her, but perhaps he had been motivated by greed, not sentiment. Men often grew jealous over their possessions, hoarding them. She could be simply an object to him, an object he would not share. He had freed her, too. Took up a sword against his friend in defense of her.

He had not looked at her like a thing. When he found her at the field, more than covetousness heated his gaze. He had been very happy to see her again. But there had been more in his eyes, in the tension shimmering through his body. He'd been afraid. Truly afraid. Not merely for the loss of her, but something else. What?

Questions fled as the familiar shapes of her band's tents came into view. Her eyes heated and grew watery. She had not been certain she would ever see them again. Zora neared, and what she saw made her heart leap: the fire in the middle of the encampment. It cast flickering light over the face of the man tending the flames. He was alone. It was Oseri, her cousin.

He jumped to his feet as Zora rode into the camp. Shocked at her sudden appearance, he only stood there as she flung her arms around him. They had never been close, Zora and Oseri, but at that moment she did not care. Only that he was familiar and she was back—for now.

"*Vitsa*," she said, clutching him tight. He smelled of smoke and horse. Smells of home.

"My God, Zora." Slowly, Oseri's arms came up to hold her awkwardly. "We all thought . . . We did not know what to think. The *gorgios* were here, and then you went after them, and then you disappeared." He put his hands on her shoulders and held her away to stare into her face. "Your father and every man in the band has been searching for you. They looked all over."

She could just picture her father tromping across the countryside torch in hand. A bullish, determined man, not unlike his daughter.

Without taking his eyes from Zora, Oseri yelled, "Wake! Everyone wake! Zora has returned!"

She looked to the fire, and felt it: a surge of primal power.

Yet before she could explore it further, the peace of the camp shattered as men, women, and children came tumbling out of their tents, blinking, confused. People swarmed around Zora, everyone talking at top volume, shouting praise and exclaiming in wonderment. It had been so long since Zora had heard the Romani tongue, and it sounded like the finest music. Perhaps not sweet, nor melodic, not with dozens of Rom speaking at once, but lovely and welcome just the same. Heedless of taboos surrounding the touching of women, hands came up to pat, pinch, and pet her in welcome. All the familiar faces . . . all the sounds and sights of home . . . it overwhelmed her.

When she found herself enfolded in a woman's arms and pressed tightly against a soft, plush bosom, the tears Zora had fought finally released. She wept openly in her mother's embrace. Litti wept, too, and mother and daughter held one another, crying tears of relief and joy to be reunited.

"*Mam*," Zora hiccupped.

"*Kaulo durril*," Litti cooed, calling Zora by her childhood nickname: blackberry.

Her grandmother Shuri demanded the same right to smother Zora, as did every female relative. Zora was pressed into a succession of bosoms, engulfed in womanly warmth and softness. When, at last, she was presented to her father, he scowled fiercely, his arms folded across his barrel-shaped chest.

"What mischief have you been up to, *chavi*?" he demanded.

"No mischief, *dado*," answered Zora. "Not of my own making," she amended. Conscious of time being lost, she darted another glance at the fire. She felt its power resonate within her. Was that all she needed? To be in its presence? Would that be enough to sustain the magic once she had left the encampment?

Her father continued to frown at her, until Litti snapped, "For the love of Our Maker, Wester, you've been out of your senses with worry. And *this* is how you welcome our *chavi* back?"

His stern façade crumbled away, and he opened his arms. It had been many years since Zora had been held by her father—at her insistence—but she went to him now and allowed herself a moment to be his child again. He rocked her and murmured soothing endearments into her hair.

After a while, Zora resurfaced from her brief trip to her youth. Standing on her own, she pushed her disheveled hair from her face as she looked over the gathered band. She must leave them soon, but first she said, "Everyone, you must pack and leave this place at once."

Shocked exclamations rose up from the crowd. The joy in everyone's faces faded, replaced by puzzlement.

"Why?" her father demanded.

"It isn't safe here." Zora started toward the tent she had shared with her parents. She needed to gather her own belongings.

"Safe from whom?" This came from the leader of their band, their king, Faden. He blocked her path. "Your wealthy *gorgios*?"

Zora fought down her impatience. "They may be coming from London. That is where I have been, too. Held as a captive by one of those *gorgios*." It felt strange to refer to Whit so impersonally, with so much distance, for he had come to be much more than a rich, bored *gorgio*.

He needed her, even as he had cut the rein that kept her trapped. Something had pulled him out of his magic-induced euphoria, and he had been badly shaken in the field south of the river. She needed to go back, as much as she hated the thought of getting anywhere near the city.

"Captive?" her father repeated. A look of horror came over him. "Did he . . . ? Are you . . . ?" Wester could not finish his sentences, for a Romani woman's honor and virtue meant everything.

"He did not touch me," Zora answered. That was not a

complete truth. In fact, Whit's kiss had been more potent, more sensual than all of the lovemaking Zora had ever experienced. Thinking of it now brought new heat to her cheeks. At least the darkness hid her telltale blush.

Her father, and all of Zora's male relatives, exhaled in relief. To exact vengeance against rich *gorgios* meant imperiling the entire band, resulting in either hanging or a rougher kind of justice.

"Why are they coming here?" asked Cousin Oseri.

Curse it. Zora did not know where to begin, how to explain or indeed if she *could* explain what she had seen. Superstition and fear ran deep in the Rom. She had been, up until a few days ago, one of the few skeptics in her band. If she told them everything, she could incite panic. If she told her family and band about the magic she possessed, they might brand her a *chovahani*, a witch. Her power meant she had a responsibility to fight the Devil. Should she ever return to her family, she would be an outsider amongst her own people.

"Well?" Faden prompted.

No hope for it but to tell the truth. Better for everyone to know all the details. Then they could get moving and out of possible danger.

Zora took a deep breath, hoping to make her long and strange tale as short as possible.

Her mother screamed.

Chapter 8

Whit heard the screaming before he saw the encampment. A woman's scream, followed by many more, from women *and* men, and the shrieks of children. His blood iced, but he spurred his exhausted horse onward. One of those screams could belong to Zora, and the thought of her in danger urged him toward greater action.

He rounded a bend in the road and instinctively pulled up on the reins in disbelief. What he beheld resembled a painting of the underworld, only this was no painting—it was real.

The Gypsy camp was being attacked. Not by angry peasants, nor men of the law. The things attacking the encampment were not *men* at all, but demons. Actual demons. Two dozen of them.

The fire revealed everything in macabre contours. Some of the demons had the forms of twisted men, their hands and feet clawed, mouths gaping, and skin the color of charred wood. Their mouths were three times normal size, running literally from ear to ear. Their eyes were inflamed and sickly, oozing opaque matter. Just as their mouths were oversized, so were their hands, with long, stretched-out fingers and sharp, iron-gray talons at the tips. The demons ran through the camp tearing apart tents and striking at terrified Gypsies.

A loud buzz grew deafening as enormous creatures

swooped and darted among the panicked crowd. The things were a monstrous amalgam of wasp and bat, nimble and insectlike, yet covered with fleshy membranes over their bodies, wings, and dangling legs. Gypsy men tried to fight back the creatures using pitchforks, torches, and other makeshift weapons as many of the women huddled or attempted to flee with their children. Most everyone bore wounds, from scratches to deep, bleeding gashes.

Not all of the women tried to run or cowered in fear. Zora stood in the midst of the chaos, swinging a torch at any beast that tried to get within striking distance. A cut gleamed red on her cheek, and her clothes were grimy, but she appeared unhurt. For now. As she fought back two of the clawed demons, more gathered.

Whit's vision narrowed to just Zora. He saw nothing else but her, imperiled. He kicked his horse forward. Just before he thundered into the encampment, he drew his saber.

The weapon was perfect for attack from horseback. Whit had practiced only on hay targets before, never actual living things. A different sensation entirely to feel muscle and flesh and bone against his blade. He resonated with a dark, primitive thrill as he slashed at the massing demons, chopping down at them without stopping his onslaught. Bodies fell heavily like rotten meat.

Not everyone in his path was an enemy. He held his hand as terrified Gypsies ran hither and yon, seeking escape. Thank God Whit trained and had honed his instincts—he was no former soldier like Bram, but he kept his body and responses sharp. A gambler ready for any eventuality.

Zora glanced up from her struggle. Her eyes widened when she caught sight of him. Fierce triumph briefly illuminated her face, but it did not last long as she struggled against an advancing demon. She swung her torch at it, and it scuttled back, yet the creature did not retreat.

Whit pushed his skittish horse forward, trying to reach her. Hot pain blazed through his shoulder as one of the enormous flying insects swooped down, and tore at him with its giant mouth. Whit swung his saber at the demon, but the cursed thing kept coming at him. His horse grew more and more panicked.

Zora shouted in anger and fear as the clawed demons pressed closer. Whit had to get to her. He could use his one shot with his pistol, but in this pandemonium he might hit an innocent, might hit Zora. If only he had some other weapon. . . .

He *did* have another weapon. *Probability.*

Drawing his pistol, Whit took aim at one of the flying demons hovering above the camp. He fought to steady his horse and calmed his racing heart. Then he delved into swirling patterns of probability. It was *his* to manipulate, *his* to control. The *geminus* said he could win only things of importance. Nothing was more important than keeping Zora safe.

He cocked the hammer. Took a breath. And pulled the trigger. Flint struck steel. The igniting powder flared, bright and white, followed immediately by the explosion in the pistol's breech. Then a thick clot of smoke as the bullet tore from the barrel. The pistol's report disappeared in the surrounding noises of terror.

The bullet slammed into the insect demon, hitting the creature exactly in a vulnerable space just behind its front leg. It screeched, lurched, then fell from the sky.

The wide-mouthed clawed demons closing in around Zora did not have time to jump out of the way. The winged demon's enormous body plummeted down onto them, smashing them beneath its carcass. Zora barely missed being crushed. Instead, she stared down at the bloody, broken heap before her, stunned by her close call. Her stare traveled from the slain demons to Whit.

They locked gazes, with chaos all around them. Fierce, brutal exultation burned in him. He had taken his gift and used it not for selfish intent, as Mr. Holliday had intended, but to help another. To help Zora. Perhaps there was some good in the magic, after all.

Her gaze suddenly darted from his to something right

behind him. Whit wheeled his horse about, but too late. A clawed demon leapt and dragged him from the saddle.

Whit found himself on the ground fighting off the hulking demon's slashing talons and cavernous mouth. The thing stank of putrid flesh. Whit gritted his teeth to keep from shouting in pain as the tipped claws tore through the fabric of his coat, his shirt, to his skin beneath. Distance was needed in order to make proper use of the saber; otherwise he would do as much harm to himself as he would the demon. He struggled to push the creature back. The cursed thing did not budge, but redoubled its attack.

A blast of heat and flame above. One moment, the clawed demon slashed at him, and the next—it vanished. Whit raised himself up on his elbows to see. No, the creature had not vanished, but it was now a smoldering heap of carbon. Ash coated Whit.

He rose gingerly, searching for the source of the killing fire. Turning in the direction from which the blast had originated, he saw Zora. She held a torch in one hand. Her other hand *was engulfed in flame*. Good God, had she accidentally set fire to herself?

Whit took a step toward her as he pulled at his coat. He planned to throw the coat over her, douse the flames, but stopped when Zora held up her fiery hand. She stared at the fire on her skin in fascination. Her flesh did not blister. She did not scream. She looked, in fact, *pleased*.

Above the anarchic din, halfway across the camp, he heard her say in wonderment, "I was right." She glanced between the torch in one hand and the torch that *was* her hand and smiled. "It needs *this* fire."

He had no idea what she meant, nor how it was possible for Zora to burn without actually burning. More of Mr. Holliday's doing? It could not be. Zora had proven herself stronger than the Devil's temptation. What, then?

The time for mulling this remarkable, unsettling turn of events was not now. A roaring clawed demon charged at

Whit, and he found himself battling creatures on every side. He lost himself in a frenzy of combat, slashing and hacking at the demons on the ground and above. The hides of the clawed demons proved thick, difficult to pierce with a single cut. Yet he still had mastery over the odds and drew its power into himself to find the demons' most vulnerable spots.

As he fought he caught glimpses of Zora learning and using her own magic. Tentative at first, then with growing strength and confidence. She darted between running Gypsies and evaded the claws and bites of demons. She wielded fire like a whip, lashes of flame leaping from her to strike at attacking creatures. Had he not been so occupied with cutting down demons, he would have gladly focused his full attention on Zora in her beautiful, lethal dance. The fire lit her face in crimson and gold, as though she were an ancient war goddess receiving burnt offerings.

An insect demon swooped down close to an older woman who bore a striking resemblance to Zora. There wasn't time to prime another shot, so Whit darted forward, blade at the ready. The woman screamed as she threw her arms up to shield herself from the demon's attack. Whit stabbed the demon just as Zora lashed it with flame. The beast shrieked as Whit's saber tip pierced its abdomen, but its shriek was cut off abruptly as the demon turned to ash.

Whit and Zora shared another look. Whatever dark gifts they each had, they fought well together. Her willingness to fight, her skill and grace as she did so—it heated his blood more than any flame. And he and Zora complemented each other, acting together, taking up the defense when the other needed support.

A frightened whimper sounded behind him. Whit turned and carefully helped the older woman to her feet. She had several years on him, but that did not dim her beauty, only added patina to an already lovely surface.

"You are safe now, madam," he said.

"Please," she gulped, "help my daughter." She looked

toward Zora, where the last remaining demons concentrated their attack.

It made sense now, the resemblance, the unique beauty. "Get yourself to safety beneath one of the wagons."

"Protect her," Zora's mother pleaded.

"I will, but you must seek shelter."

Assured, Zora's mother did as Whit directed, gathering several terrified children and hurrying off toward the wagons.

Whit plunged back into the fray. He slashed and carved his way through the demons, feeling the splash of their thick black blood as he hacked a path to Zora. The creatures fought back, and he parried their strikes, twisting, lunging—all the skills he had practiced in genteel fencing academies but never had true use for, until now. Now it seemed as if those many, many hours he spent bruised and sweaty at the fencing school had but one purpose, and that purpose had finally arrived.

He felt the heat of Zora's fire as she, too, battled the demons. As he got closer to her, the very tip of his queue sizzled, and he smelled burnt hair. His own.

Zora looked briefly apologetic as he reached back to clutch the end of his queue in his fist, effectively putting out any persistent burning.

Down to two demons, one on the ground, one in the air. "The one on foot first!" Whit shouted to Zora.

He drove his saber into the clawed demon's back, straight through until the blade appeared sticking from the creature's chest. At the same time, Zora lashed the demon around the neck with her fire. Flame burned through the neck, as sharp as a wire garrote. The demon's head toppled from its body, face contorted in rage.

The insect demon possessed more intelligence than one would have supposed in such a loathsome creature. Seeing slain demons and their charred remains dotted throughout the encampment, the one in the air rose up higher, then darted away. The last Whit saw of the thing, it flew northwest, and its wings buzzed angrily in the predawn air.

A moment passed. And then another. Everything was quiet—save for the whimpers of wounded and frightened Gypsies. The attack was over.

Whit wiped the blade of the saber on the grass before sheathing it. Zora cast her torch into the campfire. The flames surrounding her hand shrank, then died.

They faced each other, panting, as the Gypsies came out from hiding all around them. In the aftermath, Zora's hair hung wild and loose about her shoulders. Her clothing sustained tears, revealing glimpses of dusky flesh scored by demon claws. Blood had dried on her face. Her eyes were dark, fierce. She was indeed a warrior goddess, the loveliest—and angriest—thing Whit had ever beheld.

More than anything, he wanted to wrap his arms around Zora and hold her tightly, if only to assure himself that she was whole and well. Common sense prevailed. If he tried to touch her, she would burn him to cinders.

It might be worth it.

"They came for me," Zora said, her voice curiously toneless.

"Seems as such," Whit answered.

She cursed, a florid string of English and Romani oaths. Whit knew half the words, and those that he didn't he could easily surmise. He also knew that at least some of the curses were intended for him. He couldn't blame her for her anger.

Bodies of slain demons lay everywhere, and men and women skirted them warily. Gypsies crowded around Whit and Zora, pressing close, all speaking in the same half-English, half-Romani patois. Wails, imprecations, pleas, questions. A deluge of people and words that buffeted and made his head swim after the madness of fighting actual demons. Women tugged on Zora's arms, entreating, and a small child clung to Whit's boots. Some of the Gypsies looked with fear at Zora and her hands. Her magic frightened them. It *had* been a terrifying sight. Terrifying and also remarkably exciting—for Whit, anyway.

He wanted to know where her magic had come from, but

now was not the opportunity for questions, not when nearly fifty agitated Gypsies massed around him.

One burly man pushed forward to glare at Whit. "You are the *gorgio* who kept my daughter, who took her." He balled one hand into a fist, readying to smash it into Whit's face.

Whit braced himself for the blow. God knew he deserved it. Yet the hit never came.

Zora's mother grabbed her father's wrist, staying his hand. "The *gorgio* helped us, Wester. Saved me—and Zora."

"He still needs his handsome face beaten in," Wester growled.

Glancing toward Zora, Whit saw that she neither acted in his defense nor urged her father on. Her expression had become distant, resolved.

"I must go," she said.

Her father, mother, and everyone else in the camp exclaimed in horrified surprise.

"*Kaulo durril*, no," her mother cried, expression stricken. "You have only just returned to us."

A shimmer of sadness gleamed in Zora's eyes, though she fought ruthlessly to suppress it. "I never meant to stay. There's work that needs doing. He needs my help." No question as to whom *he* was.

Whit's skin heated with a combination of pleasure and shame. Pleasure because Zora would remain with him. Shame, too, because he had brought her so much torment and yet she planned to help him.

"No," her mother said once more.

"It must be, *Mam*. If I remain, more of these creatures will come. I can't let them hurt you. Hurt the tribe."

"But they will hurt *you*," her mother wailed.

"They will not, madam," said Whit.

"How do you know?" Wester had dropped his fist but had not uncurled his hand, ready to use it in an instant.

"Because I will be with her," answered Whit. He inhaled deeply, the scent of burnt demon flesh acrid in his nostrils, enforcing how very close he and Zora danced on the edge of catastrophe. "I swear to you, sir, madam, I swear to everyone here." Whit raised his voice so that he could be heard. "I shall do everything in my power to protect her."

"Protect her?" Zora's father snorted in disbelief. "This, from the *gorgio* who kept her like a beast in a cage."

Whit wondered what, exactly, Zora had told her parents and tribe about her captivity. About the complicated push-pull of attraction and defiance. He deduced that she did *not* mention the kiss they had shared. If she had, Zora's mother would not have prevented her father from beating him senseless. Yet Whit's face and gut burned with deep, abiding shame. It was uncharted territory, especially for a man who had lived every one of his days with concern for no one, not even himself.

Yet she had said she had not intended to remain with her family. Did that mean she was returning to him? Could he hope for that?

He stared at Zora, who impassively watched the interplay between him and her parents. He suspected that she had retreated far within herself as a means of self-protection. Only her eyes betrayed emotion, an intricate mingling of fury, determination, sorrow.

Zora turned away. "I'll need to gather some things to take with me." She strode off toward one of the tents, her mother and several other women following, leaving Whit alone with the rest of the band and Zora's male relatives. A tight, weighted silence descended.

"You ought to burn those," Whit said, gesturing to the demons' strewn bodies.

Someone piped, "They will come back to life?"

"No idea," Whit answered. "But let us not take chances."

A man barked out orders in Romani, and men began to gather up the carcasses. The creatures were big and ungainly, particularly in death. Whit helped, hauling bodies to the bonfire. It was tough, unsavory work, for the demons had already begun to decay. They stank in life and smelled even worse in death. Whit hoped the fire might cleanse the air, but fed by so much fuel, it blazed and poured thick, caustic smoke into the dark gray sky.

A week ago, perhaps less, the Gypsy camp had been a scene of revelry. It had rung with the sounds of laughter and song. Now it was a charnel house. And Zora voluntarily exiled herself from her home, her people.

His doing.

How did saints manage it? Sin and atonement? Carrying with them the leaden weight of remorse? It seemed an impossible task, a cannibalizing of self as one gnawed upon one's own bones. Of a certain, Whit was no saint. Yet he would find a way to make right the wrongs he had done.

Responsibility. This, too, was new.

A humorless smile tugged at his lips. Thirty-one years old, and he was finally growing up. All it took was making a bargain with the Devil and preventing a horde of demons from killing a woman he . . . he what?

Zora reappeared carrying a battered satchel. She had washed the blood and soot from her face, plaited her hair, and changed into fresh clothing, including a thick, warm cloak. She looked much as she had when Whit first met her except for the new vigilance in her expression. Both of them were profoundly altered. He had always thought himself incapable of change. Or, if it did come, it would be a slow, gradual process that happened by incremental degrees. Never in a single night.

Zora strode to her horse; it had been John's, but Whit doubted if the animal would ever be returned. John could easily afford the loss. Whit only hoped that his friend would choose not to prosecute her for theft. Whit planned to speak with John on her behalf, then stopped the thought.

There would be no speaking with John. Nor attempts by John to entice Whit into a scholarly debate. Whit would not play billiards with Edmund as they discussed horse racing.

He would never again sit across from Leo at the coffeehouse debating the latest intelligence and scandals. And Bram . . . When had Whit done anything in the last few years that did not involve Bram? When had more than two days gone by without them speaking with one another?

Loss hit him. He didn't know himself without the measure of his four friends. His identity bound up in how they saw him, how he saw himself with them. Gone now. Now, he must learn who he truly was.

As Zora must learn who she was, away from the shelter of her family. She affixed her satchel to the saddle, her shaken mother beside her.

"You will come back?" her mother pleaded. "When the trouble is over?"

The satchel secured, Zora turned to the older woman and put her hands upon her shoulders. "As soon as it is over," she said. "But you must pack everything and move the camp at once."

"We can move to—"

"Don't tell me. It's safer if I do not know."

"But how will you find us?"

"Nothing can keep me from my family."

She looked past her mother to hold Whit's gaze. The shared look told him everything. When Zora left her family and Gypsy band, she did so knowing she would never see any of them again.

From his observations, Whit understood that Gypsies were a close-knit group. It seemed as though they stayed together for the whole of their lives. Aside from the few days Zora had spent—*held captive*—in London, Whit did not know if she had ever been apart from her family. Forcibly removing herself from them must cause her unbearable pain. Yet she bore it with remarkable stoicism, a bravery Whit respected in anyone, man or woman.

Zora and her mother embraced tightly. Then, one by one, every member of the tribe came forward to bid Zora farewell. Their sadness at losing Zora was redoubled by the

fact that she had returned to them less than an hour earlier.
Though Whit had played savior moments earlier, many
people in the camp shot him glares, effectively deducing that
somehow he was responsible for everything. Including
Zora's self-imposed banishment.

Christ. Whit did not think he could feel worse. Every
moment was an education.

After each man, woman, and child had bid her farewell,
Zora swung up fluidly into the saddle. Whit immediately
went to his own horse and mounted up. As he rode slowly
through the camp, some called out thanks. Others muttered
curses. Champion and pariah—he played both roles.

He caught up with Zora just beyond the edge of the camp.
They rode in silence for a few moments. She did not once
turn around for a final look, her shoulders straight, her chin
upraised. Whit did look, however. He saw the Gypsies gradually disperse back into the camp, righting collapsed tents,
tending to their wounded. Zora's father stood with her
mother at the periphery of the encampment. After wrapping
a consoling arm around her waist, he let go and drifted back
to help the others repair their damaged homes. Zora's
mother did not move. She stared after her daughter and continued to do so until Whit and Zora rounded a bend and the
Gypsy camp disappeared from view.

Zora's shoulders finally slumped. As daylight faded the
sky from black to gray like a fading bruise, he saw exhaustion inscribed plainly on her face.

"Did you come to drag me back to London? For I'll fight
you if you think to imprison me again."

"Some gamblers are cheats," he said. "Mostly, we're
honorable men. I own that my own ethics have been . . .
variable."

She snorted.

He reached over and grabbed hold of her horse's reins,
stopping both his mount and her own. She made a shocked,
angry sound.

"But I seldom give vows," he continued, "and with good

reason. When I swear something, I hold true to my vow. I swore I would never take you by force or through magic, and I did not. I shall not. I vowed that I would do everything in my power to protect you. And I will, Zora. You have my word, my blood, on this oath."

She held his gaze for a long moment. He felt her gaze resonate deep within him, primal and strong. It was still there, the connection between them. Now made even stronger since they fought side by side. It was a connection she resented. He saw this. But he could not regret it.

"You took everything from me," she said.

Such simple words, yet so wounding. They burned far more than the demon-inflicted cut on his shoulder. "I'll kill anything and anyone that seeks to harm you. Drown the world in blood." He had never meant words more.

"I will help in your fight against *Wafodu guero*, but I can't give you forgiveness." Her eyes blazed.

Her refusal to capitulate did not surprise him. He would have to work for absolution, the first time he had ever truly worked for anything.

Whit let go of her horse's reins. She blinked at him in surprise.

"You *have* turned from him, haven't you? Finally."

"I've learned things," he said. "My own blindness, for one."

She exhaled, but the tension between them did not lesson.

"I have also learned that it is much more satisfying to wield a saber against a demon than a hay bale. And that Gypsy women with whips of fire are fearsome, indeed." He urged his horse forward. When she did not move to follow him, he brought his horse back around until they were beside each other. "You're nigh dead with fatigue. I'll find you someplace safe to sleep."

She only stared at him.

"Once I make a vow," he said, "nothing shall break it."

"Not even death?"

"That has yet to be tested," he conceded.

She kicked her horse forward. "Let's put you to the test."

* * *

Warmth and softness enveloped Zora. She drifted through filmy states of waking and consciousness, allowing herself these unburdened moments when she was neither fully alert nor entirely asleep. Dreams had plagued her. Dreams of hideous, hellish creatures with insect wings and animal claws and giant mouths that shredded apart the fabric of her family. Everything was left in bloody tatters. Fire, too, scoured her dreams, and she gladly escaped them into partial wakefulness.

She felt the bed cradling her as she lay on her back. A true bed, not the pallet she had fashioned for her imprisonment, yet this was far too luxurious for her simple, portable bed she used at home. Lavender scented the abundant linens.

Languorous, she stretched, lifting her arms up and then out. Her hand met solid, warm flesh. Someone lay beside her. Curious, eyes still closed, Zora's hand explored. It found a man's corded arm, a broad-capped shoulder, the rise of a bicep and taut forearm. Moving past the arm, her hand discovered a tightly muscled torso. Firm pectorals lightly covered by hair, then lower, ridged abdominal muscles as hard as Spanish mahogany yet heated and satiny. Rather miraculous, those muscles, and she allowed herself the luxury of running her fingers over them, feeling the twitch of response at her touch. *Like a prized stallion's flank*, she thought with an inward smile.

Eager to explore more of the delicious male specimen next to her, Zora rolled onto her side. She stroked up and down the man's torso with her palm. Dimly, she heard a masculine groan of pleasure. She made her own sound of contentment, almost a purr. It had been so long since she had touched a man. Felt his heat and virility, and desired it. Yes, desire. It crept up through her on velvet paws, weighting her limbs, stirring sensitivity back to life after . . . months . . . years? She did not know. She knew only that she was a woman too long denied her own passions, and a

perfectly delectable man lay beside her, gladly accepting—
and enjoying—her caresses. For days now, she had been
sharpened against the whetstone of need for Whit, honing
her into a blade of wanting. Wanting, and denying, for there
was always an impediment between them.

She had been denying herself, but she would no longer.
Her explorations of the man beside her continued, and she
allowed herself the indulgence of pretending this man was
Whit, that she could yield at last to the beast of her desire.

A fine trail of hair wended its way down his flat stomach,
and her fingertips followed it until it disappeared beneath
the waistband of doeskin breeches. The leather was supple,
soft, and it clung to the man's body like another skin. Her
hand moved lower. And now she truly purred, for she encountered the thick length of the man's cock pressing tightly
against the doeskin. The man sucked in a breath and rocked
up into her touch.

A gorgeous cock, even if her knowledge was gained
through touch and not sight. She traced her fingertips over
the head and the ridge just beneath it. Then down the broad
shaft. Oh, it would fill her most wonderfully, almost to the
point of pain. Hot slickness gathered between her legs at the
thought of taking this cock into her, stretching herself to accommodate its length and thickness. She wanted that. She
tugged at the breeches' fastenings.

"God, Zora. Yes."

Her eyes flew open. Whit's bright blue gaze burned
into her.

For a moment, her hand paused in its work. They stared
at one another. His bristled jaw was tight, his nostrils were
flared. He was shirtless, clad only in his doeskin breeches.
Zora wore her chemise—she must have stripped before collapsing into bed. Shadows suffused the room in which they
lay. It was dusk. She had slept all day. And now she was fully
awake. As was Whit.

Whit, the man who had cut through her life like that
curved sword he wielded. Who had been her captor, her

tormentor. Yet he had been respectful, in his way. In the moments when she forgot the nature of their relationship, she had found in him a kindred spirit, a clever man with a hunger for understanding. Though swathed in darkness and often hidden, his soul was good. Worthy. She and Whit had desired each other. He had wanted to give her things, anything she wanted. But the terms . . . the terms had been terrible.

He had ridden to her rescue before she could ride to his. However, he had helped save her from creatures that he had unwittingly unleashed.

Lying beside him now, in this inn, sharing a bed . . . a maelstrom of emotions crashed through her. Desire, yes, always that between them. Gratitude for his courageous strength against the demons. But there was anger, too.

She wanted to take from him. As he had taken from her, leaving a smoldering ruin in his wake. Strip him of everything, even gentleness, even mercy. Until, like her, he had nothing left.

Her hand cupped him through the snug fabric of his breeches. His cock jerked beneath her hand, and she squeezed. Hard.

He groaned hoarsely, the sound midway between ecstasy and pain. Yet he did not push her away or stop her. His broad hand actually came up to cover hers, pressing her even closer.

Power roared through her. She wanted more.

Zora levered herself up on one elbow and leaned over him. They continued to stare at one another as she stroked him roughly, pleasuring and punishing him.

"Ask me a question," she demanded.

His gaze was hooded. "Do you want me?"

No magic pressured a truthful answer from her. She could say whatever she wanted now. His hold over her had been broken when she escaped.

"No," she answered.

She lowered her head as he raised his own, and their mouths met. Their last—and only—kiss had been a slow, deliberate seduction, an exploration of each other's tastes and textures that had left her breathless with wanting. This kiss was not slow. It was not deliberate. It was . . . animal. Ravenous.

She plundered his mouth, just as he savaged hers. They let slip the tether that bound their basest feral natures. Tongues tangled, stroked. His lips were full, firm, devastating. He nipped at her and she bit back, like two wolves locked in a mating battle. They growled.

With one hand, Whit continued to hold her tightly to his thick erection, his hips moving against her. His other hand came up, tangling in her hair, tugging just enough to sting. The sensation traveled from her scalp all the way through her body, to gleam brightly in her breasts and her quim. Never before had she linked pain with pleasure, but now, the subtle fire of it heated her already burning body. She could feel her wetness, her need for him in her innermost place.

She maneuvered her free hand up onto his chest. Her fingers brushed against something small and cool, metallic. A ring, hanging from a cord around his neck. Her ring. The one she had flung out the gaming room door to test the magical prison. All this time, he had been wearing it close to him. Proof of his ownership? Or something more, something deeper?

Her nails raked a path, not enough to draw blood, but they would mark him for a while, her anger and desire leaving red trails on his flesh. The thought excited her mightily. And it excited Whit, too, for he rumbled like a wild creature at her scratch.

His fingers loosened from her hair, and he trailed his hand down her throat, over her collarbones. She gasped into his mouth as he cupped her breast through the thin chemise. Pleasure shot through her in hot, sharp jolts. His clever gambler's hands stroked and rubbed, the heat of his palm burning through the fine fabric. With his thumb, he teased her nipple into a firm point. Then he took her nipple between his thumb and forefinger and pinched.

Zora moaned. Again, they tread on the narrow boundary between pain and ecstasy. One fueled the other, just as anger fed lust. And something more. Something beyond the need to punish and take. Beneath the complex web between them, something glimmered, bright and true, free from the darkness that ensnared them.

She did not want to know what that glimmering thing was. She wanted only to exorcise the rage pulsing through her, and hopefully banish her desire for him.

As Whit rolled her nipple between his fingers, she fumbled for the fastenings on his breeches. Their hands tangled as he helped her. His cock was freed and she took its naked length in her hand, gripping it tightly. He was velvety and hard. She scraped her nails down the shaft, and he shuddered in ecstasy. A bead of moisture gleamed at the very tip. She rubbed the tip in hard, small circles.

"Keep doing that," he grated, "and I'll spend in seconds."

Which would give him release far too soon. She lightened her touch until she stroked him with delicate, fluttering caresses.

"Ruthless." He spoke the word half in admonishment, half in admiration.

"With you, yes." But she didn't want words, for they contained too much intimacy, which led in directions she dared not follow. She took his mouth again, and he both gave and took in response. She slid her foot up his calf, testing the feel of his flesh against hers.

When his large hand clasped her ankle, she shivered. When his hand stroked up her calf beneath her chemise, she gasped. When his hand moved over her knee and up her thigh, she could not stop her groan. He touched her leg boldly, possessively, as if her body had been created for him and his pleasure alone. She badly wanted his touch between her legs. She needed his fingers delving into her quim, wet and eager for him. With absolute understanding she knew that the moment he touched her there, she would come. It would take only one stroke.

He lifted his head to watch her. His hand drifted higher, closer. *Yes.*

His hand stopped. She urged her hips higher, encouraging, demanding.

"Now, Whit," she commanded.

"I can't."

"Why the hell not?" She opened her eyes to glare at him.

His gaze was fixed on something over her shoulder. "Because there is a *ghost* watching us."

She twisted around. Sure enough, a ghost *was* watching them. Rather avidly.

Zora released her hold on Whit. Wary, she sat up and protectively crossed her arms. "Livia."

"Why do they stop?" The specter frowned. "Over a millennium has passed since I have seen such a magnificently carnal display. Makes me wish for a body of my own." Her hands came up to stroke her neck, and her frown deepened into an angry grimace. "Nothing. I feel nothing. Not even the touch of my own hands."

Zora felt Whit beside her tucking himself back into his breeches. Given his hiss of discomfort, the process was not an easy one. He'd been so thick and hard.

"The Roman ghost has a name," said Whit. "You know the ghost's name. And it is *talking.*" He eyed Livia warily as she angrily muttered, carrying on a conversation with herself in a corner of the room. Night had fallen, so she glowed whitely in the darkness, the only source of illumination.

"Unpredictable as gunpowder, too," added Zora.

Strange how only a day had passed, but things such as demons and ghosts were almost familiar. The world had truly gone mad. Or Zora was mad, like Livia.

Zora did teeter on the edge of sanity, if from unsatisfied desire alone. In too slow increments, arousal began to fade, echoes of heat leaving her body in gradual pulses.

"Why are you here now?" Zora demanded. "You disappeared."

Livia struggled to break from her muttered raving. Her

eyes focused more clearly on Whit and Zora. "I . . . am pulled. From this place of brightness into shadow. The world between worlds. Even now, I feel it. Drawing on me." As she spoke, she guttered like a flame in a breeze.

Whit rose up from the bed. "Talking to a ghost," he said, still amazed.

"Delicious male. A brand glowing in the darkness." Livia eyed him, longing clearly written upon her spectral countenance. Though Zora understood to some extent that the priestess missed human contact, she still disliked the idea of Livia ogling Whit like a lioness sizing up a potential mate.

Good God, was Zora *jealous*? Of a *ghost*?

Livia's shape flickered. "It drags me back. Too much time, now too little. They must know—before it takes me again." Raising one ghostly hand, Livia pointed at Whit. "The glowing brand. His soul is the key."

"Key to what?" Whit and Zora demanded in unison.

"Unleashing Hell on earth."

Chapter 9

Zora heard Whit moving through the dark room. He seemed remarkably calm for a man who learned his soul was crucial to creating Hell on earth. Yet with his usual grace, he went to the candle stand, opened and closed a box, then struck a flint to light the candle. The glare temporarily blinded Zora, and she felt her pupils contract painfully.

Her eyes adjusted by degrees until the room came into focus. Compared to the opulence of Whit's home, this bedchamber appeared spare and plain. It held the minimum necessary for a night's stay: bed, table, battered clothes press. Yet it was still a *gorgio* room, heavy and immobile, and so she could not feel comfortable. Her gaze moved from the details of the room to something more . . . not comforting, but familiar, in his way. Whit.

Clad only in his breeches, he stood at the foot of the bed, his attention fixed on Livia. Zora had already seen the priestess's specter, so for her, Whit without his shirt was the greater wonder. She had touched him, learned his form and feel and knew from this exploration that his was a body worthy of adoration. Here was visual proof.

Gorgios, she had learned over the years, were soft. Especially the wealthy ones. Some of them played at being hunters, at sportsmen, but that's all it truly was: play. Their bodies bore the imprints of this charade. Even their young men at the height of their vigorous masculinity seemed fragile, vaguely unwell from a life deprived of air and sunlight. Looking at a partially clad Whit, Zora thought she might have underestimated *gorgios*.

No, she corrected herself. Whit was unique. She had known that at the encampment days ago, and she knew it for certain now.

The fire of himself had burned away everything excess. He was all lean muscle, ridged and firm, his body arranged in precise shapes, gilded by candlelight, and she wanted to stare. She needed to touch, to see *and* feel the beautiful masculine composition—chest, abdomen, the lines from his hips angling down, offering the most enticing shadows. He radiated physicality much like a horse bred for racing radiated speed. Truly, there was something almost animal about Whit, so that the façade was not his playing at being a sportsman, but rather a primal male playing at being a gentleman. His clothing had hinted at but not fully revealed what lay beneath costly silk and linen. Now she knew otherwise.

Surely he did more than hold dice or cards, for his arms were powerful sinew, his forearms tightly muscled, sprinkled with dark hair. The bones of his wrists formed hard, sharp juts beneath his skin. She already knew the seductive quality of his large, dexterous hands. Zora's gaze traveled up the length of his arms to his wide shoulders. Doubtless his tailor bemoaned having such a strapping client, for it required the cutting and fitting of his expensive shirts and coats into feats of complicated design. Gentlemen didn't have shoulders broad enough to fill a doorway.

Her gaze stopped on his left shoulder. She had seen something there when Livia had first appeared but dismissed it as a fault of her sight in a poorly lit room. Now she saw that it hadn't been a trick of the light.

Zora rose from the bed and approached Whit. He watched her, his gaze wary, as she reached out toward him. Her fingers hovered but did not touch. She felt a vine of fear knot around the base of her skull.

An angry wound marred the back of his shoulder, evidence of their battle against the demons. He had cleaned the wound at some point, and it looked as though it might leave a faint scar. Evidence that he had fought for her.

Yet her attention was snared by something else on his body. A pattern of flames covered his shoulder and ran down to the very top of his bicep, as though someone had drawn on his flesh. The design itself deeply troubled her. The flames snaked and twisted across his skin, as if they were trying to devour him. It was only a drawing, yet a malevolence imbued each line, each shape. Zora thought the candle must be guttering in a draft, for it seemed as if the illustrated flames flickered. She half expected his skin to give off an even greater heat.

"These pictures," she whispered.

He grabbed his shirt from the back of a chair and shrugged into it, hiding the design. "They appeared after I and the other Hellraisers made our bargain with Mr. Holliday. Since that day it has . . . grown."

She felt her jaw slacken in horrified surprise.

"His mark." Livia uttered this pronouncement bleakly. The candlelight had dimmed her own glow, and the struggle to remain fixed in this world showed as she shimmered. "Each moment the Dark One possesses the glowing brand's soul, his mark grows."

"And when it covers me?" Whit demanded.

"He asks for answers when I have none to give."

"Hazard a guess," he said tightly.

"When the flames cover him . . . the glowing brand is lost. His soul will never be his."

Zora seized the glimmer of hope that shone between Livia's cryptic words. "Your soul might still be recovered."

"Tell us more," Whit urged.

A laugh like broken glass shattered from Livia. "These hot

little children. Believing I have answers when the question is barely known."

Seeing that the ghost was scarce on information, Whit turned to Zora. "How does she know any of this?"

"Livia summoned *Wafodu guero* long ago," Zora said. "He tempted her with power, and she yielded."

A humorless echo of a smile canted Whit's mouth. He rubbed at his marked shoulder. "Not an uncommon occurrence."

And the reason why Zora was here in the first place. Why her whole life had become a Guy Fawkes bonfire. She did not return Whit's smile, looking away toward the window, and the night beyond.

"The Dark One feeds," said Livia. "His chosen fare is not bread nor meat. Souls. They strengthen him, give him power. Those souls capable of good . . . they are the most potent. The Dark One gobbles them up and grows in strength. Too late. I learned this too late." Her form quavered, fading in and out as her agitation grew. "Are we lost before we have begun? How can it be stopped?"

"Calm yourself," Zora urged. "Tell us what needs to be stopped."

Livia stared down at the ground as if the flames of Hell licked at her hovering feet. "Darkness from below. Drinks the light. Steals the brightness. This world shall become his own. The underworld no longer beneath but all around."

"What happened at my family's camp is a taste of what may come." Zora's head whirled at the possibility, and she leaned against the wall to support herself.

Concerned, Whit moved toward her, but she held him back with an outstretched hand. She needed her own strength just now, for she could not yet rely on him, not when he had been the unwitting agent of future calamity.

Whit kept his distance, though the tension in his body revealed how difficult it was for him to do so. Tormentor or solace—he was both.

"I see it." Livia looked up, but her horrified gaze was distant. "Each soul makes him stronger. His armies massing. Marching. The world covered in flame and darkness. Misery without end. Eternal suffering."

Hell on earth, thought Zora, shuddering.

"Then I have to stop it," replied Whit at once. "Stop Mr. Holliday."

"The glowing brand thinks it a simple matter." Livia broke from her trance to stare at the scrapes and cuts on Whit and Zora, cuts made by the demons. "Already blood is spilled. My life lost."

"We battled his minions and won," Zora noted.

The priestess made a very unholy sound of derision. "A trifle, a tame little dance. He is a strategist. Player of games. The glowing brand knows games, how to win. Everything is not learned with the first roll of the dice."

"Mr. Holliday is just testing us," said a grim-faced Whit. "Discovering our strengths, our weaknesses. For the next time."

So much certainty in that statement. *Next time*. It *would* happen. More of those awful beasts. More chances to fail, to die.

More chances to win, Zora told herself. She had to believe that she and Whit could succeed. Or else she would give in to despair. Precisely what *Wafodu guero* wanted.

"What do we need to do?" Zora asked.

"The tokens are taken," said Livia, "but not lost."

"Brilliant. More puzzles." Zora clenched her fists in frustration. "This ghost has all the makings of a fortune-teller."

Yet it seemed to make sense to Whit, for he nodded with understanding. He spoke lowly, though steel and anger threaded his voice. "The *geminus* showed me a token for a soul it had won. It must have mine, as well. It mentioned something about a vault."

He began dressing quickly, lacing his shirt and shoving it into his breeches, pulling on his boots, shrugging into his waistcoat and coat. He gathered his unbound hair to tie it back.

"I know how to find the *geminus*," Whit said. "I have the means to summon it. All I must say is, *Veni*—"

"Silence!" Livia darted forward, floating above the ground, with her hand outstretched. She moved to cover Whit's mouth, but she passed right through him. For a moment, both stood motionless in surprise. The ghost whirled away, staring angrily at her spectral hand. Her eyes flashed enraged, pure white. "Taken from me. It is so cold. So blasted cold." A seething ball of light took form above her open palm.

Zora grabbed Whit's arm and pulled him back the moment that Livia, shouting in fury, hurled the glowing orb at the far wall. It slammed into the timber and plaster with the noise and force of a thrown boulder, narrowly missing Whit. Chunks of wall fell to the floor.

He raised his brows at the close call.

"Mad ghost," Zora snapped. "Allies don't throw deadly magic at one another like footballs."

"Is it wise to ally ourselves with her?" Whit asked under his breath.

"For good or ill," answered Zora, "she's all we have."

Livia calmed herself, though the cost of summoning the ball of light sapped her, and she faded even more, as did her voice. "The *geminus* . . . will not come alone. The double's face . . . holds his master's eyes. Sees what he sees. If it is summoned by the glowing brand, the Dark One will find him."

"Then *we* must find the *geminus*," said Zora.

Whit looked thunderous. "If the *geminus* keeps company with the Devil, you are going nowhere near that damned creature."

"My fate is knotted with yours. *You* tied the knot that bound us together." When she saw that Whit meant to object again, she added, "*Wafodu guero* knows I'm a threat. That is why he sent those demons to my camp. If I threaten him, I can fight him."

"And die." He crossed his arms over his chest, a forbidding sight.

"Or live." She planted her hands on her hips. "The answer is me, is you and I together. We've always known it to be so, else you wouldn't have chased me from one end of London to the other."

Time stretched out, as tense as wire, as Whit glowered at her. She had no doubt that he had used the same glower on lesser aristocrats and at the gaming table with great effectiveness. Were she not so deucedly stubborn, she might have crumbled under such a look. But, she reminded herself, she was Zora Grey, a Gypsy vixen. She had willingly given up married life so she could honor her own judgment, make her own decisions and even her own mistakes. They were *hers* to make, and no one else's.

Many times, she had gotten into arguments with Jem, or her parents or other members of her family. They wanted her to obey, yet if she disagreed with their logic, she could not comply. No one ever tried to use reason. They shouted, or, in Jem's case, bullied. Her attempts at discussion were roundly ignored. Daughters and wives—women—obeyed. That was all she was supposed to know, or so the Rom believed.

Would Whit be the same? Would he *listen* to her when no one else did?

Whit's gaze held hers, and she beheld the swirl of conflicting thoughts and emotions there, as intricate as a constellation. Gambler's eyes: assessing, weighing, examining every outcome and possibility. Most astonishing, he was truly considering what she had said. He might not agree with her stance, still, he did not dismiss her or shoulder her aside.

She felt a strange lift of gladness, too, realizing that he did not immediately capitulate. He was not a weak-willed man, instead meeting her strength with his own. It might not make for a peaceful association, yet it certainly made things more interesting. More . . . exciting.

At last, he drew in a long breath and slowly let it out. "As we pursue the *geminus*, will you do as I say?"

"No," she answered immediately. "Blind obedience is for horses and children."

A corner of his mouth turned up, a rueful smile.

"You are neither," he said.

They stared at one another, finding their way toward a new understanding, no less complicated than anything that had come before. Each of them resisted neat definitions, both within their worlds and to each other. Yet things that were neat and easily understood were often dull. Nothing had been dull since Whit swept into her life, and she had the distinct impression that nothing ever would be again.

Before he had met Mr. Holliday, and Zora, Whit's life had settled into a kind of routine. Admittedly, what he deemed routine found a different definition in the scandal sheets: the wild revelries engineered by Bram, midnight brawls, fortunes won and lost at the gaming tables. Yet for Whit, such things had long ago lost their sheen. His hours in sundry clubs and gaming hells proved the only aspect of his life that gave him any exhilaration. Even that could develop a pail. He had begun to wager larger and larger sums to seize a measure of excitement.

Since that night almost a week ago, nothing in Whit's life had been standard. The discovery of magic, of supernatural beings, of demons and ghosts and sinister twins and the Devil himself—it tended to recontextualize one's old perspective, so that what had been thought of as the entire world was, in fact, a child's marble. Easily displaced, knocked aside by something larger, with the potential to roll away and be entirely lost.

The past twenty-four hours destroyed any sense of stability. He was no longer James Sherbourne, Lord Whitney. His title meant nothing. His estates and their vast incomes did not matter. No one cared if he attended Parliament. He was only a man. Battling for his very soul, trying to prevent the Devil from creating a literal Hell on earth.

As a gambler, he knew that the odds were against him. He had his ability to manipulate the odds—though that could not be relied upon—and his own skill as a fighter.

He also had, as an ally, Zora.

They shared a meal in the tavern's lone private dining room. They were both famished, and the mad Roman ghost—a *ghost*, with whom he had *conversed*—had exhausted her supply of energy. The spirit had winked out suddenly. Whit and Zora had been left alone in the room, and the air had shimmered not just with the ghost's residual magic, but also with the tangled desire he and Zora felt for one another. A meal was a much easier and less complex hunger to satisfy.

More curious and suspicious gazes followed them as they moved through the inn's main taproom. Whispers buzzed like dung-loving flies around the fine gentleman and the pretty but certainly devious Gypsy. Considering that not twelve hours earlier Whit had battled with genuine hellspawn, such petty comments by rustics ought not to trouble him.

"You and I have far greater enemies to contend with than these *baulos*." Zora kept her voice low, her words only for him.

Yet it *did* trouble him. As he guided Zora through the taproom toward the stairs leading to the first floor, he sent every one of the whispering fools his coldest, sharpest, and most aristocratic stare. It was a look that said, quite plainly, *You are nothing. You are all nothing.*

The taproom fell silent, and many pairs of eyes returned guiltily to contemplation of shoes.

He wrestled with the notion of standing in the middle of the room and announcing that Zora had shown more valor and character in a week than any of those miserable curs might demonstrate in the course of their entire lives. She had claw marks from *demons* on her flesh. The best the patrons of The Red Hart might claim was a gouty leg or an abscess from a rotten tooth.

"Come upstairs," Zora murmured. "These situations get

dangerous quickly." She glanced around the room. "Out-numbered, our chances here are bad. *Wafodu guero* isn't the only creature with darkness inside."

He let himself be led, her fingers threaded with his. Followed her up the stairs, where shadows were thicker and smoke from the taproom hearth gathered. Voices downstairs recommenced, first with trepidation and then returning to usual levels. Gossiping, no doubt. Speculation. Whit decided that he didn't care. There *was* far too much at stake besides the good opinion of The Red Hart.

At the top of the stairs, in the dark hallway between rooms, Whit stopped. Zora, feeling the tug on her arm, also stopped walking. She half turned to him, and he saw in the dim hallway that she raised one questioning brow.

"Zora," he said, because saying her name gave him pleasure. It was so like her. Hard and soft. Exotic yet accessible.

"Whit," she answered.

He went to her. Stalked her. She kept her ground until their torsos met, and they moved together—he forward, she backward—stopping when her back met the wall. She tipped her chin up, keeping her gaze locked with his. Enough firelight filtered up from the stairs that he saw the gleam of her eyes, as dark and alluring as secrets. The light also revealed tantalizing glimpses of her throat, her upper chest, and the delicious rise of her breasts above the neckline of her blouse.

They pressed close together. He felt the rise and fall of her breath, a counterrhythm to his own. His hand rose up to trace from her jaw to her neck to just above her breasts, then back up again. She felt like hot silk.

He lowered his head. Their lips met, mouths opened. Their tongues stroked against each other.

Her lips were silken beneath his, full and warm. Within, she tasted of wine and her own flavor. Spicy and lush. His head spun, and he let himself spin with it.

Their hands still clasped, and he brought his other hand down to claim hers. Arms straight down at their sides, bodies pressed fully against each other, chest to chest, stomach to stomach. Her thighs beneath his. Her hips cupping his. Only their mouths moved, drinking deeply of one another.

Need for her spiraled through him in torrid currents. He had wanted her from the moment he had seen her. Beautiful girl. Wild thing. Dark hair and dark, taunting eyes. It had been a covetous wanting, based on instinct. He saw. He wanted.

Now . . . now he knew her. The cutting edge of her temper, the forged steel of her spine, her clever mind and pleasure in cunning. And it stoked the fire of his desire, for she was not a novelty but a woman, with the depth and frailties and strength of a woman.

Balance shifted, and she met his power and insistence with her own, her body alive and demanding. An unexpected equality.

He deepened the kiss, and she made a sound, part moan, part growl. The sound traveled directly to his groin, drawing on his cock with invisible velvet hands.

All he wanted was to be inside her, yet the sound of a footstep on the stairs below caused him to break the kiss.

Her eyes were heavy lidded, her mouth was swollen. They walked together to their room. Hand shaking, he found the key and unlocked the door. As he did so, he calculated the number of paces from the door to the bed.

The door unlocked, he slipped inside, Zora right behind him.

Livia, the mad Roman ghost, waited for them.

A week earlier, Whit would have disputed the very existence of ghosts. Now, he not only believed in ghosts, he hated them.

"Is there a rule that ghosts must appear at the most inopportune moments?" Zora demanded as Whit lit the candle.

Livia eyed both Zora and Whit, her gaze lingering on Zora's swollen lips and mussed hair, then traveling down the length of Whit's body, dallying at his groin.

Zora risked her own peek and wished she hadn't. The

bottom of Whit's waistcoat perfectly framed the thick length of his erection pressed tightly against his doeskin breeches. A mouthwatering sight. She tore her gaze away, knowing that she would be denied use of that gorgeous cock for the foreseeable future.

"The heat of them," Livia murmured to herself. "The brand and the girl of flame. They draw me." Her eyes closed in misery. "Remind me what I cannot have, what I crave. Flesh to flesh. I cannot remember their names, those men I took to my bed, but I remember their bodies. Memories . . . all I have. Not even a body. Nothing. Only deprivation and want." She pressed her knuckles into her eyes.

Zora understood the priestess's torment. Livia had no physical body, but Zora did, and it literally ached with need that, once again, would go unsatisfied. An ongoing condition, ever since she had met Whit.

He appeared no better, looking as though on the verge of leveling the inn with his bare hands. Yet he seemed to gather his focus through force of will. "You said we cannot summon the *geminus*. Yet we need a means to locate it without Mr. Holliday knowing."

Livia lowered her fists. "Magic finds magic."

"A spell?" asked Zora.

The ghost glanced around the room, the trappings of mundane life. Bed, washstand, chamber pot, curtains to block the morning sun. "Not here. Heavy and small. Too much mortal incredulity."

"Behind the inn stands a forest," Whit noted.

This seemed to satisfy the ghost. "There it shall be, in the shade of night." Her shape dimmed, and just before she vanished, she called, "It seeks to drag me back into oblivion. We must act quickly, quickly before—"

And then she was gone.

Whit and Zora stood alone in the bedchamber. She glanced longingly at the bed. The bedclothes lay in twisted heaps, holding the patterns her and Whit's bodies had made as they had writhed together. By *gorgio* standards, it was not a large bed, but it would be more than sufficient for two to lie close together, if not atop one another.

"Don't," Whit warned lowly.

Muttering curses in Romani, Zora gathered up her few belongings. She had not taken much, only changes of clothing, needle and thread, small mementos of home such as her mother's hairbrush and her grandmother's ebony fan.

Whit also had a pack, which he slung over his shoulder after buckling on his curved sword.

"You did not take any of the gowns I had made for you."

"Impossible for me to accept them." Though it had been torture not to do so.

His face was carved of candlelight and shadow as he stared at her. "I cannot help but picture you in that golden silk dress. How like an otherworld enchantress you would have looked, all dark and gold. I would have been the envy of every man who beheld you."

She fought against a surge of longing, not just for the beautiful gowns, but for a path she and Whit could never walk together.

"Envy is a sin," she said, hefting her satchel. She stepped back when Whit tried to take the bag from her. "I carry my own burdens."

He sent her a speaking glance but did not again attempt to take her satchel. They exited the chamber and moved quickly through the hallway, past the memory of themselves kissing passionately, then down to the main floor of the inn. Silence from the taproom greeted their reappearance. Whit did not bother to settle with the landlord. Instead, he left a pile of coin on the desk.

They left the inn without speaking, and the ostler soon brought their saddled, rested horses from the stable and secured their baggage. Whit handed the man more coin, which the ostler received gratefully.

Whit turned to her, but Zora had already swung herself up

into the saddle. Rom men were most adept with horses, and
many Rom women knew their way around the animals. Zora
had been riding soon after she learned to walk. Her cousin
Ajan had even secretly taught her a few trick riding moves,
though he begged her not to tell anyone lest he incur ridicule,
a thrashing, or both.

She watched Whit leap into the saddle with an agility and
speed any *Romani chal* would envy. Once he was mounted,
they walked their horses out of the yard and toward the forest.

Had she been inside too long? Trapped within *gorgio*
walls? For she never did find the woods a frightening place,
not until this moment. They loomed dark and sinister just
beyond the ring of light thrown by the inn. To her, the trees
were tall skeletons rattling their bones in anticipation, expecting her.

She began to talk. "I saw a play about a knight and a lady
at a fair. A wicked sorcerer kidnapped a lady and had her
guarded by a pasteboard dragon. The knight killed the dragon
while the lady screamed."

They guided their horses off the main road and onto a
lane that led toward the waiting forest. Wind stirred the
branches, and they scraped against each other like fingernails scratching the inside of a coffin.

"What good does screaming do?" Zora could not stop her
tongue. She talked to beat back her fear, though it was a
paltry defense. "At the least, she could have distracted the
dragon so the knight could get a decent shot with his lance.
But no, she just stood there and shrieked while the knight de-
feated the sorcerer, too. Then he brought her the dragon's
head and she still spurned him for letting her be kidnapped
in the first place. He lay down on the floor and died from a
broken heart. Then she died. It was the most ridiculous spectacle I'd ever seen."

Whit had been silent, but as they entered the forest, he
spoke. "The world is not so easily divided into heroes and
villains."

"No," she said. "Not so easily divided."

Deeper they went. The woods were not particularly dense, but night made the shadows thicker and the path soon disappeared. Darkness engulfed them. Zora glanced over her shoulder and could still see the lights of the inn, and hear the laughter and voices within. When the trees swallowed the last of the light, she had no choice but to face forward and peer into the darkness. Her prattling had done nothing but make her feel silly and small. Anything could be lurking in the shadows, and she had been fool enough to let whatever was out there know she was coming.

She could just make out Whit at the lead, his wide shoulders and straight back. From the sound of his horse's hooves, he was not that far ahead, yet the distance between them felt huge. If something happened to her, could he reach her in time? She had her fire magic—and hoped it was enough.

The horses shied. Zora fought for control of her mount as she reached inside herself for the flame of her magic. Whit's sword hissed as he unsheathed it, and dull moonlight glinted off its blade.

Livia flickered into being, standing in their path. The horses' panic grew. Both Zora and Whit grappled to bring their animals under control while the ghost stared at them coldly.

Zora felt the horses' fear, shared it. To be trapped between the mortal realm and the infinity of death was profoundly wrong, a state in which no one should ever dwell. Would Livia remain trapped as a ghost for eternity, watching the world change around her, but never being a part of it? Denied human comfort, human touch? The possibility horrified Zora. She patted and soothed her horse as a means to calm herself.

Livia turned and sped away.

Quickly, Zora and Whit dismounted and secured their horses. They trailed the ghost yet deeper into the forest. The night was thick around them, and Zora found herself keeping close to Whit, her eyes on his broad, strong shoulders.

Finally, Livia stopped in a small clearing, with Zora and Whit facing her. "Now. Before I am dragged back into nothingness . . ." She turned to Zora. "The girl of fire. She shapes the spell."

Before Zora could protest that she knew nothing of creating actual spells, the ghost fixed her barely lucid gaze on Whit. "Something from the brand, as well."

"Tell me what I must do," he answered.

"*Geminus*. The dark self. Feed the spell with something of the body."

"Blood," said Whit.

"Blood," echoed Livia. "Hair. Seed."

There was a very long pause. Finally, Whit said, "Hair it is, then." He pulled a small knife from his boot and quickly cut a lock of hair from his queue.

"The fire must burn," the ghost intoned.

This was Zora's part. She shut her eyes and reached for the source of fire within, a strange inward spiraling. At the encampment, she had the campfire from which to draw, but now she had to locate its heat and strength inside herself.

"The girl must make haste," Livia cried, her voice thinning as she dimmed.

"The girl is trying," said Zora through clenched teeth.

"You've the power, Zora." Whit's words were grave but assured. "All along it has been in you."

She steadied herself, focusing on the gleam of flame that burned inside her. Yes. There. It illuminated the darkness, beat back the shadows. She reached for it, her hands cupping together. Heat filled her and the space between her palms.

"Yes," said Whit.

Opening her eyes, Zora saw flames gloving her hands. The forest's gloom retreated as firelight painted trunks and branches. She glanced at Whit, and he, too, was bathed in light. He did not smile, but his eyes shone with admiration. The flames in her hands burned brighter. She expanded with power. *This is mine. This is me.*

Urgency gathered Livia's scattered mind. "In the fire, now!"

Whit strode forward and dropped his shorn lock of hair into Zora's hands. The acrid scent of burnt hair rose up as the lock swiftly burned. At the same time, Livia chanted in that strange language, her words coming faster and faster until they blended into formless sound without end.

With a gasp, Whit suddenly doubled over. He toppled to the ground, his body rigid with pain.

Zora fell to her knees beside him. The flames surrounding her hands vanished. Darkness engulfed them. She gripped his shoulders, trying to ease the tremors of pain that rocked through him. His face contorted as he struggled against an unknown, unseen agony.

"Livia, what is this?" Zora cried. "What do we do?"

But no answer came. The ghost had disappeared.

Chapter 10

Zora held Whit's shoulders as he writhed. As she knelt beside him in the darkness, she felt how agony tightened his features, his long body, his eyes shut as if to block out the pain wracking him. Most frightening was that he made almost no sound, just a barely audible groan through clenched teeth.

Damn that mad ghost, leaving Zora without any means of helping Whit or knowledge of what was happening to him. Seeing him in such pain tore at her own heart, made worse by her complete helplessness.

Perhaps there was a canteen in his satchel. She didn't know what a drink might do for him, but it was better than the nothing she offered him now.

She cursed. The satchel remained with the horses. If she went to retrieve it, Whit would be alone. She could not abandon him, not for a moment.

The tremors harrowing him suddenly stopped. Her pulse stuttered as Whit went lax beneath her hands. Was he . . . ? No. He breathed. Deep, even breaths. He groaned softly, coming back from that place of suffering.

Thank God. Relief turned her bones to jelly.

She brushed back strands of hair clinging to his damp

forehead. "Whit," she whispered. "What do you need? Are you well?"

"Perfectly well," he said after a moment. His voice sounded oddly distant, and darkness cloaked his expression.

"What happened?"

"Something quite extraordinary." He moved to get up.

"Don't tax yourself," she admonished. "You've just gone through . . . I don't know what . . . but it scared the hell out of me."

Despite her warning, he rose to standing. Against the inky night sky, he made a large shape of deeper shadow. "No call to be frightened. Everything is exactly as it should be."

Unease plucked at her. She needed to ensure that Whit truly was unharmed by that horrible seizure. Kneeling, she gathered some twigs and bound them together with a vine. She found the gleam of fire within herself, nurtured it like one might tend a smoldering ember. This was not the heat of battle, but deliberate intent. It took her a moment to grasp the fire. *Concentrate.* A quick spark of triumph when flame appeared on her fingertips, and she touched them to the torch. The twigs were dry and caught quickly, flaring.

Red engulfed her vision as her eyes adjusted to the light. She stood, her legs unsteady beneath her, and turned to Whit.

He looked exactly the same as he had a few minutes earlier. Same sharply handsome face, same lean strength. Even his clothing remained unchanged: dark green coat, plain doeskin waistcoat and breeches, cuffed boots that came to just above his knees. His hair had come undone from its queue, fell around his shoulders.

But his eyes. Heaven preserve her, his eyes. Though they were still that remarkable summer blue, warmth had drained from them, so they were now the chill reflection of sky. He stared at her, smiling a little, and the profound coldness in his gaze made her gasp.

This isn't right. This *isn't Whit.*

"I must thank you," he said. "You have made my task much easier."

The *geminus* stood before her.

Whit struggled to clear his swimming vision. His head felt light, his stomach heavy. A vertiginous sensation that mired him in nausea before his balance returned.

Light. Light everywhere. After the darkness of the forest, he was blinded momentarily by the glare of dozens of candles. Heat pressed in on him, too, and sound reverberated around him in discordant crashes. Voices. Laughter. Shouting.

He was inside somewhere.

How did I arrive at this place? Where is Zora?

Those thoughts fled from his mind, pushed away by a driving hunger. Zora was gone, but there were others around him. People enjoying themselves, unwary.

Prey.

Yes, prey. Blindness receded, replaced by hard clarity. Whit took stock of his situation. A low, timbered ceiling dark with smoke stains. Settles hunched along the walls, and tables crowded the floor. Red-faced men argued and laughed over their tankards. Someone sawed at a fiddle. The smell of wet wool, beer, and human bodies lay thick in the room. A chalkboard on a post by the front door showed tallies of who owed what for drink.

Many of the patrons wore academic gowns and tasseled flat caps—these were not men, but boys, barely old enough to warrant razors scraped across their faces. When they shouted and guffawed, it was with the overly loud voices of freshly minted manhood. All of them so young. So vulnerable and open to temptation, easily led. Perfect.

He tasted it like wine on his tongue: the potential for these new lives, their energy and possibility. Rich, heady, the flavors. Where should he begin? His body hummed with excitement and anticipation. Truly, sometimes beginning the hunt could be the best part.

Or perhaps the hunt had already begun. A boy in a gentleman commoner's gown stood beside him looking up at him with imploring eyes.

"Do you speak truly?" the boy piped. He could not have been more than sixteen, his face still round with the lingering traces of childhood.

"Every word," he said.

"You've no idea." The boy shook his head. "Don't know why Pater cares about university. Nobody else does. Fred Thursby was rounded up by the proctors five times this term alone, and *his* father didn't threaten him with disownment."

Whit made a tsking sound. "Unjust."

"So I said, but he stops his ears." The boy glowered with the righteous indignation accessible only to the very young. "Stops his purse, too. Not a farthing, not a shilling if I am taken before the proctors again. But I can't help it, can I? I'm not a commoner, not a servitor."

After looking longingly at his carousing friends, the boy brightened. "But that won't happen, will it?"

"Not with my influence. I can ensure that no matter what you do neither the proctors nor your tyrannical father need ever know."

The boy actually giggled. "Most wonderful. Yet my tutor won't give me my allowance, not until Lady Day."

"Shall we wager? If you win, I promise to give you the protection you need." Whit pulled a pair of ivory dice from his waistcoat pocket and gestured to an empty table. They sat, the boy's robes settling around him like dust from a grave. Grime had settled into rings atop the table's surface, years of spilled ale collecting years of filth, until the table became a record of lost years and fallible, transient lives. The men who had created those marks were long eaten by worms, their names forgotten, with only aged circles of dirt as their legacy.

"Shall we?" Whit asked again. "A simple game. Highest roll wins."

"I don't have any blunt," the boy admitted. "All my drinks are on credit."

"A small token will suffice."

"Such as this?" The boy rifled through his pockets and produced a small wooden bat, the sort used when playing trap-ball.

Whit suppressed a smile. This boy was truly a child, as fresh and unsullied as morning.

"Acceptable."

The lad placed the bat upon the table. "And I get your help keeping the proctors and my father at bay if *I* win. You go first," said the lad.

Whit obliged, taking up the dice. They felt like miniature worlds in his hand, and he the omnipotent creator-destroyer. With deliberate negligence, he rolled the playing pieces. They tumbled over the wooden surface before coming to a rest, the pips showing that he had rolled a three and a two.

The boy looked smug. Five was easy to beat. He scooped up the dice, gave them a shake, then cast them onto the table.

Movement and sound reduced to the confines of the stained table. The lad bent forward, eagerly following the movement of the pieces. He could not see nor feel the patterns of chance being manipulated, altered. Why would he? The boy was only that, a mortal child with no understanding of the dark forces lurking beneath the surface of his mundane, ephemeral world. But it was a simple matter, merely the rearrangement of a few strands of probability, and it was done.

The boy gaped at his roll. A four.

Whit took the bat from the boy, then placed it in his own pocket. A simple gesture, yet not so simple. Bright, glistening energy surged through him. Delicious, made all the more so by its relative purity and unrealized potential. It did not matter the number of times the transaction occurred—

each exchange filled him with power barely contained by
the limits of his corporeal body. He kept his negligent posture in his seat, trained by millennia of service.

The boy, however, slumped in defeat. "Damn me."

"Do not trouble yourself," Whit said. "I may have won the
game, but I shall do as I promised."

"Truly? You'll take care of my father, and the proctors?"

"Of course. You can go now, lad. Your friends are waiting."

A boisterous shout rose up from the settles, calling for the
boy.

The lad jumped up from the table, ready to join his companions, but did not yet go. His childishly ruddy cheeks
turned even more red. "What you've done for me . . . such
a service . . ."

"Gratitude isn't necessary. I would do the same for
anyone. If any of your friends need assistance, they've but
to say the word."

After bowing, the boy scampered off to sit with his co-
horts. He beamed triumphantly as he lifted his pot of beer.
Of course he felt victorious. The lad believed he had out-
smarted his father and university discipline, and all it had
cost him was a silly toy.

A good beginning. Whit left the main taproom and
wended his way through a narrow, dimly lit passage. Warped
floorboards made traversing the hallway a hazard, but he
had his footing secure. He stopped at a doorway on his right.
Long ago, someone had made a perfunctory gesture toward
decoration, for a framed print of Christ Church Cathedral
hung beside the door. The glass was cracked, the picture
askew. Indulging a caprice, he adjusted the picture so that
it hung straight.

He glanced around. No one else was in the hallway. He
opened the door and stepped inside.

The room was cavernous, far larger than one might sus-
pect on the other side of the door. Its carved ceiling arched
far overhead, curves disappearing into murky gloom. No

windows. No other doors. Heavy stones comprised the walls, each stone wider than a man's arm span. Neither black powder nor cannon could hope to shatter the stones.

Shelves lined the walls and large, heavy tables filled the center of the room. The only source of illumination came from the few objects lined up on the shelves and upon the tables. They glowed brightly. All of them were newly taken.

Through a variety of means, he had won them. Guile, trickery and deception, and his favorite method, gambling. Everything within this chamber belonged to him, and his master. Yet it did not matter how much the room contained, the hunger for more never ceased. An appetite that could not be sated. He was as inexhaustible as his hunger, though, and pursued his prey relentlessly, continuously.

He allowed himself a moment to simply enjoy the room and what it held. The sum total of his few days' existence, its contents precious. The walls must have been thick. Everything in there needed protection. No place in the whole of this world could claim to be as secure.

His vault.

As he strode into the strong room, the sound of his boots on the floor echoed off the arched ceiling. Someday, these shelves would be crowded, but he had only recently begun his collection.

He found an empty shelf, then reached into his pocket and removed the small wooden bat. He murmured two words— *Veni, animus*—and the toy changed. Its form became blurred as it shifted. A warm, clean glow filled his palm and bathed his face in its radiance. He smiled down at what he now held: a soul.

His fingers clenched around the soul. Its warmth spread up through his arm and through his body. Strength flowed through him. To pick up and heave one of the giant tables would be an easy matter, as effortless as throwing a leaf. And that was merely his physical strength. With each new soul he claimed, his ability to gather more souls increased, drawing them to him with less and less effort on his part.

Stepping back, he admired his work. Only a few souls, but there would be more. The spoils of desire.

He walked farther into the vault until he came to his first and most valuable acquisition. The soul shone fiercely, almost aggressively. The Earl of Whitney's soul. He picked up the token and felt a vivid surge of strength. A little sun, this soul, and such a crucial addition. Its energy fed him now, giving him the power to move onward and continue his important work. There was so much to do, but with this soul nourishing him, there was no doubt in his mind that he would emerge victorious.

Zora lurched back, trying to put distance between herself and the *geminus*. The thing stared at her with Whit's face, Whit's body, and when it spoke, it used Whit's voice. Monstrous.

"Where am I?" It glanced around at the dark forest canopy.

Her mind whirled. If the *geminus* had been summoned, it might know its location through the act of traveling—just as Livia had feared. But the spell had brought the creature there directly. It had no bearings, no means of learning her whereabouts. Her only consolation.

"No words from the opinionated Gypsy? Such a change." It stepped closer. "What is most impressive is the measure of your courage. None of us anticipated the fight you put up. Surely you had some training in magic."

She did not answer as she moved stiffly backward. Her bones were made of ice, freezing her from the inside out. Even back in London, when she had been kept prisoner inside Whit's home, he never looked at her the way the *geminus* did so now. A butcher contemplated a carcass with more tender feelings.

"How did you come by such power?" The *geminus* was all courtesy, speaking to her gently, politely. As though they weren't standing in the middle of a forest, with dark, threatening night all around. She did not miss the way the creature draped one hand loosely upon the hilt of Whit's sword.

"No? Not forthcoming with the details?" It made a dismissive wave. "Whatever its origin, it shall not remain upon this earth long. Neither will you."

"Where is he?"

"More importantly, where am I?"

"Tell me where he is," she demanded.

"Lord Whitney?" The *geminus* shrugged. "I cannot say."

She struggled against panic. Whit could be in danger or hurt, and she was alone, without aid.

"Cannot? Or will not?" When the creature did not answer her, she pressed, "Give it to me. His soul."

The *geminus* smiled its echo of Whit's smile. "Child, they aren't handed out like Christmas oranges."

"I'll take it from you." She waved the torch toward the creature, but it did not shy back.

"Observe." It opened its coat, revealing pockets sewn into the gray silk lining. To her trained eye, it was easy to see that the pockets hung flat and empty. Dipping its fingers into its waistcoat pockets, the *geminus* again came up with nothing. "You are welcome to search me, of course."

"Tell me where it is."

The *geminus* smiled. "What I find most charming is your belief that you can make demands." Its smile faded, and its expression turned cutting. "But you prove yourself a danger, and that cannot stand."

It glanced down at the hilt of the sword as if just remembering the weapon's existence. "This may prove amusing."

She jolted at the sound of steel drawn from the scabbard. Did the *geminus* truly mean . . . ?

Her answer came as the *geminus* swung its blade. Dropping her torch, she dove to the side and narrowly missed the slash. The creature not only had Whit's shape and voice, but his skill with a sword as well. Whit's expertise and athleticism made the *geminus* dangerous. She dodged behind a tree as it swung at her again. The blade's edge cut into the side of the tree, sending pieces of bark flying. She had seen that same sword used against demons, knew what kind of damage it could do to living flesh.

Gorgio men fought one another with swords, yet she had no similar weapon with which to defend herself. Not true. She *did* have a weapon. Her fire. She did not need to draw power from an existing fire; she found the power within herself.

Heat gathered inside her. Flames curled around her hand. She leapt out from behind her cover and sent a bolt of fire hurtling toward the *geminus*. It spun to the side, avoiding the flame. But the edge of the fire caught its arm, and it hissed in pain as a smoldering cut crossed its bicep.

Its grimace shifted into a smile. "By all means, burn this mortal body. As long as I possess Whit's soul, whatever damage inflicted on me also injures him."

She stared at the *geminus*, horrified. It might be speaking lies, but was she willing to take that chance and hurt Whit?

It swung again.

Damn and hell. She could only leap away and do nothing to defend herself. Her mind worked frantically as she kept sidestepping and dodging the *geminus*'s strikes. What could she do? How could she fight this thing?

She couldn't, not without risking Whit's life. Leaving her with no recourse, no means of attack or defense. The flames around her hand vanished, useless.

The forest, which had been dark and threatening moments earlier, now became her only means of defense. When the *geminus* lunged toward her, she dove to the ground. As she rolled, she scooped up a handful of earth. The *geminus* whirled around. Springing up, she threw the dirt into its eyes. The double might be a minion of the devil, but dirt and twigs in its eyes temporarily blinded it like any creature, just long enough for her to dart into the woods.

She ran into the dark. Branches scratched at her face and pulled at her cloak and skirt like ravenous ghouls. Shadows engulfed her, and the sounds of her own labored breathing and snap and crash of broken branches filled her ears. Behind her she heard the noisy approach of the *geminus* as it pursued. The fact that it did not try to conceal itself made her blood even colder. It did not care if she knew it was coming—her fate was inevitable.

How long? How long until the *geminus* tired of this game and used its magic against her? The devil knew what kind of power it possessed.

Her eyes burned and her body ached from its countless lashings. No way to attack, no means to defend or hide herself. Curse that mad ghost to leave her here alone without answers or help.

More than Livia, she needed Whit. His presence and his strength. The goodness she knew existed within him and his warrior's spirit. Despite the tumult between them, she could not truly doubt his honor or determination. She felt herself reaching out to him, wherever he was, stretching toward him like a ship reaching for the shore.

"Whit!" His name sprang from her instinctively. It did not matter if she shouted and gave away her location, for the *geminus* knew where she was regardless. She cried out again. "Whit!"

Somewhere out in the large, dark world, he had to hear her. Or else she was lost.

Whit felt a sharp tug in the center of his chest. Something pulling at him. His palm rubbed circles over his breastbone, seeking to ease the sensation, but the feeling did not stop. It wasn't precisely pain, yet it drew on him—hard. A bright hand curled around his heart, the touch distant but also unbearably intimate. Again, it tugged, and he staggered back.

What black sorcery is this?

Glancing around the vault, he looked to the souls upon the shelves as if they could help him. His prizes, his treasure. They did nothing. As he stared at them, his vision dimmed.

The glow of the tokens faded. No, they did not fade, but his greed for them did. The claws of his hunger for more released. Rather than wanting to devour them, when he looked upon the souls, pity and shame inundated him, a flood of unexpected compassion.

No! How . . . ?

The pull came harder now. He gasped, sinking to his knees. His hand scrabbled with the buttons on his waistcoat, pushing them open, then the same for his linen shirt beneath. Looking down at his chest, he cursed. Warm radiance centered over his heart, the size of his fist and as luminous as one of the souls upon the shelf. But he had no soul of his own. What was happening?

A voice rang out. A woman's voice.

"Whit!"

No one was in the vault with him. Only he had access to it.

The voice called his name again. He recognized that voice. It knotted tightly into his mind, his being. Longing rose up within him, a yearning to be with the woman. She alone possessed the answers. She had fire and spirit, and he needed that, needed her. Not the souls upon the shelves, but *her*.

He gasped once more as the pull gripped him harder, warmth enveloping him. Around him, the vault faded, receding from his senses. Everything plunged into darkness.

All around him was black. Had he gone blind? No—forms emerged from the gloom. Tall shapes stretched upward, and at their tops . . . branches. Wind rustled through foliage. Beneath his feet, twigs snapped and fallen leaves rustled. Above arched the night sky smeared with clouds. Cold air bit at his cheeks.

Whit stood in a forest. He could not remember where he was nor how he got there. Images and sounds danced through his mind. He had gone into the woods. The ghost had appeared and fashioned some kind of spell to find the *geminus*. Then Zora—

Good God . . . Zora. Where is she?

Primal need and panic roared through him. He had to find her. She could be in danger. Hurt. Damn him, he'd vowed to protect her.

He moved to draw his saber. Yet it was already in his hand. The forest's darkness hid whether or not the blade was wet. He touched his fingers to the metal. At the least, they came away dry. Didn't mean he had not used it, though.

His fear ratcheted higher. Everything that had happened between Livia's appearance and this moment was a confusing tangle of images he could not decipher. Had he gone mad? There had been times when he had been deep in his gambling mania when the world surrounding him fell away. He had been aware of the cards or dice and nothing else. During those times, he forgot to eat, to drink. Ignored his body's need to rest. Yet that was not madness.

A swath of his memory didn't exist. He had fleeting impressions, but these were insubstantial, destabilizing. What if he had done something awful to Zora? The thought that he might have hurt her in his madness scoured him.

Something ahead of him ran through the forest. The woods filled with the sounds of someone plunging through the branches and shrubbery. As though the person was being chased and sought only escape, not concealment.

Pursue, or keep his distance?

His decision was made in the next instant.

"Whit!" Zora, frightened and desperate.

A moment's relief. She was alive. He had not hurt her. As he charged toward the sound of her voice, he bellowed her name.

There was silence, and then . . . "Whit?" Her voice was tentative, so very unlike her.

"Do not move." He pushed his way through low-lying branches. "I'm coming for you."

At last, he neared what had to be her. Shadows encompassed everything, and she wore a cloak, but he instinctively recognized her shape, her presence, there in the forest. An unseen but deeply felt resonance surrounding her. Both of them were panting with mingled fear and exertion.

"Zora?"

"Stop there." Her voice was hard, even as it wavered.

Light flared, dazzling him. He squinted in the glare until he could see her—*thank God*—standing in front of him. Flames traced over her hand, and she warily held it closer to him. Scratches ran across her face and her cloak and skirt sported tears. Her flight had been a reckless one born of fear. Cautiously, her gaze searched his face, and though he needed to go to her, he held himself still under her examination. If she was wary, there had to be good reason for it. She stared into his eyes, peering closely, searching for something.

He sheathed his saber, waiting.

Without warning, she launched herself at him. The flames covering her hand vanished. Her arms wrapped around his shoulders, her hands pressed against his back, and she buried her face in the crook of his neck. His own arms came up instinctively. He pulled her tightly against him, feeling her slim body tremble. He shook, too.

For a moment, neither spoke. They simply allowed themselves the pleasure of holding one another, reassuring themselves that they were both whole and well. He stroked her night-cold hair, soothing them both.

"You were gone." Her breath puffed warmly against his neck. "It was you, but it wasn't you, and I didn't know where you were."

"Here. I'm here now." He wanted to draw this moment out for as long as possible. His heart pounded and he sensed the answering throb from Zora's chest pressed against his. It stunned him how good it felt simply to embrace her like this, wanting only to have the proof of her, safe and complete. What he experienced was not desire, nor the need to take and possess. Solely to have her here, in his arms. She fit him perfectly, as if he had been fashioned for this alone—to hold her.

Too many unanswered questions hung in the air. Gently, he held her away from him. "Tell me what happened."

She took a few deep, steadying breaths. Her trembling subsided as she drew upon the courage he admired. "After you collapsed, the *geminus* took your place. It wanted to know where my magic came from, but I wouldn't say. Then . . ." She fought a shudder.

"Then?"

"It tried to kill me."

Rage the color of blood poured through him. He had sworn to protect her, and when a threat had arisen, he was nowhere to be found. Where had he been? More images flitted into his mind: an overcrowded room, young men laughing, a vast chamber with stone walls. When he tried to reach toward these impressions, they retreated.

"You fought back," he said to assure himself.

"I tried. But I stopped." He felt her fingers at his sleeve, and he hissed when she brushed against a wound on his arm. The injury pulsed hotly. A burn.

"It's not like you to halt an attack."

"And hurt you if I went on?" She gripped his shoulder. "The *geminus* said that as long as it has your soul, any damage inflicted on it hurts you, too. So, we can't do anything to it. Can't hurt the damned creature. Can't kill it. Our hands are bound."

He cursed. There had to be something they could do to strike out against the *geminus*. The *geminus* might have been lying, but that was a gamble he was not willing to take. Yet something Zora just said troubled him. He struggled to grasp at it. What?

"You said that as long as the *geminus* had my soul, if we harm it, *I* am harmed, too."

"If we can believe it."

His fingers threaded with hers. This, too, felt wondrous, the press of palm to palm. Incredibly, despite her scare, she no longer trembled. Instead, she was warm and steady.

"We need your light to guide us back to the horses. Our path leads northward. To Oxford."

* * *

As they picked their way carefully through the forest, Whit's deep voice and the feel of his hand steadied Zora.

"I was myself, but I was the *geminus*, as well. Living inside it. Thinking its thoughts, sharing its feelings."

She shuddered. "Awful."

"It wasn't." The firelight from her hand sharpened his frown. "It felt . . . incredible."

"A trick, some kind of enchantment. Making you feel something that wasn't true."

"*Power*. That's what I felt. The hunger for it, the sources of it all around me." His jaw tightened at the memory. "I was in an alehouse in Oxford, a place I'd gone to countless times when I'd been at university but too young to sit in the senior common room."

"You revisited a memory?"

"I was *there*. Nothing had changed. The tables, the stains. There were students everywhere. And all I could think was how they were perfect victims, how easy it would be to steal from them."

"Steal money."

"Steal souls. Feed upon them. Each of them belonging to me." He narrowed his eyes as he recalled the sensation. "A greed unlike anything I'd ever experienced, yet I recognized it, too."

She stared at him, aghast.

"I'd known it at the gaming tables. In my need for more." His footsteps slowed. "Zora, the *geminus* is *me*. It couldn't exist unless that darkness and greed was already within me. And what it offers, what it seeks . . . it tempts me. Stronger than words could say."

She heard the struggle in his voice and wondered what that must be like, to inhabit the dark side of oneself, and feel those dark feelings without reserve. He was not far from that. Only a few days ago, his darker self had kept her imprisoned in his home. Her captor hadn't been the *geminus*, but Whit.

The divide between him and the *geminus* was no thinner than a playing card. Was it the same for everyone? Were their own darker selves just a whisper away? She thought of her own wicked impulses, the deeds she had done, the desire to hurt those who hurt her, and sometimes worse.

She had to believe everyone felt those things. The trick lay in not giving in.

"Whatever the *geminus* offered," she noted, "it wasn't enough. You came back."

He stopped in his tracks, holding her gaze with his own. In the shadowed forest, with only her fire magic illuminating him, his sinner's face was beautiful. "Because of you."

Her mouth dried. She had reached out to him, called his name, and somehow she had breached the distance between them. This was another kind of magic existing only between her and Whit. A kind of magic for which she wasn't fully prepared.

Once, Whit had been her jailer, the man who had dragged her into a sinister world of demons and stolen souls. Now, nothing was as simple as captor and captive, as hate and affection. She knew only one moment from the next, a series of small steps that led in a mysterious direction.

They must move forward. That much she understood. She tugged on his hand, and they resumed walking. "If the *geminus* was in Oxford, likely it's moved on by now. Especially if it's aware that we know where to find it."

If he wanted more from her, he did not press for it. "Perhaps. Something did happen when Livia cast that spell, something other than the *geminus* and I changing places." He was silent for a moment, then spoke again. "Mariners employ a thing called a bearing compass to find their way at sea. It uses magnets to locate direction."

She did not know anything of devices called bearing compasses, nor of magnets. It sounded like magic to her. "You have some kind of bearing compass that shows where the *geminus* is."

He rubbed a knuckle between his ribs. "Here. I can *feel* where the *geminus* is, as if we were magnetized, and I am drawn to where it is."

"So that mad ghost's spell worked," she murmured to herself. The initial result of that spell had been terrifying. Never would she forget the icy determination in the *geminus*'s gaze as it stared at her, nor its resolve to crush her like a bark beetle. The fact that it had Whit's face, his eyes and voice had been the worst part. Even in his darkest moments, he had never looked at her like she was a worthless object.

"What we're seeking isn't the *geminus*."

"That was the point of the spell."

"Perhaps originally. Yet I saw something when the *geminus* and I traded places. I took—rather, the *geminus* took—a soul into a room in the alehouse. It was a vault, not a room. Impenetrable stone walls. Shelves reaching as far as I could see, and some of the shelves held more souls. Including mine."

Her heart began to pound. After what felt like a lifetime of being chased and being at a continual disadvantage, here at last could be their chance of taking the lead against *Wafodu guero*.

"If we can reach that alehouse and find that room—"

"We can reclaim my soul."

Chapter 11

The Rom seldom traveled at night. Their caravans were too cumbersome—dozens of wagons, scores of tents, horses and donkeys, families with children. It was easier to move during daylight hours, when no one might accidentally get left behind, and the hazards of poor roads could be navigated. There was another reason, too, more than the coordination of transporting a large band of people and animals.

Evil wandered freely after dark.

Zora had long ago dismissed Romani superstitions. There were so many, they cluttered up one's life like dusty bottles rattling on a shelf. Menstruating women were *mochardi*, unclean, and forbidden to cook or touch food intended for a man. To see a dead crow in the road presaged bad tidings, and the traveler would have to turn back. Countless others.

As she rode beside Whit through the night, she thought of all the cautions against being abroad after sunset.

Passing through a grove of willows, she hunched her shoulders protectively.

Whit sensed her unease. He raised up in the saddle, his hand straying toward the hilt of his sword. "What do you see?"

"Shadows." She pulled her cloak closer. "Stories."

"Fireside tales."

"At night, willows uproot themselves and walk the countryside. Frighten the unwary." She glanced cautiously at the branches. "I heard many warnings about swarms of evil creatures roaming the dark, searching for victims, for the incautious."

He, too, looked up at the swaying trees, his gaze assessing. "Any truth to those stories?"

"Once, I thought *baba*'s reprimands were only to keep me stuck beside the campfire. Now . . . I wonder how much might be real." A shiver ran through her.

She thought of her fire magic and took strength from it. Should anything happen, she was not defenseless. Even before she had been given her magic, she had power. Perhaps not physical power, but her mind was its own weapon, as sharp as a blade. Still . . . she liked knowing that she could summon fire when necessary.

"The world has changed," she murmured.

"*We* have changed," he said.

Whit's hunting coat bore marks of battle: tears, bloodstains, the singe on his sleeve. His snug doeskin breeches were not new, his boots scuffed. Yet the set of his shoulders, his upright confidence as he rode, even the tilt of his jaw revealed him to be a born nobleman. This was her traveling companion, the man she knew would battle beside her when more danger inevitably arose.

She was Romani. Her mother gave birth to her in a tent. She owned almost nothing, save for the gold around her neck and on her fingers. Under normal circumstances, she and Whit might meet once, briefly, before continuing on in the arcs of their lives.

These were not normal circumstances. Something was loose upon the world, something evil, and instead of running from it, she ran *toward* it.

"Everything has gone mad," she said, "and we have gone mad, too."

"Merely a different kind of madness."

"Maybe *you* were mad before," she answered, "but I wasn't."

He slanted her a considering gaze. "I saw how you looked at me when I rode into your encampment."

It felt a thousand years ago, yet her face heated as the memory returned with vivid clarity. Whit on horseback, with his dashing friends beside him, all of them full of barely restrained energy, dangerous, alluring. He, most of all. She had not been able to take her eyes from him the moment he had emerged from the darkness.

"I can't deny I thought you handsome."

"You saw into me, but I saw into you, as well. Admit it, you were on the verge of going mad from boredom until I showed up."

His insight alarmed her. *She* was the one who read faces, who saw what people tried to hide. This . . . unsettled her. "Rich *gorgios* don't need any more flattery."

"You think of me as more than a rich *gorgio*. Just as I think more of you than a Gypsy girl."

The heat and intensity of his words ran like a dark caress down her spine. "*I* don't need flattery, either."

Miles had passed. The horses' energy was flagging.

"Damn," Whit muttered. "The horses need resting." He surveyed the land around them. A few farm outbuildings hunched at the crest of a nearby hill, but beyond that, the signs of habitation were scarce. "By the time we reach a coaching inn that might have horses, we'll be dragging these animals behind us."

Clearly, he burned with impatience to reach Oxford, but Zora knew horses well. The animals would run until they were dead unless someone told them to stop. Given how the horses' flecked sides heaved, another hour at a punishing speed meant they very likely *would* die.

He pointed to a lane leading off the road. "We can follow the lane to that structure on the hill. If we're lucky, we might find a farmer and some willing hands to help cool the horses."

"The odds are yours to control," she noted.

He gave a humorless laugh. "I've discovered limits to my gift."

At the top of the lane, she discovered this, as well. Not a house, nor a farm. Its conical roof revealed it to be an oast house. She and Whit dismounted and, after they discovered the wide double doors to be unlocked, peered inside. Zora summoned her fire magic to investigate further.

"I don't know when I will get accustomed to that," Whit said. A corner of his mouth turned up, softening the hard edges of his face. Stubble darkened his jaw, and hours in the saddle had pulled strands of dark hair loose from his queue. He looked part aristocrat, part highwayman. A lethal combination.

"Always be on guard around me," she said.

"Love, when I'm around you, there is no danger of complacency."

She did not like how easily he called her "love," nor did she like the spike in her pulse to hear him call her that. To regroup her thoughts, she held her hand aloft like a torch and appraised the structure.

No one was within. Light weakly filtered in, revealing enough room for them to bring the horses in from the cold.

The air inside smelled of bitter hops. A few dried blossoms crunched underfoot.

Zora doused the flames around her hand. Wordlessly, she and Whit removed their horses' blankets and saddles. The animals steamed, their hides glistening with sweat. She swallowed her groan of frustration. They would have to wait until the horses dried before putting the tack on again. Knowing that Whit's soul awaited them, less than thirty miles away, tried her patience strongly. It had to be a thousand times worse for Whit.

He made a tense, shadowed shape in the darkness. Though he said nothing, she felt his restlessness, his need to move forward, like an invisible flame giving off heat. Zora watched his swift, efficient movements, unable to look away.

The burning brand, Livia called him. A perfect name, for he blazed, and he scarred. However long Zora walked this earth, she would always bear the unseen marks of his touch upon her innermost self.

He stilled, and though darkness filled the oast house, Zora knew he stared back at her. She felt his gaze on her, that burning brand, and she turned away. She busied herself with removing her horse's bridle, then patted the animal's velvety nose as it eagerly released the bit.

Lucky beast. It took so little to make a horse happy. Zora supposed that if she spent most of her day with a metal bit in her mouth, dictating her every move, she would relish having it taken out, as well.

Being a Romani woman, she sometimes felt as though she had a bit clamped between her teeth. Always someone trying to control her, pull her one way or another. Whit had seen that, when no one else had.

She handed her horse's lead rope to him. When he sent her a questioning look, she glanced meaningfully over her shoulder toward the open doors. Outside. Privacy. He nodded with understanding and a silent admonition to be careful. In response, a flame enveloped the tip of her forefinger. He smiled, but his eyes remained sharp with caution.

Once outside, Zora tended to her personal needs. A nearby pump yielded water, and she did not mind the water's frigid bite upon her hands. Her stomach growled. It had been many hours since her last meal back at the inn. She remembered the suspicious looks she had received in the taproom, and Whit's unexpected fury on her behalf.

She spotted a shape a short distance from the oast house and smiled to herself. Hearing Whit inside walking the horses, cooling them, she slipped off noiselessly. Her people could make a lot of noise, but they could also be very quiet when necessary.

Moments later, she stepped back inside.

Whit still did not speak, but his expression indicated that he had been growing concerned.

In answer, she held up her hands, revealing several ripe pears. She tipped her head toward the direction from which she'd just come. A pear tree grew nearby, and she had helped herself. He made a low chuckle of appreciation. Their fingers brushed as she handed him some fruit, and the contact of skin to skin ran like liquid flame through her body. His breathing hitched.

They had been clawing at one another hours before. A simple, brief touch ought not to stir her after the intimacies they had shared. Yet it did. Instantly.

She took back the lead rope for her horse. They continued to walk the animals, cooling them, as they ate their pears. The pears were sweet and musky, autumnal. An unexpected pleasure in a night fraught with tension. When the fruit had been consumed, Whit pulled a canteen from his saddlebag and handed it to her. The wine warmed her throat, and watching her drink from the canteen warmed his eyes. They traded it back and forth, and if their hands touched more than once in its exchange, Zora did not mind. Between the wine and these fleeting touches, the night's chill soon left her body.

When the horses were cool enough, they secured the leads to a post supporting the roof. There was nothing to do but wait while the animals rested. Whit went to the sacks of dried hops stacked against one wall. He hefted a sack, then brought it over and laid it upon the ground. He gestured for her to sit and use the sack of hops as a cushion for her back. She sank down, grateful. He eased to sitting beside her, stretching out his long legs with a groan. A laugh escaped her.

Despite her eagerness to be on the road and reach the *geminus*'s vault in Oxford, her eyelids drooped. Weariness made her head heavy. She caught herself nodding several times, and snapped awake, but then fatigue would overtake her again.

Whit tugged on the edge of her cloak. She glanced over,

and he patted his shoulder, offering it to her as a place to rest her head. Her brow raised. *What about you?*

He waved his hand. *I'm fine.*

For a moment, she hesitated. His frown indicated that he would brook no refusal.

Her immediate response was rejection. But then she hesitated. Maybe just this once, she would allow someone to be in charge. It was only because she was so blasted tired that she permitted it.

She edged closer and tentatively put her head on his shoulder. She barely rested against him, more of a cautious lean than a repose. With a growl of command, he wrapped an arm around her, his large hand cradling her head, and pressed her closer.

Arrogant man! Yet, even though she bristled at his literally heavy-handed attitude, and even though his shoulder was far too hard with muscle to make a really comfortable pillow, her eyes drifted shut, as if in secret alliance with him.

She started at the brush of his fingers upon her cheek. She must have slept. Shifting slightly, she glanced up through her lashes to find him watching her, their faces barely inches apart. He scanned her face, his gaze like a possessive touch, both tender and fierce.

His fingers moved from her cheek, lower, to stroke her mouth. Only the smallest of movements, the back-and-forth of his fingertips against her bottom lip, as if testing its softness, its warmth and texture.

Her tongue darted out. Quickly. Then retreated back into her mouth. But not before she tasted his flesh, salty, and the lingering traces of pear juice that sweetened him.

He sucked in a breath, as if burned.

Some spell must have taken her, for she could not move, could not breathe. She could only wait, staring up at him. All that moved was her heart beating thickly in her chest.

One of the horses snorted and shook its mane, as if reminding them both that they needed to get back on the road to Oxford. Where Whit's soul was being held.

At the sound, the spell broke. Zora rolled away and to

her feet. Whit did the same. They stared at one another in the dark oast house. A tremor passed through him, and his breathing came quickly, as though he fought to keep something inside. Whatever it was, he mastered it, and his breathing returned to normal.

Once the animals were saddled and bridled, she and Whit led them out to the pump. A bucket was retrieved, and some moments were spent watering the horses. The mounts could not be fed, not with more hours of travel ahead of them, but their thirsts could be quenched.

At least some of us are satisfied, Zora thought as she watched Whit.

He sent her a look fraught with understanding.

She mounted her horse. Whit strode away and leapt into his own horse's saddle. As he did this, she allowed herself the indulgence of watching the flex and pull of muscle beneath his doeskin breeches. Of particular note were his taut, hewn buttocks, revealed when the tails of his coat flared up as he moved.

Caught looking, she tipped up her chin, refusing to be embarrassed. He gave her one of his slow, wicked smiles that set fire to her very blood, then pulled his horse around and set the animal into a gradual trot. She did the same. They trotted away from the ruined house, down the lane and back onto the main road.

It was only later that she realized they had not spoken the whole time they had rested the horses. Yet more surprising, the silence between her and Whit had been charged . . . but not entirely uncomfortable. They had easily communicated without words. No one, not even her closest kin, understood her half as well as Whit did.

The thought troubled her. Here was a man who readily admitted the darkness within him, who had tasted sinister power and found its flavor to his liking. If this man understood her so easily, as easily as she understood him, what did that say about her?

She was not certain she wanted to find out.

* * *

Whit consulted his pocket watch. It was a battered thing, hardly the finest timepiece a gentleman of his means might possess. Yet he owned no other.

His grandfather's watch. The timepiece was old now, the luster of its case long worn to dullness by the hands of James Sherbourne, and his son, also named James, and eventually his grandson, the latest James: Whit.

This was the watch he always carried. Especially now, in the midst of chaos, it comforted him, somehow, to feel the permanence of his family, of their lands and legacy, manifested in one simple, rather battered object. *You will survive this.* The implicit promise offered by the watch. How far lost was he that he gripped at the hope offered by a tiny arrangement of metal parts.

He stared at the timepiece now, turning its face in the last of the moonlight, as his weary horse walked on.

"Dawn's an hour away," he said. He slipped the watch back into its case and then into his waistcoat pocket.

"Lil-engreskey gav is half mile distant," said Zora.

"What is Lil-engreskey gav?" He mangled the pronunciation. Romani was not half as easy as French.

"The Rom's name for Oxford. It means 'book fellows' town. We've Romani names for every city. There's a whole other country within England. A tiny country with its own customs and language and names for places."

"But it's a country without borders, without cities and a king."

"We have our kings, and they are just as useless as yours. As for borders and cities, those are things only *gorgios* value."

"Values change." His own, for example. He had lived, not so long ago, only for the gaming table. The winning of money and things—that had been his greatest pleasure, his sole pursuit.

The stakes were higher now. What he played for could not be counted.

He looked at Zora in the remains of the moonlight. She stared back at him, boldly, for everything she did was done boldly. If he licked his lips, he thought he could still taste pear, and he remembered her tongue lapping at his finger. A thick swell of desire coursed through him. It had not lost its edge, but had somehow grown sharper, more ravenous.

He tightened his hands on the reins. His time as the *geminus* echoed through him in waves that flooded and ebbed. There were moments when he felt controlled, balanced.

Then the *geminus* within him would surge forward. His hungers demanded, *wanted*. It had taken more strength than he knew he possessed to keep from having her in that oast house, to fight the demon inside. Even now, despite hours in the saddle and no sleep and tension everywhere within him, he fought. To keep from pulling her down from the saddle and taking her right there. To lay claim to everything she was, everything she possessed, body and soul.

Before the demands overtook him, he wrestled them back, clenching his hands so hard they ached. He had no soul and would not feed upon hers—much as he wanted.

Would this monstrous need to utterly possess her vanish once he reclaimed his soul? He prayed it was so, for his sake, and hers. Yet he knew that every moment without his soul drew him farther and farther into darkness. Until there would be nothing left of him, save malevolent hunger.

He kicked his horse to go faster. Behind him, he heard Zora speaking the Gypsy language to urge her horse on.

When the dark shapes of Oxford's spires and the Radcliffe Camera's dome appeared on the horizon, he allowed himself a brief sigh of relief. Soon. He would have his soul back and sever his link with the wickedness seeping through him.

They crossed Magdalen Bridge over the river and headed into town. Stillness and shadow hung thick in the streets. He had not been back to Oxford for more than a decade, and the sights of its mullioned windows and Headington stone buildings brought back . . . not nostalgia, but half-remembered impressions of someone else's life.

He felt the *geminus* everywhere, a sinister web clinging to the faces of the buildings. With a silent roar, the darkness within him answered, nearly blinding him. *Prey here, ready to be hunted. Take from them.*

Some servants, bakers, and dairymaids wended over the cobblestones toward work. *They have nothing of worth.*

Yet the hunger shrieked at him as two senior college fellows staggered toward him down the middle of the street, their velvet caps with gold tassels listing over their eyes, bright silk and gold lace gowns hanging off like molting plumage. Noblemen lurching back to their chambers after a night's carousing in the senior common room.

He locked his thighs tight against the saddle and made his horse walk around the drunk students. *But they would be so easy to take from, to trick into betting more than they realized.* Money, possessions. A quick game of cards and he could ruin the young men.

Fight this. An icy sweat clung to his forehead and filmed his back. Yet he let the students continue on.

"Yes," he said once he and Zora had passed the fellows. "That was me."

He had continued that venerable tradition after graduating university. At the least, he and his fellow Hellraisers took carriages home rather than stumble about the streets.

Those days, and the Hellraisers, were gone from him now. What he had now was this monstrous, dark hunger.

His pulse came too hard in his throat to speak anymore. It was here. His soul was *here*, and the nightmare would end.

But the exhausted horses moved too slowly. When he passed a sleepy crossing sweep, he whistled at the boy. The child immediately shot to his feet.

"Watch these horses." He tossed the sweep a thrupenny bit and dismounted. As he handed the reins to the boy, Whit glanced up at Zora. "It will be faster on foot. You can stay behind if you want."

She shot him a speaking glance that said under no circumstances would she remain behind. He did not expect otherwise.

Once the horses were tended to, Whit set off at a run. He couldn't control his movements any longer. Either find his soul or else give in to the predator within. Memory and the dark energy of the *geminus* pulled him along. He sprinted through the maze of streets, both wide and narrow, that wove around the university. Dimly, he heard Zora's light, running steps behind him.

He ran past a gowned proctor patrolling for errant fellows. "Oi there!" the proctor shouted. Then, "Beg pardon, my lord."

The proctor exclaimed in surprise when Zora sped past. Whit rounded a corner, Zora following him, and they left the proctor behind.

Whit came to a stop. Zora skidded to a halt beside him. They stood together outside an alehouse, *the* alehouse. It was a freestanding building, two stories, squat, with a listing chimney. A sign hung from its post, depicting a painted bird perched atop a swayback horse. The Grouse and Nag. He'd thought it a very clever name when he was a callow boy. Not a trace of humor touched him now.

"Doesn't look as though they're open," Zora said quietly. The narrow windows were dark, and no sound came from within—no music, no laughter.

He strode to the door and pushed. It rattled on its hinges but did not open. *Damn.* He thought the odds were his to control, but not this cursed night. His fist came up to pound upon the door.

Zora's light touch on his sleeve stopped him. "No need to wake the house."

"I have to get inside." His voice was a growl.

"A moment." Then she slipped away into the shadows.

He scowled at the place where she had just stood. This

seemed a badly timed moment to sneak off somewhere for
God only knew what reason.

The hell with it. He lifted his fist again to hammer on the
door but stopped in midgesture as he heard the bolt sliding
back. The door opened on a creak and Zora's face peeped
out at him. Before he could mutter his surprise, she grabbed
his sleeve and pulled him inside.

She shut the door as quietly as she could and slid the bolt
back into place.

"Your fire magic," he whispered.

Her smile was a silver gleam. "No magic but the wiles
of the Rom."

They stood in the main taproom, and the room was just as
he had seen it during his time as the *geminus.* But the settles
were empty, and no one sat at the tables over pots of ale. The
fire had gone cold and dead. A thick smell of people, smoke,
and spilled ale filled the dark room. Stronger than this,
though, the *geminus's* black energy choked the space,
choked him.

"It was here, then," she said softly.

"I . . . *it* . . . stood there." He pointed to a spot in the room.
"And made a bet with a fellow no more than a boy. He didn't
know what we gambled for. I took a token from him—the
pledge of the boy's soul."

"And after?"

But he was already walking. Vaguely, he knew he ought
to have removed his boots so he'd make less noise upon the
floor, yet he could not wait any longer. He paced through the
taproom and entered a cramped corridor. Just as he had
seen, a few doors lined the passageway, and on the wall
hung the cracked print of Christ Church Cathedral. *It's here.
I will be whole and free soon.*

He turned to face the door leading to the vault. Zora appeared beside him. With his hand upon the doorknob, he
took a deep, steadying breath. Opened the door.

And stepped into a tiny storeroom.

* * *

There were shelves lining the walls, to be sure. He saw this in the illumination from the flames surrounding Zora's hand. But the shelves held cider jugs, ceramic canisters, and a bowl full of candle ends. No gleaming souls. Further, not only was the room *not* stone, it was plaster, and hardly big enough to accommodate Whit, let alone Zora, wedging in.

His jaw clenched, hard.

"Maybe it's one of the other rooms," she suggested.

He shouldered past her and pushed open the door across the hallway. All he found was a wet larder, reddish brown meat hanging from ceiling hooks like sinners in eternal torment. Flies stirred as the door opened before settling back down again in black clumps.

The final door opened into a bedchamber, where an old man started up from his bed at Whit's entrance.

"Who's there?" the man shrilled. "Murder! Thief!"

Before the old man could yell the house awake, Whit and Zora fled. She doused the flames around her hand as they sped down the hall and through the taproom. He slammed the bolt open and they ran off into the coming dawn, leaving shouts and confusion behind them.

Yet as Whit ran, confusion clung to him—and fury. *Damn hell bastard.*

Noises of pursuit followed. Men, and a dog. As a nobleman, he could easily intimidate his way out of a situation, or offer enough financial inducement to have the constabulary look the other way. His name and title might shelter Zora, but there was always the chance that some zealous magistrate would use her to set an example, and that, Whit could not allow.

He and Zora approached a wall. He vaguely recognized it, another reminder of his youth, when the proctors had chased him from some unsavory tavern and he had needed a means of evasion. The wall stood some two feet taller than him—it had seemed higher back then. Before Zora could protest or utter any word, he clasped her waist and all but threw her over the wall. She recovered quickly, managing to control her fall down the other side. He braced his hands atop the wall, pulled himself up, and vaulted over, into a small courtyard garden behind a town house.

They both pressed their backs against the stone, panting, and waited. Men's heavy footfalls sounded on the other side of the wall, and a dog's frantic whine. Only when the pursuers' angry shouts faded did Whit feel an infinitesimal easing of the tension gripping him.

The sky turned to ashes with the dawn, washing color from everything. The garden seemed made of stone plants and hedges, as cold and lifeless as the dry fountain that formed its centerpiece. Someone, whoever lived inside, had brought out a chair, but it had tipped over like an animal frozen in its death throes.

Only through force of will did he keep from stalking over to the chair and smashing it against the flagstones. Instead, he turned so that he faced the wall and beat his knuckles against the stone.

"It was there. Hell's fire, it was *there*."

"Another alehouse, maybe?"

"We were at the right place. I saw it. I *felt* it."

"Perhaps the *geminus* wanted to trick us. Plant a false idea so we would chase at phantoms."

"The vault is real."

"Whit, your hands." She tugged him away and made a sound of shock when she saw crimson dripping down his fingers. With a patch of her cloak, she dabbed at the raw, open flesh.

He did not want tender ministrations. Not when anger and despair turned his chest into a hot battleground. He swung away from her and paced the confines of the garden.

Damn and hell, he'd been so bloody close. With the opening of a single door, this entire nightmare might at last have begun to end. But, like everything the Devil promised, the rotten flaw consumed hope. Whit was no better than he had been the night he and the Hellraisers had found the temple. Worse. For the *geminus* had its claws in him now.

He wrenched his arm from the sleeve of his coat, then pulled at his waistcoat and shirt to reveal his shoulder and arm. In the pallid light of daybreak, he saw it. The flames that marked his flesh now engulfed his shoulder and twisted farther down his bicep, almost to his elbow. The Devil's mark grew.

In three strides, he stood in front of Zora. He loomed over her and grabbed her wrist.

"Burn it." He pressed her hand against his marked shoulder.

Her eyes went round. "What? No—"

"Burn it from my skin. Char my flesh. *Get. this damn thing off me.*"

"It doesn't work that way." Her cool, steady fingers curled gently over the curve of his shoulder.

"You do not know." He was hot and seething and her touch maddened him, yet he would not release her.

"I do know that *Wafodu guero* is not a problem with an easy solution."

His laugh scraped his throat. "Setting oneself ablaze is not an easy solution."

She winced. "If I thought it could truly help you, I would. I'd gladly take the torch to your skin."

"And gain a measure of retribution."

Her gaze turned fierce. "There are other ways I'd rather hurt you." She pressed her fingers against him, then tried to pull free from his grip. "Let go of me."

She scowled at him when he did not release her, and tugged harder. Still, he wouldn't relent. They stared at one another, gazes locked.

"This will solve nothing," she said.

"Fire with fire."

She tightened her mouth. He thought she would refuse, but then the cool skin of her hand warmed, growing hotter and hotter. His shoulder blazed with pain, as did his hand grasping her wrist. Yet he continued to hold her tightly. The pain traveled in searing currents through his body. An extraordinary transformation from hurt into something else, something . . . pleasurable . . . playing upon his senses in a strange alchemy. Lead into gold. Pain into pleasure.

Heat of another kind pulsed within him. His cock thickened. She caught the shift from pain to arousal, and her breathing hitched, coming in shallow gasps.

Cinnamon stained her cheeks, and her lips parted. Here was another surprise: she was as excited as he. They continued to hold each other's gaze, a contest of wills and a prelude to desire.

The thrill of risk heated him as much as her burning hand, if not more. A gamble, and his gamester's blood craved it. How far would they take this? Who would submit first?

The acrid scent of his flesh burning drifted up.

"Whit . . ." Her voice urged him to be cautious, yet her hand did not cool.

He let her go. They gasped at the release. She took a small step back, slowly lowering her hand. Their gazes broke apart as they studied his shoulder.

The flames marring his skin still twisted over his shoulder and down his arm. *Damn.* Yet a deep red mark remained, as well: the shape of Zora's hand. She had branded him.

Only vicious restraint kept him from spending there and then like a boy with no control. Her mark on his flesh. Nothing had ever been as erotic as that darkening handprint.

He stared down at the hand-shaped mark. "If a sinner like me can pray, then I pray this scars."

Her eyes flashed. She curled her hand in the folds of her cloak, as if sheathing a weapon.

Slowly, wincing a little from the pain, he righted his clothing, layer by layer. Until everything was as it should be, save for the sun of pain that glowed and throbbed within his shoulder.

A crash sounded nearby. He moved Zora to the wall, and they crouched behind it.

"Where is she?! Where's that damned slut?!" A woman's voice, shrieking. More crashes reverberated, the sounds of shattering ceramics and metal objects falling to the floor. "Out of my way! I don't care what hour it is. That trollop is here."

Whit stood and stretched up to peer over the edge of the wall. He did not see anyone on the street, but the noise continued. He glanced toward the town house, yet it, too, was still. Another smash resounded. It was close by, but where? He moved carefully to the side of the garden and looked over the wall that separated the yard from its next-door neighbor.

There was no one in the adjacent garden, but when he looked toward the town house, he finally saw the source of the commotion: the neighbors' home.

Zora appeared at his side, yet she wasn't tall enough to look over the wall. He wrapped his arms around her slender waist and lifted her just enough to see. Windows gave them a perfect proscenium for watching the scene unfold.

A woman of middle age forced her way into a bedchamber. The furnishings of the home and the disordered clothing of the women were of good quality—this was not the home of a fishmonger, nor was the female intruder a ballad-seller. A girl in servant's drab tried to pull the intruder from the chamber, but she was too small to do anything but tug ineffectively on the woman's waist.

The woman stalked to the bed and shoved the curtains open. The man and lady within, clad only in their nightgowns and caps, screamed.

"Vile whore!" the intruder shouted. She grabbed the woman in the bed by her hair and dragged her out. Screams the likes of which Whit had never heard from human or animal came from the nightgown-wearing lady as she clawed to free herself. "You may be in bed with your husband here, but it's *my* husband you preyed upon, and in *my* bed."

"Help me, Christopher!"

Her husband only looked on in terror, clutching the sheets to himself.

"Have you no shame, Arabella?!" the intruder screeched. "Are you so unsatisfied with Christopher that you must turn your filthy wiles on Philip?" She shook Arabella by her hair.

"A mistake, Maria. I never—"

"Deny it? Is this not your garter? And did I not find it in my husband's bedclothes?" She flung a scrap of ribbon in Arabella's face.

"It is mine, but . . . but I have no idea how . . ." She screamed as Maria shook her again. More shouting came from inside the house, the sounds of either manservants or a constable. Or perhaps Arabella's errant husband, Philip.

Zora wriggled in Whit's grasp. He obliged by releasing her, and the slide of her down his body was delicious. She mouthed the words, *We have to leave.*

They ought to. But something rather vicious in him wanted to see more, to watch these respectable ladies tear each other apart. See the chaos unfold.

"*Now*," Zora urged lowly. "Before someone spots us out here."

He tore his gaze from the spectacle and nodded. Within a minute, they crossed the garden, and he and Zora were back on the street. The shouting and sounds of breaking furniture could still be heard. A maid carrying her brooms gasped at the foul language and hurried on her way.

The sun had risen higher, brightening the sky. Whit placed Zora's hand on his arm as if they were merely out for an early stroll. But the day was anything but routine. He remembered the patterns of morning from his more clear-headed stumbles back to his chambers. Instead of the usual wagons bringing food to market, the craftsmen heading purposefully toward their businesses, and dairymaids with pails of milk balanced on their shoulders, the streets were oddly derelict. As if abandoned. Yet, from open windows fronting the lanes, the sounds of arguments and tears tumbled out.

"Seems Arabella and Maria aren't the only ones caught in domestic troubles," Zora murmured.

As Whit and Zora moved down the street, they passed three arguing men. These were not students in the middle of a drunken brawl, nor rough country men in homespun and mud-stained boots. The men were clad in the sober, well-made clothing of staid tradesmen. Yet their faces purpled in rage as they yelled and shoved. A professor in his robes and old-fashioned, full-bottomed wig stood in the middle of the arguers trying to keep order. To no avail. The fighting men continued to hurl insults and accusations at one another.

"The man in the middle is Dr. Hammond," Whit murmured as he and Zora moved past. "He tried to teach me philosophy. Now he's mediating brawls between respectable burghers."

A fragment of the doctor's lectures popped into Whit's mind. "*Malitia unius cito fit maledictum omnium.* Publilius Syrus." At Zora's blank expression, he translated, "'One man's wickedness may easily become all men's curse.'"

His heart stuttered and he stared unseeingly at the roofs of Oxford, the homes and university buildings. Much of the university had been built hundreds of years ago, at the direction of monarchs and clergy, monuments to enduring legacies.

"It's all so damned fragile," he said.

Zora gazed up at him, understanding written plainly in her eyes. The chaos—the *geminus* had created it. Wherever the *geminus* went, destruction followed. Even here, this seat of learning and reason.

Good men like Dr. Hammond could not hold back the tide of ruin. Futile—a single, brittle leaf trying to dam a flood. But it had to be held back, for the alternative was too appalling to contemplate. Devastation on an incomprehensible scale.

He stopped walking.

"Are you all right?" Zora peered up at him with a frown of concern.

"It cannot continue."

She nodded with understanding, yet she couldn't know the full weight of the burden. It was his to bear.

But *where* was the *geminus*? Ever since he had switched places with the creature, he'd felt its presence, the echoes of where it had been and its forward trajectory. Staring at the venerable buildings of Oxford, he did what he hated to do: reach out with his inner self to connect with the *geminus*. Its traces were everywhere in the town—smears of filthy energy he felt rather than saw—but went no farther.

"It's not here." He scowled. "The *geminus*'s traces are here in Oxford, but the *geminus* itself has just vanished."

"Perhaps it's gone for good." But even she did not sound convinced.

"Gone from this town, but it *will* turn up somewhere and wreak more devastation." He knew this with a terrible certainty. "Yet where the creature will next appear, *that* eludes me. In this quest, we are lost."

Chapter 12

Zora woke alone. She lay in darkness, staring up at the ceiling. Glimmers of lamplight flickered across the beams as people crossed back and forth outside. There were shouts for fresh horses, for ale and food, for passengers to hurry up with their meals before the coach departed without them. The sounds of *gorgio* life seemed more familiar to her now, and it felt like the last time she heard Romani had been years, not days, past. She had left the tiny country she called home and traveled as a stranger in an unknown land.

Another inn. This one in Lil-engreskey gav, Oxford. With no trace of the *geminus*, they could not move forward. Even if they had a trail to follow, both she and Whit were exhausted. They had needed food and rest.

She pushed herself up and sat on the edge of the bed. Once again, she had slept away the day, and night had already fallen. A candlestick perched atop the nightstand, so she touched the tip of her finger to the wick and lit the taper. She smiled at how familiar her magic felt to her now, as though it had long been part of her and only now could it come forward.

At the washstand, she poured herself a basin of water and quickly cleaned herself. A small mirror hung above the washstand. She undid and then braided anew her hair. As she did, she caught sight of the bed's reflection, and Whit, asleep in a chair. His sword lay across his lap.

She had offered him use of the bed. They could sleep beside each other. His eyes had blazed, his jaw clenched tight, a sinister intensity radiating from him.

"I do not trust myself," he had said through clenched teeth. "Now get into bed."

She had taken one look at his face and done exactly as he demanded.

He battled something. Ever since he had switched places with the *geminus*, a burning shadow clung to him. Unmistakable hunger smoldered in his gaze, especially when he fixed it upon her.

With him asleep, she could admit it to herself: that hunger and shadow called to her. She stared into her own eyes reflected back at her in the mirror. Her other self—the one who craved power over others, who yearned for dark pleasure at any cost. She no longer knew who she was, only that each moment the world changed anew, and she with it.

She turned and studied him as he slept. Even in slumber, that dark edge shaped him. He was just as volatile as she, yet, for all that, he remained her constant in the midst of uncertainty, perhaps *because* of his unpredictability. In some bone-deep way, she knew him. All his faces, all his facets. As he knew her. And they both needed to undo or stop the damage wrought by the *geminus*, before it spread like sickness to other towns, other cities. Before it was too late to regain Whit's soul.

His eyes opened. His body tensed. Instantly alert.

They held each other's gazes for a long moment. She kept very still, like a fox waiting for its hunter to move. Suddenly, he stood, secured his sword, and left the room.

Shaking, she washed, using the basin and ewer. The water was cold enough to steal her breath, but she used its chill to cool her heated blood. She doused the candle and left the room. The carpets and gleaming lamps in the hallway testified to the inn's quality, far better than that of the inn of the previous day. The quality of patron was better, too, as evidenced by the many curious, suspicious, or outright hostile glances she received as she went downstairs.

Whit was not in the dining room. Those who sat in it hunched over their sausages and chines of mutton, their glasses of wine and bowls of green soup, moodily sawing away at their food and speaking no more than necessary. A peculiar tension hung over the chamber, evidenced by the sideways glances being exchanged, and mutterings like a river on the verge of flooding.

A woman in a server's apron and bearing a tray walked past. Her eyes flicked up and down Zora. Open hostility soured her expression. "Didn't know we let filthy Gypsies in."

"Insult me again," Zora urged softly, "and you'll wake up tomorrow with a gourd for a nose."

The *gorgie's* eyes widened. "That's not possible."

"Are you willing to take that chance?" She waved her ring-covered fingers at the serving woman as though conjuring up a Romani curse.

"No," squeaked the *gorgie*, clapping her hands over her nose.

"I'll be watching you with my third eye, reading your mind, so if you even *think* another insult, I will know. And act." She waved her fingers again, and the serving woman fixed her gaze on the floor.

With a regal nod, Zora glided outside.

As she crossed the torch-lit yard of the inn, she felt it again, that tension and disquiet hovering over the town. She heard it, too—the sound of many voices raised in restless humor, arguments and accusations flung like so much pottery to shatter upon the walls of empathy.

She darted to the side as two ostlers in the yard actually threw punches at one another. Briefly, she debated trying to separate them but decided the safest course of action was to stay out of their fight. In her experience, fistfights never lasted long. Hopefully, the ostlers would burn themselves out faster than they could hurt one another.

She found Whit inside the stables, in the stall that accommodated his horse. He had removed his coat and stood in his shirtsleeves, tacking up the horse to prepare it for anticipated departure. He wanted to leave, and soon. Yet she kept silent, watching him at work, the strength of his body and play of muscles beneath his shirt. Lamplight lined his clean profile in gold.

She shifted, and he turned at the sound.

"I haven't felt the *geminus*'s pull." Whit growled a curse. "It's gone, the bloody vault is gone, and I've nothing. No direction." He looked grim.

She muttered her own curse. Livia was nowhere to be found, and the mad ghost had been their only source of information, jumbled and rambling as it had come. Now she and Whit stumbled in darkness trying to solve a riddle without fully knowing the question.

The ostlers' fight outside grew more heated as someone slammed against the stable door. Whinnying in alarm, Whit's horse tossed its head, but the lead rope tied to an iron ring in the wall kept it from rearing up.

Whit murmured to the animal, soothing it, even as tension hardened his shoulders. "It's been like that, according to taproom gossip. A near riot on Broad Street. Students smashing the windows of coffeehouses—these were commoners and servitors, not noblemen or gentlemen commoners. Half the populace is in the street; the other half is barricaded in their homes."

"I thought the *geminus* was gone."

"Chaos breeds wherever it goes, and even when it has moved on, the turmoil continues." His scowl was bitter—and directed at himself. "Oxford is a powder keg. One spark is all it needs to explode. And wherever the *geminus* goes next, whatever village or town or city, the same thing will happen. That's precisely what it wants. Madness. Literal pandemonium."

She eyed the saddled horse. "When do we leave?"

"Immediately. But I don't bloody know where to go." He slammed his fist into the stall's wooden partition.

The horse snorted in alarm. Zora edged back. It was a large animal, and she knew full well the kind of damage an errant hoof could cause. Whit was a large animal, too, just as unpredictable, and even more dangerous.

"You and the *geminus*, you're bound together somehow."

"Ever since we switched places." His voice was tight. "Except I cannot feel it now."

"The . . . what did you call it . . . bearing compass. The one within you that draws you to wherever the *geminus* may be. What Livia was trying to create with her spell." She held his gaze. "Try that compass now so we can track the *geminus*."

"It isn't here," he said through clenched teeth.

"But it's *somewhere*." At his silence, she pressed, "Don't fight your link to the *geminus*."

He scowled. "If I let it go, give it free rein, it will take over. I'll be lost."

"You won't." But she was not so certain as she pretended.

"And if I hurt you—"

"I can protect myself." She glanced down at her hands. "What I did before, in that garden, that was nothing."

He stalked out of the stall, with Zora close behind him. They faced one another in the main chamber of the stable, the musky smell of horse, leather, and hay all around them.

She moved quickly, drawing Whit's sword from its scabbard. The hiss of metal slid through the stable, cold and purposeful.

His expression tight, he stared at the blade she now held.

"I'm not giving the *geminus* a chance to swing this at me again," she said.

With the tip of his finger, he guided the sword's point upward, making it ready. "Use this if I do *anything* to hurt you."

She prayed it did not come to that, but she nodded. He shut his eyes and exhaled, long and slow. Tension left his long body in a wave. He appeared to reach inside himself, searching.

She watched him, carefully, cautiously. This needed to work, yet she also feared its success.

For several breaths, nothing happened as Whit stood, eyes closed, silent, reaching through unseen space for the bond between himself and his dark half. To Zora, every moment felt a painful eternity. What might happen? Could she truly hurt Whit, if she had to?

A horse kicked the door of its stall. She jumped, almost dropping her weapon. The other horses shifted restlessly, nickering in apprehension.

Whit opened his eyes. He smiled at her.

She secured her grip on the sword, readying to strike.

The *geminus* was back.

For all the darkness within himself, the difference between Whit and the *geminus* was stark—the difference between the night sky and the pitch-black depths of a bottomless chasm.

It took a step toward her. She held the sword higher, pointed at the creature's chest. But it was still *Whit's* chest. His heart beating in his chest.

The *geminus* eyed the sword. "A fine welcome for an old friend." It pressed one of its fingertips to the sharp tip until a trickle of crimson ran down its finger.

"Stop," she said, for the creature wounded Whit as much as itself.

Surprisingly, it did, then wiped its finger down the front of its waistcoat, staining the doeskin with a band of blood. The *geminus* glanced around the stable with a grimace of distaste.

"There's nothing here but animals. Hardly worth my time." Then its gaze returned to Zora, chilling her. "But you, my child, are a delightful prize. My master will be pleased."

"I'll sooner drag this"—she hefted the sword—"across my own throat."

The *geminus* clicked its tongue at the gesture. "Either way, a threat is eliminated."

She seized this bit of information for the advantage it was. "So I am a threat to *Wafodu guero*."

"Are we to play chess now? Strategies and gambits?" The creature shrugged. "Well may you try, but no matter your cleverness, there's truly nothing to you but an ignorant Gypsy girl. Whereas I have my master's unfathomable experience and knowledge." Its smile turned cutting. "The advantage will always belong to me and my master."

It stepped closer, and Zora angled the tip of the sword against its chest, holding it back.

"Tell me where you are," she said.

"In this repulsive stable. Wherever it is."

"Where were you *before*?" she demanded through clenched teeth.

"So you may undo my beautiful work?" Despite the sword's keen top, the *geminus* moved yet closer, its expression cold and hungry. "I rather like it here. Wherever we are. The company is vastly entertaining."

It would not stop at the threat of the sword. She held tight to the hilt, keeping the blade up, feeling the solid resistance of the *geminus*'s chest. Whit's chest. If the creature came any nearer, she would have to either stab it—stab Whit—or flee.

The creature saw her hesitation, and smiled again. It pressed still closer. The sword's cutting tip pierced the doeskin waistcoat and shirt, but the sharp metal hadn't yet punctured the flesh beneath. The *geminus* kept its gaze locked with hers.

Her palms grew damp. In a moment, she would have to do it. Stab the creature. She wanted Whit back from wherever he had gone.

"Whit," she said.

The *geminus* stopped in its advance, its expression hardening into an icy mask.

"Whit," she said again. She had summoned him once

before. He had told her, upon his return, that somehow *she* had brought him back.

Her arms shook, yet she forced her mind free, searching for him like a loosed bird seeking warmer climes before the onset of winter. The strangest sensation: she knew herself to be standing in the inn's stable, holding the *geminus* at bay with a sword, the sounds of agitated horses all around. Yet she was also winging across the darkness, a place that was *felt* rather than seen. He appeared as a gleam in that darkness, something bright and sharp, and she sped toward that brightness, calling his name. *Whit. Whit.*

And then . . . an answer. His voice, formless, soundless, but resonating within her. *Here. Zora, I am here.*

She reached out with an invisible hand. *Return with me.*

It is very dark here. I am lost.

I'll guide you back.

She was suspended in these twin moments. In the stable with the *geminus*. In a veiled landscape with Whit. And she was afraid, but not afraid. For she felt Whit slide his hand into hers, his brightness joined with hers, and they sped back so quickly that her head spun.

Then she was only in the stable. Dizzy, but there. And facing her was Whit.

He glanced down at the sword, a gasp away from piercing his flesh. She shoved it into a nearby hay bale.

Ashen, drawn, he sank to his knees. She did the same, bracing his bowed shoulders when he would have fallen forward. Relief weakened her legs.

He drew a breath, and then another. Gradually, color returned to his cheeks, and his eyes lost their glazed cast. His shoulders straightened. Slowly, his hand came up to touch the hole in his waistcoat. Fury carved his face into something brutal.

"You never hurt me," she said quickly. "It never got the chance."

"The next time," he rasped, "do not hesitate. Not for a moment."

"It wasn't necessary. I brought you back." And she thanked the heavens for it.

"What if you hadn't?"

"But I did."

"If it happens again, I command you to use the saber against me."

She shot to her feet. Her relief turned to fury, both fed by the same river of emotion. "*Command* me? If you think you can order me around like one of your *gorgio* lackeys, then you can go to Hell."

He rose to standing, slower than her, his movements stiff and without his usual grace. "I will never mistake you for a lackey. As for going to Hell"—he lifted his marked shoulder—"that has already been arranged."

"You aren't being dragged off by demons," she countered.

"Not yet." He retrieved his coat and slowly pulled it on.

She was torn between pulling him into her arms and kicking him. Instead, she watched as, with an exhausted groan, he undid the tie binding his queue and dragged his fingers through his hair. Whatever the process for switching places with the *geminus* was like, it had to be grueling. Only veteran soldiers moved as wearily.

Still, with his hair loose about his shoulders, he was everything alluring and dangerous. And the more time she spent in his company, the less she could resist him.

He was not bent on seduction at the moment, drained by his ordeal.

"Come into the inn," she said. "Warm up by the fire and have some wine."

"Wine, I'll take. But I cannot go inside yet." He rubbed his forehead as though it ached. "All those people."

She understood. Quickly, she left the stable and crossed the now-deserted yard to reach the inn. Ignoring the stares from the men in the taproom, she walked up to the counter.

"Wine," she said to the publican. "And quickly." Before the man could object, she twisted one of the coins from her necklace and slid it across the battered counter. The coin was worth far more than a glass of wine, or even the full decanter the publican gave her in exchange. She plucked an empty glass from behind the counter, and, heedless of the gawking taproom patrons, strode back out to the stables.

She found Whit still there, though his hands were braced against the wall and his head was hung low in weariness. He looked up at her approach.

"I'm still not your lackey," she said as she poured him some wine.

"I still don't think of you as one." He took the offered glass and she watched his throat work as he took several deep swallows of wine. "My thanks."

Very strange. She had always hated waiting upon the men of her band, fetching them food or drink or tobacco for their pipes. Her resentment had not lifted during her brief time as a married woman—she had still brought and carried, only she had added a husband to her duties. The men sat around the fire, laughing, telling stories, while the females attended to them, refilling cups, bringing plates of roast mutton. It smacked of male laziness, and a belief that men's leisure held greater value than women's work.

Her feelings had not changed in the intervening years. She did not want to be a man's servant. Yet what she just did for Whit felt very different. It wasn't serving; it was balance. He saw to her, protected her, and she did the same for him. A rare equality. And as she watched him revive with a glass of wine that *she* had provided, an unfamiliar tenderness unfurled within her, as unexpected as meadowsweet growing in a barren plain.

"I felt it." Hard satisfaction honed his voice, weary as it was. "The *geminus*. North of here."

Having direction and a goal pleased her. She wanted to hurt the *geminus*, as it hurt so many others—especially Whit. "We'll lay a trap for the whoreson. Force it to reveal the location of its vault."

"Force. That implies some level of violence."

"It does."

His brow rose, either from her language or from her eagerness to make the *geminus* suffer. "On whose account are you so bloodthirsty?"

"Does it matter, when the results are the same?"

He studied the bottom of his glass, swirling the film of wine collected there. "I wonder now if there is any shade but gray."

"I am Grey," she said.

"Neither of us would have survived this long if you weren't."

It was an unusual compliment, yet it pleased her. She did not think any man in her band would ever have praised her for her ferocity.

"An interrogation might not be required," he noted. "The creature *is* the vault. When I became the *geminus*, I saw the chamber again. Behind a different door."

She tried to make sense of this, as though he had given her one of the wrought-iron puzzles blacksmiths sold for extra coin.

"Wherever the creature is," he continued, gaining strength, "that's where we find the vault. Any door it wants—the door to a bedchamber, a granary, even a stable—whichever it picks leads to the vault of souls."

"Opened only by the *geminus*." What Whit proposed made a contrary kind of sense, which seemed exactly in keeping with how *Wafodu guero*'s minions might operate. She retrieved the glass from him and filled it, then took her own drink. Just as she had hoped, the wine helped steady her and sharpen her thoughts.

She glanced at Whit. He seemed deeply intrigued by the sight of her licking wine from her lips.

"Getting the *geminus* to open it for us," she said. "That's the trick."

His slow smile intoxicated her far more than wine

ever could. "If anyone has a storehouse of tricks, it will be a gambler and a Gypsy."

In the public dining chamber, they bolted a hasty supper of bread, cold beef, and wedges of pale, buttery cheese, having little time for private dining rooms. Between Whit's torn, bloody clothing and Zora being Romani, the other patrons gave them wide berth. She did not mind. At the least, it gave Whit some respite from the press of voices.

Whit frowned as the serving woman saw Zora and started. The tower of empty plates the *gorgie* carried toppled to the floor.

"Sorry, my lord." The *gorgie* shot Zora a panicked glance from beneath her lashes. She gathered the fallen plates before scuttling off to the kitchen.

With their meal concluded, she and Whit went to gather their belongings. He left their room to settle their account. A few moments later, she also headed back down and felt a thrill of unease when she could not find him waiting for her. He was not in the dining room, nor his room, nor the stables.

The beginnings of panic curled around her spine as she stood outside in the yard. The *geminus* might have returned, or sent demons to attack. But there were no signs of a fight—not of the demonic variety—and she had heard nothing. Where was he?

She strained her ears for something, some clue. Behind her, someone opened a window to the taproom, letting out the thick smell of smoke and beer. The clattering sound of dice rolling across a floor caught her attention. Turning, she saw men crouched in a circle on the floor of the taproom. Dicing. Their eager eyes fixed on the little wooden pieces tumbling over dusty planks. From the sound of their shouts, the game was hazard.

And Whit hovered over them, a tall, sinister shadow. He looked like a wolf about to leap into a pen of goats. Nothing would be left but blood and bones.

She darted inside. Whit did not notice her standing beside him, no matter the number of times she said his name.

The men on the floor looked up, their hands arrested in the middle of their game. They eyed her with curiosity, but it was Whit who made them start in their buckled shoes.

"We've a journey ahead of us." Urgency tightened her voice.

"One round," he answered in a monotone. All that mattered were the dice. "I'll play one round."

She couldn't tell if the hunger in his expression came from his connection to the *geminus*, or his own need for gambling. It did not matter. One round would inevitably lead to another, and another, until he would find himself so deep in the maze he could not find his way out.

A man saw the signet ring on Whit's finger, and the fine quality of his clothes, despite their worn state. Used to reading the tiny expressions that flitted across faces, Zora saw the man assess Whit, no doubt thinking to himself, *Rich pigeon ready to be plucked.* "Join us, my lord?"

These poor bastards, she thought. *They have no idea what danger threatens them.*

Before Whit could lower to a crouch, she bent down and scooped up the dice. She strode to the fire and made a show of casting the dice into the flames, but, in truth, all she threw were ashes. The dice had burned to nothing in her hand.

Shouts of displeasure and anger rose up from the men. She ignored them, her gaze fixed solely on Whit. He looked thunderous.

Boots heavy on the floor, he stalked toward her. She forced herself to remain where she stood, though her every instinct screamed for her to run. His hand gripped her wrist, iron tight, and he dragged her from the taproom. Cheers came from the men.

She tried to pull away, but his strength far surpassed hers, and all she accomplished was having her arm ache. The fire she kept within roiled through her, concentrating in her wrist. Burning him. Forcing him to release her. Yet he did not react to the burn at all and kept his grip tight around her.

He strode from the inn, hauling her behind him. She wondered if she had, at last, pushed him to his breaking point, if the need to gamble and the influence of the *geminus* trumped everything—including her.

They headed toward the stables. "Let go," she said.

He swung around so quickly, she slammed into the hard wall of his chest, her hand trapped between them. His grip did not loosen, but his hot gaze moved over her face as if he were seeing it anew, as if, up to that moment, she had been a stranger to him, or disguised, and the disguise had fallen away and he recognized her at last.

Finally, he released her. Stared down at his burned hand, then up at her.

She stared back. The fevered glaze faded from his eyes.

"Solace or torment." He tugged off the linen stock encircling his neck and wrapped it around his hand. "I cannot decide which you are."

She checked to make sure the makeshift dressing was secure. "My family would say I'm your punishment."

"God knows I deserve it. Just the same"—he flicked his gaze to her mouth—"it is a sweet penance."

She tilted her head back as she considered his mouth, the shape of his lips. He had kissed her . . . when? Yesterday? Years ago? Either was too long to go without the taste of him—this nobleman, this gambler.

He reached out, stroked his thumb where her pulse fluttered in her wrist and her skin was sensitive. A contrast from how he had grabbed her roughly just moments ago. Now he plied her with a surprisingly gentle caress, the pad of his thumb along her wrist, for all the clawing and grappling they did with one another. This touch revealed more than incendiary lust. If she had to name the feeling, she might call it . . . affection.

Something loosened within her as he stroked her wrist, a knot of vines around her heart releasing its stranglehold.

Male voices echoed in the street. She thought nothing of them, but Whit's thumb stopped moving.

He turned his head, listening, his brows drawn down. The voices came nearer, as did the sounds of horses on the cobblestones. A group of men traveling together, by the sound of it, approaching the inn. Nightfall and scattered torchlight hid their appearance. Yet, as they drew closer, something about their voices sounded familiar to her, though she could not place them.

Whit could. He growled a curse. Keeping his eye toward the street, he pulled her toward the stables. His free hand went to his sword.

They reached only halfway to the stables when the men rode into the yard. Light from the taproom spilled out, revealing the travelers on horseback. Mutual recognition stunned Whit and Zora as well as the men. For a moment, they stared at one another.

"Hellraisers," Whit said, his voice even.

"Whit." The dark one with the scar along his neck dismounted. He began to stride toward them, and the flare of his long black coat, with its many capes and high collar, made him resemble a great raven.

The Rom feared ravens. Zora let her fire magic thread into her hands, keeping it ready should she need it.

"No farther, Bram." Whit tightened his grip on the pommel of his sword.

Bram stopped in his tracks, his gaze never leaving Whit's face.

One by one, the other men swung down from their saddles. They, too, stared at Whit, their expressions as tense as bowstrings.

Whit broke the silence first. "Mr. Holliday has you acting as errand boys?"

The youngest of the men, a lean blond man with shrewd eyes, answered. "No errands. We used our gifts to find you, at our own behest. It's friendship that had us seek you out."

"After everything, Leo, you still consider us friends?"

"Always," came the immediate reply.

"It isn't too late," said the third man. He had a pleasant

face, and Zora remembered how readily he had laughed when he had visited the camp. "The way to London is straight and fast. All of us may return, take up exactly as we had been before."

"*Better* than we were before," said Bram. "We've gifts now. Anything is possible."

"Come back," the pleasant-faced man urged, "and there will be no harm to any of us."

Her stomach clenched as she glanced at Whit. Would he accept his friends' offer? Would he slip back into that world of darkness and vice?

"Whit," she whispered so softly only he could hear.

His gaze found hers.

Stay with me, her eyes said.

A moment passed. A lifetime. She could not breathe.

He turned back to his friends. Though his expression did not change, his gambler's mask in place, she knew him now and could read the smallest change in the set of his mouth and the lines around his eyes.

She did not exhale in relief, but she wanted to. His friends' temptation left him unmoved.

"No harm?" he repeated. "Edmund, you have a mark somewhere on you. A mark of flames."

The answer came when Edmund gingerly rubbed his thigh.

"If we bear such marks," said the fourth man, narrow faced and thin, "they mean nothing in exchange for what we have received. The ear of the Prime Minister—it's mine. The Chancellor of the Exchequer, too. Leo reaps benefits, as do Edmund and Bram."

The men all nodded, and Zora felt sick dread slithering in her stomach. *Wafodu guero*'s influence had snared them, and nobody looked eager to be free. If what the Devil offered them held as much dark allure as it did for Whit, then only the purest of men could refuse. Whit's friends were far from pure.

"Political influence is not worth your eternal soul, John."

Whit looked at each man, those who had once been his friends. "None of it is worth the price."

"Is that what *she* has told you?" asked John. "The thieving Gypsy."

Before Zora could fire back a retort, Whit spoke. "I trust Zora now as much as I once trusted you."

The men looked stunned by this statement, especially Bram, who grimaced as if Whit had slid a blade between his ribs.

"There's more at stake than your own desires," Zora said. "You've seen it, riding into town. The destruction, the madness."

"Perhaps the fellows have run wild," murmured Edmund. "A common occurrence."

"Not on this scale," Whit countered. "And it's not only the students. All of Oxford runs wild. Only the slightest provocation and it descends into complete chaos. Imagine that chaos spreading like a pestilence. The smallest village all the way to London. Traveling beyond England's shores. Riot, devastation and ruin."

"Hell on earth," said Zora. "Unless you turn from the Devil."

Bram scowled, his sharp features turning severe. "You sound like that mad Roman ghost."

Zora straightened. "You've seen her? Livia?"

"Damn spirit harasses me," Bram muttered. "The others, too. Always speaking in broken riddles, but the message is clear enough. A shame, too. She'd be a beautiful woman . . . if she wasn't demented."

"And dead," added Leo.

"Deranged she may be," said Whit, "but she is trying to help."

Bram's scowl deepened, shifting toward a menacing snarl. "It isn't helpful. It's bloody maddening." He took a step toward Zora and Whit. "End this nonsense. Return with us, back to London."

"No going back." Sorrow edged Whit's voice, but it

quickly hardened. "And if you come any closer, this saber comes out of its scabbard."

Rather than cooling Bram's temper, Whit's threat only fueled it. His mouth twisted, and shadows crept into his eyes. "Unsheathe it, then."

Whit did not move.

His stillness seemed to goad Bram. "Do it, Whit. Or do you gamble only with dice and cards, like a coward?"

Zora felt the tension within Whit, saw his jaw tighten and his fists clench. She knew some of *gorgio* ways, enough to understand that Bram's insult demanded retribution. Yet Whit battled this demand, for the sake of tattered friendship.

Seeing that his taunts did not work, Bram growled. From beneath his overcoat, he drew a sword. Torchlight licked along the blade.

Zora reached for her fire magic, and flames curled over the fingers of her free hand.

"You want me to fight you?" Whit could not keep the disbelief from his words.

Bram smiled unpleasantly as he brandished his sword. "I not only want it, I insist."

Chapter 13

The directive built inside Whit's brain, in his muscles. He did not want to fight Bram, nor any of the Hellraisers, though he had prepared himself for the possibility. If he had to, if it meant protecting Zora, he would let steel ring against steel. As corrupted as his friends had become, however, he had no desire to hurt them.

But with Bram's words, Whit's choice dissolved. Dimly, he understood that it was Mr. Holliday's gift that forced Whit to comply. Bram could persuade anyone to do anything. And what his old friend wanted from Whit was a fight.

"You may control the *what*," Whit said, drawing his saber, "but not the *how*." He positioned himself between Zora and the others, shielding her, and advanced in a vigilant side step.

Bram's smile gleamed like wolf's teeth as he also advanced. "Nothing by half measures for me. Friend or enemy—one or the other, but nothing in between."

Whit and Bram drew closer. More steel hissed as John and Edmund drew their swords. Leo held a pistol. Their faces were hard, distant, so different from the close companions he had known. Mr. Holliday had them now, so they were no more than automata with familiar faces powered by diabolical machinery.

He felt more than saw Zora trying to edge around him,

but he had to protect her. No telling what any of the men might do now that Whit no longer knew them. The *geminus* wanted her eliminated, and the Hellraisers might be all too happy to oblige.

Bram attacked first. His rapier flashed, quick and deadly. Whit countered the blows, though his heavier saber hadn't a rapier's speed. He and Bram used to practice their fencing together in an academy near Fleet Street. They wore no padding now, no protective masks. They came together in a fierce clash of blade to blade, the force of the blows reverberating up Whit's arm.

He blocked a strike—barely. Though Whit practiced his swordsmanship like any nobleman, Bram had the advantage. He had been a soldier, and a damn good one. The Indian who had given Bram the scar tracing down his neck had not lived long after bestowing the souvenir.

Bram moved with swift precision, striking, parrying. "I always beat you at the academy," he said as he sidestepped Whit's swing.

"This isn't the academy," Whit answered.

"Masks are off now."

Whit did not know what was the disguise—the friend with whom he had shared every confidence, or the vicious man giving free rein to his taste for blood. Long had Whit suspected that beneath Bram's licentious façade was a dark core of brutality, barely contained. At that moment, he had his answer.

"Back away, Whit," Zora urged, her hands wreathed with flame. "I can't get a decent shot when you're so close to him."

But Bram's attack came on relentlessly, leaving no room for even the slightest strategic retreat.

Out of the corner of Whit's eye, he saw movement, almost distracting him. The other Hellraisers moved in. It would be four against one in a moment. John and Edmund hadn't Bram's skill with a sword, but Whit could not hold back all of them. Leo might not fire his pistol, but he could box like a born brawler. Leaving Whit with exceedingly unpleasant odds.

Odds. Damn him, he *did* have a skill Bram did not.

When Bram moved to strike, Whit blocked the blow, then redoubled the strength of his own hits. Bram possessed speed and skill, but his lighter rapier could not hold up under attacks from the heavy saber. Whit reached into the interlaced fibers of probability, probing its configuration until he found what he sought. Minute weaknesses in the rapier's blade. He struck hard at the steel.

The sound of metal snapping rang through the yard. At the same time, Leo moved to skirt around Bram. Leo stopped his intended assault, biting out a curse as five inches of broken steel pierced his shoulder. Blood welled, a black stain on his fawn coat. He fell back, swearing and clutching his wound.

Bram stared at his broken rapier. The sight stoked his anger, and he launched into another volley of attacks. Whit barely had enough speed to counter. He found himself retreating, struggling to hold Bram at a distance. He delved back into the maze of chance, and found another weakness. A further hard strike broke off over a foot from Bram's rapier. John and Edmund dodged the flying steel, and it lodged into the wall of a town house across the street.

Though Bram's sword had been reduced, he still fought well, using it like a cutlass. He came in closer for his offensive. The fire of bloodlust gleamed in his eyes. He feinted. Whit moved to block but felt a blaze of pain as the shortened rapier gouged his side, just beneath his ribs.

They circled one another until Bram stood in front of the inn and Whit had his back to the Hellraisers.

Out of his peripheral vision, he saw John and Edmund taking advantage of their opening, edging nearer.

A burst of light flared. "Back," Zora commanded, her hands aglow. "Or I will burn you where you stand."

The Hellraisers stopped their advance. Whit would thank her later, but he still had to contend with Bram. Having scored first blood, Bram fought harder.

He and Whit crossed blades, grappling for the upper

hand, swords locked just above the cross-guards. Both men bared their teeth, grimacing, as they struggled for mastery. Whit was strong, but so was Bram. They planted their feet, leaning into each other, every muscle tensed.

Whit delved back into the intricate patterns of probability swirling around them. They shifted and transformed at his urging, the reticulum of probability his to command. All it took were slight adjustments, and chance lined up in precise order. *Yes.*

With a surge of energy, he threw his fist. He smashed the saber's thick hand guard into Bram's jaw. The blow snapped Bram's head back, dazing him. It would take more than a hard punch to the chin to lay him out, but the force of the blow did cause him to readjust his footing. Bram took a minute step back. As he did, the heel of his boot caught on a loose cobblestone. His balance faltered, and he slipped backward.

He fell against the front wall of the inn, swearing roughly. Seeking equilibrium, his arms flew out, and his left hand knocked into a lamp mounted on the wall. The lamp tumbled down. Its glass shattered on the stones, and flame touched a scattering of hay. The tinder caught immediately, creating a tiny blaze.

Then the fire was everywhere, roaring up in a wall. The four Hellraisers' panicked horses ran off. Whit glanced over his shoulder and smiled. Zora stood beside him. She had flung back her cloak, and, with hands outstretched, she guided the flames, creating a barrier of fire encircling the Hellraisers. Her lovely face was fierce, unrelenting. With her hands wreathed in fire, and fire reflected in her dark eyes, she was an avenging goddess, and nothing had ever been so beautiful.

"Call off your witch!" John shouted above the blaze.

"No one controls her," Whit answered.

He cast a quick look toward the inn. Faces crowded the windows. With wide, disbelieving eyes, people watched the spectacle as firelight danced on the glass. Witches had not been burned in England for thirty years, but he did not want today to see the practice resume. It would not take much urging for the citizens of Oxford, having seen their town descend into chaos, to blame Zora.

One hand still holding his saber, he held the other out to her.

She glanced between him and Bram, who was pinned and held back by the wall of fire. An unspoken question. Whit reached into himself and found that Bram's command no longer bound him. The hit to the jaw and subsequent fall must have broken the magical directive. Whit did not have to fight Bram any longer.

"We leave this place. Now."

The flames around her hands disappeared, though the fire continued to blaze and imprison Edmund, Leo, Bram, and John. She took hold of Whit's hand. Together, they ran into the stables. It took some doing to mount the frightened horses, but they managed the task.

Whit's side throbbed, and blood dampened his skin. He ignored the pain and urged his horse out of the stable. Zora did the same, as fleet as lightning, her cloak billowing behind her.

For a brief moment, they paused, taking in the scene. Leo, wounded. Bram, staggering and snarling as he rose. John and Edmund, shielding their eyes from smoke. The strange, hellish image of fire encircling his erstwhile friends, while onlookers within the inn stared back, pale and aghast.

With a wave of Zora's hand, the flames guttered, then died. She flicked her gaze toward the inn and then the stables. He grasped her meaning. The fire could not be allowed to spread, could not touch any buildings, lest innocents found themselves caught in an inferno. Only a diversion had been needed, not a holocaust.

Leo could not run, and the other Hellraisers could only follow on foot.

Whit refused to allow them the possibility of pursuit. He and Zora shared a glance. They set heels to their horses' flanks and rode hard into the street. Shouts rang out behind

them, but the voices soon faded. The havoc in the streets of
Oxford matched Whit's heart. If there had been any possibility of reconciliation with his friends, it was now gone. A
line of fire had been drawn. On one side stood the Hellraisers. On the other stood Whit.

But he was not alone. Zora was with him. As they crossed
Folly Bridge, he felt her bright, fierce presence beside him,
and the shadow of loss dimmed in her brilliance.

"We were at school together."

Zora glanced up from where she knelt beside a stream, a
strip of muslin dangling from her hand.

"Winchester," said Whit. He sat upon a fallen log, his legs
outstretched to relieve the ache from hours in the saddle.
Nearby, the horses dipped their heads to the ground, crop-
ping grasses and taking their deserved rest. Whit blessed the
need both he and John had to buy only the finest of everything, including horseflesh. Any other lesser animals would
have collapsed into quivering meat after such a rigorous,
taxing pace.

Zora dipped the muslin into the water. A quiet, intimate
sound. She gracefully rose and walked to him. He followed
her movements as if the sight of her could somehow prevent
his slide into greater darkness.

She perched beside him, and he caught her scent of night,
wind and smoke. As he inhaled, she motioned for him to
remove his coat, waistcoat, and shirt.

He obliged, and did not miss the way her gaze roamed
over his bared arms and torso. Even in this moonlit meadow,
he saw and felt her hungry perusal. Her gaze lingered on the
hollow of his throat, where her ring rested. He still wore it.
A low throb moved through his body, settling in his groin
with warm expectation. He allowed himself to sink into the
need, a distraction from the injuries riddling his body.

"Bram and I." He watched as she dabbed gently at the
wound beneath his ribs. The cold water made him hiss, but

he eased his breathing. "I'd been there for two years when he arrived. Eton and Harrow had already thrown him out." He smiled. "Wild, he was. Even then."

"And you were great friends right away." The muslin in her hand darkened as it swabbed away crusts of blood. Bram's rapier had made that wound. It was deep enough to leave a scar.

Yet it could have been much worse. Bram's skill with a blade could not be matched by any of the professional maestros in London. Not for the first time in the past few hours, Whit wondered if Bram had truly fought as hard and ruthlessly as he could.

"The first time we met, I teased him about his shoes. One of the buckles was loose, and it jingled when he walked, so I called him a cow. A cow in the field. He punched me in the stomach. Whenever we saw each other—in the refectory, at lessons, on the football pitch—we beat each other bloody. A month that went on."

"Something changed." She peered closer at the wound, her breath feathering over him.

He forced his concentration on the stream rather than her head bent low, or her braided hair brushing the tops of his thighs. "There was another boy, a liar and bully. Bram and I beat *him* bloody one day. And then we were friends."

Her chuckle curled over the flesh of his abdomen. "Nothing strengthens friendship like a shared beating."

"After that, we were inseparable. But when I went to university, he bought a commission. Saw each other often enough when he had leave. Cutting a swath through the assemblies of London—a young earl and an officer in His Majesty's Army."

"What *gorgie* could resist?"

Few did, but he was not much inclined to tell her that. "He was different back then. So was I. That's the callowness of youth and privilege. He went to the Colonies to fight the French, and came back . . . changed. Wilder than ever. I couldn't even attempt to keep up with him. He seldom talked about what happened over there. It left him profoundly altered. Almost . . . broken. It . . . hurt to see."

"Did you ever speak to him of your concerns?"

He looked at her, raising his brows. "Have you no knowledge of men?"

Her smile was rueful, and she dipped her head in acknowledgment. "Despite your silence, you stayed friends." Satisfied with the cleanliness of the wound, she reached for a broad leaf. A grassy, herbaceous scent rose up, slightly astringent, as she dabbed a green paste over the injury. Saint John's wort, she had said as she had gathered the plants and ground them into a salve.

It was a double sensation: the stinging of the wound, and the gentle press of her fingers. Yet that was how it played out between them, in the intermingling of pain and pleasure. He enjoyed the edge. Everything else seemed too soft now, too pale and enfeebled.

"I met John and Edmund at university, and Leo much later, in London. If there were founding members of the Hellraisers, they would be Bram and me."

"Prestigious." She wrapped more strips of muslin over the wound, her movements deft and practiced.

He scoffed. "A dubious distinction. Yet it's who we are." H quickly corrected, "*Were*. Now . . ."

She tucked in the ends of the muslin to secure the dressing. Satisfied, she looked up and held his gaze with her own. In the darkness, nothing possessed the depth of her eyes, black and as rich as velvet. "Now you must learn yourself all over again."

He found that he could not hold her gaze, and his own moved restlessly over the moon-glazed field, touching briefly on the mercury gleam of the stream, the slivers of grass ruffling in the cold breeze—anything to distract him from the truth he now faced. None of it worked.

In a kind of daze, he spoke. "I keep seeing them, the burning ruins of my life. Whole edifices charred and collapsing in the wake of my entanglement with Mr. Holliday." Shaking his head, he amended, "No, that's not entirely true. There had been foundations, but the structures themselves were built of nothing more than diversion and dissipation. Hardly the sturdy materials in which one could take shelter. If I now stand upon a scorched wasteland, I have only to blame the architect: myself."

Ahead lay shadows and yet more uncertainty. He had only two forces guiding him: the black chains binding him to the *geminus*, and Zora.

Bram had been his closest friend. Yet, for all their shared experiences, for all the long nights they had spent with cigars and brandy in hand, speaking of everything and nothing, not once had Whit confided in Bram as he now did in Zora.

He was a gambler. He kept everything close, revealed nothing of himself, by either design or habit. Yet, when he was with this woman, words came from him as if from a cask finally tapped. The wine within had turned acrid and bitter, and it needed out.

Instinct guided him. If there was anyone who walked this blighted earth to whom he could reveal himself, who could see his weaknesses and doubts without using them against him, that person was she.

"I've spent my life doing exactly as I pleased. Hardly a word of contradiction spoken against me."

"Until you met me," she said.

He discovered he was smiling. He looked down at the wound beneath his ribs, the bandages pale against his skin. "Broken he may be," he murmured, his smile fading, "but I envy Bram. He went to war, proved himself."

"You aren't going to fail," said Zora, heated. "*We* aren't." Hers was a spirit that could not be crushed or extinguished. Stronger than fire.

Yet she needed to understand that nothing was certain, especially where he was concerned. "Shall I tell you stories? The kind told around a campfire? Stories where the handsome prince defeats the wicked beast."

"I have seen those plays, as true as the pasteboard dragon."

"Gambler I may be, but I don't lie. At the end of this, there is no happy ending." His words were brutal, yet he knew that their brutality did not target her. He had to remind himself that as heroes in tales went he would never be what was required. Heroes did not have monstrous hungers clawing them from the inside out. They had noble hearts, pure intentions. He possessed neither.

The flames marking his skin twisted their way down to just above his wrist. An inexorable devouring. How long did he have left before they covered him entirely?

She studied the hand-shaped burn on his shoulder. Softly, she traced its perimeter. The pain of it branched out like thick vines of heat, filling him with fire-laced pleasure.

"Every tale changes with each telling." She blew lightly over his singed flesh, cooling him. "You can't foresee how this will end."

She dabbed more of the slick and aromatic herbal paste upon his shoulder, then applied it upon his injured hand. She took more fabric and wound it around his shoulder, covering the burn and the paste, and wrapped his hand, as well. Each brush of her fingers jolted through him.

He shoved his clothing back on but could not find the wherewithal to redo the lacings and buttons. As he stood, his waistcoat and coat gaped. His open shirt revealed his chest, his stomach. A man undone. He had nothing to hide behind, not his wealth, not his title, and certainly not his deeds.

"You deserve better."

"I think we deserve each other." She smiled up at him.

His laugh felt hard in his throat. "So we are both being punished."

She shot to her feet, and her lush mouth was tight with anger. "You set too low a value on yourself. *This* is the time we prove ourselves. *This* is when we show who we are. You say your life is in ruins? Then rebuild it. However you want. Stone by stone. Brick by brick." She laid her palm across his jaw, and her touch was steady and sure. "You're strong enough."

All he could do was stare at her in wonder. He had bared himself to her in many ways, trusted her as he'd never trusted another. He had gambled the most valuable stake he had ever pledged. Not money or possessions, but the core of himself.

In games of chance, someone won, and someone lost. One player had everything, and the other walked away with nothing.

Not this time. He had taken his biggest risk, and both he and Zora were all the richer for it.

Lights from the assembly hall spilled out onto the walkways. Inside, townsfolk danced to the music made by fiddle and viol. Local gentry, landowners, prosperous shopkeepers, the parson. The town was small, yet sizeable enough to support its own elite. In London, such folk would hardly get past the front door of the humblest aristocratic gathering. But the world did not revolve around London—shocking as the idea might seem.

Whit and Zora rode past the assembly hall, watching the patterns made by the dancers. Circles and lines. Back and forth. The music was merry. The people were not. All of them wore tight, distant expressions. They clasped each others' hands overlong, or barely touched. Their eyes spoke of mistrust, caution, fear. None of them wanted to be there, sweating beneath their powder and finery, chandeliers dripping wax upon their self-dressed hair. A girl wearing yellow watered silk cried in the corner, yet no one noticed, no one cared. Those men who did not dance paced up and down the length of the hall eyeing one another mistrustfully.

"A wonder any of them bothered to come," murmured Zora.

"They seem . . . compelled." Pushed by invisible hands, tugged on by unseen strings, like toys or marionettes.

Much like himself, following the *geminus*. The creature's presence in this town filmed the cobbled roads, gathered in the oily puddles, and clung to the mistrustful faces of the townsfolk. In a town where the greatest unrest came from squabbles over who sat in which pew on Sunday, a deep, cancerous anger now ate at its soul.

They had no direction but the dark binds around Whit's heart. He did act as their bearing compass, leading them down roads, through towns and villages, following what he could of *geminus*'s course. Which wasn't a course at all. The damned thing didn't travel as humans did, upon roads, linearly moving from here to there. It appeared and disappeared at will, alighting like some damned predatory bird.

Wherever they rode, evidence of the creature blighted the landscape. Broken windows, raised voices, angry throngs massing in streets and squares regardless of the hour, or, as it was here, an assembly on the verge of collapsing into diseased chaos.

Whit had investigated each town, but he knew with a growing instinct that the *geminus* remained always ahead of them. It *had* been in this town, that much was certain.

"The *geminus* is gone," he clipped as they rode away from the assembly hall.

She had her own impressive vocabulary of curse words, most of them in the Gypsy tongue, and she used them now. He knew the words were low and vulgar, and yet, in spite of, or perhaps *because of* that, his blood heated. No one would ever confuse her with one of the pastel silk–wearing girls who haunted the corners of assembly halls.

"It leaves this . . . coating . . . in the air," he said when she had run through her litany of Gypsy oaths. "Like ash after a fire."

"We need to see what *will* burn, not what *has* burned." She glanced at the darkened windows around them and had to wonder, just as he did, if more shadowed shapes lurked just on the other side of the shutters.

He guided his horse close to hers, then pushed up the cuff of his coat and shirt, revealing his hand. Her gaze widened. The flame markings covered his hand, trailing up his fingers, and curving around to snake across his palm. The marks obscured the lines on his palm, making them impossible to read. Only hours before, his hand had been bare of everything but his rings.

"The thing that continues to burn is *me*."

The rest of the night's journey proved fruitless.

He surveyed the latest village, where a group of men were too busy accusing one another of offenses both real and imaginary to notice Whit and Zora slowly riding past. On a nearby hill, a farm outbuilding burned. The predawn sky glowed red.

It must stop. It had to stop. He submerged himself in the dark, sharp greed coiled around his heart, followed it. Sentient to nothing else, yet feeling the edges of danger on every side, and the tendrils of flame that grew over his body, claiming him.

Something pulled at his awareness: a buried memory rising up like a ghoul.

He looked about him, turning in the saddle. The sun had cleared the eastern horizon, revealing that the land had grown rockier, sharply undulating. The bent humps of limestone hills rose up, with the road being little more than an attempt to scratch a path between mountains, and dawn light could not penetrate the shadowy dales.

"I know this place. There." He pointed to a peak half a mile away. "It marks the southernmost boundary of Whitney holdings."

"Derbyshire." She gazed at the rolling hills, dotted with gorse and ash.

A thrush burst from the hawthorn scrub in a tiny explosion of wing beats. The bird darted away, until it disappeared into a stand of alders atop a hill.

Whit's heart beat as fast as the bird's wings. Chill sweat filmed his back. "My family's estate." The *geminus* had been here. What did it want? What would it take from him on his ancestral lands?

He urged his tired horse into a trot. They reached the crest of the peak, affording them a view of the hills, faded to paleness with the advance of autumn. Crofts huddled in the vales, and sheep formed white specks as they grazed. In the still of early morning, their bleats carried all the way to Whit and Zora.

After the chaos they had encountered over the past few days, everything seemed remarkably peaceful. But Whit wasn't comforted. He felt the echo of the creature's presence like burning ice.

"Whitston Hall is that pile of stone by the lake."

She stood up in her stirrups to get a better look, then sat back down on the saddle. "Maybe someone there has seen the *geminus*."

"There's only the steward in residence, and a skeleton staff. No one else. I'm seldom here."

"Is it here now, the *geminus*?"

He reached through the dark haze, searching. "I can't feel its presence," he said after a moment. "Not anywhere. But I do know that it has been here. And the Devil only knows what destruction it has wreaked."

Chapter 14

They could not urge their weary horses to go any faster than a walk. Whit had no idea what they would find once they reached Whitston, and apprehension gnawed at him in relentless, slow bites.

Unanticipated memories sifted into his mind the closer they came to Whitston. Playing knights with his brother, Michael, on the heather-laced hills. Laying Michael to rest in the funerary chapel after the fever took him. Returning to the chapel to entomb his mother, and then his father. His sister, Sarah, weeping into an embroidered handkerchief. Walking back from the chapel, hat in hand, as his father's man of business explained that the title belonged to him, and all the privileges and responsibilities that came with being an earl.

He had accepted the privileges, but not much of the responsibility. He'd seen Sarah married, and well, with a substantial dowry. She'd born four children, three of them still living. The last he had heard, she was increasing again. So her marriage turned out as well as anyone could hope—though he supposed he was the last person she would confide in. In one of her more recent letters, she upbraided him for his wild living, his life at the gaming tables.

Was their family's home now a ruin? The agonizing, slow

pace of the horses would not allow him to know, not soon enough.

Wearily, Whit and Zora's horses plodded up the winding lane leading to the Hall. He tried to distract himself by studying the lands. The pastures and hills looked well cared for, and the farmers he passed raised their hats in respectful greeting. The laborers stared at him with wary awe—several of them did not know who he was, until informed by others—yet they had robust health, full cheeks rather than gaunt. Some comfort there, knowing his tenants prospered, even in the shade of his benign neglect. He had Mr. Reynolds, his steward, to thank for their prosperity. His correspondence about the estate came regularly, and when Whit bothered to read it, what he found bespoke careful stewardship.

The farmers stared more guardedly at Zora. As always, a Gypsy attracted mistrust. Yet more than a few of the laborers looked at her with something else besides suspicion: admiration. She sat in the saddle, straight and proud, dark, windblown hair coming loose from its braid, unconcerned by the attention she attracted. There was no denying her exotic beauty.

One young, hale man leaned upon his scythe and gazed at her with open desire. He tried to catch her eye, and puffed out his chest to draw her attention.

Thick, pungent rage poured through Whit.

Mine.

He wanted to leap off his horse and beat the man. He would not even use the scythe, but wanted the pleasure of the swain's blood on his hands rather than a blade.

Mine.

If he could, he would forbid the sun from shining upon her, so that he and he alone could have the pleasure of seeing her.

Tension knotted his shoulders, his body. It must be the *geminus*'s influence, this black, possessive fury. He had to keep tight restraint on himself. The effort singed him from the inside out, making him ache even more than days and days in the saddle.

Past the outlying fields, he and Zora rounded a bend and emerged from a copse of birch trees. Zora audibly gasped.

"That *can't* belong to you," she said.

"It belongs to the current Earl of Whitney. For now, the earl is me." And if he produced no male offspring, one of Sarah's sons would assume the title, the lands, and everything else.

Given Whit's chances of surviving the near future, it seemed more and more likely that one of his nephews would one day be known as Lord Whitney. At least he could see that no external damage had been done to the Hall.

"You cannot live there alone," Zora said.

"I hardly live there at all." He didn't know how many servants were in residence during his long absences. Half a dozen? A dozen? Mr. Reynolds saw to those details.

Whit searched for the *geminus*'s presence. Nothing. It hadn't been here. Gratitude flooded him.

"It didn't reach the Hall," he said.

Zora exhaled, mirroring his relief.

The original Whitston Hall had earned its name, built three centuries earlier of local pale limestone. As a child, Whit had played in the grass-covered remains just behind the main house. In the aftermath of the Restoration, his great-grandfather had razed the old Hall and built a new one of brick, with an abundance of modern sash windows that testified to the title's wealth. The structure was perfectly symmetrical, consisting of two identical wings connected by a central hall. A balustrade ran the perimeter of the roof, and a cupola stood at the very top.

"I used to pretend I was a sea captain," he said, pointing to the dome. "I'd stand at the windows of the cupola and imagine the hills to be waves, and the house was my ship."

Zora nodded, smiling a little, but did not speak.

As they rode up the circular drive leading to the main

entrance, Whit took a shallow pleasure in seeing the look of wonderment on her face. He admitted it to himself: he preened. Whitston *was* his, a physical embodiment of his affluence and prestige. She knew him as a gambler and had seen his home in London. But Whitston stood as a testament to his privilege, generations of his family firmly entrenched as one of England's most esteemed. Even if the latest scion was a gambler whose soul belonged to the Devil.

The thought brought him back to full alertness. They had been granted a temporary reprieve, but the *geminus* would appear again. He would have to find and destroy it.

Before he and Zora brought their horses to a stop in front of the house, the large double doors opened and a man in a dark brown coat, buff breeches, and gray wig jogged down the wide stairs.

"My lord," he panted, adjusting his waistcoat. He bowed. "This is an unexpected pleasure."

"Mr. Reynolds." Whit swung down from the saddle. Habit had him turning to help Zora dismount, but, yet again, she saw to herself and already stood beside her horse. "This is Miss Grey."

The steward bowed once more. As Reynolds murmured his welcome, Whit glanced up to the open door and saw several curious faces peeking out. He did not recognize them.

"The post must have mislaid your letter, my lord," the steward said. "None of the rooms are prepared, but that can be quickly remedied."

Whit offered his arm to Zora. Her brows rose in surprise. They were both exhausted, hungry. Wounds of various kinds covered his body. Hardly the image of a lord and his lady retiring into the aristocratic comfort of the manor. Yet she tucked her hand into the crook of his arm, and together they ascended the stairs, regal as lions. Reynolds trotted beside them, and a groom appeared to lead off the weary horses. The servants inside scattered, disappearing into the dark recesses of the house.

"I sent no letter," Whit said. "This visit was . . . unplanned."

"Of course, my lord." The steward gained the top step a moment before Whit and Zora and held his arm out, gesturing for them to come inside. "I shall inform Mrs. Kinver of your arrival. How many guests shall we anticipate?"

"Only myself and Miss Grey." They crossed the threshold to stand in the entry hall. Whit's voice echoed off the vaulted ceiling, and he followed Zora's gaze up to the windows set up high. Early morning sunlight slanted in from the east, leaving squares of gold upon the paneled walls. Her eyes were wide. He'd no doubt that this was the largest and finest home she had ever been inside. "And just for the day."

Though Reynolds was a well-paid professional whose job description included largely humoring the whims of his employer, he blinked in astonishment. "The day?"

"Long enough for food, baths, and rest. Then we must resume our journey." They moved from the entry hall to the staircase hall, where the carved oak stairs rose up two stories. He turned to Zora. "Will that content you?"

She inclined her head. "Yes, that is sufficient."

Her imperious tone nearly made him smile. Gypsy girl she might be, yet no one could deny her confidence and pride.

"My lord," Reynolds murmured, reddening. "How many . . . how many bedchambers shall I have Mrs. Kinver prepare?"

Whit gazed at Zora, and she returned his look. She said nothing, but a flush the color of Baltic amber crept across the high contours of her cheekbones.

He opened his mouth to give his answer, but Zora spoke first.

"One bedchamber," she said.

Time was needed before the master bedchamber could be of use. It needed airing out, linens on the bed, the rugs beaten. In the meantime, a meal was being prepared. The cook insisted on making a full dinner. Whit couldn't regret the cook's dedication. Hasty meals at inns and roadside chophouses had lost their appeal long ago.

While the bedchamber was made ready and the meal prepared, he guided her through the Hall. Most of the rooms were shut up, and holland covers draped over the furnishings like ghosts.

"It's not looking its best," he said, opening the doors to the Red Drawing Room. He strode in, with Zora trailing after him, and pulled open the heavy velvet curtains. He lifted the sash of the window so a gust of cold air swept inside. Dust swirled, dancing along the sunlight, and more spun through the air when he tugged off a holland cover to reveal a desk of carved mahogany. One by one, he stripped off the covers, until all the tables, chairs, and cabinets were revealed.

"The color suits you." He glanced between her and the blood-red damask covering the walls. The hue did not flatter her so much as underscore her vivid beauty. "Passionate."

In truth, the room had been anything but passionate. The wall coverings were merely dyed fabric. The room had always seemed hollow, filled with unused furniture and bereft of purpose. Zora was a brilliant flame, alive and radiant. And the room came to life when she stepped into it. The curtains moved in the breeze as if the house took its first breath.

She trailed her fingers along the inlaid surface of a side table, but gave it little notice. Her attention was fixed on *him*, not the room. Looking for something within him— but he did not know what she sought.

He watched her circle the room, skirting the edge of the Savonnerie rug as if it were a chasm waiting to swallow her up. Yet she was not afraid. This room, this house, to her they were merely things without meaning.

Even in her silence, she transformed this barren place. He saw Whitston Hall through her eyes, saw its emptiness. His own emptiness.

"What this room needs," she said, her gaze on him, "is something green and living."

"Gypsies aren't farmers."

A secret smile curved her mouth. "I'll make something grow here."

Brutally intense desire flooded him. He wanted to pull her down onto the chaise, throw up her skirts, and sink into her. His body was hot with it, hard and demanding. *Take her, claim her. Now.*

The *geminus*'s influence, or his own black hunger—he could not tell the difference, and that was enough to cool his need. Barely.

She saw his hesitation, and walked toward the door. "Show me more."

He did. The large Saloon, with its gilt-wood mirrors reflecting views of the fountains and the lake. The Tapestry Room, so named for its Mortlake tapestries of impossibly bucolic scenes. The study, and the Yellow Drawing Room. Not wanting to stir up more dust, he did not open the curtains through the rest of the house. Everything felt mired in a continual twilight gloom. Holland covers haunted the chambers and the hallways. He pointed out various features of each room, but the words tasted of ash and felt hollow. She spoke very little but watched him closely.

They ascended the stairs to the Library and Long Gallery. He knew these rooms, this house, yet her presence made everything strange, alien, as though he suddenly could not speak his native tongue. Whitston was well tended, yet through her eyes he saw its neglect. Its history had always stifled him. He'd fled it as soon as he had been able.

In the Long Gallery, he decided to pull back the curtains so that the rows of portraits could be seen. She walked slowly down the gallery, examining each painting of waxen-faced ancestors in their Elizabethan ruffs, their Cavalier wigs, their full-skirted coats, posing in satins with favored spaniels at their feet.

Whit rubbed the back of his neck, prickling with unease. He had the oddest sensation that he and Zora were being watched. But no servants were in the gallery. No one was there but him and Zora. The only other eyes were those in the portraits. He actually caught himself turning around quickly, as if he could catch one of the paintings *looking* at him. Yet all that met him were flat, painted eyes, forever unmoving.

She stopped in front of one painting. He did not need to look to know which one caught her attention.

"You were very skinny," she said. "Someone wasn't looking after you."

"It took a steady diet of beef and beer at university before I filled out." He did not care to look at the portrait, for it reminded him too much of the intervening years spent in riotous pursuits.

She turned to him, her gaze moving over him in a thorough perusal. Everywhere she looked, his body lit with a thousand invisible fires, until he became a pyre of need.

"And filled out well." She glanced at the portrait, at the gallery, then back to him. "Do you know why the Rom don't like houses?"

He shook his head.

"Because they are cold. Dead. You can't know yourself when penned in by walls. Out there"—she nodded toward the window and the land beyond—"with nothing around us but earth and sky, that's where we find the true measure of ourselves."

His breath snagged. "I trapped you. In London. I took that from you."

She smiled, holding up her hand. A delicate lace of fire wove around her fingers. "I got free."

The elemental power of this woman, he craved it. Craved her. She could burn the house down, and he would not care. All he wanted was to be consumed by her fire.

* * *

Zora stood before a window, holding up a nightgown to the sunlight. The silken fabric was so fine, she could see right through it, nearly as clear as the window. Through the pale haze of silk, she made out the garden and lake that lay behind the house. She put her hand up into the gown. The fabric revealed every line on her palm.

If she put the gown on, she might as well be naked.

She *was* naked. Standing in the middle of a small room that adjoined the bedchamber, Zora wore nothing, not even her necklaces and rings. The strands of gold gleamed softly, piled carefully on a little table beside the bathing tub. The water was cloudy, cold, evidence that until a few minutes ago, she'd been as filthy as a beggar.

In a vast room dominated by a huge mahogany table, she and Whit had eaten a meal so rich and sumptuous, she had nearly dropped beneath the table and fallen asleep. Both of them had been dusty from the road, yet the servants had brought them platters of food with the same blank-faced dignity they would show to any respected *gorgio*.

Whit had spoken to the servants with an aristocratic reserve. He did not mistreat them, but they were not his equals. Both he and the servants understood this. Only Zora found herself strangely at a loss. This was not her world: the echoing hall, its empty rooms, the thick walls.

Only when she had looked at Whit and he had stared at her with meaningful heat over the rim of his wineglass did she feel comfortable. No, not comfortable, for there was no mistaking the sensual promise of his gaze. Yet looking at Whit made the house disappear, its walls dissolve. With him, she felt both secure and free.

They had finished the meal and gone upstairs, neither of them speaking. The air around them had been too thick with desire to permit anything more than the simplest actions and the fewest words.

More servants had brought bathing tubs—the luxury of having not one but *two* tubs astonished her, and hot water for both, though the scarcity of servants meant that it took longer to bring up and fill both—and Whit had adjourned to his bedchamber to wash himself, whilst she was given this smaller room for her own bathing.

As she washed, a woman servant had brought her the nightgown. Zora had no idea where the gown had come from, who owned it. Not one of Whit's former mistresses, for it was clear he never came to this house. That gave her some comfort. She would sooner wear nothing than the discards of Whit's past lover.

In a few minutes, his lover will be me.

Heart beating thickly, mouth dry, Zora slipped the gown over her head. It settled around her like a cool mist, smelling of lavender and the inside of a clothes press.

She went to the door that separated the two rooms, and softly knocked. Whit's deep voice answered, bidding her enter. She did so, thinking with an inward smile that this was one of the few times she would obey a command.

Earlier, she had briefly been inside the bedchamber: a large room with cream-colored walls and a row of windows that faced the lake. Like all *gorgio* rooms, it left little impression in her mind, but something within it *had* captured her attention: the bed. Tall and canopied, its expanse could easily fit ten adults.

But it didn't need to fit ten adults. Only two.

Whit stood at the window, his back to her, but he turned when she entered. For a moment, they did nothing more than stare at each other. The curtains were open. Sunlight filled the room. They saw one another plainly.

A robe of dark green silk clung to the width of his shoulders, and the sash tied at his waist attested to the narrowness of his hips. His feet were bare. Beneath the robe, he wore nothing; the fabric draped over the hard, tight shapes of his muscles. Arms, torso, legs. Hinted at, but not fully revealed. Yet, as he looked at her, she could not miss the stir of his cock under the silk.

His jaw tightened, and his burning gaze moved from her

face to her chest. Glancing down, she saw that her breasts were almost completely revealed by the sheer nightgown. Her nipples, dark as plums, beaded under his attention, and the slight brush of the fabric against them sent shivers of awareness through her.

His breathing came hard and fast. So did hers. Neither spoke. Neither moved.

"Come here and touch me," she said.

"Can't." His voice was an animal rumble, so deep that it resounded low in her belly, in her most secret places. His hands knotted into fists.

She frowned. "I want you to."

"I don't . . . trust myself. Want you too much." He shook with suppressed hunger, on the verge of violence, reminding her of a stallion she had once seen. The horse had been wild and without a mare for a long time. When it caught the scent of a mare, instead of racing toward it, the stallion had been frozen in place, overcome with need. Only a slap to its flank had pushed it to action.

Zora was no passive creature waiting to be claimed.

She strode across the chamber until she stood before him. At this close distance, she could see the cost of his effort in the tightness of his mouth, the cords of his neck. His pupils were large, like those of a predator. He smelled clean and musky and delicious.

"I'm not porcelain," she said. "Not even steel. I won't break." She slid her hands up the front of his robe, feeling the solidity of his chest and the pound of his heart.

"Don't want to hurt you." His voice was a growl.

"You can't." She threaded her fingers together behind his neck and stepped closer until their bellies touched. His cock was thick and upright, hot as iron even through the layers of silk, and he rumbled when she tilted her hips against him. "Take this gamble with me."

His eyes darkened. Then his lips came down onto hers. It felt as though it had been years since they last kissed, and their ravenous mouths demanded more, demanded everything. It could have been a battle. Or the best kind of seduction. All she knew was the taste of him, the wet heat of his mouth, the rasp of his tongue against hers. They drank each other up and clamored for more.

He moved from her mouth, and his teeth scraped along her neck. His breath came hot against her throat as he groaned her name. She pulled the tie from his hair. It sifted over her fingers, redolent of male arousal. She dug her fingers into his hard shoulders, but stopped when he hissed softly. Her fingertips traced the shape of the bandage around the shoulder where she had burned him.

She moved to pull her hand away, but his own came up and pressed her against him.

"I don't want to hurt you." She echoed his earlier words.

"Everything you do, every way you touch me is exquisite." He lowered his head and took her lips in a deep, dizzying kiss. One of his broad hands cupped her behind, urging her against him. His other hand stroked the aching swell of her breast. She moaned into his mouth.

The sound spurred him. He pulled the nightgown from her body in one swift, deft movement. Cool air danced over her heated flesh, yet she did not feel cold at all, not with his heat surrounding her.

He stared at her, the savagery in his gaze almost frightening. "*This*. How I've always wanted you. In my bedchamber. Naked."

"I want the same." She tugged open the robe's sash, and pushed the garment over his shoulders and off his body. It fell in a gleaming green wave to pool on the floor.

Until that moment, they had never been fully nude together, and she was glad that they had waited until full daylight could show them everything and nothing could be hidden. Lean and hard, he radiated male strength. The perfection in his form was marred only slightly by the fresh bandages wrapped just beneath his ribs, around his shoulder, and on his hand.

Two of his injuries had come from her.

He followed her gaze to the dressings, particularly those that covered the wounds she had inflicted. His cock thickened even further, twitching high just beneath his navel, and a small bead of moisture appeared at the tip.

Slick heat flooded her. Her quim felt made of liquid fire, achy with need.

They surged together, bodies hot and tight and straining. Frustrated with the bandage on his hand, he tugged it off with his teeth, and it joined the robe and nightgown upon the floor. Then his mouth was on hers and his hands roamed everywhere, stroking her, learning her curves and hollows, all the sensitive places on her body that made her gasp when he touched them.

She found herself walking backwards until the mattress met the backs of her legs. Whit and Zora tumbled down together, his mouth never leaving hers, his long body atop hers a wonderful weight. The soft mattress cradled them as they stroked and caressed one another, fevered, lost to everything but the demands of passion.

"Zora." Her name was a growled prayer.

She gasped when he captured her wrists and pinned them over her head. He leaned over her. Sunlight gilded him, tracing each rounded muscle, the hard line of his jaw, his parted lips. The mark of flames now completely covered his shoulder and his arm, and tendrils of flame had begun to spread across his torso. The Devil's mark, yet it emphasized the hewn contours of his arm and the planes of his chest. With his eyes as bright and hot as burning sapphires, raw desire sharpening his face and tightening his body, he was a myth, a creature from a girl's darkest dreams.

Light gleamed on the ring he wore at his throat, where his pulse beat fast and hard. The sight transfixed her.

He held her tightly, restraining her, and she twisted, determined to break his hold yet reveling in the strength of him. Strength that matched her own.

She could summon the fire within her and force him to

release her. She did not want to. He kissed her again, possessive, and then his mouth moved hotly down her neck, over her collarbones, lower. When his lips fastened around one of her nipples, sensation arrowed through her. She arched up, wild, but he kept her pinned in place, even as he licked and sucked her into a frenzy of excruciating pleasure. And when he took her nipple between his teeth, biting down very slightly, she veered dangerously near to climax.

"Let me go," she gasped. "I want to take you. I want you inside me."

She felt the silken brush of his hair over her breasts as he shook his head. "Not yet."

"*Now*. Or I'll burn you."

He raised up so that he stared deeply into her eyes. His skin was lighter than hers, so she saw the stain of arousal across his high cheekbones, and even on his throat and chest.

"You have burned me," he said roughly. "Burned me to my soul."

Her pulse throbbed in her neck and between her legs. "Whit—" She pushed against his hands holding her wrists.

"No. I have to give you pleasure."

"You do, you will—"

"More," he rasped. "Even more pleasure. Because when I am inside you, I won't be able to hold back." Dark need shadowed his face. "Do you understand? I'll take you, Zora. Not tender and gentle, but rough. Hard."

She thought she might set the bed on fire. "I'll take you, too, Whit. Hard and rough." Exactly how she wanted it, how she wanted him.

His eyes flared. "Let me give you this." He released her wrists, leaving a sweet throb, but before she could move, he trailed kisses down her stomach. Pushing herself up onto her elbows, she watched him widen her already open thighs. The bedclothes rustled as he shifted to kneel between her legs.

He gripped her hips, and as she watched his large, clever gambler's hands holding her tightly, her arousal climbed even higher. For a moment, he simply knelt there like a pagan about to perform a holy ritual, his gaze on her devouring, possessive.

He bent forward, and his breath came hot and quick against her wet, intimate flesh. With his gaze fixed firmly on hers, he put his mouth on her.

The sound that ripped from her throat was unlike any other she had ever made. A long, husky cry. He kissed her deeply, learned her with his tongue, tracing her folds. Around, and within. He consumed her, licking, stroking, softly at times, before becoming greedy and demanding. His greed spread to her. She grabbed his head, and she held him to her. Whenever his touch lightened, she fisted her hands and pulled on his hair, enough to hurt. Yet he fed on that pain, groaning, lapping at her readily.

Behind the fire of her closed eyes, she felt him slide two thick fingers into her passage. He circled and sucked at her pearl as his fingers moved within her. Stretching her, filling her. Two thrusts of his fingers and she came, screaming.

Yet he wasn't finished. He continued his onslaught, and his tongue joined his fingers within her passage, circling inside her.

"Oh," she panted, *"mi Duvvel—"* Another climax exploded through her, brilliant and decimating.

Even as she continued to find her release, he sucked harder at her clit, then pulled back.

"Are you coming for me?" His voice was deep, hoarse. "Are you, Zora?"

"Yes," she moaned.

"Again. Come again." He would brook no refusal.

Her climax had leveled her. She draped over the mattress, her hands falling limply to her sides. She barely knew herself. "I can't."

"Yes, you can," he said, edged and unyielding. "You can and you will. Come for me. Or must I punish you, as you punish me? I think I must." He withdrew his fingers and tapped them sharply against her agonizingly sensitive clit.

Pain and pleasure tore through her like a lightning storm. She moaned.

"You desire more punishment, my wild Gypsy? I shall give you more." He lightly slapped her bud. Once, twice. Again. She lost count—knowing only that fiery pleasure filled her beyond reckoning. Her hands found her breasts, and she tugged on her nipples, rolling them between her fingers. All the while, Whit continued his erotic onslaught with his hands and his words, telling her in a rough, low voice how delicious she was, how she was *his*, and he demanded that she never stop coming, that she never leave this bed. The way he touched her, the way he spoke, she didn't think she ever *could* stop climaxing, for it had her in its teeth now, devouring her.

She screamed so loudly her throat hurt. Yet even that added to her pleasure, and her orgasm rolled on and on, seemingly without end.

Some time later, she surfaced, dazed, wrapped in a thick cocoon of repletion. Barely able to lift her head, she saw Whit poised above her. She might be satisfied, yet he was anything but. His face, his body—everything was tight and hard. Especially his cock, dark and thick, straining upward. Wanting her.

She thought her arousal entirely spent. But as she witnessed Whit's desire, hers renewed itself.

"Cannot wait." His voice was guttural, throbbing. He was braced on his forearms, his legs between hers, caught in a moment of suspension before the storm. "Can't be gentle."

"Don't." She hooked her heels around the hard muscles of his calves.

He groaned her name, and plunged into her. White light flickered behind her eyes as he filled her completely. They each took a moment to feel one another, her all around him, and him deep within her, stretching her. Fortunate that she was so wet for him, for he was thick and large. All she felt was pleasure. All she knew was him.

He thrust. Hard. The massive bed actually shook. Each glide back and thrust forward sent waves of ecstasy through her. She gripped his shoulders, but he demanded more. He grabbed her wrists and pinned down her arms, so that he was fully atop her, their arms outstretched as if in flight.

Held down by his hands on her wrists, the weight of his body, the thickness of his cock. It felt . . . wondrous. The dusting of hair on his chest abraded her breasts as he rocked into her. She used what leverage she could to meet his thrusts, her own hips moving in eager rhythm.

As he promised, he was rough, pounding into her almost violently. And it was good. So very, very good. All it would take was a few more strokes, and she would come again.

Yet he stilled.

"Don't stop," she gasped.

He shook his head. "Not enough. Too soft."

She made a noise of loss and complaint when he withdrew and rose up from the bed. He cupped her elbows and brought her to standing. Her complaints died, though, when he led her to the wall. This, she understood. He positioned her so that the wall braced her back. His arms came around her, lifted her up. She wrapped her arms around his shoulders, her legs around his waist.

With a fierce growl, he thrust up into her. The wall against her back kept her supported, far more than the soft mattress. He plunged into her, again and again, savage.

"Yes," she panted. "Let go, Whit. Don't hold back."

He growled as her words broke the last threads of his control. His thrusts grew quicker, ferocious. One of his hands cupped the back of her head, protecting it, as the other held her hips to the wall. Despite his precautions, she knew she would be bruised, but she did not care. Feral, he drove into her. She dug her nails into his back, and came apart with a climax as expansive as destiny.

A groan tore from him as he came. His body clenched, every muscle becoming rigid. For many moments, they were like that, locked together as his climax went on and on. He pressed his head into the damp, warm crook of her neck, gasping his release.

Zora held him close as shudders wracked him. Sunshine poured through the windows, and she shut her eyes to its brilliance, lost in the radiance she and Whit had created.

Chapter 15

The day passed unlike any other. Zora knew only the bed, and Whit's body, and her own body. They slept. They made love. Mostly in bed, but they made use of other pieces of furniture, too. A bureau. A long sofa. Sometimes they made love with an aching slowness, other times with that hard, furious heat that rose up so easily between them. They would collapse in a tangle of damp limbs, the bedposts still shaking around them like a storm-wracked forest. Sleep overtook them. Then one would wake, touching and stroking the other, and the fire would renew itself all over again.

Wafodu guero and the *geminus* were still out there. She and Whit had to seize what pleasure they could in the time they had left. After building for so long, they needed to release the desire between them. As such, they sank into an undulating sea of pleasure, knowing that they would have to surface at some point. But not just yet. Their every touch was imbued with urgency.

A tray bearing bowls of food showed up on a table. Zora didn't see anyone come in to leave it, but then, when she did succumb to slumber, it was deep and dreamless. Whole processions of drum-banging musicians could pass through the bedchamber and she would not notice. It was either Whit, or sleep, and once, both together.

If not for the heavy slackness of her arms and legs, and the constant, pleasurable ache in her quim, she might have thought it all a dream. Surely nothing in her life compared to this.

As the sun began to lower, deepening the sky's hue, she and Whit lay upon the bed, naked, with the tray of fruit, cheeses, and sugar-laden cakes between them. Glasses of wine glowed as red as blood. The sheets piled around them in soft white hillocks, and his body formed a long, hewn shape amongst them, a shape she could not help herself from admiring.

"Such temptations." She plucked a grape from a pale china bowl. "Luxury, and you. Coaxing me to stay like this, here in your home, in your bed. Forever."

"We could." He took the grape from her and rolled its cool, smooth skin over her lips. Gently, he urged the grape between her lips, and his eyes darkened when she took it and his finger into her mouth, sucking at both.

She broke away. "The cost is too high. Not only your soul, but mine."

"It's almost worth it. Today has been extraordinary."

"I would think such sensual indulgence was common for a Hellraiser."

"Truly, Zora," he said, his voice low, "for all my wicked ways, I've never had a day like this before. Nor a night like this, either."

She raised a brow, skeptical.

"Since university, I've had but one vice, and it involves cards and dice, not mattresses and headboards."

"I can't believe you lived chastely."

To his credit, his cheeks darkened only a little. "I won't deny that I've enjoyed the privileges of my sex and station." He peered closer. "And that angers you."

"It doesn't." But her heart beat strangely, painfully, when her mind conjured up unwanted pictures of Whit and some faceless *gorgie* doing the same wonderful, indecent things she and Whit had been engaged in all day.

"Neither of us came to the other innocently." His brow lowered. "Thinking about you with anyone else—I'm not normally given to violence, but if I ever meet those men, I will yield to my violent impulses. Gladly."

Having seen Whit fight, she didn't doubt him. Not his intent, nor his ability.

"We'll never test that. Unlikely that you'll ever cross paths with them. They aren't men of your circle."

"How many?"

She drew herself up, no longer relaxed or flattered. "Does my lack of chastity bother you, my lord? It didn't an hour ago. Or the hour before that, or the one before that." When he didn't answer, his jaw tight, she made a small noise of annoyance. "Men want pristine angels with nary a lewd thought in their heads. Except when they get the angels into bed, and then they want bawdy strumpets. So, which is it, my lord? Do you want the saint or the slut?"

He, too, raised up, and pushed aside the tray. It fell to the ground, clattering, sending bowls of cakes and apples rolling across the floor. Wine spilled like blood in a battle. He did not notice, surging toward her so quickly she did not have time to move. Steel tight, he gripped her upper arms, his look utterly possessive.

"You," he said through clenched teeth. "I want *you*."

"Here I am." Her fingernails scored down his chest, leaving parallel red lines. Lines of ownership, she realized. As if any one person could own another. "Here you are."

She expected their kiss to be hot, aggressive. And so it started, but the heat softened from a conflagration to the warming glow of a campfire. Life-giving, sustaining. They were not destroyed but nurtured. He tasted of the sugary cakes, spicy wine, and him. Nourishing.

They were content to let the kiss be itself alone—a prelude to calm. They were more than a ravaging firestorm. From each other, they now gained sustenance. They lay back against the headboard, shoulder to shoulder, hands clasped, and watched the room turn dusky with the approach of twilight.

In the stillness, she felt herself unlocking, like a strong-box that had finally found its key.

"I was married," she said.

His grip around her hand tightened. "My sympathies."

She looked up at him. "Why?"

"It's not an easy loss to bear," he said gently. "After my mother died, my father . . . dimmed. They were fond of one another, I think."

"Jem didn't die."

Gazing down at her, he frowned in puzzlement. "You said you *were* married. I assumed . . ."

"He's married now. Has several babies, and another coming." She could not quite keep the bitterness from her voice. Not that she desired being Jem's broodmare, but he embraced his next role as husband to Kimi with a good deal more enthusiasm than he'd ever shown Zora.

"Divorce is only possible by private act of Parliament," he said. "Unless it is different amongst Gypsies."

"No, no different. But the *gorgios*, they don't have trial marriages?"

His eyes widened. "God, no. Haven't you seen all the miserable married people?" He pulled back a little. "Do Gypsies allow provisional marriages?"

"Yes, but the courtships are short. The bride- and groom-to-be are hardly permitted to hold hands, let alone kiss. Not until after marriage" She looked down at her hand, still joined with Whit's. The interweaving of fingers. It *was* an intimacy, though it had never seemed so before. Not with anyone but him.

"Thus a rush to the altar," he said, wry.

"I don't know how you *gorgios* stand it. Never knowing if your husband or wife is a terrible lover, or if you hate the sound of them coughing in the morning, until it's too late."

"And you discovered that you and this Jem"—he said the name as if it tasted of rancid mutton—"did not suit."

"A shared discovery." In truth, it had been more Jem's decision than hers, but she did not fight hard to keep him. She had thought he would be different from other Rom men, and at the beginning, he had been. He liked how independent she was, how little she courted the opinion of others. His vixen, he would call her. Until he realized that her independence extended to him, as well. If he wanted a fawning drudge to fetch his tobacco and agree with everything he said, he would have to look elsewhere.

So she did not argue or hold tight. He slipped away, a wispy shadow of the man she thought she had wed. She received a few more offers, mostly from men who did not know her well, and she did them the kindness of refusing.

You will become a spinster, her mother had scolded.

Better that than some man's trained hound.

Is that what I am? What your grandmother is? Her mother had slapped her, hard enough to burn. *You're not a child, Zora. This is the world as it is.*

But she knew now that the world could change, and change utterly. And all because of one man.

"Shared decision or not," said Whit, his words deliberate, his gaze on hers, "that Jem was an idiot. He didn't call your bluff. A terrible gambler. And I'm glad." He ducked close and kissed her softly.

Well, when Whit said things like *that*, and kissed her as if she was impossibly valuable but certainly not fragile, what could Zora do but feel the thick growth of protective vines around her heart wither away?

For some time, they lay together, silent and thoughtful. Shadows lengthened in the room. Everything was still, almost suspended, as if in waiting. Time moved unceasingly forward. They would have to leave, end this idyll, and soon. It hurt to think of it.

Whit suddenly rolled off the bed and onto his feet. Nude, save for the bandages around his chest and shoulder, he tilted his head, listening and alert.

His caution radiated out, and she caught its tension. Slowly, she rose and stood beside him. She strained to catch whatever it was he heard.

"I don't hear anything," she whispered.

"Nor I. That troubles me."

No footsteps in the hall. No voices down the stairs. Anxiety and foreboding tightened the skin on the back of her neck. She wrapped a sheet around herself, as if the fine cotton could protect her. "You said that it was a skeleton staff here."

He picked up his discarded robe and slid it on. "There should be *something*, some sound, no matter how few servants are about." From a small table, he removed a pistol and quickly loaded it with powder and a bullet.

At the sight of the weapon, her heart began to pound painfully within her chest.

In a few swift strides, he crossed to the door. "Do *not* go anywhere," he warned her before guardedly opening the door and slipping out, pistol at the ready.

She stood motionless beside the bed, fighting down swells of fear. Flames danced around her free hand, a ready weapon.

Moments later, he returned. His face was a hard mask. "Get dressed."

All of her clothing was in the dressing chamber. After allowing the flames around her hand to disappear, she darted into the smaller room, scooped up her clothes and jewelry, and hurried back into the bedchamber. Whit tugged on fresh clothing found in a press: buff doeskin breeches, a laced shirt, matching russet wool waistcoat and coat.

"What did you find?" Her hands flew at the laces of her bodice, drawing the crimson wool closed.

"Nothing." He pulled on a pair of supple brown jackboots, buckled his sword, and tucked the loaded pistol into a pocket. "I couldn't find a damn soul. Whitston is empty."

Alarm crawled through her. She did not know what it could mean, but concerning *Wafodu guero*, anything could happen. None of it good.

She stood by the window, using the last of the daylight to tie her cloak. As she did, movement caught her attention.

Glancing up, she looked out over the deserted, formal garden, its clipped hedges mostly bare, the fountains dry. Nothing there. She must have been mistaken, or confused the flight of a curlew for something more sinister.

Then her gaze drifted farther. To the lake that lay just beyond the garden.

"Whit." Her dry mouth made her words barely more than a rasp. Licking her lips, she tried again, this time with more force. "Whit!"

He was at her side in an instant. Followed her gaze, and swore.

Dark shapes moved just beneath the surface of the lake.

"Fish?" she asked. "Otters?"

"That lake isn't stocked for fishing. There are no otters near Whitston."

"What—what are they?"

The shapes held mass, and water moved around them in thick ripples. Whatever they might be, they were large. Numerous. And heading toward the closest shore.

"I think I see some kind of *claws*," she breathed.

Whit moved from the window. He grabbed his satchel and swung it over his shoulder. "Do you have everything?"

"Yes." Her hand closed around the handle of her battered rucksack.

He gave her a clipped nod, and they both slipped from the chamber into the hallway. They moved so quickly, she hadn't time to glance over her shoulder and consider the room that had, for the span of a few hours, contained her greatest happiness. Now a heavy drape of malevolence hung over everything.

Silence heavy as eternity choked the house. No one had lit any lamps or candles, not even a rushlight. Whitston Hall had seemed empty before. In the growing darkness of sunset, it became a yawning black cave. The white sheets draped over furniture glowed dimly, and no matter how much she and Whit tried to muffle their footsteps on the thick carpeting, even these soft sounds echoed far too loud.

Together, they hurried down the main stairs. Not a single person met them there, nor in the entry hall, where the marble floors rang with Zora's and Whit's departing footsteps. She winced at the sound.

He pulled open the heavy front door. Colder evening air stung her mouth and nose, but she paid it little mind. They hastened down the steps to the gravel drive.

"The stables," he said tersely, and she followed him as he jogged swiftly away from the main house. As she ran, she did glance over her shoulder and barely suppressed a gasp. The house was entirely dark, not a single light appeared in any of the windows, yet she was certain that hunched, shadowed shapes moved from room to room on the second story. Where she and Whit had been not a minute earlier.

Whit led her to a long stone building, also unlit. Inside the stables, nervous horses chuffed and stamped in their stalls. She and Whit saddled two fresh horses, the task made difficult by the near blackness. He handed her the reins to his mount. He moved swiftly from stall to stall, opening the gates and urging the remaining horses out. The panicked animals cantered from the stables, disappearing into the night.

"Don't know what's happening here," he said low, "but I won't leave those beasts to be hurt or worse."

She made a final adjustment to her mount's tack before leading the animal out of the stable. They hurried out of the stable with full night descending. The moon had not yet risen. Everything was dark.

Shapes rushed toward them. The horses shied and whinnied in terror. The animals pulled hard on their reins and broke free. She lost track of them in the darkness. Whit drew his sword.

Zora reached for her fire magic. A weapon, and illumination. Yet she almost wished she could unsee the creatures that surrounded them now. They were an unholy mix between men and legged serpent. The creatures held the vague shape of humans, standing upright on two legs. Glistening scales covered their bodies, firelight tracing the jagged edges.

The heads and faces . . . they were the most horrible. They had no hair, only more scales running in a ridge from the crown of their heads all the way down their bodies. Slits for ears and nostrils. Mouths full of yellow fangs. And each had a single, monstrous eye. Not a serpent's eye, but a human's, as large as a saucer and webbed with blue and red veins.

One of the creatures lunged. Whit struck back, parrying the blow with his sword. The blade only glanced off the demon's scales.

Several creatures darted toward Zora. She pushed them back with a blast of flame, yet their bodies didn't catch fire, only smoldered.

Whit attacked more creatures that circled close. His blade struck them all hard and true, but all he managed was to shove them back a little. None of them were cut or wounded, though the sword was sharp.

Three paces in any direction was all she and Whit would have before coming up against the encircling demons. Not nearly enough distance from the creatures. The demons showed no signs of retreat, waiting almost patiently for either Whit or her to make a move.

The foulest betrayal—surely Whit felt it, for this had been his ancestral home. Now defiled by the Devil.

"The horses." She pointed to a hedge about fifty yards away, where the two saddled horses had stopped and nervously pawed at the ground. If she and Whit could just make it to the horses, they might have a chance of escaping with their lives.

Neither her fire nor his sword had enough strength to fight the two dozen creatures encircling them. Not on their own . . .

"Give me your sword."

He shot her a warning glance. "The pistol fires once. This is my only weapon."

"Not for long." She held out her hand.

Yet he hesitated.

"Trust me," she said.

And just like that, the sword was in her hand. She couldn't marvel at the fact that he did trust her so readily, so completely. All she had was this moment, when she drew deeply on the fire within her. She reached for it now, concentrating on the sword in her hand.

Flames raced down her hand, over the hilt of the sword, then covered the blade. She held it out to Whit. "It won't burn you."

"It's *them* I want burned."

He took the sword from her, gave it an experimental swing. The flaming blade cleaved a path of light and heat through the air. His smile was sharp, deadly, full of killing intent. With the blazing sword in his hand, his body coiled and ready, and his face hard, he was the scourge of the underworld—more terrifying than the creatures surrounding them.

In an instant, the stalemate broke.

Four demons rushed Whit. He stepped into the attack, striking in a fast series of slashes. The creatures shrieked as his flaming sword now cut into their bodies. One lost an arm. Another took a wound to the throat and fell to the ground, black blood pouring from its neck.

Whit snarled, darkly triumphant. He sent Zora a quick glance of thanks before turning his attention to a new group of charging demons. His movements came swift and lethal, tracing patterns of fire and black blood through the air. She once saw a stained-glass window showing Archangel Michael with his fiery sword. Whit was more beautiful, more magnificent, for he wasn't glass, but real.

He wasn't the only one who could fight. Rather than depleting her power, endowing Whit's sword with fire magic had renewed it. As two creatures darted toward her, Zora lashed out with a bolt of flame. She cleaved them apart into stinking, smoking pieces, their bodies writhing in mindless death throes.

Yet there were more. Always more. Fast and thick on every side. They lunged forward, claws swiping, and she beat them back. Again and again. Her fire was strong, yet it could not reach far enough to take down more than a couple of demons at a time. They swarmed like locusts, the air filled with the sounds of demonic gibbering.

The creatures wanted blood. Her blood, and Whit's.

Not in a million sodding years.

"Throw me your powder!" she called to him.

Without taking his eyes off the three demons he battled, he snapped the leather cord of the powder flask that hung across his chest and tossed it to her.

"Gun, too?" he shouted back.

"Won't need it."

He *did* look at her then, briefly, questioningly, but the demons pressed closer and his attention returned to his own fight.

With her teeth, she pulled the plug from the powder flask's spout. She gripped the flask and flung her arm wide, throwing an arc of gunpowder into the throng of demons. At the same time, she used her other hand to shoot a bolt of flame directly into the gunpowder.

A fiery blast split the air—and tore into a dozen demons in a wide, blazing scythe. The creatures howled as explosive flames ripped through them, shredding their bodies. Blood sizzled as it sprayed. Zora threw up an arm to shield herself from the force of the explosion. Dark drops splattered over her clothes, her face. Looking up, seeing the devastation she had wrought, she didn't mind the mess.

With the demons temporarily stunned by Zora's improvised weapon, Whit seized his opening. He cut a swath through the creatures trying to flank him.

They recovered enough to lash back with claw and fang.

A demon edged closer to Zora. She danced away, avoiding its talons, but her cloak caught on the creature's scaled arm. The fabric ripped into tatters. It swiped at her again, and she winced as its wrist grazed her arm. Scales sliced into her. At once, pain boiled through her, hot and thick.

At the sight of her blood, the demons' frenzy grew.

"Keep them at a distance!" she shouted to Whit. "Their scales cut like knives!"

He swore when he saw the ugly wounds on her arm. Fury rekindled, Whit launched into a series of attacks. He spun and slashed, cutting down creatures with calculated rage, carving a path of escape.

Pain was everywhere within her, clouding her eyes, burning her veins, but she wouldn't give in. She sent another arc of gunpowder out into the remaining demons, set it ablaze. A blast of devastating fire. Half a dozen more fell, another half dozen retreated, cradling their wounds.

"Zora, now!"

She and Whit ran, dodging claws and scales. With the demons in hard pursuit, they sped toward the horses.

Her vision misted with pain, everything was a blur of sound and movement. She stumbled and fell to her knees. Strong hands pulled her up. Whit's worried, blood-smeared face swam into her vision.

"Keep going," she gasped.

He nodded, tight-lipped and grim. Whit's grip was tight and steady as he held her hand. Until, at last, they reached their horses.

Zora tried to mount up, but her limbs were pain stiffened. Once, twice. An action as easy and instinctive as breathing became clumsy, foreign. Then Whit was with her. He swung up into the saddle, then pulled her up to sit behind him.

"Arms around me," he ordered.

She managed to get her arms up and wrapped around him. He felt hard and solid, and she leaned against his broad back as one might lean against a stone battlement. He tied the reins of the other horse to the saddle and took the powder flask from her hand.

"Hold tight to me. All right?" When she didn't reply, he said again, harder, "Zora. Answer. Will you hold tight to me?"

"Yes," she said, but it came out slurred. Still, it was enough, for she felt him kick the horse into motion.

The world became small, the world became giant. She

knew Whit's strength, felt his taut stomach beneath her hands, the tight yet fluid movements of his body as he moved. He twisted in the saddle, striking down attacking demons with his flaming sword. The horse surged below her, and all around came the sounds of the demons hissing, shrieking.

Up ahead, in darkness, lay freedom. The demons were all earthbound, could run only as fast as a human. If she and Whit could make it far enough on their horse, they could outpace the creatures. But she felt them close behind, the force of their rage and need to kill.

Whit sheathed his sword as they rode beneath the large, outstretched branch of a huge oak. The moment they passed the tree, he turned in the saddle and threw the powder flask up toward the branch. He pulled his pistol, drew a breath, and fired. Smoke and a flash from the pistol's breach, but a larger explosion from the powder flask. It caught the tree branch in exactly the right spot at exactly the right time. The thick branch came crashing down onto the pursuing demons. Only a few were caught beneath the branch, but the rest screamed and reared back.

"Lucky shot," she mumbled.

He didn't laugh. They rode deeper into the night, and the demons' shrieks of frustrated anger faded.

Gone. Escaped. They had done it.

There was a rushing sound in her ears, and her veins felt full of burning pitch. Agony, everywhere. She closed her eyes to it, closed her mind. She just wanted to drift away where there was no pain. Where there was nothing . . .

"Damn it, Zora," Whit snarled. "You're staying right here." He grabbed her wrist and shook her.

She cried out, feeling as though the blood that coursed in her veins had been replaced with broken glass.

He hissed, and she knew her pain hurt him, as well. She wanted to tell him that it would be all right. If he just let her go, the hurting would stop. The darkness would be over, and everything would be sunlit rooms and massive beds and the wonder of their bodies and their hearts and nothing could get to them, nothing could pain them anymore.

She tried to speak. No words came from her mouth. She tried to tell him with her eyes, but they would not open. Her arms were locked around him as if in spasm.

Can't move my fingers my hands can't see can't talk this is what dying feels like or maybe this is death and there's too much to say and too much to do Whit Whit please Whit . . .

They had fled the demons but she could not escape the darkness. It took her. The world disappeared.

Chapter 16

Whit rode on, searching for shelter. The night and empty road stretched out, limitless, treacherous. He needed to find somewhere safe, somewhere he could tend to Zora's wounds. He refused to think of her as a dead weight. She was injured. Unconscious. He would hunt down a refuge and nurse her back to health. No other option existed. He shut his mind down to anything else.

The demons did not give further chase—his one consolation, when all others were gone. Lights flickered in the distance, signs of habitation. Once, he might have ridden toward them, believed they offered safety. He trusted nothing now. Not the promise of security. Not himself. Only Zora. And she lay quiet and motionless against his back.

Rage and fear the likes of which he'd never known pulsed through him. The demons had hurt her. Badly. And in the shadow of his ancestral home. The basest desecration. He vowed that he would hunt down the rest of those creatures, flay them as they yet lived, then give them the rare privilege of choking on their own intestines.

A shape emerged from the darkness. Riding closer, he discovered it to be the ruins of a church. He remembered the place from some of his youthful ramblings. Crumbling stone walls rose to pointed gables, and black, empty eyes stared where round windows once admitted heavenly light to the worshippers within. A relic from the time of England's papacy. The roof had long ago vanished. No one would be inside.

Outside the arched doorway, he pulled the horses to a stop and swung down. Zora was a still, slight weight in his arms, her head lolling back to expose the fragile pulse in her throat. She had always been fire and strength—had fought the demons like a warrior queen—but as he carried her into the church, he felt the vulnerability of her body. The terror frosted around his heart, piercing that muscle with spikes of ice.

He strode up what had once been the center aisle of the church. The wooden pews had either rotted away or been carried off by looters. Weeds poked through the remaining pavers on the ground. Beneath his boots were patches of long brown grasses. Above his head, stars shone cold and distant.

The nave was empty. His toe connected with something that went flying. It shattered against a transept wall. A bottle. Acrid fumes of spoiled wine spilled out. He vaguely remembered coming here as a youth to drink wine pilfered from Whitston's cellars. So the church had not always been deserted. But tonight, only Whit and Zora took shelter here.

A brazen sinner such as he finding sanctuary in a church. The irony might have made him smile, could the muscles of his face move into any form other than a grim scowl.

No stone floor remained where the altar had been. Some particularly idolatrous image must have adorned its surface and had not survived the purging. Wild grasses now composed the floor. Kneeling, Whit carefully laid Zora down. A brittle, autumn scent rose up from the ground.

He pulled off her torn cloak, tugged the laces of her bodice to loosen it. She lay still and compliant as he pulled up her sleeve. Ugly wounds scored her arm—black, foul gouges marring her dusky skin. Bending closer, he cursed his lack of light, but to strike a flint might attract unwanted attention. He had to make do with his imperfect vision. What he saw made him curse again.

These were not the simple cuts of a sword, not even the burnt and torn flesh of a bullet wound. Her skin was lacerated as if her arm had been pulled through a thicket of razors, and dark liquid seeped from the countless wounds. It gave off a rank, sulfurous smell, vaguely chemical. Poisonous.

That demon poison now invaded her body. He leaned closer still and felt the faint feathering of her breath against his ear. Too faint. Too shallow. His own breath came quickly, his pulse a riot.

God curse him, he didn't know what to do.

"Clean the wound," he muttered. Needing a voice, any voice, directing him, even if he commanded himself.

There was no water, but he had a flask of brandy he'd taken from his chamber at Whitston. It would have to suffice. He poured the brandy over her injuries. They bubbled and hissed, black ooze washing away. Zora did not stir.

"A poultice." Yet he hadn't her knowledge of simples and herbs. Perhaps if he scraped off the mixture she had used to dress his wounds . . . No, he might have polluted it, if he hadn't drained the mixture of its benefit.

A learned physician in his long full-bottomed wig and with an air of superciliousness would have her bled. Drain her of the poison.

Whit pulled a bone-handled hunting knife from his boot. Held the blade suspended over the tender inside of her arm. His hand shook. As ignorant as he was of simples, he knew almost nothing of proper medicine, had not trained in Edinburgh, as all the best physicians had. He could make the wrong incision. He might take too much blood, if such a thing was possible.

He could not cut her. Spilling her blood was an anathema.

Swearing foully, he stabbed the knife into the ground. The bone handle stuck up like a grave marker.

He gathered her up in his arms, cradling her. Stared down into her face as he brushed away strands of damp black hair. Her skin was pallid, and the dark fringe of her lashes trembled slightly as she battled the poison. Even in the depths of oblivion, she fought.

"What the hell do I do?" This powerlessness tore him apart, choked him with rage. The woman he had sworn to protect at all costs lay in a deathlike slumber, and actual death beckoned.

"No," he snarled. "There is no forfeit. You're *mine*." She had been his the moment he saw her, just as she possessed him utterly.

Damn and hell. There had to be *something*. He dove head-long into the patterns and labyrinths of chance, seeing an answer there. But this was beyond the realm of his power.

The demons were creatures of darkest magic. Her cure would need its own magic. Aside from the other Hellraisers, he knew of no one with magical power.

He did. The mad priestess. She had not appeared for many days, but in Oxford, Bram and the others had complained of her haunting them. Surely she had not disappeared to some realm beyond. And if she had, then he'd drag her back from Heaven or Hell or some pagan place of eternity. If the ghost held the answer to healing Zora, he would cross this world or the next to find her.

"Livia!" He threw his head back and roared for her, his breath misting in the frigid air. "Livia! Show your cursed self!"

He waited, hearing his own panting, the wind moaning through the empty church. Nothing else. Peering into the darkness, he saw no ghostly glow. No coalescing shape of a Roman priestess.

Another shout proved just as useless and went unanswered.

There had to be a way of conjuring the ghost. It was not so simple as summoning the *geminus*, which proved all too ready to ferret them out. How?

A fragment drifted through his memory. Livia's mournful words. *The heat of them . . . They draw me. Remind me of what I cannot have, what I crave. Flesh to flesh.* The ghost had appeared when Whit and Zora had unleashed their passion for one another.

The thought of pawing at Zora whilst she lay insensate repelled him. Yet he needed the heat of desire to draw Livia from her cold, nebulous place.

Whit gazed down at Zora, held tenderly in his arms. He stroked his fingers down her cheek.

She looked like an effigy of herself, robbed of her fire, her essence. But he knew her—her shape, her feel. He knew the dark glow of her eyes and the sharp edge of her will. All of that, all of *her* was still here, within this fading form. Her breath, slight as it was, still warmed her lips.

His breath—he would give it to her. He pressed his mouth to hers. She was quiescent, unresponsive, yet the feel of her lips against his was a bittersweet wonder. So faint, her breathing, and fading.

He kissed her. Gently, sweetly. She would not hear his words. *This* had to convey what words could not. A kiss unlike any he had given or received, that asked for only the aching joy of knowing another. His Zora. The meaning of his existence. He had been a shell before she came into his life. Without her . . . there was nothing.

Holding her close, he fed her his breath, his heat. The world narrowed to only the touch of their lips.

Something flared through his closed eyelids. A glow. He raised his head and beheld a ghost.

Livia stood before him. Still clad in her Roman garments, she appeared more substantial, less transparent than before. And she gazed at him with eyes far less clouded by madness.

She stared at him, at Zora. Raw longing in her face.

"Here is passion," she whispered. "Here is . . . love."

The word shot through him like the best kind of pain. "You came now, but not when Zora and I made love."

"You two were alone in your passion," the ghost answered, "but I was there, hiding in the sunlight."

Disturbing, knowing that the priestess had watched as he

and Zora had reveled in the most profound intimacies. He could not dwell on it now. "Help her," he rasped.

Yet the specter's attention wandered. She drifted away to stare at the walls of the church, and the empty trefoil window above the altar. "This place. The three-part god that crushed all others. But they could not know how much more lay beyond the bounds of their dominion. They have come to learn, as everyone must."

"Damn you, none of your opaque madness! She's hurt." *Dying.* No, he wouldn't think that. "I need your help."

The ghost floated back toward him in the chancery, her expression remote. "Show me."

Gently, Whit held up Zora's wounded arm. Even in the dimness of night, he could see the dark poison staining her veins, black lace beneath the surface of her skin.

Livia curled her lip. "Foul is the work of the Dark One's beasts."

"You will help her. Cure her." This was a command, not a request.

The priestess shook her head. "I am air and memories. Little can I do."

"You gave Zora her fire magic. You cast the spell that made me trade places with the *geminus*. You can heal her." Desperation and fury deepened his voice into a growl.

Livia frowned, considering. Whit could decipher expressions, no matter that Livia was no longer a living person. He saw the minutest change in her face, and leapt on what it might mean.

"There *is* a way," he said. "Do not deny it, for I read it on you."

"A possibility," conceded the ghost. "The faintest chance."

"Whatever it is, do it."

"Some power is mine, yet I have no body, no corporeal form." She drifted toward the chancery wall and stuck her arm straight through it.

"Tell me what needs to be done," he answered at once, "and I will do it."

She moved away from the wall and once more surveyed the ruined church.

"Priestess . . ." He could ill afford her mind wandering.

"Silence," she snapped. Then, a moment later, she pointed and spoke again. "Where the font once stood. Gather up the plants growing there now."

Carefully, Whit laid Zora back onto the ground, then sprinted down the length of the church to stand in the nave's entrance. Centuries earlier, a basin had stood there, filled with holy water and reminding the faithful of their baptism. Like everything once venerated within the church, the font was gone. A faint stone ring on the ground was all that remained.

Within that ring grew small purple wildflowers. It seemed improbable that anything could blossom so late in the year, yet there they were. Whit plucked every last flowering stalk and brought them all to Livia.

"A bowl," she said when he held them out for her inspection. "And water."

His satchel produced a small silver cup, worked all over with a pattern of vines. "No water, but some brandy remains."

"Crush the plants and mix them with the spirits."

He was no apothecary, yet he did as she asked, pulverizing the flowering stalks with the handle of his retrieved knife. Green sap stained the white bone handle. This he combined with the brandy, swirling it all together in a pungent brew.

The ghost appeared satisfied with his handiwork. "Hold the cup between your hands. Do not let it go, do not drop it, whatever may transpire." When he obeyed, she closed her eyes and let her own hands hover over the cup. For a moment, she was silent.

"Make haste," Whit grated.

The ghost scowled, but did not open her eyes. After another pause, she began chanting, words in a tongue that might have been a dialect of Latin, words that he did not know or recognize. But he felt their power. Charging the air, firing through his every nerve. Wind billowed within the confines of the church, careening from wall to wall like a penned beast. The heavy stones shuddered, and Livia chanted on and on, her voice growing louder, her words faster.

Whit sent a quick glance toward Zora, but she lay as motionless as before. Only her hair and clothing stirred in the wild wind.

He turned back to Livia. The priestess continued her chanting above the shrieking wind. Her eyes opened. They burned with silver light, nearly blinding him with their radiance.

The mixture within the cup glowed, as well. It shone as brightly as Livia's blazing eyes.

Then, as her chanting reached a crescendo and the wind screamed, the light in the priestess's eyes flared, as did the light within the cup. The cup itself burned him. Whit could barely stay upright, buffeted by the force of the wind and the ghost's power. *Keep standing. Do not loosen your grip. This one chance . . .*

Silence. Stillness. As abrupt and forceful as the tempest that had preceded them.

The light from Livia's eyes and within the cup faded away. The silver cup cooled in his palms.

"Tell me what to do with this." He held up the silver vessel. "Put it on her wounds? Make her drink it?"

"Into her mouth."

He eyed the mixture in the cup. "And this will work."

The ghost offered a noncommittal wave of her hands. "Perhaps."

"Perhaps?" He gritted his teeth, fighting for calm. "I do not need *perhaps*. I need certainties."

"Either it will heal her, or be her final push into death." The priestess sounded mildly concerned, as if she were discussing the outcome of a child's game.

"I won't gamble her life," snarled Whit.

This snared her attention. "Would you gamble your own?"

"Of course," he said immediately.

A small, edged smile curved her mouth. "Then drink. A sip only, and you will know. If you survive, then she shall, as well. If you do not . . ." She gave a fatalistic shrug. "It may be that you will meet again in the next world. However, as the Dark One has your soul, the greater possibility is that you will journey one place, and the girl will go elsewhere. Many likely outcomes. Who knows how fortune will favor you."

Fortune. He delved into the patterns of probability, only to find himself rebuffed, thrown back into the world as others knew it. Arbitrary, uncontrollable.

"The Dark One's power will not help you here," tutted Livia. "This hazard is all your own. What will it be, gamester? Will you gamble your life to save hers?"

He did not waste a moment. Whit lifted the cup and drank.

Everything hurt.

Her arms, her legs. Skin. Tongue. Her eyes were a merciless weight pressing into her skull. Her *hair* ached.

In slow increments, Zora tested every part of her, cataloging, measuring. She could find nothing that did not cause her pain. It inhabited her completely, and she wondered if she had ever known life without this unending hurt, or if she ever would know it again. It did not seem likely.

She drew a breath. Her throat ached and more pain spread in branches through her lungs.

This could not be death, could it? Death meant the end of pain. Death also meant that one didn't need to breathe. Yet she did.

Alive, then. Vividly alive, if this agony tied her to life.

Her eyes opened. She bit back a cry, from both the torment of opening her eyes and the brightness of the sun.

The sun . . .

She stared at it. The sky was a brilliant blue, cloudless,

hard and cold as glass. Framed by crumbling stone walls. The sun glazed her with chill light. It seemed uninterested in giving off warmth, an unwanted habit it had discarded like drinking or gambling.

Whit. Where is he?

Turning her head sent swords of anguish through her entire body. She could not stop her moan, then, and to her own ears her voice was a weak and piteous thing.

Yet it was strong enough, for suddenly Whit was there, filling her vision. His face was taut, ashen, and deep lines bracketed his mouth. But he was alive, as was she, and to her eyes, no sight could be more welcome.

He knelt beside her. His gaze moved across her face. Fierce joy gleamed in his eyes, eyes that were warmer and more blue than the sky overhead. His lashes were spiked. Wet.

"Whit," she said, yet it came out barely a whisper, and the effort of speaking cost her. Sound moved in painful ripples through her muscles.

"Zora. Oh, God, Zora." He bent forward, his forehead touching hers as his eyes closed. The feel of his skin against hers was agony. She did not want him to leave.

Warm drops trickled onto her face. Not from her. Him. Salty against her lips. His hands caressed her hair, face, arms. This was too much, and she cried out in pain.

He snatched his hands away.

"Forgive me, forgive me," he murmured.

"Nothing to . . . forgive." She tried to look around, but to move meant a fresh wave of anguish. "What . . . ?"

His hands hovered above her, as if, being unable to actually touch her, he dared allow his hands as close as possible.

"We escaped the demons. You were injured. Poisoned."

It came back to her in pieces, shards of a broken nightmare. His estate. Demons. Fire. Flight. And the venom that spread through her body, dragging her into a half-world of darkness, neither dead nor living. She should not have survived. Yet she did.

Whit saw the question in her eyes. "Livia. Her doing."

"And yours," Zora whispered.

He looked away. That was when she noticed it. Dried blood in the corners of his eyes.

Slowly, her hand came up. She felt it in piercing darts through her arm, but she pushed herself on, until the tip of her finger touched the outer corner of his right eye. He started at her touch, and his own hand came up to rub away the dark flecks collected there.

"Had to test the antidote," he explained after a moment. And that was all he would say.

But she read people, just as he did. She saw in his silence what had transpired. The bodily suffering he had endured to make sure the antidote was safe. Blood crusted beneath his fingernails, dark crescents proving that whatever he had borne had been beyond understanding.

For her.

Her own eyes heated, and she could not blink fast enough to clear away their dampness.

He would not linger on the subject. "You must be hungry. Thirsty."

The thought of eating anything sent a wave of stomach-churning pain through her. "Water," she croaked.

He pressed a silver cup to her lips, and though the water was cold and sweet, she could barely swallow it. Most of the water dribbled from her mouth, but she was too exhausted and hurting to care how feeble she must look.

"There's a spring not but a dozen yards from here." He gently dabbed at her lips with a scrap of linen. "I think that's why this church was first built. It must have been an ancient sacred spring. The church followed, supplanting the pagan."

He spoke as if testing what it might be like to talk about meaningless things. His voice was hoarse, unused.

"How long . . . ?"

"Two days."

She absorbed this, shocked. For *two days* she had lain like this? And he had watched over her the whole time. As the *geminus* consumed how many souls?

"The *geminus* . . ."

"To hell with the *geminus*."

His words were fierce, but they made her smile. As much as she could smile—which wasn't a great deal.

"Either we'll find the damned creature," he said, holding her gaze, "or we won't. But understand this: *I will never leave you.*"

Her body was filled with pain, yet it was distant, someone else's suffering. "Never . . . would I have . . . guessed."

"Guessed what?"

"You and I. This." She clasped his hand with hers, ignoring the agony, feeling only him. "The odds . . ."

Blue, his eyes. Impossibly blue. Impossibly warm. His hand, steady and strong. "Were great. They still are. Precisely how I like them." He lightly pressed his lips to hers, profoundly tender.

She wanted more than a soft kiss, but her body would not allow it. "I need this . . . sickness gone . . . from me."

She struggled to rise up, prop herself on her elbows. The lingering poison tore through her with razored claws. She fell back, shaking, as much from pain as from frustration and anger.

"*Rest*, My Lady Firebrand," he said gently. "That is what you need."

"Not rest . . . but action," she insisted. Summoning all her strength, she held up his hand. Upon his skin were images of flame, marking him as the Devil's possession. "*Wafodu guero* . . . has something of mine. And I'm . . . taking it back."

Wanting to be well and *getting* well were very different. Especially when one wasn't recovering from a bout of catarrh but rather poison from the scales of a demon. Zora could not use horehound tea to cure herself of a venom born from Hell.

Her strength grew moment to moment, the pain receding

in tiny increments, yet she couldn't sit up unassisted, let alone stand or ride a horse. But they needed to move, and soon, for already two days had passed and the *geminus* was out there, somewhere, wreaking chaos.

"Doctoring wasn't covered in my 'gentleman's education.'" Whit sat beside her as she lay upon her cloak on the ground, giving her sips of cold spring water. Late afternoon sunlight filtered through the nave windows, gilding his face. With his hair unbound, his clothing disheveled, and several days' worth of stubble darkening his jaw, he looked rough and untamed. Yet she suspected that this was more his true face than the one of the polished *gorgio* who haunted the gaming clubs of London.

"Drinking, gambling, idleness, and indulgence," he continued. "That's all I ever learned at Oxford. And even if I *had* bothered to study, Cicero and Heraclitus wouldn't help us now. Long-dead chatterers. Prattling on about things that have no relevance in the modern eighteenth century." He smiled wryly. "Though maybe my callow boy's brain hadn't the means to make sense of their wisdom. Heraclitus believed that we never step in the same river twice, for the river constantly changes, and so do we."

That seemed sensible. "Maybe schooling is wasted on the young."

"Maybe *everything* is wasted on the young. For they never place value where it's most required." He spoke as if from experience. A man who had transformed utterly from the boy he had been. A man who was not the same as he'd been only a few weeks earlier.

His gaze grew pensive, and she watched the play of thought across his face.

"Fire," he said, breaking his musing. "What Heraclitus thought was the origin of all other elements. Through fire, everything comes into being or expires."

"Fire changes things." She knew this well. Fire had changed her profoundly.

"It's the symbol of constant change. Transforms one thing into another. Burns away its old form."

Understanding hit them both at the same time. Their gazes held, alight with possibility.

"Can you do it?" he asked.

"If it makes me recover faster so I may tear that *geminus* into rags, I'll do anything."

His expression darkened. "Should *anything* go awry, you must stop at once."

"I will." Yet she wasn't certain if, once she'd begun the process, it could be stopped. She kept silent about her concern, knowing that he would attempt to prevent her from trying. As much as anyone could prevent her from doing anything.

She was resolved. He had risked himself for her. She would do the same for him.

"Tell me what to do," he said.

"Stay close." When he took her hand, she added, "But I wouldn't do that." Much as she savored his touch, she might hurt him unwittingly. "These need to come off, too." She glanced down at her clothing. Flammable.

He raised a brow. "Presenting me with a hell of a lot of temptation."

"Thank the heavens you've a strong will."

"Not where you are concerned." He brushed his lips across hers, and even weakened as she was, heat and need sped through her. "Irresistible."

She wanted nothing more than to thread her fingers into his hair and pull him close, taste him, feel him. But she couldn't, not in her current condition. Which made her break the kiss—reluctantly.

"Please," she said. "I need your help to . . . undress."

His eyes blazed. "One condition. You make the same request again when I can truly take advantage of the situation."

"We'll take advantage of each other," she vowed. She would enjoy that. Very much. She knew now how it was between them, the soul-shattering ecstasy they created. "For now . . ." Her hands shaky, she pulled at the lacings of her bodice.

Quickly, with a minimum of lingering caresses, he helped her disrobe. It felt strange to be so exposed, baring her flesh in this ruined house of worship, and Whit fully dressed. The late afternoon air held autumnal chill. Bumps stippled her skin.

When they were done, she lay naked and exhausted. His breath came quickly, and his jaw was tight.

"You look like a pagan offering," he rumbled. His gaze traveled over her, possessive and hungry. "Nude upon an altar. Yet I'd rather worship you, not sacrifice you."

"Worship me." She said this with far more liveliness than she felt, for the effort of removing her clothes as well as concerns about what she was about to do left her drained. "Later. Now I just need silence. And whatever happens, *don't touch me.*"

"You might need me."

She shook her head. "To fight the *geminus*, you must be as powerful as possible. No injuries, no wounds. The creature is strong, but you need to be stronger. Promise, Whit. Promise not to touch me."

After a long, tense moment, he gritted, "I promise." Though he kept his word and did not touch her, he kept as close as possible, understanding instinctively that she would need his strength—not to use, but simply to know it was there.

On a deep breath, she closed her eyes. Drew into herself. The process wasn't easy, for distractions abounded. The cold air on her shivering skin. Trees rustling in the wind. Even Whit, a source of power, yet so compelling it was all she could do to keep focused on the task at hand. For him, she did this. And for herself.

She found the poison within her body. Not difficult to do. It seeped through her in black, noxious tendrils, sapping her, stealing from her and replacing her strength with pain. But this poison was not her; it was foreign and unwelcome. The truth of her lay deeper, centered within the terrain of her soul, her heart. There. Bright and burning. Fire.

This was her and hers. Livia had brought it to the fore, but Zora knew it had always been within her. She had been named for the dawn, the rising sun breaking through the darkness, born at first light just like the day. Now it was time to draw upon that fire and use it not simply as a weapon, but as a way of reclaiming herself from the evil that sought to destroy her. She did not need another fire's power to feed her own. She could summon it now as she willed, hers alone.

She fanned the flames, summoning the fire. At first, the fire responded as it had in the past, flowing to her hands in preparation for battle. She channeled it back into herself. The battle was within. She guided the flames through her body, through her veins, where the poison seethed.

Fire met venom. A brutal clash. The poison hissed and raged as the flames attacked, heating her blood to burn away sickness. Agony tore through her—the demons' venom fought back. Hazily, she heard her voice cry out in pain, felt her body arch up from the ground.

She wanted to give in. It was too much. As the fire battled the poison, venomous thoughts seeped into her mind. *This is just a small sampling, a taste of what's to come. You cannot imagine the suffering. You cannot fight something with our strength. This struggle is useless.*

The thoughts were right. She couldn't endure the agony any longer. Or know why she fought so hard in the face of such overwhelming odds. Maybe she could simply surrender, sink into the wave of darkness and let oblivion take her. Then the pain would be over.

Nothing is worth this torment, the voices whispered.

The voices were wrong. She never heeded anyone's foolish counsel before.

I am worth this, she fired back. Whit *is worth this. For us both, I'll do anything.*

She pushed back against the poison, urging the fire higher, stronger. Her blood sizzled. She could not imagine what the battle must look like from outside her body, but within, it felt as if each and every vein and vessel glowed white hot, searing her.

Burn it away. Every last drop.

She became a cauldron, a crucible. And felt the poison melt away in minute traces. Slowly, slowly. Time dissolved like a pearl in vinegar. All she knew was this—the battle-ground of her body, fire and poison locked in combat, and she the general that rallied her troops to beat back the invader. Reclaiming herself.

Then, suddenly, it was gone. Fled. The fire had cleansed her, leaving her free from sickness, from poison.

Her eyes opened. And there was Whit, waiting for her.

"Can I touch you now?" His voice was a harsh rasp.

Turning her head, she saw a pattern of scorched earth surrounding her, shaped like her body. She flexed her hands, tested the temperature of her skin and found it to be normal.

"I want you to," she said.

No sooner were the words past her lips than she found herself held in the power of Whit's arms, pressed close and tight to him. Her own arms were strong as they came up to wrap around his shoulders. For long moments, they simply held one another. The wind was cold on her bare skin, yet she knew the warmth of him, and she knew her restored strength.

No matter what was to come, the dangers ahead and very real possibility of defeat, *this* victory was theirs.

Chapter 17

"It's stopped."

Zora looked up from packing her bag to see Whit staring fixedly north.

"The *geminus* is gone?"

"Stopped moving." His gaze lingered on an unseen point beyond the church's walls. Dusk was falling, and the stars were on the verge of appearing in the deepening sky. The borderlands between day and night. "It's found a good place to dig in. Abundant prey."

The word sent a chill along the curve of her spine. Not so much the word, but the way Whit said it, as if savoring the taste of stalking and claiming victims. No matter what deeds he had performed in her service, he still fought against the darkness within himself.

And that made her all the more determined to find the *geminus* and reclaim Whit's soul.

"Gives us time to catch up." Bloodlust clamored through her, an unfamiliar sensation. Yet one she now embraced. She wanted to make the damned thing pay. "Where is it?"

"A city. North of here." He shook his head as if coming out of a trance, but his expression was shadowed. "If I try to get too far into its mind, its heart, I'm not certain I can come back into my own."

She crossed to him and took his hand. "Stay with me."

"I've no wish to be anywhere else." Yet in the dusk, his eyes were haunted. He attempted a smile. "How disappointing to have you clothed again."

"Naked horseback riding is much less appealing than it sounds." She searched his face. "Have we enough to track the *geminus*?"

"It's feeding often. Growing stronger."

Which meant that, even without deliberately trying to reach the *geminus*, its link to Whit also grew stronger. She saw it now in the crystal darkness of his gaze, the hard beat of the pulse in his throat.

They had not a minute to lose, for every moment meant a little more of Whit was lost. Zora gave his hand a squeeze before hefting up her bag and striding out of the church to her horse waiting outside. She untied its reins from a makeshift post and lifted up into the saddle.

Whit came out of the church and placed his hand on her calf. His gaze was hard, focused, as he stared up at her. Atop her horse, she might be higher up than he, but his potency did not diminish. "You need to heed your own advice."

"I give a large amount of advice."

"To face the *geminus*, both of us need to be as powerful as we can be. No injuries. No wounds. No lingering illness."

"I've never felt stronger." She spoke truly. Something had happened to her, changed her, when she used her fire magic to cleanse herself of the demons' poison. Like a sword forged in flame, she had a cutting edge, ready to carve the world apart. Gleaming and deadly.

Whit looked at her for a moment, then reached up and cupped his hand around the back of her neck. He was a tall man, so there was no awkwardness when she bent at his touch, bringing her mouth close to his, nor did he rise up onto the balls of his feet. He simply claimed her mouth as she demanded his.

The kiss was hard and hot. His tongue swept into her mouth and she sucked on it, wanting to feast on him, to consume him. She knew his taste now, sultry and masculine. Craved that taste with every part of her, not merely her body's needs but her heart's wants, as well.

He broke the kiss first. An animal growl sounded low in his throat. Grimacing as if in pain, he released the back of her neck and stepped away. She tightened her grip on the reins to keep from reaching for him. Distractions came all too easily when he touched her.

Soon, they were back on the road, riding hard for a northern city. She hoped that this time, as they tracked the *geminus*, they were no longer the prey but the hunters.

Zora had never been this far north. Other Rom bands wandered these lands, but hers had always held close to the south, its towns and villages, fairs and markets. Whit, however, knew these roads, and as she traveled beside him, she used his confident posture and alert gaze as her means of guidance. The *geminus* pulled them forward, yet Whit led the way.

In the hours before dawn, they reached the outskirts of a city. Smaller than London, and not as dignified as Oxford, yet still impressive to her outsider's eyes. Rows and rows of stone buildings lined the avenues, and a broad, grand street led to a towering church. Though the lamps were dark and everyone was still in bed, Zora could still make out a fine white fluff hazing the cobbled streets. It couldn't be snow, for the weather held far too much warmth, and no clouds filmed the sky.

"Cotton," Whit said, seeing her curious gaze. "Manchester's newest trade."

She saw now that many of the buildings were new, as yet unmarked by coal smoke.

"Then there's money in this place," she said.

"Where money dwells, gambling follows." He spoke from experience.

They rode through the quiet streets, passing a few coster-mongers and masons with their long-handled brick hods on their shoulders, readying to raise more new structures. Despite the stillness, Zora sensed a peculiar tension in the air and humming along the surface of her skin. Through shuttered windows came the sounds of voices, muttering and low, agitated.

"The *geminus* is here," she murmured.

"It's like a second pulse beside my own." Whit's lips compressed into a hard line.

At that moment, a finely dressed man rounded a corner and drew up sharply in front of their horses. Drink or drowsiness made him sway, fighting for balance. He adjusted his crooked wig as he stared up at Whit in surprise.

"How'd you get here so quick?" the man demanded.

"Took a shortcut," answered Whit. "But I left something of mine behind, and I've forgotten my way back."

The man snorted. "Going back to drain other coffers, more like."

"That shouldn't matter to you. Not with yours already empty."

Removing his wig, the man scratched at his shaved head. "I'd like to see you clean out Mundy and Coburn. They wouldn't be so damned smug with nary a ha'penny in their pockets."

"Point us in the right direction," said Zora, "and he will."

"Down this street, next left, another left, and then it's on your right." He gestured his words, tired lace drooping over his hand. His bloodshot eyes narrowed. "Mind, if you do clean out Mundy and Coburn, I want a share for leading you to 'em."

"You'll get nothing," Whit said. "Go home and lose consciousness."

Whit's voice was as cold as steel and just as hard. It shocked her to hear him speak so callously, for though he sometimes had a wealthy man's reserve, he was never cruel. It had to be the *geminus*'s influence, this heartlessness that sprang up so readily.

Whit's words affected the drunken man even more. He clapped his wig back onto his head and tottered away as quickly as his unsteady legs could allow.

Wordlessly, she and Whit followed their informant's directions. Their path took them off the wide streets, into the narrower, winding avenues. Here, the cotton fluff had mixed with dank residues and muck, creating a gray paste that smeared the ground. A clammy wind shuddered down the lane. It smelled like a burial shroud.

She and Whit passed men as they rode. Walking singly or in small groups, most of them were drunk, and all of them were angry, muttering about losses and throws of the dice and how they'd return again on the morrow to win back what they had lost.

Whit stopped his horse. He silently dismounted, and Zora did the same. They both peered around the corner. Whit's hand lingered above the hilt of his sword.

A house faced a small courtyard, its windows shut up tight. It seemed a perfectly ordinary *gorgio* house, if a little shabby, with paint peeling off the shutters and weeds choking the flower boxes. From within, masculine voices rose and fell in a muted din.

As she and Whit watched, the door opened. Glaring yellow light spilled out as a man stormed down the stairs. He turned and shouted something toward the house. A giant filled the doorway, blocking the light. Though the big man said nothing, the irate shouting stopped abruptly, and the shouter hurried away. The door slowly shut.

"There. Where I must go." Whit's voice was only a whisper, yet tense and grim. "Hell."

Zora frowned as she stared at the building. "I thought Hell would be surrounded by demons and three-headed dogs. I don't see any demons, and that"—she pointed to a cur slinking across the street—"has just one head."

Whit almost smiled, even as he fought against the rising tide of darkness within him. Trust her to discern the truth. "Not Hell itself. A gaming hell."

"It should be called a gaming heaven. Attract more customers."

"Nothing heavenly about it. Gaming hells earn their names." He'd been in far too many, and whether they had crystal chandeliers and French wall hangings or guttering rushlights and warped walls, they were essentially the same. Places where bored or desperate men frantically grabbed at meaning. He had been no different. Even now, the hunger rose up in him, demanding he cross the filthy courtyard, walk up the short flight of steps, and enter the building. The familiar, tempting peril of gambling, made all the more enticing by his power over probability. He could have anything he wanted. . . .

Not everything. As if sensing his pull toward darkness, Zora's hand came up to rest on his arm. The barest touch, yet it anchored him.

The *geminus* was within. This was a certainty. It stood between Whit and eternal damnation. He wanted to kick down the door and slam through the gaming hell until he came face-to-face with his dark double. Run the creature through. Whit envisioned the blood of the *geminus* on the blade of his saber. A vicious pleasure he craved.

"It can't be killed." Again, Zora knew his thoughts as they formed within his mind. "Not until we've gotten back your soul."

He turned away, frustrated not with her but the truth of

her words. He needed to think. This was not the place to do it. Not with the *geminus*—and temptation—so close.

"Whatever we plan," he said lowly, "it must wait. Soon, the hell will be closing up for the day. Come." He held out a hand, and it gratified him how readily she took it. "Nothing's safe here."

The glen was a sheltered spot, tucked between hills that lay a short distance from the city. Finding it had not been easy. Manchester grew like a beast, eating up the countryside as cotton fed manufacturing. In the years since Whit had last been in this city, it had changed, turning colder and colder with the onslaught of industry. Which made locating a piece of isolation all the more difficult.

He knew Manchester only a little, and the countryside around it not at all. But Zora possessed abilities he could not, and though she had never been to this part of England, she guided them both to this dale with confident ease.

Trees sheltered the small valley, their branches forming a canopy. Most of the trees' limbs were bare, though a few hardy leaves still clung in resilient little groups that checked the cool wind. A breath of warmth lingered here, like the last inhalation before stepping out of doors and into a storm.

Consulting his pocket watch, he noted that the sun was still nearly an hour from rising. Soft violet light filled the glen. Zora made a slim, elegant shape as she glided through the tall grasses, seeing to the horses. Neither she nor Whit had spoken since they had left the gaming hell.

He felt the lure of gambling, felt the *geminus* within him, wanting to feed on the weaknesses of others. Yet he had to fight it.

She had taught him that, how to fight. He watched her move, her straight shoulders, her uptilted chin, as if she was ready to take on any opponent.

Now was no different. "We can't attack the *geminus* head-on." She moved to stand beside him.

"Gamblers always have a strategy. If you bet too aggressively, no one will play, and you've gained nothing."

"So you think ahead."

"Not so far that you cannot concentrate on the game being played at that moment."

Her gentle, bold fingers traced along the line of his jaw. "There's something we Rom call the *hokano baro*, the great trick. A confidence trick. It's spoken of with pride, and whoever carries it out successfully is the object of much admiration."

He tried to concentrate on her words, but her touch kept leading his thoughts—and body—astray. His hand came up to capture hers, and she smiled, a small, cunning smile, as if she knew precisely how she affected him.

"The *hokano baro* has three parts," she continued. "Simple parts, truly, but it's the simplest things that prove most challenging. Only the wisest and cleverest can perform them properly."

"Including you."

"A time or two. I don't like to boast."

"Tell me these three parts, my modest Gypsy." He risked temptation by pressing a kiss to her fingertips, and was either rewarded or punished by a catch in her breath.

"First, find a way into the home of your gull." She *did* sound a little winded, as affected by his touch as he was by hers.

"Break in."

She shook her head. "Too messy, too dangerous. The *hokano baro* is about confidence and cunning, not brute force. There are other ways into someone's house."

"Ruses."

"Ah, the *gorgio* is clever. Perhaps you've some Romani blood." With her free hand, she stroked down the lapel of his coat as if unable to stop herself from touching him. "Usually, all it takes to get into your quarry's home is to offer to *dukker* for them, but there are other ways, as well. Once inside, we come to the second part of the *hokano baro*. Remove the goods."

"Which brings us to the third part."

"Make sure the gull can't do anything about what you've just done."

He captured her other hand, too, yet he knew that while his physical strength was greater she had her own power. "I think you might be the most dangerous woman in England, Zora Grey."

"Do you think so?" She tilted her head to the side, considering.

"The idea pleases you."

"Only because you're a dangerous man. It's only fair."

He needed this. This play and banter. Reminding him that there still existed a part of himself beyond the darkness, and Zora brought it to the fore with her soul of fire.

"*Wafodu guero* is sharp," she continued. "We'll be sharper."

He took her hands and brought them up to link behind his neck. "What I have in mind requires a little more magic than either of us have."

"We need Livia." She raised a brow. "Or maybe it's the summoning of her that you're after."

"Gamblers always have ulterior motives." He ducked his head to kiss her. As their lips met, she raised up, pressing herself against him. He gave himself to this, to the feel of her slim, lush body, warm and alive. To the flavor of her, spicy and as sweet as cinnamon. To the heat and energy they created. To the hunger that grew with every taste and every touch. She responded to him like no other, stealing his breath, hardening his body.

Breaking the kiss was a torment, yet he saw a spectral glow in the corner of his vision. He exhaled.

"I almost wish our ghost had a less reliable means of summoning," he muttered. For of a certain he could not stop himself from touching Zora. Passion between them was inevitable.

Livia raised her chin. "It is not by my design. I have little desire to watch what I cannot possess." Haughty, her words, yet underscored by loneliness and yearning.

"We've need of you." Zora stepped back, her hands sliding away. He wanted to pull her against him.

"Observe me," said the ghost. She gestured to her elegant tunic and the golden circlet in her hair. "A high priestess and daughter of Rome. Not a lackey to fetch and carry as determined by your whims."

"Reclaiming my soul is no whim." His own anger came quickly. "This is to fight a dark power that *you* first summoned."

Livia's eyes narrowed; she was all readiness now. "My power gains slowly, but I shall endeavor to do whatever is required."

In measured and deliberate words, he outlined his ideas. Zora quickly understood his objective, and provided her own additions to the scheme. Indeed, she knew the mechanics of the ploy far better than he, though they needed tailoring for the circumstances. Between them both, they strategized a plan. It was perilous, and it was all they had.

"You are both as mad as I," the ghost said after they concluded, a note of admiration in her voice.

"Can you do it?" Zora pressed.

"The working of such a spell will drain me. If you do manage to face the *geminus,* I shall be unable to assist you."

"I will see to the *geminus.*" The creature was Whit's to destroy. He glanced toward the eastern horizon, where the sun lightened the sky from black to indigo. "The gaming hell opens its doors again at nightfall. We will need you then."

"How shall you make use of the intervening hours?" asked Livia.

He reached out and threaded his fingers with Zora's. A

blush stained her cheeks, but he saw in the brightness of her eyes that hers was the blush of arousal, not embarrassment.

The priestess smiled, wry and sad. "I shall stand guard."

"Thank you." There was no irony in Whit's gratitude. Safety, he had come to learn, was scarce. If not unattainable. He would seize whatever fragments of it he could.

With a regal nod, Livia flickered, then disappeared. Likely her disappearance was only an illusion. Yet he would gladly suspend his disbelief if it meant having these last moments with Zora, more precious than anything he had ever won.

Pulling Zora closer, Whit felt a tension in her arm. Yet it was a drawing out of the moment, not reluctance, that made her slightly resist. Proving that neither of them led the dance, but moved in the steps together. Slowly, steadily, he brought her nearer. When only a few inches separated them, he released her hand. She held his gaze as his fingers moved over her face, down her throat, around the delicate architecture of her ears.

"I envy these," he said, circling an earring. He leaned close and touched the tip of his tongue to the soft flesh of her earlobe, tasting her flesh and gold. "They touch you every moment of every day."

She stroked up his chest, where his heart thundered. "If there was a way for you and I to have the same . . ."

"I'll give you everything I can." His hand covered the back of her neck and he urged her mouth to meet his.

They kissed, liquid and deep. The control for which he ruthlessly fought broke apart into hot, jagged pieces. He held her close, one arm around her waist, the other still cradling her head. She pressed into him, wordlessly asking for more.

He cupped the curve of her buttocks and brought their hips together. A groan ripped from him as she moved against the thick, hard length of his cock. She was perfect, exactly what he wanted, what he needed. She felt the desire between them and reveled in it. Womanly, unafraid, hungry—she was this, and more as she cradled him, her hips writhing in an echo of what they both desperately craved.

If he could touch her everywhere, he would. But he was only a man, bound by the limitations of his body, so he had to relinquish one part of her to touch another. His hand slid from her neck down her throat, over her collarbones, lower. He undid the lacing of her bodice, loosening it. Then he allowed himself a reward for his patience, filling his hand with the faultless weight of her breast.

Through the fabric of her blouse, he stroked and rubbed, teasing the hardened point of her nipple. Her sounds of ecstasy shot straight to his groin as his other hand performed the same service for her other breast.

Yet she was neither idle nor passive. Her hands moved over him boldly, taking in his muscles and the structure of his body. A body that seemed to give her pleasure, and so he was grateful for it. She stroked his shoulders, his chest. She undid the buttons of his waistcoat and pressed her hands to the hard planes of his pectorals. His breath came staccato as she tugged his shirt from the waistband of his breeches, then stroked his bare skin.

She knew him. As he knew her. Not simply what gave each other pleasure, but the *why* of it. It sheltered them now, protected them. *I give myself to you. My body. My heart.*

When her hand glided down to stroke him through his breeches, he made a low, feral sound. Her confident touch brought him close to madness. His wits disappeared entirely when she opened the fall of his breeches and wrapped her hand around his cock. God, the feel of her fingers on him . . . She stroked him as if he, and his cock, belonged to her.

She made a sound of protest when he took his hands from her breasts, but her protests fell away as he gathered up her skirts. He found her wet, tropically hot. She was soaked silk beneath his fingers as he caressed her, and knowing how to touch her made everything all the sweeter. *Here* she wanted a firm stroke. *Here* she wanted just the tip of his finger. He knew the sound she would make when he sank two fingers into her heat, and when he did, and when she did, deep satisfaction rolled through him.

A cry broke from her. She tightened around his fingers, her body taut and beautiful in its release.

He moved to bring her over again, but she nudged his hand away.

"I want something, too," she gasped.

He was tense and dazed, sharp edged, yet he allowed her to lead him. She guided him to a stout tree and wordlessly directed him to lean back against it. For a moment, he felt a little ridiculous leaning against a tree with his hard, upright cock jutting out. Then she knelt in front of him, and he didn't feel ridiculous at all.

For a moment, she stared up at him, and he down at her. Neither of them believed that her kneeling gave her any less power.

She wrapped one hand around the base of his shaft. Lowered her head. Took him into her mouth.

Was it possible to die from pleasure? He'd known nothing like this, like her. She swirled her tongue around the head, then dipped lower, taking him more fully. His fingers dug into the rough bark of the tree trunk, yet his hips would not remain still. As she licked and sucked, he pushed forward. She did not retreat, but lapped at him eagerly.

Dawn lightened the sky, and he stared up at the branches limned in gold, both transported out of his body and deeply, richly immersed in sensation. This was everything . . . and if it went on much longer, he could not put off his release.

He lifted her off and up him. They kissed with aching tenderness.

He lowered them both to the ground. As she stretched out on her back, he leaned over her and gathered up her skirts.

Briefly, very briefly, he indulged himself in looking at her: mouth red, bodice undone and dark nipples visible through the light fabric of her blouse, skirts at her waist, legs spread to reveal her slick, ready quim. She was both vulnerable and impossibly powerful. Her hips tilted up in invitation.

He settled between her thighs. She wrapped her legs around them. They were like that for a few moments, breath and heartbeats aligned, their gazes held.

He sank into her. They both gasped as he penetrated her deeply.

"Yes." Pleasure and emotion suffused him. "Here."

He drew back and thrust forward again. She bent up, moaning.

"Whit. *Acoi.*"

All around him, she was drenching heat, tight and flawless. He gave her slow, measured strokes, letting them feel one another. Though his body shouted for speed, for climax, he would not give in. The sun would rise, and when it sank down again, both he and Zora would face the possibility of death—or worse. The need in him was primal, to give her this pleasure now, to brand himself upon her from this moment and all the moments after, through eternity.

"I'm yours." His voice had never been deeper. He plunged into her again and again. "Understand that, Zora. *Yours.*"

"*Miro*," she gasped. "Mine."

All he wanted was to belong to her, and he did. "Yes."

She was flame beneath him, making wordless sounds of pleasure.

His tempo increased, the speed of his thrusts. Her moans urged him on. The glen filled with the sounds of flesh to flesh, a communion of bodies, of more than bodies, but hearts and souls.

She gripped the earth and bowed up, moaning her release. His own followed heartbeats after, beginning low in his back and pouring through him in long, brilliant pulses until he reached the very edge of oblivion, impelled onward by pleasure beyond reckoning.

When the very last of his orgasm faded into hot, red echoes, he withdrew. He carefully rearranged their clothing, enough to preserve a trace of modesty, then lay down beside her. She went willingly into his arms, curling against him with an ease that took his breath. Her murmurs were drowsy, barely intelligible, and she quickly drifted off to sleep.

Sated exhaustion pulled at him, yet he forced himself to stay awake just a little longer. This might be his final day. Surviving the coming night was not a given. If given a single day, how might one fill those hours? Such a question was the kind posed by students of philosophy in the senior commons, whiling away the dark, wine-soaked hours before dawn. He avoided such hypothetical discussions, preferring to consider what *was* rather than what might be. Theory and possibility he engaged only at the gaming tables, and even there, the outcome was real, not speculative.

This was not theoretical. Truly, this might be his final hours alive. Leaving him with the question: What was he to do with himself?

He glanced down at Zora, asleep in his arms.

Here, then, his answer. If he had a single day of life he would do precisely this.

Chapter 18

They spent the day in the glen: sleeping, lying quietly together, talking of unimportant things. Neither wanted to risk going into the city for food, so Zora foraged and found apples and wild greens, and this made up their simple meal as the day crept unceasingly onward.

She watched the sun's progress across the sky. Time slipped away, measured in golden light and high, scattered clouds, in the patterns of birdsong, and, very distantly, human voices. She and Whit pretended not to notice. They fed one another slices of apple, spoke about plays—those she had seen had been performed by strolling actors at horse fairs and markets, while he had attended Drury Lane and the Haymarket Theaters Royal—and favorite games of chance.

They made love once more, slow but fierce, holding one another's gaze until pleasure overtook them and their eyes closed in ecstasy.

These moments of privacy and safety were brief and deceptive. She tried to grab at them with both hands, yet they slipped away. Neither spoke of what was to come, yet they both understood that, at sunset, they would undertake a gamble worth far more than money, more than their very lives. No future was discussed, or what might be. A silent agreement not to hope for too much.

Shadows deepened in the glen. Zora shivered from the growing chill, and found warmth in Whit's arms.

That was how Livia found them, wrapped together. The priestess appeared as twilight fell, her ghostly light a little paler before the onset of full darkness.

"The time draws near," she said.

Zora was amazed at how far Livia had come since first she appeared to her in Whit's gaming room; her eyes and wits sharpened with each manifestation. Perhaps the more the ghost interacted with the world, the more her mind anchored. Whatever the cause, Zora was grateful that her and Whit's lone ally could finally speak sense—even though Zora did not much want to hear sense right now. She wanted this day to last forever. It didn't.

She and Whit got to their feet, brushing leaves off each other and plucking away stray bits of grass clinging to their hair and clothing. As if they were merely returning from a picnic.

"Have you everything needed for this scheme?" the ghost asked.

Whit drew his pocket watch from his waistcoat. He ran his thumb back and forth over the silver case, his expression brooding. An old watch, much used and, in its way, much loved. Zora remembered seeing him with it soon after he'd taken her to London. The Rom knew the value of objects— not merely their worth in coin, but significance. As roving people, they did not prize land, nor anything too large to easily move, yet what could be passed from one generation to the next was deeply cherished.

Whit had land. He owned many objects, small and large. And seemed to give none of them any thought. Not so this pocket watch. He had told her that it once belonged to his grandfather, a man with the same name as Whit. She had studied him when he had revealed this. Despite the distance he felt from his family and birthright, the pocket watch held meaning for him, a connection even he did not fully understand.

"I have this," he said, "and my control of the odds."

"Don't forget, you have me," added Zora.

He ran the backs of his fingers down her cheek. "I never forget, and I never assume."

Zora tried to speak and found that for the first time she could not. Her throat ached with unsaid words, and something more.

"If you are prepared," said Livia, urgent, "we must begin. Now, while my power is strong enough."

"One moment more." Whit brushed a kiss across Zora's lips. He might have meant it to be sweet and tender, yet nothing between them could last in so mild a state. The kiss grew hungry. It couldn't be ignored any longer: this might be the last time they would ever touch.

They pulled back just enough to take each other's breath. His lips hovered less than an inch from hers.

"A Gypsy and a gentleman gambler," he murmured. "An unlikely pair."

"An unbeatable pair," she said.

They both smiled ruefully, for though she spoke with bravado, neither truly believed her. But that was the nature of the bluff—pretending just enough to reach the desired outcome.

Reluctantly, they stepped apart. Zora signaled her readiness with a nod.

From this point on, there was only moving forward. By the next sunrise, Whit would be either saved or eternally damned, which would damn her, as well.

Having walked into town, Whit now stood in the grimy square outside the gaming hell. His pulse beat thickly, his mouth was dry, and his skin was taut over his muscles and bones. He resisted the impulse to touch the timepiece in his waistcoat pocket. If anyone watched the street from within the gaming hell, the person would surely take note of any gesture he made. He had to appear as any gentleman eager to risk fortune.

He smoothed his hair in its queue and tugged on his coat. Yet before he took a step, a voice stopped him.

"You've the same needs, despite your claims to the contrary."

Turning, Whit watched Bram emerge from the shadows. In his long black coat, his hair dark and his eyes haunted, his old friend seemed *made* of shadows, separating only a little from their veiled darkness to stand three paces away.

Whit's hand hovered near his pistol in his coat. "Whatever your purpose here, I have not the time to indulge you."

"This place"—Bram tilted his head toward the gaming hell—"it's no different from what can be yours in London."

"After slicing me with your blade, you still want me to return to you and the other Hellraisers?" Whit could not keep the suspicion from his voice. "Why? To what purpose?"

"Because that is how it is *meant to be*." Bram took a step closer, and weak lamplight chiseled his face into a collection of sharp surfaces. "You and I, the others. We carve the world to suit our needs. Almost nothing stopped us before, and with our gifts, nothing can ever stand in our way."

"*We* stand in our way. No matter how deeply we've fallen, there yet exists in us some honor."

"I saw enough *honor* in my military service to know that it's valueless."

"But *you* have value, Bram."

Bram's mouth twisted cruelly. "I thought us friends, that you above all knew me. I was mistaken."

How had Whit not seen it? The corrosion eating his friend from the inside out? Surely Mr. Holliday had known, and preyed upon that, as he preyed upon all of the Hellraisers' weaknesses. The Devil saw what Whit either could not or refused to see.

"I did you a disservice," said Whit. "And for that, I am sorry."

Whatever Bram was expecting, it was not an apology.

He could only glare at Whit with a mixture of hostility and confusion.

Whit took a step toward the gaming hell. He could not linger outside, for there was work to be done within. Yet Bram stopped him once more.

"That Gypsy wench. The fiery one."

Whit tensed. "What of her?"

Bram made a show of looking around. "Her absence is conspicuous."

"Women aren't allowed in gaming hells."

"Then she is nearby." Bram smiled predatorily. "She might need companionship."

"Spare her your excellent company." The edge in Whit's voice could cut through bone.

Yet Bram *was* a predator, and when he sensed a weakness, he attacked it. "Here's a dilemma for you, Whit. Either indulge your need for gaming, or keep me from your woman. Which is it to be?"

When Whit said nothing, holding himself taut and still, Bram's smile widened.

"Enjoy your night's sport. I know *I* shall." Bram sauntered away, his long coat a black wake as it billowed behind him.

It took several moments, but Whit eventually unclenched his fists. He could do nothing for or about Bram. Now, his only goal lay on the other side of the gaming hell door. He strode up the steps, conscious the whole time of the slight weight of his pocket watch.

Before he could raise his hand to knock, the door opened. The gaming hell's bully filled the doorway, then stepped back and, with his giant hand, waved Whit in.

"Lord Whitney."

Of course they knew him, and his intentions. Whit only hoped that was all that comprised their knowledge.

He straightened his shoulders and stepped inside. The door shut behind him.

* * *

For all that he had anticipated what might be inside this place, he still gave an involuntary start when he saw the face of the bully. It wasn't a man, not even a very big man.

It was a demon. Dressed like a man. The creature had leathery red skin, a protruding brow, horns and tusks. Yet it wore a waistcoat, shirtsleeves, and breeches. No shoes upon its huge, taloned feet. A demon footman in Manchester.

"Down the hall, to the back," it grunted. Sounds of play rang out from the gaming room, the cacophony of men's shouts, coins clinking, and the rattle of dice. That, at least, was familiar.

As Whit moved toward the gaming room, a heavy clawed hand gripped his shoulder.

"Weapons with me, my lord."

He did not want to disarm himself, but it was to be expected. He divested himself of his pistol and hunting knife. Now he was armed only with his mastery over probability and the plan. They both could not fail.

Satisfied, the massive demon jerked its head to indicate Whit could move on. He gladly did so.

He walked down a corridor lit by dozens of reeking tallow candles. Framed pictures portrayed men surrounded by wealth, food and drink worthy of a feast, and soft, pale women largely bereft of clothing, smiling beguilingly. Every man's fantasy. Peering closer, he noticed that the women had snakes' tongues, the food was rotten, and the piles of coins were tarnished. He wondered how many patrons bothered to look carefully.

Certainly none of the men he passed in the corridor gave much thought to their surroundings. They staggered in from smaller side rooms, holding cups of wine, roaring with laughter or cursing one another.

Whit followed the growing din. Until at last he found himself in the gaming room. His heart kicked, to be back amidst the world he knew so well, the thrill of chance that continued to pull at him. And here was chance in abundance.

Blistering heat. A press of bodies. Sulfurous candlelight turning desperate men's faces into sweat-filmed, red-eyed grotesques. They crowded the tables, waving fists, throwing dice and slapping down cards. The chamber shook with their voices, harsh and discordant. He could taste despair and hopelessness in the air, turning the atmosphere rancid. At the far end of the chamber, a blaze burned in a massive fireplace, throwing long shadows over the walls.

In all of this, the chamber was much the same as a multitude of gaming hells. The men were a little rougher than his usual London crowd—though most here had means. The gestures toward decoration were minimal and poorly kept, yet the tables for hazard and piquet were familiar. Even the looks of desperation on the patrons' faces were recognizable, if less disguised than normal.

The patrons did not surprise Whit, but the staff did.

More demons. Of every size and shape. They were clothed like men, but there was no escaping the fact that they were, indeed, demons.

Some were small, bat-winged imps. These creatures fetched wine on dented pewter plates. The piquet dealers stood the same height as men but had the bulging eyes and gray, bumpy skin of toads, their hands webbed, their mouths filled with jagged teeth. Other creatures were bones—not skeletons, but collections of bones held together by some sinister power in the rough shape of men. Finger bones and ribs and teeth and bones belonging to parts of the anatomy Whit could not begin to speculate. Embers burned in the eye sockets. Dice rattled in their bony hands as they presided over the hazard tables.

This truly was a gaming hell.

None of the men within it noticed. They continued on in their play, deep in their games, and entirely unaware that they gambled amidst creatures from the underworld. They had no idea that what they staked was more than money.

The crowds parted and a man appeared, as if summoned by Whit's thoughts. Even across the room, Whit recognized him. The man was no man, yet it shared Whit's face, his shape, his gestures. His dark self.

His *geminus*.

"Excellent timing, my lord." The creature played the affable host, smiling, arms open. "The game is about to begin."

"What is it to be? Piquet? Vingt-et-un?" The *geminus* guided him forward, offering anything a gambler could want.

"Hazard," said Whit.

The *geminus* smiled wider. "Of course. I should have known. This way, my lord."

Whit followed the creature to a corner of the room, near the colossal fireplace. The flames within threw off blistering heat, and as he neared, sweat coated his back and his clothing stuck to him like someone else's skin.

He and the *geminus* took up their places at a table covered in dark red baize. A bone demon stepped forward and bowed, its body creaking with every movement. It presented Whit with a pair of dice. The carved ivory pieces were almost indistinguishable from the bones of its hand, save for the small black pips marking the dice.

Cold bones brushed Whit's hand as he took the dice.

"What shall we play for?" The *geminus* maintained its cordiality, and, in a way, Whit was glad, for it meant that the creature suspected nothing.

"A thousand pounds."

Disquieting, seeing the *geminus* offer the precise expression of careful boredom Whit implemented so often at the tables. "Trivial," it drawled. "Yet a fitting way to commence."

"If my lord would be so kind as to call your main." The hazard table attendant's voice was a rasping scrape, the disturbing sound of bone against bone.

"Six." Whit rolled the dice. As he did, he delved into the patterns of probability, knowing he would have to play his strategies carefully.

The dice came up a five. This number would now be his chance. He would have to roll again, and hope for a five.

"A side bet," said the *geminus*. "Two thousand pounds that your main will come up before your chance."

"Done."

He rolled twice more, letting control over the odds go as slack as a cast fishing line before reeling it in. His chance came up.

"Five," intoned the bone demon. "A nicks. You win, my lord."

Whit indulged in the briefest pleasure—he still enjoyed winning, no matter the circumstances.

The *geminus* yawned. "These bets are inconsequential. And, I'd wager, not why you came here this evening."

"Higher stakes would add some piquancy." He, too, could affect the proper boredom, even as his ribs felt tight and his mind raced.

"Then wager something of significance."

"If I'm to risk something I value," Whit said leisurely, "it is only fair that you, too, make a meaningful wager."

The *geminus* laughed—Whit's laugh, the same he utilized at the gaming table, the one that showed superficial amusement.

"By all means," the creature said, smirking, "let us not waste time on the preliminaries. If you win this next round, I shall grant you fifteen more years on top of your original life span."

Whit was tempted to ask how long he was slated to live, but he did not truly want to know the answer. He did know that fifteen more years merely delayed the inevitable, if Mr. Holliday still possessed his soul.

"And if you lose this next round," the *geminus* continued, "you shall give me the Gypsy girl."

Whit's hands ached as he gripped the edge of the table, struggling to keep from beating the creature senseless. At that very moment, Bram prowled the streets of Manchester in search of Zora. Whit spoke through clenched teeth. "She isn't mine to wager."

The *geminus* raised a brow. "The latest intelligence suggests otherwise."

"Whitston. That is my wager. Unless you have taken it already."

"My subordinates ran your servants and tenants off, and have made themselves comfortable. You have already met them."

Whit struggled to keep from choking the life out of the *geminus*, remembering the demon-borne illness that nearly cost Zora her life. He took some comfort in knowing that the staff and tenants had not been truly harmed. As for the house and lands, they were valued but hadn't the worth of human life.

The estate had belonged to Whit's family for centuries. It provided the source of their wealth, the foundation of their power. He had other estates, yet none of them carried the significance of Whitston.

The *geminus* knew this. It grinned, an awful parody of himself. "What is left of the house and its lands is still yours. Yet, at this juncture, there is something I must disclose. Only sporting of me."

"Yes?"

"The gift that Mr. Holliday granted you. Power over probability. It operates differently in this gaming establishment."

Whit stilled. "Tell me."

"In here, your mastery over the odds is reversed. The more important the wager is to you, the less control you have over probability."

Whit took a moment to absorb this. "I will lose," he said tightly.

"Perhaps. Perhaps not. It is truly *gambling*, not certainty." The *geminus* gave another ghastly smile. "You remember gambling, don't you, my lord? There was a time when you lived for nothing else. So, shall we play?"

He stared at the creature. Continue on, or turn back? His gaze moved down to his left hand, covered by the Devil's mark. He thought of Zora, his vibrant Gypsy, the heat in her

eyes and fire in her soul. He wore her ring around his neck.
Retreat was impossible when it meant losing her.

"We play." He scooped up the dice. "Eight."

He cast the dice, diving into the shifting structures of
probability. Just as the *geminus* had predicted, he now found
the structures of probability difficult to hold. Like wriggling
snakes, they struggled to slip from his grasp. As the pieces
of ivory rolled across the table, he fought to hold and shape
probability as he needed it.

The dice came to a stop. Two sixes.

"Twelve," announced the bone demon. "A nicks. You have
won again, my lord."

A thin smile from the *geminus*. Yet Whit did not feel
much sense of victory. He was about to take his biggest
gamble.

Zora hated this, hated knowing that Whit was out there,
alone. His strength and skill were never in doubt, but he
faced an enemy that obeyed no rules and had limitless power
at its disposal. Even with his fighting ability, his manipulation of probability, he was still at a huge disadvantage. He
needed someone at his side, someone to watch his back,
face the inevitable treachery with him.

She burned with impatience. *This has to end now.*

Yet there was nothing for her to do. For now, all she could
do was wait. Her time was coming. Soon.

"Only preliminaries, as you say." Whit braced his hands on
the table. He drew upon his wellsprings of calm, the gambler's lack of affect that was at one time more familiar to him
than open laughter or anger. Zora had dragged him from his
self-imposed impassivity, the blank emptiness within giving
way to unbridled feeling. True, it was easier to feel nothing,
free from true pain or loss, yet that meant living less than
half a life.

She had blazed into his world, waking him from cold dormancy. Blood and sensation filled his body. His thawed heart. Because of her.

"My purpose is doubtless clear to you," he said.

"To gamble for your soul." Thoughtful, the *geminus* frowned. "Why should I wager my master's valuable possession? It already belongs to him."

"Think of the risk. The fortune you tempt, and what *I* am risking." Whit's voice was smoothly persuasive. He understood the scrupulous ways in which he essentially manipulated himself, for the *geminus* was fashioned of the selfsame material. The creature and he were not merely similar, but identical, and he played upon that now.

"You have something I want," he continued. "Very badly. Is it not thrilling to watch me make this desperate gamble? To know that *you* hold the power here? Especially as I have no advantage."

Dark excitement gleamed in the creature's eyes. Like any veteran gambler, it quickly hid its emotions. "What stand I to gain by accepting this bet? There is nothing more valuable in your possession." It added, sulky, "And you will not wager the girl."

Here, as planned and hoped for, was his moment.

"This." He pulled the pocket watch from his waistcoat. His fingers curled tightly around the timepiece, instinctively protecting something so precious.

Like a jackal sighting prey, the *geminus*'s pupils widened, its eyes darkening with greed. As Whit's double, it knew the significance of the pocket watch, what the timepiece truly meant to him. Nothing material in his possession held as much value; it was his only true link with his family and birthright.

"Should I win," said Whit, "I regain my soul. And should I lose, you put the pocket watch in your vault."

The *geminus* raised a brow, suspicious. "You know of it?"

"We share most everything. I have seen with your eyes. Felt with your heart. Just as you have seen and felt what I have."

"Including the Gypsy girl." A venomous smile followed the *geminus*'s words. "The pocket watch in my vault. I rather like picturing that. The bright token of your soul beside that battered old watch, where no one can see it, no one can touch it. You will spend your remaining days knowing that the last of your legacy is beyond your reach. And you will also lose the chance to ever again reclaim your soul."

Sharp pain sliced through Whit as he considered this. There was no choice, however.

"Do you agree to the terms of the wager?" His voice was rough.

"I do."

Whit stuck out his hand. The *geminus* snorted at such a quaint, honorable gesture. Yet it shook Whit's hand—an uncanny moment for Whit, shaking hands with himself. The creature was cold, so it felt as if he shook hands with his animated corpse.

The *geminus* released Whit's hand. "Let us commence."

"Call your main, my lord," the bone demon creaked after Whit took the dice.

He considered it. "Seven."

"The main with the greatest probability of winning," noted the *geminus*.

"I *am* a gambler, but I take whatever advantage possible."

"Naturally," said the creature.

Whit blocked the sounds of the room from his mind. His sole focus became the dice in his hand. Small cubes of ivory that bore the full weight of his eternity.

This was no game with something as negligible as wealth or property at stake. This was Whit's soul, and his future. He finally understood how much he wanted that future— with Zora.

For her, then, and himself.

He cast the dice.

As they tumbled, Whit tried once more to plunge into the swirling vortices of probability. Now, when so much depended on the outcome, he found the patterns more complex than ever, impossibly convoluted. This was no mere shifting of the odds, for if one fragile element changed, a tidal wave of unwanted outcome followed. The smallest miscalculation could cause disaster. The lacework of probability covered him, pulsating against his skin and inside his body, his mind.

Nothing would hold in his grasp. He could *see* probability but could effect no change upon it. It simply existed. Independent of him. What it would do, what form it might take, he could not predict or alter. It was true chance.

As Whit's heart beat thunderously, the dice slowed. Stopped their roll.

"Three," pronounced the bone demon. "A throw-out."

The *geminus* smiled its death's-head grin. "You lose, my lord."

For several moments, Whit stood motionless, silent. He stared at the dice, and their markings. Two, and one. Three. By picking seven, his cast of the dice could not be three, else that meant he lost the round. And so he did.

The *geminus* held out its hand. "The terms were precise. Now you must forfeit."

Whit unclenched his fingers from around the pocket watch. He had clutched it throughout the round, and it left an imprint in his palm like a memory soon to fade. His arm felt made of rusted iron as he held out the watch, and he found it strange that his muscles and bones didn't shriek with the movement.

The pocket watch. Everything that he was and would ever be. Held out to the Devil's eager minion.

As fast as a striking scorpion, the *geminus* snatched the timepiece. Once the watch was in its grasp, however, the creature took its time. It held up the watch, admiring its prize. Firelight gleamed across the metal surface, as if the flames of the underworld clamored to consume it. A circle of reflected light shimmered over the *geminus*'s eyes. It grinned as it stared at its new treasure.

"Another round," said Whit.

But the *geminus* merely smiled. "Come now, my lord, those were not the terms of our agreement. We shook hands like gentlemen."

"Neither of us are gentlemen."

"Several hundred years of the Sherbournes' selective breeding begs to disagree. And, as I am merely a part of you, the same rules apply." The creature closed its fingers around the pocket watch. "So I will do you the honor of ignoring that insult to us both."

Whit knew that nothing he might say could convince the *geminus* to give him another chance. He remained rigid and still, his every muscle coiled, ready to spring.

"Now," said the creature, brisk and cheerful, "I will take my prize to its new home." It strode from the table.

Whit followed, shadowing the *geminus* as it wove through the chamber. The heat and sound crushed down, and there were men everywhere, red-faced, riotous, lost in the morass of gambling. His head spun as he trailed after the *geminus*, the room awash in tumult. Faces swam toward him, twisted by darkness and firelight. Some laughed. Others shouted in rage. Demons appeared and disappeared in the chaos.

God, but he wanted to see Zora's face. To have her beside him, brash and fierce.

The *geminus* left the main gaming chamber. Whit followed close behind. Yet the creature walked leisurely, its stride easy and confident, as it entered a sparsely populated corridor. It stopped beside a door, then paused, its hand on the doorknob.

"You cannot take it back from me." Carelessly spoken, the *geminus*'s words. "Not by force, not by persuasion."

"I know."

"A final farewell, then?" The creature shrugged. "As you wish."

It held up the watch, and even though the creature had Whit's form, its hand identical to his, nausea billowed as he saw the precious object in its hand. He fought the impulse to try to seize the pocket watch, his body locked tight in a kind of rigor mortis.

"A last look," smirked the *geminus*. It opened the door.

Whit caught a glimpse of the vault within. The chamber appeared precisely as it had when he had been the *geminus*: stone walls, vaulted ceiling, shelves awaiting further souls. Hunger rose in a dim surge as he felt the *geminus*'s demands for more and more souls, more power. Whit wanted that power for himself.

Zora would urge him to fight that hunger, and it *was* a fight.

Sensing this, the creature gave him a condescending smile. "Beautiful, is it not? Alas, never to be yours. Only mine, and my master's. Your pardon, my lord, but this is the portion of the evening you are not permitted to see."

It stepped into the vault and shut the door.

Whit opened the door immediately. He found himself in a dim parlor, where two men hunched over a game of whist. A demon with a twisted face presided over the game, and it looked at him with polite disinterest.

"Shall I deal you in the next round, my lord?"

Whit closed the door.

Standing in the corridor, he envisioned very clearly what was transpiring in the vault. The *geminus* walked across the stone floor, passing the tokens of other souls it had won or stolen. Until it stopped beside the shelf that held Whit's soul. It placed the pocket watch next to the token and admired the pretty picture they made, side by side. His eternal soul, and the tangible evidence of his legacy. Both now lost to him, kept in the accursed vault until the end of time.

After a last, exultant look, the *geminus* walked through the vault. Its shelves kept filling, and Manchester would see even more treasure added. At that very moment, nearly fifty men in the gaming hell were staking their souls, and none of them knew. The master would be very, very pleased. His power grew with each soul. Once he had acquired enough, he would be unstoppable. What a marvelous day. The final day. Eternal night ever after. Hell on earth.

The *geminus* was not surprised to see Whit waiting for him on the other side of the door.

"No need to look so dour, my lord." The creature shut the door behind it. "The night has only just begun, and there are so many marvelous games to play." It held out a directing hand, urging Whit back into the main gambling room.

If Whit opened the door again, he would find exactly what he had seen before. A parlor, with men playing whist. Not the vault. Only the *geminus* could enter it.

"Yes," he heard himself say. "There are many games to play."

He followed the *geminus*, casting one last, lingering glance at the door. Behind it lay everything he'd ever valued.

Chapter 19

Within the vault, everything was quiet, suspended in eternal silence. No one ever walked upon its floor save the creature who had built the structure. The souls contained within it existed in solitude, feeding the Devil's ravenous appetite. When the time came and they were fully consumed, no one would witness their final fading. There was power here, and despair.

And stillness.

Yet not everything was still. On one shelf, beside a particularly radiant soul, sat a pocket watch. Old and battered. A perfectly ordinary pocket watch, hardly worthy of being in the vault.

The watch moved. At first, the movement was small. Barely more than a vibration. But then it began to rattle. It moved as if something were trapped inside trying to break free. The metal casing glowed. The pocket watch jolted as its case opened. Light poured out of the timepiece, pooling on the shelf and moving down to the floor. The gleaming light grew and coalesced into the height and shape of a woman. The glow faded, but the woman remained. In her hand, she held a heavy cavalry saber.

Zora stood in a large stone chamber. Its ceilings curved up high above her head. Tables ran down the length of the room, and shelves bearing small, glowing objects lined the walls. She recognized the objects without ever seeing them before. Souls.

This was the *geminus*'s vault.

Her gaze immediately flew to the shelf closest to her. What she saw there made her gasp. Whit's soul shone like the rarest of gems, casting a radiance so beautiful her eyes grew hot and damp. How lovely it was. How precious. No wonder *Wafodu guero* wanted it. The power and beauty of Whit's soul would make anyone covetous.

Beside the gleaming soul sat the pocket watch. Her means of transportation. *It worked.* Livia's spell had truly worked, as had Whit's plan to lose to the *geminus*. Granting Zora means of entry to the vault. It had been a strange sensation to be suspended in magic within the watch, able to see and hear everything outside as if from a great distance. The world felt very bright and close after she had emerged.

She had little time to lose. She took the watch and tucked it safely into her pocket. Whit's soul remained. Gently, with utmost care, she took hold of the radiant token. Living energy shimmered through her, filled her. *Incredible.* Touching the soul of her lover, holding it in the palm of her hand. She felt alive yet profoundly peaceful as Whit's wild, passionate spirit enveloped her. Even making love with him had not brought them so close. From this moment on, she would know him as she knew her own soul.

Yet his had to be returned to him. At once.

Making a pouch of her skirts, she quickly ran through the vault and gathered souls. Every one. And they were plentiful. In the brief time the *geminus* had walked the earth, it had been busy. Touching all these souls filled her with power, so much that she grew dizzy with it. Easy to understand why *Wafodu guero* coveted them for himself. Precisely why she had to take them back.

She hurried to the door and opened it. As the door opened, the souls' brightness grew. Her eyes widened as the souls dissolved into pure light, flying down the corridor in streaks of radiance. They flew out a window at the end of the hallway and disappeared into the night.

The souls were free, returning to their rightful owners. Her own heart soared. Yet her joy did not last long. A horrible, terrifying scream came from all around her. It shook the walls and froze her blood. The sound of demons shrieking in rage.

They knew. The demons knew what she had done. They would demand vengeance.

Instinctively knowing where she needed to be, she ran down the corridor, sword in hand.

Whit watched a group of men at the hazard table, barely feigning interest in their play as he waited for Zora to enact the next stage of the plan. Tension pulsed through him. He felt ready to put his fists through the walls. Giving the *geminus* his pocket watch was the most difficult thing he had ever done. If anything went awry, Zora would be trapped—either within the watch itself or in the vault. Yet he'd had to hand over the timepiece, and he had died by degrees as the *geminus* took it, and Zora, away.

All he could do now was wait—and it was killing him.

Then he felt it. A surge of energy moved through the gaming hell, as strong as a tidal wave. All of the demons stopped in the midst of motion. Dealing cards, serving wine, collecting winnings. As one, the monsters looked up and froze. Even the *geminus* paused as it urged a man toward the Pope Joan table. The creature looked baffled and then . . . enraged.

"Whit." Zora's voice.

He spun around and saw her, standing at the entrance to the gaming room. Their gazes locked. Something wild and fierce broke open within him.

In one hand, she held his saber. The other held a glowing

object. He knew what it was. It flew up from her hand and headed straight toward Whit.

He saw the *geminus* move to intercept the light. Instinctively, Whit threw out a punch, slamming his fist into the creature's jaw. Pain blossomed through his own jaw, but it was enough force to stagger the *geminus*. It reeled back just as the light hit Whit in the center of his chest.

As the light spread through him, the feeling was unlike anything he had experienced. No—that was not true. When he had held Zora, when he loved her, the feeling was the same. Completeness. An aligning of self. The darkness within shrinking away. Not gone entirely, for that would always be a part of him, but it no longer corroded him from the inside out.

She had done it. Zora had freed his soul.

As his soul filled him, a black cord within him snapped. A dark, glimmering power. The control over the odds broke away, dissolving into a shadowed miasma. It was gone. The power for which he had traded his soul was no more.

He waited for the sensation of loss he thought inevitable. It did not come. He had his soul. He had Zora. He needed nothing more.

The air filled with demons' shrieks. The *geminus* threw back its head and screamed, its face contorting with wrath.

Men in the gaming chamber trembled at the screams, throwing their arms around their heads, cowering under the tables. The noise seemed to wake them from a trance, for they suddenly looked around and saw themselves in the company of monsters. Their terrified shrieks joined the demons' howls of rage. Panicked, the men shoved one another in a mad flight to the door. Whit struggled to remain standing as he was buffeted by fleeing men.

"Tricks and deceptions!" The *geminus*'s wild, maddened gaze locked on Whit. "Your doing."

"Only a fool goes up against the Devil without a plan. I've grown much wiser these past weeks."

Snarling, the *geminus* stepped back, then shouted in an

unknown language to the demons in the room. Moving in unison, half the demons turned to face Whit. The other faced Zora, readying to attack.

He had no weapons. Not even his pistol. But he had his soul. And the knowledge that he must fight his way to Zora, protect her.

A trio of demons rushed him, talons out. He grabbed a heavy chair and swung it. The demons staggered, dazed, and the chair broke apart, precisely as he wanted it to. In each hand, he now held pointed wooden stakes. They weren't much as weapons, but to reach Zora and get her to safety, he would battle with his bare hands—and God help anyone who got in his way.

Zora admired the sight Whit made, fending off attacking demons with only two wooden stakes. He swung and parried, struck out and blocked blows, all swift motion and deadly purpose. With unerring skill, he found the demons' weaknesses, their vulnerabilities. The fiends fought and fell, yet more kept coming. He could not hold them off forever. She winced as one demon caught him across the back with a well-aimed claw. Whit spun and stabbed the fiend in the juncture between its neck and shoulder. Black blood arced up as the demon collapsed.

But there were more, and more. The *geminus* stood in the corner urging the fiends on. She had to help, reach him. Dozens of demons stood between her and Whit.

She did not need to draw on the blaze that burned in the fireplace. She had her own fire, stronger now that she was with Whit, and his soul restored. The flames leapt from her hand, forming into a whip. It snapped against a cluster of demons. The fiends howled and fell as she raked them with fire.

Three small, flying demons hurtled toward her. She lashed out with her whip of fire. They were reduced to cinders instantly, black dust scattering over the floor.

She and Whit fought their way toward each other, demons

falling, screaming, splattering blood. Until, at last, Whit stood before her. She had never seen him so savage, so beautiful.

They had only a moment to touch one another. A quick meeting of hands. Yes, he was real, and she was real, and danger surrounded them.

Zora drew his sword. Her fire power rose up like a beast unchained. Flames engulfed the blade.

"Make them pay," she said.

He took the weapon. Grasping the sword of fire, surrounded by demons, he was a conquering angel. Never had she beheld a man so powerful as Whit, beautiful and lethal. The demons, seeing the sword in his hand, screamed.

Turning, he swung out at the fiends, cleaving through them. The smoky atmosphere turned thick, filling with the stench of burning demon flesh. He slammed the hilt of the sword into a creature made of bones. The thing shattered.

A movement caught her attention, and she thought for a heartbeat that Whit had somehow gotten to the other side of the chamber and was trying to flee. But Whit would never run away. He was right beside her.

"Whit—the *geminus*."

At Zora's words, Whit turned to his true target. The *geminus*.

It was creeping along the wall, attempting escape in the midst of chaos. It hissed, revealing hidden serpent's fangs. Talons sharpened its hands. It had to be destroyed, this creature, this darkest part of himself. Whit wanted vengeance.

He began to clear a path to the *geminus*, cutting down demons with his saber. Screams and blood everywhere. He heard none of it, his focus narrowing. He kept part of himself attuned to Zora, ready to leap to her aid if she needed him. Like him, she hungered for demon blood, ready to wipe their evil from the face of the earth. And that meant the obliteration of his *geminus*.

Seeing Whit steadily approach, the creature waved its

clawed hands in the air. Flames swirled around it, gathering to form a shape in its hands. An axe of fire. Brutal, the
geminus's weapon. Whit bared his teeth. He was ready to
face anything.

His sword crashed against the creature's axe. Reverbera-
tions from the blow traveled up his arm, yet he would not
allow the hit to slow him. He pushed back, and the weapons
clashed once more.

"It can still be yours," the *geminus* panted. "It is not lost.
Say the word, and your control over probability shall return."

"Keep it," Whit said through clenched teeth.

"Any game you seek to win, you can. And if you desire
pure chance, you can have that, too." Though the blade of
his axe locked with Whit's saber, the *geminus* made its voice
silky, persuasive. "Consider—the power over probability
can fill the emptiness within you, that vast chasm in search
of *more*. Always *more*. Say but a word, and it's yours again."

Temptation. So deep and powerful, calling to the hollow-
ness within him. Once, it would have enticed him.

"The emptiness is gone." He lightened pressure just
enough to slip free from the lock, and lunged. His blade
sliced across the creature's chest. He felt no corresponding
pain in his own flesh. "I have my soul. I have love."

"Love?" Angry that its effort to tempt Whit had failed,
the *geminus* sneered, even as blood dripped onto the floor.
"Worthless."

It slammed its shoulder into Whit's chest. Whit struggled
to breathe, and as he fought for air, the *geminus* darted
around him. Axe upraised, it headed straight for Zora. She
didn't see its approach, her attention fixed on the demons
she fought.

Whit acted immediately, instinctively. Rage poured
through him as he launched himself at the *geminus*.

His saber sliced through the back of the creature's thigh.
Screaming, it went down on one knee.

Zora turned at the sound. Her eyes widened to see how

near the *geminus* was, how close it had come to hurting her. She gazed at Whit, and he was almost overcome by feeling at the gratitude and emotion in her eyes.

Then more demons moved to attack her, and she turned to fight them back. Her fire traced bright ribbons through the air. Her ferocity was more beautiful than life itself.

"Love isn't worthless," he said as the *geminus* pushed itself up to standing. "It is *everything*."

Swaying as it balanced on its uninjured leg, the creature's face contorted in rage. Whit would never return to the Devil's faction, and both he and the *geminus* knew it. One option remained: death.

He and the *geminus* threw themselves against each other. As demons fought and died around them, Whit and his dark self battled. Again and again, his saber and the creature's axe clashed. He had fought Bram and the other Hellraisers, but all restriction was gone now. He wanted—*needed*—this creature dead. For retribution. For the future.

They moved through the room together, through the growing piles of fallen demons, through the drifts of playing cards and scattered dice. He and the *geminus* lashed out, blocked hits, evaded blows. The creature swung and Whit sidestepped. He missed the worst of the strike, but the blade caught him just above his bicep. Not a deep hit, yet enough to shed blood and send hot pain through him.

A scream sounded right behind Whit. He spun around in time to see a bone demon turn to carbon as Zora's lash of fire wrapped around its body. The demon had been moments away from attacking him.

He nodded his thanks, vowing that he would thank her properly—later. For now, he had a *geminus* to kill.

Turning back to the creature, energy renewed, he launched into a new attack. The *geminus* found itself on the defensive, frantically trying to block his strikes. It wasn't enough. This had to end. He had to rid the world of the blight that he had created.

He could not manipulate chance, but he could use intelligence and strategy.

Whit edged back. Seeing an opening, the *geminus* pushed forward. It stepped onto a fallen playing card: the queen of diamonds. The creature slipped on the card, just enough to throw it off balance as it swung at Whit. The axe's blade slammed into the wall, lodging there.

The *geminus* pulled on the axe's handle, but the weapon held fast.

Whit stepped forward. He did not hesitate, did not speak. His gaze fixed on the creature's snarling face, he plunged his sword through the *geminus*'s chest. It screamed.

"Go to hell," said Whit.

The *geminus* shuddered, its eyes glassy, its fanged mouth slack. The flesh surrounding its bones burst into flame. Whit had the peculiar experience of watching himself burn to death, clothing turning to flakes, muscles and skin roasting. His own face turning to embers. But it wasn't him, not any longer, and he withdrew his sword when only a charred skeleton remained.

The blackened bones crumbled to the ground. Whit stared at them for a moment as they coated his boots with ash. He gave them a kick and they flew apart into brittle chips. Then he turned away.

He beheld Zora beating back the last of the demons. She was covered in ash and blood, her hair loose about her shoulders, and a whip of fire in her hand.

Dear God, how did I exist before her?

The final demons fell. But, no. There was another.

The hulking bully roared as it charged into the chamber. Directly toward Whit. He readied himself to strike.

Zora's whip lashed around the giant demon's neck. She pulled. Fire sliced straight through the bully's throat. An abbreviated yelp sounded as its head toppled from the rest of its body. The body crashed to the ground to lie in a smoldering heap.

Now there was only Whit, and Zora. Ash fell around them in gray drifts.

Her lash of fire disappeared. They ran to each other. Both of them filthy, exhausted, smelling of smoke.

He needed her in his arms. When she was close enough, he pulled her to him. Never before had he felt such potent, savage joy.

"Hurt?"

She shook her head. "You?"

With her in his embrace, he barely felt any of his wounds.

"I love you." He held her tightly and breathed his words into the crook of her neck.

She burrowed close. It had been only a few hours since he had seen her, held her, and it felt like ten lifetimes.

"Whit," she murmured, her voice hoarse. "*Camo tute.*"

"And in English, my Gypsy lady."

"I love you."

To say those words and have them spoken in return by a woman as magnificent as her. He was humbled. He was a conquering titan. He had truly gone through hell for her, and would do so again and again. She had her own power, as well. Together, they were an indomitable force. He bent to kiss her.

"How perfectly repulsive," drawled an urbane voice.

Both Whit and Zora turned. In the middle of the destruction, elegant in spotless black satin, stood Mr. Holliday. The Devil himself.

Zora and Whit tensed, their arms dropping so that they stood side by side. After seeing and battling so many horrible creatures, handsome, polished *Wafodu guero* terrified her. He looked exactly as he had so long ago in the chamber beneath the ruin. White hair. Black satin. Pristine and untouchable. Malevolence pouring from him in unseen waves. His diamond white eyes were cunning, cold—the evil within them infinite.

Wafodu guero surveyed the devastation, frowning as if someone had tracked mud into his clean parlor.

"A most disappointing turn of events." He glanced at the charred remains of the *geminus* before turning back to Whit. "You held such promise."

"I am happy to fail you." Whit's arm wrapped around Zora's shoulder when the Devil gazed at her.

"It would have been far better to kill you when first I had the chance."

"None of your underlings managed the task," she answered.

Wafodu guero gave a rueful little smile. "Perspicacious, my dear, as always." His glance danced back and forth between her and Whit, and she felt scoured by a freezing rain. Yet when he grinned, charming and handsome, it was difficult to believe this being ever meant anyone harm. "The door is still not closed. I can offer you power without limitation. Your hearts' deepest desires."

"We have that." Whit pulled her closer.

"Does he speak for you now?" The Devil directed this to her.

"I always speak for myself," she said. "But he knows my heart, as I know his. And in this, we're agreed. There's nothing you can offer me that I want."

Wafodu guero dropped his charm like a soiled kerchief. "As you wish. I am in all ways amenable." Dark energy gathered around his hands.

Zora had a moment's terror. Had she and Whit come so far, fought so much, only to be destroyed by the Devil's greater power? *No.* She must fight back.

Wafodu guero shot a bolt of blackest energy toward her and Whit. She acted without thought. Flung up a protective wall of fire—the first time she had ever done so.

Yet she did not act alone. Whit's sword came up to block the hit at the same time.

The dark energy bounced away from the shield they had

created. She and Whit had only a moment to realize that together they had actually thwarted the Devil's attack. The energy slammed into the ceiling, tearing a massive hole through the plaster and wood. Chunks of ceiling tumbled down.

She and Whit jumped back to avoid being struck. Groaning, the ceiling buckled.

"You have a measure of safety now," the Devil said above the noise, "but it shan't always be thus." He glanced up. Cracks in the ceiling spread to the walls, and the entire building shuddered. He smiled.

With that, the Devil vanished. Leaving Whit and Zora in a building on the verge of collapse.

They wasted no time. Hand in hand, they ran.

They fled the gaming room moments before the ceiling caved in. Tables, chairs, cards, dice, demons, the *geminus*— all were buried beneath tons of bricks, timber, and plaster. A thick cloud of dust chased her and Whit as they sped down the corridor. Walls shivered like trees in a storm. Whit pulled up short, flinging an arm out to stop her from going farther just before a section of wall collapsed in their path. They would have been crushed if he had not stopped them.

Wide eyed, she stared at him. "Your power over the odds?"

"Gone. This is simply me, protecting you."

Through the collapsing building, they sprinted, with Whit maneuvering them to avoid toppling walls and falling ceilings. The floor shook. In a few seconds, the entire structure would collapse. The dust came so heavy that she and Whit both coughed violently.

Just ahead, through the haze of dust, stood the front door. Escape and freedom.

They crossed the threshold. The cool night air felt like salvation against her overheated skin and in her choked lungs. Yet feeling Whit's hand clasping hers was best of all. They ran out into the square fronting the building and got two dozen yards away when the ground quaked, and a huge roar sounded behind them.

Zora found herself on the cobblestones, shielded by Whit's larger body. All she could hear were the noises of collapse, a three-story building toppling in on itself. It went on and on, until, at last, came silence.

A few moments later, Whit peeled himself up off of her and helped her to stand. They both stared at the smoking wreckage of the gaming hell, then were joined by numerous people from the nearby buildings. All stared in horrified wonderment at the destruction.

"Never liked that place," said a heavy man, and he spat upon the ground.

"What happened?" a woman in a night rail asked.

The old man beside her shrugged. "Bad foundation."

Whit and Zora walked away. They had gone only a few steps down an alley when a man stepped in front of them. The street was poorly lit; she saw only a few details of the man. Tall. Broad shouldered. Long, black coat. It took her a brief moment to piece together his identity, but she did, and her fire magic rose up quickly. The flames around her hand cast harsh light over the sharp lines of the man's face, and he seemed as much demon as the creatures buried within the gaming hell.

"Control your witch," said Bram.

"She does as she pleases," answered Whit, his words hard and taut.

"And if you come any closer," Zora said, "I'll turn you into a torch."

Bram's gaze flared in anger, then moved past them to stare at the wreckage. He inhaled sharply. "You damned fools."

"*We* aren't the ones who are damned." Yet Whit's voice wasn't as cutting as it had been a moment before. "Bram, it isn't too late. Not for you, nor any of the others."

His friend's smile was bleak. "Not all of us have pretty Gypsy girls fighting for our souls. I've no one but myself, and that's worth nothing." Bram's expression hardened.

"And I won't let you and this Gypsy threaten the best thing that has ever happened to me."

When his fingers drifted to the hilt of his sword, the fire around Zora's hand blazed, and Whit held his own blade in readiness.

Bram's hand stayed. But the set of his lips remained cruel. "Even with my gift of persuasion, I cannot fight you on my own. Yet when I gather the other Hellraisers, I swear to you"—his eyes were lethal—"no power in this world or any other shall protect you."

As he spoke, tendrils of light drifted around him. Almost seeking a way in. These were not stray beams of light from a lamp. They had no origin other than the otherworldly. Bram did not notice. He turned and strode away into the night.

The strange wisps of light remained.

Zora let the flames around her hand fade. "I don't know whether to pity or fear him."

"He'd never want pity." Whit stared at the shadows where his friend had stood, then gazed at her with fierce protectiveness. "I will strike down *anyone* who seeks to harm you."

She did not think it possible to contain so much love, and yet more and more grew within her, endlessly building upon itself. It would go on thus. Forever. What a marvel.

The light grew and gathered. It took the shape of Livia. She appeared exhausted, her shape barely holding.

"The Dark One . . . scurries off to . . . lick his wounds and sulk. Yet . . . he will rally. Use his newest weapons. The one whom . . . I could not reach."

"And the other Hellraisers," said Zora.

"As well as the Hellraisers' *gemini*," Whit said, grim.

Zora had not considered that. Her heart sank.

"Our small army . . . needs allies," said Livia. "Gather them. But my strength . . . fades. Too much. I need—"

Her words abruptly stopped as her image flickered. She tried to speak, but no sound came from her. Another flicker, and she was gone.

They waited many minutes, but Livia did not reappear.

"Do you think . . . ?" Zora could not finish the question.

"I don't know. But I do know that I want to get you far away from this place."

Holding hands, they walked through the streets of Manchester. Darkness lay thick over the streets, and things lurked in the shadows. Zora kept her fire magic close. Whit did not sheath his sword, but had it out and ready.

Finally, they made it to the edges of the city, then continued warily onward until it was well behind them. Seeking safety, they made their way back to the glen. It had been but a few hours since they had lain here, made love here, willfully pushing the coming threat from their minds.

They had met the threat, and survived. But the fight was far from over.

She could not think of that now. She wanted only him.

In the protective shelter of the glen, they reached for each other. They kissed, deep and long. They were bold together. Tender, too. Everything she wanted. She was exhausted, wrung out, yet he renewed her spirit with his own.

"I have something of yours," she murmured.

"My heart."

"And I will treasure it, always. But this belongs to you." She pulled back slightly and pressed an object into his hand.

For some moments, he simply stared at the pocket watch. Then he closed his eyes and gripped it tightly.

"They would be proud of you," she said.

"I think . . . they would, too." He slipped the watch into his waistcoat pocket.

She reached for his hand. "There's something I need to see."

Summoning her fire, she brought forth just enough to illuminate his skin. What she saw made her heart lift.

"Gone." He tugged at his clothing, pulling off his coat, his waistcoat and shirt, casting them all upon the ground like discarded regrets. Wonder and relief shone in his gaze when he beheld his flesh, marked only by the wounds he'd taken in his many battles. But the flames that had marked him as the Devil's possession, those had vanished.

Zora pressed her lips to his shoulder. He was hot satin, tasting of sweat, blood, and him. This sinfully handsome gambler. The man who had ridden into the Rom encampment, the man whom she had cheated at cards, and desired upon first sight. He was the same, yet entirely altered. As was she. They had traveled together and changed together, and with each stage of their transformation, they became precisely who they needed to be. For themselves, and each other.

A perilous journey lay ahead of them, and she would not deny her fear. She thought of all their adversaries, all the hazards: the *gemini*, demons, the Devil, the Hellraisers.

She gazed up at him. "To love you in the midst of danger means I have everything to lose."

"I will always be with you," he vowed, framing her face with his hands. "Fighting beside you. Loving you."

"If I have that, if I have you," she murmured against his lips, "I gladly take the gamble."

Have you tried Zoë's Blades of the Rose books?
Go back and read them all!

In September, we met a WARRIOR in Mongolia . . .

To most people, the realm of magic is the stuff of nursery rhymes and dusty libraries. But for Capt. Gabriel Huntley, it's become quite real and quite dangerous . . .

IN HOT PURSUIT . . .

The vicious attack Capt. Gabriel Huntley witnesses in a dark alley sparks a chain of events that will take him to the ends of the Earth and beyond—where what is real and what is imagined become terribly confused. And frankly, Huntley couldn't be more pleased. Intrigue, danger, and a beautiful woman in distress— just what he needs.

IN HOTTER WATER . . .

Raised thousands of miles from England, Thalia Burgess is no typical Victorian lady. A good thing, because a proper lady would have no hope of recovering the priceless magical artifact Thalia is after. Huntley's assistance might come in handy, though she has to keep him in the dark. But this distractingly handsome soldier isn't easy to deceive . . .

In October, SCOUNDREL whisked you away
to the shores of Greece . . .

*The Blades of the Rose are sworn to protect the sources
of magic in the world. But the work is dangerous—
and they can't always protect their own . . .*

READY FOR ACTION

London Harcourt's father is bent on subjugating
the world's magic to British rule. But since London is
a mere female, he hasn't bothered to tell her so. He's said
only that he's leading a voyage to the Greek isles. No matter,
after a smothering marriage and three years of straitlaced
widowhood, London jumps at the opportunity—
unfortunately, right into the arms of Bennett Day.

RISKING IT ALL

Bennett is a ladies' man, when he's not dodging lethal
attacks to protect the powers of the ancients from
men like London's father. Sometimes, he's a ladies' man
even when he *is* dodging them. But the minute he sees
London he knows she will require his full attention.
The woman is lovely, brilliant, and the
only known speaker of a dialect of ancient Greek
that holds the key to calling down the wrath of the gods.
Bennett will be risking his life again—
but around London, what really worries him
is the danger to his heart . . .

In November, we got lost in the Canadian wilderness
with REBEL . . .

*On the Canadian frontier in 1875, nature is a harsh
mistress. But the supernatural can really do you in . . .*

A LONE WOLF

Nathan Lesperance is used to being different. He's the first
Native attorney in Vancouver, and welcome neither with
white society nor his sometime tribe. Not to mention the
powerful wildness he's always felt inside him, too dangerous
to set free. Then he met Astrid Bramfield and saw his
like within her piercing eyes. Now, unless she helps him
through the harsh terrain and the harsher unknowns of
his true abilities, it could very well get him killed . . .

AND THE WOMAN WHO LEFT THE PACK

Astrid has traveled this path before. Once she was
a Blade of the Rose, protecting the world's magic
from unscrupulous men, with her husband by her side.
But she's loved and lost, and as a world-class
frontierswoman, she knows all about survival.
Nathan's searing gaze and long, lean muscles mean
nothing but trouble. Yet something has ignited
a forgotten flame inside her: a burning
need for adventure, for life—
and perhaps even for love . . .

And in December, STRANGER brought the adventure
back to London . . .

*He protects the world's magic—with his science. But even
the best scientists can fall prey to the right chemistry . . .*

LOOKING FOR TROUBLE

Gemma Murphy has a nose for a story—even if the boys
in Chicago's newsrooms would rather focus on her chest.
So when she runs into a handsome man of mystery
discussing how to save the world from fancy-pants
Brit conspirators, she's sensing a scoop. Especially
when he mentions there's magic involved. Of course,
getting him on the record would be easier if he
hadn't caught her eavesdropping . . .

LIGHTING HIS FUSE

Catullus Graves knows what it's like to be shut out:
his ancestors were slaves. And he's a genius inventor
with appropriately eccentric habits, so even people who
love him find him a little odd. But after meeting a certain
redheaded scribbler, he's thinking of other types of science.
Inconvenient, given that he needs to focus on preventing
the end of the world as we know it. But with Gemma's
insatiable curiosity sparking Catullus's inventive impulses,
they might set off something explosive anyway . . .